WATER
MEMORY

OTHER TITLES BY DANIEL PYNE

Catalina Eddy: A Novel in Three Decades

Fifty Mice

Twentynine Palms

A Hole in the Ground Owned by a Liar

PRAISE FOR DANIEL PYNE

"Deceptively explosive, *Water Memory* pairs the cleverness and precision timing of Daniel Pyne's riveting storytelling with his addictive, action-packed plotting and unforgettably vivid cast of characters."

—Karin Slaughter, *New York Times* and international bestselling author

"*Water Memory* blew me away. It's the kind of rare character-driven, adrenaline-charged action-thriller readers crave and writers dare to emulate. Aubrey Sentro is an iconic, kick-ass heroine—deeply flawed, exceptionally skilled, and exceedingly motivated. Lara Craft on steroids. A brilliant page-turner."

—Robert Dugoni, #1 *Wall Street Journal* bestselling author of *A Cold Trail*

"A deftly crafted thriller with a captivatingly complex lead character, Pyne's action-packed novel builds with each surprise twist and will keep you up late turning the pages."

—Chad Zunker, Amazon Charts bestselling author of *An Equal Justice*

"Mother knows best, even when her memory is short-circuiting. *Water Memory* has everything you want in a modern-day thriller: pirates, propulsive action, and an unforgettable female lead. Pyne's prose is elegant, evocative, extraordinary. Best book I've read in ages. Addictive."

—K. J. Howe, international bestselling author of *Skyjack*

"*Water Memory* moves like *Die Hard* but with a tragic family backstory as its heart—and with an indelible, three-dimensional action heroine, Aubrey Sentro, as the muscle and sinew. I loved it."

—Barry Eisler, *New York Times* bestselling author

"Daniel Pyne's *Water Memory* is a stylish and addictive thriller propelled by gritty action, sublime intrigue, and a brilliantly executed character twist."

—Steven Konkoly, *Wall Street Journal* bestselling author

"A mysterious woman on a mysterious path, danger in the future and from the past—*Water Memory* holds a hypnotic grip on you from the very first page. This is Daniel Pyne at his very best."

—Michael Connelly, #1 *New York Times* bestselling author

WATER
MEMORY

A THRILLER

DANIEL
PYNE

THOMAS & MERCER

"I'm an Old Cowhand (From the Rio Grand)"
Words and Music by JOHNNY MERCER
Copyright© 1936 (Renewed) THE JOHNNY MERCER FOUNDATION
All Rights Administered by WC MUSIC CORP.
All Rights Reserved
Used By Permission of ALFRED MUSIC

Published by Thomas & Mercer, Seattle

www.apub.com

Amazon, the Amazon logo, and Thomas & Mercer are trademarks of Amazon.com, Inc., or its affiliates.

ISBN-13: 9781542025027 (hardcover)
ISBN-10: 1542025028 (hardcover)

ISBN-13: 9781542025034 (paperback)
ISBN-10: 1542025036 (paperback)

Front Cover Design by Kaitlin Kall
Back Cover Design by Ray Lundgren

Printed in the United States of America

For Joan

Alas! (thought I, and my heart beat loud)
How fast she nears and nears!
Are those her sails that glance in the Sun,
Like restless gossameres?
Are those her ribs through which the Sun
Did peer, as through a grate?
And is that Woman all her crew?
Is that a DEATH? and are there two?
Is DEATH that woman's mate?

—Samuel Taylor Coleridge
"The Rime of the Ancient Mariner"

PROLOGUE

The fifth-floor hallway was darker than reported, and there was an awkward dogleg near the stairwell that their local recon hadn't bothered to map; it smelled of garlic, mold, and dry rot even though the hotel was billed as a Byzantine five-star. A milky Mediterranean twilight bled faint from hidden recesses along the ceiling, enough to cast a glow but not overly expose the shadow gliding through the shadows toward its target.

A woman, unremarkable, if a little boxy, hip to shoulder. Here on business, you might think, not worth a second look. Black slacks, T-shirt and unstructured blazer, wireless earpiece, and Zero Halliburton briefcase.

She approached a doorway with a curious surfeit of caution, stepping to one side of it while preparing to knock. But then she hesitated, stared uncertainly at the brass digits fixed to the door—six two seven— and was momentarily unable to make sense of them. A voice in her earpiece hissed, "What's wrong?"

She shook her head, forgetting that the voice couldn't see her; she glanced across the hallway at the next doorway, momentarily paralyzed with doubt.

"Suite number," she murmured, with a calm she didn't feel. "Double-check for me?"

"Seriously?" In her earpiece, an annoyed whisper: "Shit, man, did you fucking forget it?"

She didn't answer him but felt her cheeks flush hot because yeah, she had.

"Stand by."

She waited as papers rustled on the other end of her comm, a clock in her head ticking away precious seconds that she knew, from long experience, she'd regret losing however this went down, at which point a door across the hall but just behind her—six two six—opened to reveal the naked, pale, middle-aged Chinese American asset she'd been sent to retrieve, a towel wrapped around his waist and a frown on his face. Their eyes locked.

There's the plan that you make going in, and then there's what really happens—the shitstorm. Rarely do they align.

"Can I help you?"

No. It was supposed to be the other way around. But on the love-tossed bed in the room behind the towel man, a pretty, naked woman was reaching to a side table and a big black Glock that surely had been stowed in its drawer for a contingency just like this one.

The woman in the hallway felt the familiar slowing of time she often experienced at the initiation of conflict. The clarity, the narrowing of focus, her pulse in her neck, a slight dissociation, as if she were watching what was unfolding rather than actively participating in it.

She was across the corridor and falling to the side and away from the six-two-six doorway, her arm wrapped around and pulling the towel man down with her as bullets from the naked woman's gun splintered the jamb, slipped hot past their faces, and blistered plaster off the wall opposite. She felt them tear into the tactical vest under her T-shirt and bang off the metal briefcase she had raised as a shield. The narrow corridor came alive: voices, Turkish, other doors flung wide, a volley of panicked gunfire as red tracer dots from short-stock automatics searched the gloaming for her.

The towel man was shrieking. She felt the warm wetness where a bullet had grazed her neck, just below her ear.

Stress, but no panic. She whispered evenly, "Stay with me, Scott, okay?" Their Halliburton shield burst open, she lost her grip on it, and bullets tore the cash bundles inside into a flurry of pale confetti that smelled like burned rice.

She hit the floor hard. The stun grenade that exploded next was too close to her, with a roar of blinding light she'd been unprepared for.

The three-op backup who had rolled into position beyond her waited for sight lines to clear so they could cut the Turks down with little fanfare.

Close your eyes. Cover your ears. With the asset in her arms, she had been unable to follow any operational protocol. A searing scree deafened her. Curled around her man, protective, blood leaking from her neck wound, she felt dizzy, head filled with glue, and sensed a lateral movement.

The naked woman. Glock in her outstretched hand aimed point-blank down at the asset.

His dad body wasn't as heavy as she expected. Or maybe it was simply the adrenaline of fear. She levered him safely to one side, rotated while pulling the sidearm from her hip—took a breath—and aimed center mass before tapping the trigger twice.

The naked woman dropped like a puppet whose strings had been cut.

Shredded bills and bits from the broken briefcase were still wafting down on them. No more than eleven seconds had passed. It had happened so fast that the spray of the overhead sprinklers triggered by the stun grenade only now began to rain.

Her thinking was splintered and unreliable; her eyes felt fried, the hallway even thicker with the smoke and the mist. She struggled to sit up. The naked woman lay dewy and unmoving on the threadbare carpet, ivory skin between augmented breasts ruined by the two puckered puncture wounds where the bullets had made entry.

There was movement around her. She heard but couldn't understand the voices, as if she were underwater, but when her hand found his shoulder, she felt the pounding of the sobbing towel man's heart.

"Let's get you home," she heard herself murmur.

There were hands under her arms then, and she stood, finding her balance; the rank lukewarm water that ran down her upturned face felt heaven sent. The backup team got their trembling towel-clad asset to his feet and trundled both of them to the emergency stairwell and away.

Her own pulse was steady, stubborn; she'd survived.

PART ONE:
~~GIRL~~ WOMAN ON A BOAT

CHAPTER ONE

"The ocelot is a wild cat."

Only one of her assigned kids is still in residence, and in the big, noisy common room, she sits at a table helping the scruffy almost-nine-year-old boy named Damien struggle with his homework, reading aloud the paragraph she's helped him research and watched him compose.

"It hunts at night."

Little kids, she muses, sound more like spics than spies.

The creepy security guy who must never go off duty greeted Aubrey Sentro with a gap-toothed leer, just as he does every night she slips through the front door of All Saints Rescue Mission to tutor homeless grade school students. She tries to imagine herself as he sees her: not really MILF material, but he doesn't seem picky; average, then, older than she looks, not big but fit, oddly graceful, her close-cropped hair threatening to grow out, no aversion to smiling. Which she did as she breezed past him. It's a reflex. Smiles disarm and buy time. One of the few things she's sure she inherited from her mother, it's proved useful from time to time, in this case to breeze safely past the guard without having to suffer another one of his humorless jokes.

"It's got fur like a jag—a jag—a jag-u-are—"

"Jaguar."

"—and people kill them for its fur."

Since Dennis died, she's struggled to fill her time. Grown kids, empty house. Hard to make close, long-term friends when you've been living a sort of lie. Between her business trips there lurks a yawning emptiness that scares her more than any physical threat. Doing homework with Jenny and Jeremy was once borrowed time she treasured. Despite the long absences—or maybe because of them—she'd greedily spend all her free days at home with her children. It was never enough. Cramming too much into limited windows probably smothered them—out of guilt, out of need, out of her own greedy joy—and no doubt was the reason they began to push her away as they got older. It could be maddening, the way they craved you when you weren't there and evaded you when you were. Dennis would reassure her it was natural; they were a good team, the two of them, each filling in where the other gapped.

"*Their* fur. That's great, Damien. Keep going."

She had never expected to outlive her husband. She did her part, but he was the glue that held them all together. And now, if it turns out she can no longer do her work, what's left? Friday bar crawl with Lucky and his wife? Marta's book club? Her ears ring faintly at a pitch not on any scale. That and the tepid headache have become her constant companions.

"I don't understand why you won't let me use spell-check."

"You need to learn to spell."

"But that's why there's spell-check."

"What if the spell-check is wrong?"

"Wronger than me?"

"Or what if there's a power failure and you can't get online?" She hesitates—what do they call those bombs? EMPs. Electromagnetic pulse weapons, Sentro remembers. They were all the rage for a while.

Damien rolls his eyes, and as he makes the correction on the borrowed shelter laptop, Sentro reaches into her pocket, takes out a small pill bottle with a childproof cap. It was Jenny who suggested the tutoring, Jeremy who found her the venue. For a while she was coming here four times a week. But the impermanence wore on her. Homeless kids are at the mercy of their peripatetic parents; she'd just be getting started, and they'd vanish. Rarely to return.

"Jagwire."

"Close enough." She fumbles to open her bottle as Damien soldiers on.

"Jagwire. *Their* fur. The ocelot—the ocelot can live in trees, and the ocelot will fight"—he stumbles over the word—"fer-o-shus . . ."

Sentro shakes out a pair of capsules to wash down with Diet Pepsi, then sees the boy watching her, looking wary. "It's just aspirin," she says. "For a headache." She smiles her smile. "Keep going."

"My sister went to jail for pills."

"These are legal."

"They make her act scary weird."

Sentro holds Damien's gaze. "Don't worry." His mother works two jobs, trying to save enough to make first and last month's rent to move to subsidized housing. Sentro has offered to help them, but the All Saints volunteer rules prevent it.

"—and fight ferocious sometimes," he resumes.

"Ferocious*ly*."

"What?"

"Never mind."

"She sorta stabbed my mom with scissors." The little boy won't look at her. There's something else.

"What."

"What if I'm not here when you come back?"

Sentro wants to say the right thing. "I'll find you," she tells him, knowing it might be impossible. But she'd try. "Ferociously."

"Ocelots, us," Damien says.

"That's right."

"'Kay." The little boy lowers his head, makes the correction, and:
"—ferociously, sometimes to the death . . . for its home and family."

He looks up at her. This last part he knows by heart.

"But mostly ocelots live alone. They are an endangered species."

Chapter Two

I'm an old cowhand...

Several CT scans of a human head glow, spectral, on a wall monitor.

...from the Rio Grande...

Normal bone structure. Healthy tissue. No tumors. No apparent trauma.

"Did you play contact sports when you were younger, Mrs. Troon?"

"Sentro. Ms."

"Oh." The doctor looks down at his chart with what she presumes to be a practiced, professional doubt that he could ever be mistaken. "I'm sorry. It says here—"

"Sentro's my maiden name; I never legally changed it. When the kids were younger, I used my husband's name for family and medical matters because—"

"I get it." He makes a notation.

Having given up trying to convince herself that the noise in her head will fade, here she is: battery of tests, awkward questions, anxious and undone. She's determined not to tell anyone, yet. A diagnosis is what she wants. And a remedy.

A confirmation is what she's afraid she'll get instead.

MRI of a human brain. The ragged coastlines of gyri and sulci. Her head has felt heavy for days. Overcast. Migraines, mood swings, discomfiting distractions—she can't shake loose the clouds. The riot of color assigned to scanned images is merely for reference, but part of her wants to believe that they've actually mapped the tangled, uninvited memory scraps that have started chasing her through fitful nights: thunderclouds piled like soft serve, tumbleweeds the size of longhorns, a wafer-thin air freshener in the shape of a rose, faded by sun, dangling from the rearview of a station wagon doing ninety on a Texas two-lane, ruler straight from horizon to horizon. A brown Sherman Cigarettello, smoke twisting up from the glow, wedged in the pink lipstick smear of her mother's mouth, singing:

Yippee-ai-oh-kai-yay.

"Field hockey? Rugby?"

Legs dangling, feet bare, sitting uneasily on the end of the examining bench she feels a cold shiver of loss trouble through her. "No."

He's a specialist she found online, deliberately out of network. Patchwork hair not necessarily all his own, troubled skin, lab coat, skinny legs crossed, hipster socks showing, the doctor makes a few more marks with a stylus on the wireless tablet crooked in his arm, then glances up at her, pushing rimless glasses back up his nose.

"Ping-Pong," Sentro offers. "In high school."

"Your film shows evidence of multiple concussions. Serial TBI." He's fishing.

"Traumatic brain injury?" She just stares at him. The fluorescent ceiling has a faint low-frequency hum that harmonizes with her tinnitus and reminds her of something new; an image flickers, indistinct. Cairo? Apple-shaped man in a mustard-colored suit. Comic book eye patch, leather, tooled with a starburst.

Then gone in, literally, a flash.

Her hearing has, until the high scree crept into it, always been freakishly good.

. . . I'm a cowboy who never saw a cow,
never roped a steer 'cause I don't know how,
and I sure ain't fixin' to startin' now—

"At some point in your life, Aubrey," the doctor is explaining, "you received a blow to the head, and then again, and then again—more than once is what I'm saying, likely over an extended period of time, months, years. And now you're paying the price for it." His eyes keep straying to the small bandage under her ear, but he seems to have no idea how close he's stumbled toward the truth.

"Wouldn't I remember something like that?" She wonders if he can tell she's dissembling.

"You would. Until you forgot." There's a hesitation before he asks, as kindly as he can, "Abusive relationship?"

"Excuse me?"

"Did your late husband get physical with you?"

"What?" The utter absurdity of this misunderstanding is a relief. "No. Nothing like that. Not my husband or anyone. Ever." She conjures a picture of Dennis, with the easy, restful eyes, running a hand lightly through her hair. His gentle touch a glory.

"Okay. Well. What you have we call persistent postconcussion syndrome," the doctor tells her, "and it would explain your headaches, the aural distortions, mood swings, memory problems, and so forth. Unfortunately it can present long after the original trauma."

"Will it clear up?"

"It won't. No. It's . . . typically degenerative."

"Typically."

"Yes."

"And rarely?"

"There's so much we don't know," he admits.

The examining room is quiet, farthest away from reception. She feels herself detach so she can brave the only question she isn't sure she wants answered. "Is this Alzheimer's?"

"No. Different."

"Better, worse?"

"Different."

Shit. Now she just wants to wrap this up and leave. "Treatments."

"There's so much we don't know."

"Right." This is why she chose someone not in her provider network. No one at work needs to know.

"Soccer?" She avoids the doctor's probing gaze, looks away to all the wall monitors and all the film clipped to light boxes that flank the paper-covered bench where she's sitting. "All that heading of the ball, field collisions," the doctor elaborates. "You know." She respects his persistence, not just going through the motions. Part of her wishes she could tell him what he wants to know, but even if it were possible, she wonders where she would even start.

With the song, in the car?

There's an extended, uncomfortable pause; then he exhales and sits back. His eyes are too big for his face, set far apart, not unkind. "Ms. Sentro. Aubrey. Let me put this as clearly as I can. Your symptoms are still presenting; it's possible they could stabilize. Palliate. But you need to make some hard decisions. Expect the best; prepare for the worst. Work, family. Reduce your stress. Move to Iowa. Let your brain calm down, and perhaps we'll get a fuller picture, over time."

"Okay." She's become impatient with him. "Meanwhile, can you give me something for the headaches?"

"I'd like to run some more tests."

Sentro just looks at him, level, as opaque as she can manage. Refusing to give him the gift of her fear. Of this onset of brain fog and disremembering, she is very afraid, which is unfamiliar territory. She needs time to sort it out.

The physician shifts his bony weight and makes a serious face. "Look, not to overstate your condition, Ms. Sentro, but there also exists with this a possibility that another head injury could be extremely dangerous for you."

Sentro nods. "Second-impact syndrome. I read about it online."

"Online."

"WebMD." Another concussion could kill her is what it said.

"The University of Google." A withering professional grimace and sigh as, frustrated, the doctor stands up from his rolling stool. "Well, then, you read that there's also a persuasive correlation between recurrent head trauma and early-onset Alzheimer's disease and dementia."

"Which you also can't cure. Yeah, I saw that." If he wanted to touch a nerve, he's succeeded. "But you said this wasn't. Alzheimer's."

The doctor just shrugs.

She feels a hot West Texas wind buffeting her face through the open window, the gloomy blue-slate sun-split sky bearing down with its promise of a squall—how the Chevy hit a dip in the highway, how her stomach flopped when the chassis bottomed out, bumpers squawking, sparks pinwheeling out behind like shooting stars as she floated up off the seat, unbelted, how her mother's arm shot out in front of her, protective, and both of them laughing, their off-key singing interrupted, and how her mother's purse spilled off the seat and the handgun tumbled out of it, small, pink grip, lady size.

Yippee-ai-oh-kai-ay.

"I come unmoored, is all," she offers thoughtlessly.

"What?"

Sentro looks up at him blankly and remembers where she is. "If you can't fix me, I don't see the upside in running more tests."

The doctor taps his notebook screen dark and walks out.

An impasse is so often the best she can manage.

Chapter Three

"What'd the doctor say?"

Jeremy Troon has always felt hard put that he looks so much like his mother—or, well, yes, a young, male MBA version of her, but still. Lean, even lanky, strangely graceful but unathletic, a kind of puzzle in which some of the pieces don't fit, according to his ex-girlfriend Kimmy. Same troubled hair, same nose, same eyes, her unreadable gaze; gentle features not so much effeminate, he decided long ago, as somehow tentative. Almost meek. It didn't make surviving adolescence any easier. Jenny, on the other hand, got their father's infectious grin and blind confidence, which, although mostly useless over the long run, made her popular until she decided she wouldn't be.

Wearing creased blue chinos with a linen jacket for his presentation to his graduate school entrepreneurial seminar later in the afternoon, he's flung his power tie rakishly back over his shoulder so it won't get any soup on it.

"He said I shouldn't eat fries. Then he offered me a prescription sample for this female Viagra."

"Mom. Jesus. TMI."

"You asked."

The gazpacho has a kick to it. The restaurant she chose this time is lively and crowded with young, eager, hungry faces like his. Their bimonthly lunches have become habit, when she's not traveling, and he finds he looks forward to them, even if he insists to his sister that they're a pain.

His mother looks tired. "Did you talk to him about your memory stuff?"

She says, poker faced, "Oh. I totally forgot."

Jeremy shakes his head—"That's not funny, Mom"—and his mother's expression softens, and for a moment he can tell she's trying to find his father in him. He knows all her looks; he studied her greedily growing up so he'd have her in his head during the extended periods she spent away on business. Now, of course, he couldn't get her out of his head if he wanted to, and so he watches her study him to locate her husband in him, which he knows she always will. The Dennis gene is subtle: the folds of his eyelids, that frustrated downturn of mouth. He sees it, too, sometimes, looking back at him from the mirror in the morning.

But mostly he sees her.

"I don't have a problem with my memory," she's telling him. "A four-hour erection sounds lovely, though. Conceptually. Can a woman really get one?"

Nobody wants to hear their mom talk about erections. "You called me last week from the airport parking lot because you thought your car was stolen."

"I think 'missing' was the word I used."

"It was in the next aisle."

"I had jet lag. The flight from Athens was endless, some Turks kept smoking in the bathroom, and the flight attendants ran out of gin."

"You don't drink gin."

"I started, the trip took so long," she jokes, deadpan.

He gives her back her own deadpan. "You weren't freaking out?"

"I don't think so."

"I think you were. Yes." On the phone, her voice had an edge of anxiousness he'd never heard before.

"Annoyed, was all. And exhausted."

She's probably lying; he lets it go. "Right, fine." Letting go is reflexive for him—all the years of her ins and outs and extended absences. When he was little he just resented it, but as he got older, he started to believe that her work was so meaningless, so unimportant and tedious, and had cost her so dearly that she clung to it all the more stubbornly. This gave it the aura of something else, something that mattered, that made a difference, so her kids would be proud of her and understand why she couldn't always be with them.

And the truth is it *didn't* matter—she tried her best; he knows she's still trying. Other kids had a mom at home; Jeremy and Jenny had their dad. And what Jeremy really feels now, as a grown-ass adult (as Jenny would say), is the acute need to take care of his mom the way his dad would.

She gets lost. She's been forgetting things.

He pokes at his salad and returns to his soup. "Is this something I should worry about? As a matter of genetics, I mean? Gramps didn't have it, but what about your mom?"

"Died young."

"I know, but what if what happened with her was an early sign of dementia or—"

"No. Totally different," his mother adds, and then, unnecessarily, "I'm not her. It wasn't contagious." She reaches across the table and touches his arm. "It's not something you'll get."

It's always been a little awkward when she tries to nurture, because it's not her nature; his sister was the first to point this out to him. Back from another failed shopping expedition on which tweenage Jenny had been determined to find a fashion intersection with the cool girls who'd been merciless in trolling his sister because of her feral opposition to everything they represented, their mother had, unfortunately, bought into Jenny's fiction that she wanted, needed, to be accepted. Five hours and $362.45 of Forever 21 later, Jenny had a wardrobe she would never wear and was flopped facedown on her brother's bed in tears, since all she really had wanted was a mom who would tell her she didn't need to curry favor with those little bitches. That she could be loved the way she was. And their mother did love Jenny—loved them both unconditionally, no question about it. She could even say the right words, once their father helped her disentangle the Gordian workings of a twelve-year-old girl's mind.

But she nevertheless has always, in his opinion, lacked the basic tools to truly connect and console.

He doesn't resent it. Or does he? Always disconcerting, growing up, when he'd have to explain to teachers that no, his mom was away working, and his dad would be bringing the class snacks, or whatever. Kimmy, the psych major, was of the opinion that a father could never provide his children what a mother would. Jenny was of the opinion that Kimmy was a pretentious bitch and was quick to point out Kimmy also claimed she was a virgin because she'd only had anal sex.

At the time he wished he hadn't shared with his sister that intimate detail, but it turned out Jenny, in the case of Kimmy, was proved absolutely right. He was still paying off their trip to Thailand, where she'd left him for a scuba instructor and then used his PayPal account for another six months before Jeremy figured it out and changed the password.

"You don't need to worry about this, or about me. I'm just old," his mother is saying to him, trying to lighten the mood. "We seniors start to slip."

He wonders again what the doctor really told her or if she went to the clinic at all.

"You're not even fifty," he points out. His phone chimes, and he can't stop himself from glancing down at the text screen, and while his mother says nothing, he's well aware of her opinions about phone etiquette and braves her irritation at the interruption.

Message from Jenny. His mother complains that she never gets texts from her daughter; he gets from his sister at minimum a dozen a day. With a flurry of taps on the screen keyboard, he tells Jenny where he is and whom he's with and, defensive, in a variation on an old theme, multitasking with only a slight distracted delay, suggests to his mother: "Maybe you're feeling job lag."

"I like my job."

Here we go again, he thinks. "Your job." Sipping soup and talking: "Reinsurance."

"International risk mitigation."

"Reinsurance," he repeats, even more sarcastically.

"Somebody has to do it."

"And you've been there how long? Flying red-eyes to wherever, whenever, East Bumfuck. Jesus, Mom—the sleep deprivation alone. And jet lag. Long term, you know what that does to you? They've done studies of old flight attendants. It's not good. I mean, no wonder you have brain rot."

"I like my job." She says it again because it's true. "I'm fine, Jemmy, really."

A sour warning frown—it's Jenny's pet name for him, from when she was little, and his sister's still the only one Jeremy allows to make use of it. Is his mom breaking the rule on purpose, or did she forget? "Shouldn't you have gotten promoted or something? Running your own team, sending other people out to do the shit work? You're smart." He means it. Whenever she came home from a long trip and had a little time off, she would be right there to help him with schoolwork. She rocked with history and the world, geopolitics, capital cities of every country, the myriad troubles with China, Russia, the Middle East. "Dad used to always brag on how you got yanked out of basic and sent to Berlin on special assignment at, what, eighteen?"

"I think I was twenty." She says this modestly but seems pleased that Jeremy remembers. "Your father liked to spin stories."

"You're saying it didn't happen?"

"It wasn't nearly as colorful as he made it sound," she says in a tone that lets him know she doesn't want to talk about it anymore. He's trawled these waters before during their lunches, but she never takes the bait.

There's so much about her she won't let him in on. Could that be how it is with every parent? They have whole other lives before their kids are born and no obligation to share. His dad used to say their mom's guardedness came from what had happened with *her* mother. Something else she doesn't like to talk about. But at least with that, he understands why.

"Do you think it bugged him?"

"Who?"

"Dad."

"Do I think what bugged him?"

"You being the breadwinner, him staying home?"

She nods and hesitates. "I don't know so much that we made a decision as that it was just kind of how things worked out." And Jeremy marvels, irritably, at how quickly she turns it around on him: "How would you feel if Kimmy made all the money and you had to raise the kids?"

"Mom, I broke up with her almost two years ago."

An awkward pause. His mother looks momentarily caught out, and he realizes that she's forgotten.

"We talked all about it; you said it was probably for the best. Remember?"

She clearly doesn't. Color flushes her cheeks; she looks down at her empty plate.

"Jet lag, I guess," Jeremy deadpans.

Ignoring the dig, she answers a question he didn't ask. "We made a life. Your dad and I. Or tried to. We made a home."

"Where you hardly ever were."

"A home isn't necessarily a fixed place."

"Oh." Jeremy pounces. "Let's see. There was me and Jen and Dad—and, well, yeah, you sometimes, in person, but a lot of times just like swooping in with the phone call from a galaxy far, far away." He doesn't mean for it to sound so bitter, but the words just tumble out and swarm like Furies.

"We were on the forefront of Skype," his mother jokes.

Jeremy feels no need to pretend that this is funny. "You do realize that meant I never had a dad who was a role model in the business world. Good or bad. Somebody to emulate, somebody to rebel against."

She shrugs. "You have me."

"It's not the same."

His mother sits back, folding her hands on the napkin in her lap. She gets stronger, he knows, and grows calmer when she's upset. "How's your sister?"

"I don't know. Why don't you ask her? She isn't talking to me."

"Why?"

Jeremy just shrugs. An only child, his mother doesn't understand the sibling thing.

"That wasn't her just now texting you?"

"Mom. Texting isn't talking." He doesn't mean to say it so sharply. His mother falls silent. The subject of Jenny always discomfits her. "It doesn't matter. We'll make up. We always do." Then, back on point: "When was the last time you even got a raise? Or asked for one?"

"I'm paid well for what I do," she insists.

"For all those long hours, the busted holidays and missed birthdays? Disney World, Grand Canyon. Texas and Grandpa, twice. Paid well for your incredible doglike dedication to the firm?"

She says, "Now you're just being mean."

Jeremy chews and nods. Part of him regrets playing this broken record again. He's no longer interested in the salad. His phone chimes with another text message, probably from Jenny, but he doesn't bother to look at it. "You're not that old. Lots of experience. International sales. You could hire on with some K Street lobbying outfit selling almonds to the Chinese or Stingers to the Saudis. Pull down serious money; solid up your retirement."

Frowning, his mother says, offhand, "Nobody should be selling the House of Saud anything."

"Mom."

"Joke." But her unamused look suggests it wasn't. "And 'not that old' sounds like damning with faint praise. Compared to what? Flight attendants?"

He puts down his spoon and wipes his mouth with his napkin, frustrated. "Never mind."

"So"—she studies him for a moment—"would we even be having this conversation if your father had been the one who wasn't always around when you wanted him?"

Now he feels like he's nine years old, complaining about her missing his star turn as one of Fagin's orphans in a local high school musical production of *Oliver!* But he can't stop himself. "I'm just saying. Well paid? Mom, even an entry-level credit-swap trader's half-year bonus last year on Wall Street was probably more than you've made in your whole fucking career."

His mother stares at him, her eyes opaque, unreadable, but unspeakably sad, the way he remembers them looking down at him when, in the middle of the night, she was called away and woke him up to say goodbye. Suddenly he feels unsettled, his mouth dry, his hands tingling, the sounds of the restaurant rattling around them as if somebody turned up the treble. Sometimes, when he's with her, the old anxiety and resentment just boil up and over.

"You wanted me to study *philosophy*, as an undergrad," he mumbles, meaning it to be sarcastic, but she takes him literally.

"I was seventeen when you were born. I never got to go to college. I wanted you to have opportunities that I didn't."

Same old complaints, same old rationales, the broken record. Things that cannot be undone, words that cannot be unsaid.

"I know," he mumbles.

For a moment, she doesn't respond, and whatever emotion lurks behind his mother's temperate, unwavering gaze is too well disguised for him to gauge it. "Why don't you try this: whenever you look at me, tell yourself, *I am not going to bend over every day, like my mom, and let the world kick my butt.*"

Jeremy shakes his head, his face hot. "I would never say that." He doesn't want to meet her steady gaze.

"We did the best we could," she insists. More than a flicker of hurt in her eyes. "I'd like to think I played a part."

"I never said you didn't." It's all he can think to say. He loves her, he resents her, he's scared about what might be going on with her slips and misremembering, but right now he just wants to escape to the safe refuge of his campus apartment and clear his head.

"You don't need to take care of me," his mother says, still reading his mind. "Or worry."

"I won't. I don't."

"You're lying," she says. "It's sweet. I'm sorry if I ruined your life."

"That's not what I said."

"Okay." Her smile of surrender lifts his mood like clouds clearing on a windy day. He can't help it. The power of Mom. Making it okay when he dropped out of T-ball and his dad looked so disappointed; letting him pretend a cold was lingering long after it was gone so that he could stay home with her and the new baby Jenny until she had to go away on another months-long sales trip on the other side of the world. He's nine years old, flustered, frustrated, self-conscious, wanting that mom all the other kids have, who bakes cookies and cries at the end of movies. But not willing to give up the mom he has.

"You still tutor downtown?" he asks her.

"The little kids, yeah. I'm glad you and Jenny talked me into it."

"Once a week?"

"More or less. I've cut back."

"And the other nights?"

"Busy." Her eyes narrow; he can see that she's probably gun shy about where he might be going with this. "Nap. Knit. Cook. You know. Reality TV." Jeremy recalls that she and his father rarely watched television when he was growing up, and his mother was notorious for her calamities in the kitchen. "I unwind; is that okay?"

"Did you really see the doctor?"

She squares her shoulders and puts her knife and fork across her plate. "Why would I lie to you about it?"

He doesn't know. That's another thing that worries him, but he's not willing to push it any further today. "Jenny and I think you should start dating."

"What?"

He grins, enjoying putting her on her heels for once. "Swipe right on some desperate widower and, you know, have a social life, find some release."

"Release?"

"You're the one who brought the subject up. Dad's been gone for, what, almost a decade? And now you're geezing out. YOLO, Mom. Pop that female Viagra, and you go, girl." Her spontaneous laugh is infectious. "Why not?"

"Tinder?" His mother approximates a scandalized grimace. "Be a sex fiend?" The latest of her sundry smiles spreads; this one he knows is genuine. "You're funny." She reaches out, touches his arm again, and leaves her small hand on it. "You want to go, don't let me keep you."

"No," he lies, again. "All good." He pushes his salad plate back, done. They can order coffee. No harm in his staying a little longer; the seminar starts at four.

"I love our lunches," she says absently, looking around the restaurant with her restless curiosity.

Even at his father's funeral, he's never seen his mother cry.

Chapter Four

Pregnant at seventeen.

In love with a hard body: hot, dreamy, her forever boy, Dennis Troon, and his blue bedroom eyes, who too late she came to understand would do anything for her—anything, that is, except be something her father had warned from the get-go Dennis was not nor would ever be: employable.

A minor detail that Jeremy needn't ever know.

Silty Bethesda sunshine glints off windshield trim and resurrects her dull headache. Low-slung stone-and-glass buildings rise like oversize tombstones from an undulating terrain of well-fed bluegrass under the standard well-pruned arboreal canopy. The term *industrial park* is, Sentro thinks, such a free-market fuck-you.

She slips her Audi wagon through a guard gate into the fresh inky asphalt of the Solomon Systems parking lot. Her cell phone hums. Text: **Where are you? Here.** *I'm here,* she thinks. Always here. She texts back: **Walking in.** The engine ticks with heat as she gets out, and like an earworm, the rhythm hounds her all the way inside.

Baby Jeremy was not even six months old when she enlisted. She did it mostly to secure health care but also with eyes on the GI Bill to pay for her college afterward, because Dennis was getting his AA from the University of Phoenix and the high-paying medical lab job they'd practically guaranteed in their brochures. The plan was for her to work until he finished, then let him support her while she went back to school. Jenny arrived four years later, a happy consequence of Sentro's reconciliation with Dennis in the wake of the troubled Berlin posting that had estranged them. Not exactly an accident, but the second child guaranteed Sentro would re-up, since by that time army intelligence had found her, used her, and, by way of apology, fast-tracked her into a West Point program with a covert detour through Langley. It meant Pentagon pay and silver bars on her collar and sundry other officer's entitlements no family of four (carrying the sizable student debt Dennis had, while she was overseas, racked up in successive well-intentioned but unrealized for-profit-college career moves like his AA in political psychology or the bogus certificate program in elevator repair) could walk away from.

Regret never figured into it. Life unspooled, and they gathered it as best they could. It was only from the outside looking in that a more conventional world would, now and then, intrude and pass judgment. She didn't care what the world thought. The reverse-role thing that her son is so curious about? No, Dennis never felt emasculated, never ceased to find the softness in her, loved her unconditionally, called her by her maiden name because he rejected the notion that anyone should have to lose themselves in a marriage, and she steadfastly believed, more and more as she drifted deeper into the darkness of the shadow wars and became addicted to it, that he was by far the better one to raise their kids.

What would he have said to Jeremy at lunch?

Her husband.

Has it really been nine years?

Hushed cubicles and shared work spaces squared in by a perimeter of glass-walled private offices, airy, bright, plants in pots. Sentro hurries through. She has a pace she keeps, faster than the engine ticking, which began after that cataclysmic first posting in Berlin as the wall came down and the Cold War took a turn to something even colder; it comes from never wanting anything to overtake her again. When they were little, her children complained about it, falling behind her on errands, on walks to school, at museums or amusement parks during her time off, dragging their feet and whining. She'd slow for a moment, then, invariably, return to her natural pace again, and they'd have to skip-hop to keep up.

Coworkers greet her, office banter; she banters back reflexively. These are not friends so much as coconspirators, but she's comfortable here, plays well with others; they all speak a common language. Click of keyboards. Scent of burned coffee. The familiar soft compression of sound and light, low trill of landlines ringing, and her feet on the carpet dull. It reassures her, speaks of safety and civilization.

Her space is in the corner, tidy and spare, big windows overlooking the river, light streaming in. Unless they paid close attention, a casual observer would take it for middle management digs, which is misdirection but also the goal. Clients expect a high level of invisibility. And Solomon wants to afford them the illusion of calm. Just another day at the office.

Hers has few personal touches. Hand cream she never uses. Old picture of the husband and kids. A bowling trophy someone gave her as a joke, unaware that it was one of the few activities she had shared with her father growing up. In a bottom drawer, sexy blue spike heel pumps she bought on impulse once for an embassy cocktail party and never wore again but loves to look at. Corkboard map of the world with pushpins of all the places she's been. A generic abstract watercolor that matches the color scheme of the building. Bookshelf, binders with no labels. Her long career has led to this, and she's content with it. But lost in tangled thoughts of concussions, consequences, Jeremy and Jenny, and what a suddenly seemingly uncertain future may bring.

"Where the hell have you been?" A colleague she's known for years has poked his bristly head in. She has no intention of telling him. But for a moment she draws a blank on his name and feels a hollow panic. "Ready?"

"For what?"

"Peer review of your Cyprus thing."

Reno. His name comes back to her with a rush of relief. Retro flat-top that reminds her of the cut grass of the parkway; in fact, stubble encircles his head, crown to chin, like one of those head warmers you wear under a ski helmet. Sentro suspects his wife trims it with pet shears. Their little boys—there're three of them, right?—have the identical haircut but nothing on their chins yet.

"Did you forget? I texted you. Ten o'clock." Reno—someone nicknamed him "Lucky"—Elsayed. "Jeez Louise, Aubrey, where's your head?"

Where indeed?

"Reno—" The trick to improving memory for names is to use them more often in casual conversation. She read this once, in an airline seat-back magazine.

"What?"

Wait, what *was* she going to say? Is it Reno Elsayed who has the annoying habit of compressing everyone's name into a single-syllable hip-hop sobriquet? No, that can't be right.

"Earth to Aubrey."

Cyprus.

"You okay?"

"Much better now. It was mostly the jet lag." Cyprus. She laughs. "Of course I haven't forgotten the meeting; I was just . . ." She wasn't "just" anything, so she lets the thought hang. "Never mind. Tell them I'll be right in."

He lingers, though, frowning, so Sentro quickly gathers papers together from the orderly disorder on her desk. Cyprus. The hotel hostage swap and exfiltration in Nicosia. She had forgotten about the debrief. Fuck. Into a stray empty folder she slips charts, surveys, cell

30

intercepts, surveillance transcripts, and satellite imagery of the city, the Mesaoria plain, and the river Pedieos. Digital photographs of a blown-out building, dead bodies—definitely not your standard middle manager fare.

"You want me to have them push it back a half hour?"

"No." She stands up. "Good to go."

But he stays in the doorway. "What the heck happened over there?"

Sentro says, "Oh, you know." Folder in hand, she's squeezing past him. "The usual fuck the what."

Chapter Five

There's this throw rug of crushed cigarette butts back by the garbage bin, which Jenny doesn't understand, because how hard is it to put your cancer stick out and take two steps and flick what's left into the trash? Hundreds of flat cellulose cylinders with their ragged charred ends, like spent bullet casings, which, she muses as she takes another deep, unpleasant drag on her last Spirit, is totally apropos.

No, she's not trying to quit. Yes, she knows it's a disgusting habit that doesn't even give her pleasure anymore.

What's your fucking point?

A dolphin-gray Amazon Prime delivery van bounces down the alley that flanks the minimall, stirring up a miasma of Baltimore urban decay. The driver's rosacea and aspirational neck beard are familiar to her from all his chummy banter across the barista bar: his name is Chet or maybe Chuck, skinny decaf butterscotch macchiato, no foam, no tip. Now he leers at her from the open side window as he drives past. Last week she complained to her manager about Chet's relentless attempts to ask her out and got a lecture on customer primacy and a how-to on using her wit and charm to defuse uncomfortable interactions "before they start," and while doing so perhaps she should upsell to the man the apricot scones that are always piling up because they arrive from the bakery rock hard. The manager concluded with a suggestion that Jenny not wear so much makeup. And a long-sleeve shirt would cover the dueling dragons that curl down around her upper arms.

He's an asshole, sometimes.

She smokes, making the most of her illicit break to take out the garbage. Her phone chimes. Text from Jeremy. Her brother had his monthly lunch with their mom; no insight into the memory lapses. Because they both share the suspicion that she hasn't actually seen a doctor, Jeremy was going to call the neurology clinic directly to find out if their mom made an appointment. Jenny was pretty sure it wasn't going to get them anywhere. Her brother's message confirms it: if they want to know about her private medical matters, the receptionist told him they should ask their mother directly.

Jenny sends a shrug emoji. Then the smiling pile of poo.

Texting her brother is so much better than talking to him, and this is why she invented the argument that she's been able to string out for the past three months. Its catalyst was a typical Jeremy Troon harangue on how Jenny was pissing her life away on sybaritic indulgences in childish defiance of their mother's stolid and cautious career path. This rapidly devolved into a shouting match in which Jenny accused her brother of feigning ADD in high school to buy more time for his SAT tests so he could get into Johns Hopkins, something she didn't really believe but had always been jealous about because her own test anxiety had resulted in mediocre scores and, by this same theory, doomed her to the third-rate state school she'd dropped out of junior year. Jeremy countered with a dig about weed stealing her ambition. She insisted weed helped her anxiety and accused him of only dating sociopaths, citing Kimmy, then kicked him out and cut him off except for texting, which didn't count as real conversation but enabled her to keep tabs on him since that was one thing she had promised her father before he'd died.

With her mother, the communication blackout has been longer than three months, and Jenny didn't need to invent anything. The last time they were together was Jenny's birthday, just the three of them. Her mother has made a point of mustering "the family" on special occasions for the past few years; Jenny finds this super ironic, considering that they're all adults now and that her mother missed so many important family milestones back when they were important. When they were kids. *Her* kids.

They were never close, Jenny has decided, never had the mother-daughter thing Jenny assumed all her friends had. The lunches, the intimate girl talks, shopping for prom dresses, and sharing little secrets. Her grandfather once told her, in his blunt, declarative style, that the reason she didn't get along with her mom was because they were so much alike. "Coupla ornery warrior princesses," he growled. "Two peeves in a pod."

She doesn't believe that for a minute.

Their relationship got worse after her father died, when, as irony would have it, her mother began spending more time at home. The mom phase lasted fourteen uncomfortable months, and then Jeremy moved back from the dorm to be Jenny's adult surrogate for the remainder of her high school while their mother (the professional Aubrey Sentro) went back out into the world of commerce and crisis and did whatever it was she did there.

On the one-year anniversary of Dennis Troon's funeral, still grieving, Jenny slipped out with her friend Rachel and got her father's portrait tattooed on her back, left shoulder. First ink. She didn't tell her mother, and her mother didn't notice the bandage that covered it for the first few days. But when Jenny finally uncovered and looked at it in the mirror, she was horrified at what she saw. Although she'd given the tattoo artist her favorite photograph of her father, what she discovered on her shoulder was some sort of black-and-green wolverine—not the X-Man, the animal, and badly drawn at that. So badly rendered that Jenny burst into tears seeing it, and her mother heard her and forced her way into the bathroom (how did she know how to jimmy the lock?) and thus discovered Jenny's ugly secret.

Not that her mom was judgmental; she offered to take her daughter to have it removed. Jenny, however, in her grief and embarrassment, insisted that she didn't want to lose it; she wanted it fixed. Which she now knows was impossible, but the reflexive willfulness she inherited from her mother caused her to dig in and refuse any help.

At least, she thinks, *in every other way I'm nothing like her.*

A couple of years later, stoned and moody after dropping out of college, she tried to have another artist turn it into a rose. Her brother says now it looks like a hallucination broccoli. And ever since, Jenny just doesn't take her top off except when she's alone, not even for sex, although that hasn't been much of an issue. She's told her few hookups she has a hideous scar from a childhood kitchen grease fire, and she used to hope they would think this was something her mother had done to her.

Lately, she's just ashamed of the whole fiasco. And sometimes wishes her mom would bring it up and offer again to go with her to have it removed. Or does she not remember that?

Shayda bangs out of the back door and into the alley, dragging two black plastic twist tie trash bags and looking surprised to find Jenny already back here. "You on break?"

Jenny takes one final drag on her cigarette and mashes it out on the bottom of her shoe. "No. Why?"

"We're short behind the register. And somebody just did an online order for, like, ten gazillion variations on venti mocha frozen frappe shit." Shayda takes some scarlet lipstick from her pocket and applies it blind, like a slash, to her mouth.

Jenny flicks her cigarette butt onto the ground and helps heave the trash into the bin. One of the bags splits open on a sharp metal flange and spills half its contents back out onto the pavement. "Dammit."

The Amazon van rolls back up the alley, passing them, slowing to a crawl, Chet's face in shadow in the driver's side away from them, but his eyes are turned this way and bright, like they're backlit. "Hey, ladies."

"Ew. I know that guy."

"Chet," Jenny says.

"Chuck," Shayda corrects. "Creep cupped my butt the other day when I was restocking napkins."

A claret tongue splits the lips of the Amazon driver, and he waggles it at them lewdly.

Something in Jenny snaps. She reaches down and picks up the first thing she can find: a stale scone sopping with milk so spoiled she nearly retches as she reels back and throws through the van's window a perfect spitball strike that hits Chuck on the side of his head and breaks into pieces that will be hard to clean out. He howls. Jams on the brakes. Throws open his door.

"Fuck fuck fuck."

Shayda says, "Oh Jesus," turns, and runs back inside.

Out of his vehicle, spitting, coughing, one eye clotted with viscous scone bits and half-shut, Chuck is holding one of those steering wheel lock bars, with which Jenny assumes he's going to try to clobber her.

"The fuck are you doing?" he's shouting, doing a stagger-walk around his van, clawing fetid crumbs from his collar. "The fuck do you think you fucking are?"

What Jenny thinks is she needs another weapon, and there's an awkward length of rebar under the trash bin that, once she's yanked it free, is way too long to be practical, but for one brief breath she imagines herself lifting it and running Chuck through, like a warrior princess would.

"I'm your worst nightmare," Jenny barks at him, because she remembers it from a movie. "I'm Chuck the Creep's hell on earth, a bitch with balls."

"What's going on here?" Dimitri, her manager, has stepped down from the back door.

"I'm pressing charges," Chuck whines, letting the wheel lock fall to his side and starting to dig in his jacket for his phone. "Assault."

Now that she can compare Chuck to a normal-size man—in this case Dimitri, but could be anyone, really—Jenny confirms what she suspected all along: Chuck's smallish. His saggy chinos, rolled up, still manage to pool over his trainers.

"I threw a scone at him," Jenny confesses. "He's the serial dick I told you about, D. He grabs ass when we come out from behind the bar."

"She assaulted me with a biomuffin."

"Stop embarrassing yourself, man." Dimitri has only two interests: handpicked mycotoxin-free fair trade certified-organic Nicaraguan beans and cross-training. His forearms are bigger than Chuck's legs. The manager may be an asshole, but he's her asshole for once.

"Get out of here," Dimitri tells the Amazon driver. "You buy your coffee beverages somewhere else from now on."

After one defiant, disgusted sideways spit, Chuck turns and swaggers with all the dignity he seems able to muster back to his van, and they watch him climb in and drive away. Could be Jenny's imagination, but she would swear she hears Chuck screaming as he pulls into traffic.

"You smoking out here, Jennifer?"

"No, sir."

"Good." This is the longest conversation she's had with Dimitri since he hired her.

"Thanks," Jenny says and means it.

"Shayda thought you needed help." He glances at the rebar she's still clutching, then spies the mess at the bin. "Put your sword away, and clean that shit up."

CHAPTER SIX

A baker's dozen of Sentro's colleagues, the usual bridge mix of retired military in work-casual civilian clothes and exiled government bureaucrats in everyday suits, have gathered in the big pleather chairs around the conference table to browse her written report on the Nicosia exfiltration, which all were supposed to have read by now.

A senior man, his coiffed silver hair a Beltway cliché, starts in, "This was supposed to be a simple acquisition," before Sentro can even sit down. Another lost name. Shit. Valdez? Falcone? Why does she forget some things while other stray memories crash in uninvited?

"I know." The debrief has evidently started.

The senior man's eyes tic-twitch when he looks up at her. Hector something. His eye situation is the unfortunate consequence of a nerve gas snafu in Tripoli when he was with the DIA. She remembers that. The Russian GRU was trying to kill another one of their own peripatetic ex-spies, and senior man got caught in the middle. His last name another anxious mental blank.

Was she ever good with names?

"I mean, jeez Louise, Aubrey, we're trying to move in the direction of risk reduction and cost containment, and it's like you're out there, mountains to molehills, throwing money off the back of a train."

How many metaphors can a man mix? "I know. I know."

And she does know. All of it. It cascades back in harrowing detail: the dark hallway; the switchback no one had mapped; the stench of garlic, mold, and dry rot; the way she'd blanked on the suite number at the door.

"A number of complications arose," she says. "Variables out of anyone's control."

The client was a multinational cloud-storage provider whose encryption-code team supervisor had traveled to Greece for a conference and disappeared from the hotel bar late one night. The ransom demand had been made through intermediaries; Solomon's online investigation unit had identified the source as a Turkish terrorist organization that was, no doubt, engaged in another round of typically violent and aggressive seasonal fundraising.

This was the crisis. Solomon's job was to manage and resolve it. Once the asset was located, she took a team to the island to facilitate a rescue and exfiltration.

Listening to the operation audio feed over the conference room's sound system, Sentro hears what her communications earpiece picked up of her own steady breathing while the remote audio-control op rustled papers with irritation while he looked to provide suite-number confirmation; a short delay, then the sound of a door opening to reveal the middle-aged Chinese American asset she'd been sent to retrieve, followed by the question he'd asked of her.

Can I help you?

For the big mission-review flat-screen in the Solomon Systems conference room, someone in support has prepared a PowerPoint of the Nicosia hotel-hallway confrontation. On an adjacent whiteboard are diagrams of the hallway's events as they unfolded, positions of the principals, timeline, photographs: bodies on the ground, walls chewed up by high-caliber bullets.

The audio becomes badly distorted with all the hell that broke loose.

A studio publicity portrait reveals the asset fully clothed, from his firm's corporate annual. Buttoned down and smiling. "Scott Chang," Sentro narrates. "Forty-one. Father of three from Minnetonka. His wife is an Amway Silver Producer. He was in Cyprus to negotiate a cloud-sharing software license for the client, met some hot-girl honey trap in a bar, and confused a blue-ribbon blow job with true love. Lost three days in a GHB daze and didn't, in fact, even understand he'd been kidnapped and ransomed by the Bozkurtlar Grey Wolves."

The audio maxes out when the flash bang explodes.

"All I could do was embrace the suck," she admits and looks around the table, hoping that those present, partners and peers, will understand, from their own experiences in the field or elsewhere, what she's talking about and let her little memory glitch at the doorway slide.

"Happy ending, of course," Sentro tells them. "Our client got its valued employee back. Amway wife still has a husband. And three little girls in Minnesota will grow up with a wiser, repentant dad."

A sober silence, some shuffling of papers. Nobody wants to go first; nobody smiles.

The overhead sprinklers triggered by the stun grenade whisper on the ambient audio, raining down.

Sentro fills the awkward quiet with a comment: "That water felt heaven sent."

No one around the table reacts.

Adrenaline and endorphins laid down underexposed snapshots that flood back to her, of Grey Wolves spilled in the hallway, of the naked female shooter she was forced to put down. As is her habit and means of self-protection, Sentro chooses not to think of them as dead but rather erased. No longer active obstacles.

But she remembers nothing of their flight from the hotel, the city, the island, their airlift back to Frankfurt, or the next thirty-six hours of her cool-down. And this is why she has, privately, gone to see the brain doctor. If there's a decision that has to be made about her ability to do her job, going forward, she wants to make it herself.

"Why the hesitation in the hallway prior to contact?"

Shit. Sentro touches the Band-Aid covering where the bullet nicked her and looks down the conference table to the former NSA woman Lucky calls Lady Bug, but only behind her back. "Sorry?"

Okay, okay, don't panic, but what's Bug's real name?

Tap-tap-tapping her mechanical pencil on the open report, the NSA woman looks back at Sentro, quizzical. "You asked your control for confirmation of the suite number." Her taupe lipstick matches her No.6 clogs. Who does that? When the Bug—*wait, got it: Laura, Laura Bugliosi*—when Laura came aboard at Solomon Systems, Sentro hoped they might be friends. Discounting support staff, there are still only a handful of women on the Solomon Systems employee roster.

It didn't happen; will never happen. Laura Bugliosi worships in the church of SIGINT. Sentro is a heretic.

"Eight seconds pass"—the senior man, Falcone, picks up Lady Bug's thread—"and then the asset comes out of a different suite, and he seems to have surprised you."

"I didn't fully trust our intel," Sentro lies. "The local recon was sloppy. I didn't want to stumble into the wrong room."

"You were out of position for what followed?"

"No. In position but requesting confirmation."

"Had you not paused for it, might this all have transpired differently?"

Sentro's been asking herself the same thing. The truth is she doesn't know. And that scares her. "The world turns. There are no sure things or do-overs," Sentro says a little defensively, and the room falls silent again, save for more idle flipping of pages. She likes her colleagues; they mean well. Like her, they've had to come to terms with a chosen profession rife with ethical and moral contradictions. Everyone finds their own way through it, and no one emerges unscathed.

Jenson, from operational finance, clears his throat. "Okay. So. Our total exposure . . ."

"Will greatly exceed our fee, yes," Sentro concedes. "And that's on me. I apologize. The cleanup, the local payoff, the necessity of an emergency exfiltration of the whole team after the event went south. It was just one of those days." Of course it was. But she's bothered by how much she suddenly wants them to believe this.

"The baseline goal for this operation was to facilitate a clean exchange," someone says. "The money for the man."

"Didn't happen as planned, but we got a good result," Sentro reminds them and looks for the source of this flinty criticism.

"You seem to be having more and more of 'those days' than any of our other active field operatives. Of late." Bob Drewmore is the critic, a former ranger who, absent army fitness requirements, has been slowly eating his way toward an approximation of Jabba the Hutt. His assessment stings, because he was the one who first recommended Sentro go private sector with Solomon as she was mustering out, back in the day.

"A clean exchange happens between rational parties." Her temper flares. "But I'm sorry—nobody calls us to deal with rational people, do they? We go in when all the other options have failed. And once in, if there are lives in play and I can save them, I do it. Goes where it goes. But I think my record speaks for itself."

"Port Isabel."

"What about it?" Drewmore just stares at her, smug, as if he's just played an ace. In a way, he has; hardly a day goes by when Sentro doesn't think about Port Isabel and wonder what she could have done differently. Better. "The boy was alive when I delivered him."

"I guess you can look at it that way, sure. But we're still paying on that civil suit."

"Fuck you. That was one of my first jobs here, Bob, and I recovered the asset. You shouldn't have settled."

"Just saying."

But he's not. "For the record, you weren't even there; you were sitting on your fucking thumbs in Islamabad, letting teenage soldiers get sent into an unwinnable sectarian civil war."

The folds of Drewmore's chin and jowls clench and shift. His stubby hands flutter up, defensive, backing off. "Hey. Okay. Sorry. Nothing personal, Aubrey." He's a good guy, she reminds herself, still married to the wife he met while in basic, commemorative rings from West Point and his multiple Middle East tours on almost all of his fingers. "It's just, business-wise, we gotta factor the optics. Our investors don't do nuance, nor give a runny shit about your record, or mine, only how it affects their bottom line. And you've become reckless, girl."

Has she? Sentro takes a deep breath. Reminds herself that ever since the Solomon board decided to seek venture capital, these operational reviews have become public shamings.

"Caracas, Lagos. That rat fuck in the Bahamas. Now this?"

"Wasn't me who ran the op in the Bahamas."

"Still. History. Liability. Exposure. It's a new game, Aubrey. I mean, hell, if you weren't practically a founding partner here, wouldn't we be likely looking to find cause to fire your bony ass?"

"My ass has never been bony."

There's some uneasy laughter, allowing release.

"Back off, Bob. Point taken," Bugliosi says, in a friendly tone. She trades a blank look with Sentro, who is a little astonished that the Bug has stood up for her. "Don't be an armchair quarterback."

"Maybe if she took a stretch of time off," Falcone suggests, trying to de-escalate. "Until we get this all sorted out. Cooler heads and whatnot. She's earned a break. Full salary."

"Maybe you shouldn't talk about me in the third person," Sentro tells the room, thinking that the last thing she wants is a break. Another job is all she needs. The discipline, the narrowing down. The comforting sense of purpose. Her mind will settle down.

"I'm with Laura. What the hell is all this?" Elsayed asks in Sentro's defense. "She's not operating in a vacuum. We're a team."

Falcone spreads his hands in a vague gesture of helplessness. "We have three dead Turkish right-wing militia to explain to State. Weapons violations the Cypriots are squeaking about. Extensive damage to the hotel premises, ditto the leased vehicles used during the operation and subsequent exfiltration. Local fees and fines. NATO has been inquiring about an unauthorized dark flight through restricted airspace of four member countries."

"Not to mention the bureau is threatening to sanction us for violating federal law prohibiting paying ransom for foreign hostages," Lady Bug adds drolly, because everyone in the room knows that Solomon does this regularly; it's fundamental to their sales pitch to clients.

"The feds themselves think that policy is horseshit," Elsayed says. "Hell, the White House just bought back a couple of Christian missionaries using highway-department funds."

Two words are rattling around Sentro's head: *time off?*

"The client should have to cover all incurred overages. It's in the standard contract. There's no exceptions." Elsayed shoots Sentro another sidelong look of support, and the argument swirls sans Sentro. Her thoughts skip, and suddenly she wonders, mortified, if during her wild years after Jenny was born, when she spent so much time away from Dennis—maybe Tripoli, or Mogadishu, where they worked so closely together and drank so much more than they should have—she slept with Reno Elsayed and can't remember that.

"You want to be the one to educate the client, Lucky?" Falcone drawls.

"I would. I doubt you'll want me to," Elsayed drawls back.

Drewmore cackles. "He's right." The tension in the room is easing. The requisite hazing, to Sentro's great relief, has come to an end.

"Look, Vic, I'm fine," Sentro insists. *Vic, not Hector.* Vic Falcone. She's said the name automatically, before she recalls it, like that awkward delay in a bad cell connection. There. Her memories aren't lost; some of them are just slow finding her. "I'd rather get right back onto something new," she adds, still slightly troubled by the suggestion of time off. "A simple wiretap op, if you're so, you know, worried I'm going to start World War Three."

A crushing weariness washes over her. What if the work is all that's holding her together?

Falcone nods, neutral. "You must have a boatload of vacation time coming, though, huh?"

It's not a suggestion.

CHAPTER SEVEN

Another half hour unspools before the meeting breaks up. The Bug goes quiet, lips pursed, eyes hooded, returning again and again to Sentro like surveillance cameras. Peers and partners delve into other business: a Case Western archeologist who needs site security in Cape Town, the partisan attacks dogging East Timor, how to monetize the ongoing White House obsession with Tehran, a dispute with Raytheon over incidental expenses during what all agree was a regrettable circle jerk in Honduras.

And the ill-fated events of Port Isabel shudder back to Sentro in installments, raw.

———

It didn't help that her marriage was fraying.

The Yoder boy's kidnapping had been Sentro's first private-sector caper after the seemingly bottomless largess of government-funded work for one agency or another. Lean crew, just her and Falcone, with a Houston-based gearhead freelancer named Unger providing remote tech support; but there was an unusually robust posse of rubbernecking hometown cops and bottom-feeding feds sent from Houston to babysit. Sketchy Mexican extortionists out of Matamoros had been holding a young American boy hostage for six months before the parents, wealthy

Brownsville developers, had reached out to Solomon in their desperation. The kidnappers had a price; the clients were willing to pay it; the endgame was just about Sentro getting the proper proof of life, making the money drop, and ensuring a fourteen-year-old who had crossed the border with a hundred bucks and a couple of very white friends, intending only to lose his virginity to a sex worker, got set free. After testy negotiations, the G-men and the locals had agreed to stay clear until the boy was safe.

Sentro holed up in a Best Western comfort suite and waited for a call, a handgun she didn't want on top of a squeaky AC with tattered viscose strips fluttering. Falcone—his dusky-red hair a riot of defiance in those days, with the beginnings of the tattoo sleeve he now hides, old-school can headphones, and a cheap laptop—and two deputies had set up shop in an adjacent unit, impatient, listening to phone taps while Unger, back in the office, videoconferenced and provided a full complement of satellite tracking technology and computer support for when things broke open.

Gulf coast. Hellish heat. Summer squalls. This was three months before Dennis had learned his body was riddled with cancer. On her back, on a bedspread of bright-yellow tropical fish swimming in a soft blue polyester sea, open eyed, one arm outflung, Sentro waited for the extortion call and talked on her personal cell phone to her husband about divorce.

Dennis had called to tell her that he'd decided to let her go. He would just do what she wanted, he said. "Because if you love someone, you do what they want. Right?"

He was so determined to take control of their free fall.

Sentro, numb, unsure of anything back then except the job in front of her, offered that maybe she didn't know what she wanted. That maybe as soon as you stopped wanting something, you got it.

"You'll say anything," was his observation. Dennis sounded so tired. They should both have guessed why.

She remembers saying to him: "Before you called, it's stupid, but I was thinking. Well, dreaming. A daydream. About my mom."

"Again? What a surprise."

"The truth is that what I remember are just stories and her smile," she continued, letting his gentle dig roll away. "But it reminded me how pointless it all is—history, I mean."

"Dreams are history?"

"Everything is history. And you can't live in the past, and it maybe wasn't really happier anyway; you just think it was. And how, I don't know, sometimes things are just over."

Through her mobile came only a pulsing, soft static, waves of it.

"Dennis?"

"Like this is over, you and me?"

Hearing it said out loud like that was beginning to make her have second thoughts.

He asked: "Second thoughts about the divorce? Or everything you've done to make it inevitable?"

They'd traveled this road before, many times. Her job, the long absences. Why couldn't she make a commitment to her family? Sentro had no answer, except that Dennis knew what she was, who she was, when he married her.

"Sorry." He backed off. "I didn't mean . . ."

"I fly back tomorrow. Just waiting to make this one last drop and get the asset; then I'm done. And everybody's happy."

"Everybody except us."

"Don't say that." Sentro stared at the backlit window blinds. She didn't tell him that she knew he'd been sleeping with Jenny's sixth-grade teacher. Couldn't bear to hear him deny it and didn't want to risk that he would; she made her livelihood and stayed alive by parsing lies.

Plus, this was different. She didn't blame him. They'd been given a gift and squandered it, both of them. Regular life was so much more treacherous and complicated than anything she faced in the field.

"Don't say anything more," she told him, smiling sadly. "I'll come home; we'll get takeout from that bulgogi place and put the kids to bed and sneak out into the garage and cuddle in the back seat of the Odyssey and have one last angry, high, hard one."

She remembers how Dennis laughed, in spite of himself.

"And after that, hell, I dunno. I don't know what else we'll do besides telling ourselves that it's no good to let yourself die without knowing, once more, the wonder of fucking with love." She'd forgotten to breathe, so she inhaled, ragged, fighting tears, and added:

"Or something like it."

Was this how her mother had felt? Was she taking the same empty ride? Her room's landline started ringing, shrill, and she had to hang up on Dennis and pick up the receiver to answer the call and go to work.

"How is he doing?" Nothing. Just a soft huffing static on the other end. "My client, Andy. How is he?"

The voice on the other end of the call was soft, musical, comically high pitched. "You got my *rescate*?"

"I do."

"A'ight."

"Bring Andy to the phone."

"You think I'm stupid? No. I get the money; then I let the hostage go."

"I need proof of life."

The kidnapper switched to Spanish. "Are you listening to me?"

"Have Andy tell you the name of his first girlfriend. They won't release the money unless they know he's still alive."

"Señora, I am a businessman, not a murderer."

She could hear, in her communications earpiece, the freelancer telling Falcone to make her bring the gun.

She said, "Try to see it through their eyes: once you have your money—"

The caller cut her off, sounding impatient. "Yes, okay. I will have the answer for you. Proof of the boy's life. No cops. No shadow."

"You'll have the answer when?"

In Spanish: "When I'm ready. You have eight minutes to get to the lighthouse." And then, in English: "Mark, set, go."

Dial tone. Shit. Sentro was already grabbing her keys, her sunglasses, the lumpy gray duffel bag near the door, in a hurry, pointedly ignoring the handgun, despite the admonitions of Falcone.

"Unger wants you to take the gun."

"No. Just make sure they give me space."

She could hear Falcone arguing with the Port Isabel cops about a surveillance tail. "Aubrey, wait."

Sentro pulled the door open; the smothering humidity hit her as soon as she stepped out into the day.

"Lots of space, Vic."

Her rookie mistake was thinking she'd get it.

———

Elsayed stews as he follows Sentro back to their private offices. "Bean-counting bastards have no concept of dynamic truth in the field."

"They have investors to consider." She caught herself. "We have."

"The hell does Bob Drewmore have against you? Besides that you're competent?"

Where to start? Sentro thinks she says aloud, but Lucky just stares at her, waiting. *That I'm still out doing fieldwork, and he has trouble seeing the tops of his feet over his gut? That he hates women because he got passed over by the Pentagon on account of his wife fell into the opioid swamp? That he's old and scared and feels marginalized and, like the rest of us, wonders what the hell he will do when the circus shuts down?*

Changing subjects, she says, "Vacation. Wow. Dennis and the kids usually had to go without me. Even if we planned ahead. Shit happened.

Then the kids got older—sports, camp. I bet I haven't had one since
. . . I don't know. Maybe Disney World. Right after I left the agency?"

"You missed Disney World, Aubrey."

"No, I remember it."

"From your husband's photographs, maybe. It was the first time we
did a gig together. I remember you calling them every night."

She stops short outside her office doorway. Looks at Elsayed fondly;
he's walked alongside her without judgment through a lot of unforgiving and hostile terrain.

"Dennis took great pictures."

"He did."

"You came in and hit the ground running," Lucky says. "Port-au-
Prince, dropping the hammer on Cédras, remember?"

She doesn't remember. "Oh, right."

Lucky may sense this is a lie, but he doesn't press her on it. He asks
again, with real concern, "You okay?"

Sentro deflects. "So. Anyway. Vacation." She shakes her head.
"Where should I go?"

CHAPTER EIGHT

Lush green islets dawn from an azure sea.

Fouled by a nosing of fish oil and decay.

The luxury yacht floats becalmed, glorious, midday in a pristine equatorial lagoon. Silvery water licks at its sides when a wave rolls through. Rigging shivers and clicks. The quiet is unreal.

And like some tropical trope, a lean, sun-kissed young woman is reclined on a deck chair. Her flawless brown body shames an impractical white bikini dazzled with sequins and a pink spritz.

His burly shadow eclipses her; his ferret eyes scutter over her one last time before his hands send the storm of flies thrumming.

Gossamer ginger hair floats out on the midday thermals like a shredded nimbus. All the hustle on the ship she appears to be aloof to. The bite of diesel fuel in the breeze doesn't faze her. Seabirds crisscross overhead, warped in the lenses of her sunglasses.

Her arm has slipped from the chaise. Her hand dangles limp, wrist engirdled by diamond bracelets.

Blood drips from the ends of her fingers onto the screen of a smartphone and spills off into the ruby pool spreading under her chair.

Pauly Zeme lifts the dead woman in his arms like she's nothing, her blood spatting down his board shorts onto the tops of his bare feet as he shuffles across the teak deck to an open hatch that leads to the galley and living quarters. He locks his hip and shifts her weight and, balancing her, removes her jewelry before tossing her down below, where a half dozen other bodies are tangled in fleshy discomposure.

He frowns at the violent red smear she's left on the front of his aloha shirt. "Aw shit."

A voice cries up, "Oy!"

Pauly's own face seems to detach from the lower-deck shadows, blue eyes finding the light and looking up. His identical twin, Castor. Same gym-rat build, sun blond, but flashing teeth that Castor's had filed into points, and his brother's forearms are girdled with serpent tattoos that Pauly thinks immodest.

Castor says, "Give us a fucking warning, ya knob." Then he adds, "Hullo! Back atcha!" and heaves a huge ziplock bag up through the hatchway, where Pauly fumbles to catch it. Rings, watches, and jewelry jangle in the plastic. Pauly splits the seal and adds the diamond bracelet from the dead woman's wrist as his brother shouts again. "And another!"

A second ziplock bag is tossed up, this one stuffed with wallets, pocketbooks, and loose cash: dollars, pounds, euros, yen. It arcs and slaps to the deck uncaught.

"And another!"

"Piss off! Not so fucking fast, ya knob!"

Laughter and bottles of champagne erupt from below in rapid succession like a juggling act gone awry. Pauly struggles not to drop them, but a few go wide and shatter on the gunwale, spewing foam and glass. A pirate boy in a wine-and-gold jersey watches, expressionless, crouched on the lip of the cabin. Castor comes up the ladder with a clean shirt that he throws at his brother.

"You look like the meat man."

"Can I help it they were bleeders?" Pauly peels off his ruined tropical shirt and examines the label of this new wardrobe critically before trying it on.

Two small, battered aluminum fast boats are tied up along the lee side, and the Zemes' motley crew of mostly teenage pirates, with their chipped, rusted machetes and long knives, looking for anything of value, has piled both high with booty: clothing, shoes, fishing gear, espresso machine, pots and pans, perfume, electric razor, ice chest, deck chairs, instruments ripped from the helm, a couple of spearguns, and a fancy assault rifle with all the trimmings. Their ebony shoulders are rimed with sea salt, and their shorts sag, slender frames gutted by hunger, shoes flecked with blood, and empty eyes hidden by the Ray-Bans and Oakleys and Warby Parkers they've found in the forward cabins.

One thin tweaker with a scar that runs through his ruined eye and a mustache he should not have grown snakes among them, shaking out gasoline from a spout can. The madras sports coat he's owned all of twelve minutes is too big; he lets the sleeves hang down over his hands.

In the clean shirt, Pauly jumps down into the closest skiff, and the still water trembles around it. He battens the plunder under a patched tarp and starts to cast off. His brother takes the helm of the second boat and whistles. Pirates lope back across the deck like a pack of dogs.

They start to settle in the two boats, jostling for position. But as Pauly watches, Castor grabs the smallest by the scruff of his ragged wine-and-gold West Indies cricket jersey and pulls him up and shakes him so hard the toes of his sneakers squeak on the bow trim. Common dinnerware clatters from threadbare cargo shorts pockets. Knives and forks. Worthless, but—

"Hey now."

The kid is shaking, he's so scared. He can't be more than ten.

"Fuck off my boat, Zoala," Castor says.

The boy's eyes plead: *Please.* He smiles, helpless, not meaning to.

"Fuck OFF!" Castor smacks Zoala with the back of one big hand, and the kid's sunglasses shatter as he recoils and half falls and half leaps back to the deck of the yacht. Eyes welling huge.

"*Desculpa.*"

"You don't steal from me."

Castor guns the engine, and the boat veers away, and Pauly follows in his brother's wake, throwing white water and leaving the boy and the plundered yacht behind. "Little useless knob."

Pauly looks back over his shoulder. Marooned, Zoala watches the fast boats hurry into the open sea. Pauly feathers his throttle, his boat slows . . . and he cranks the wheel sharply, as if turning to go get the boy.

Zoala grins and waves. Relieved.

From the fast boat's helm, Pauly waves back. He kills the motor and makes a vague gesture to the stern.

"Carlito. *Vai*."

The boat lurches, idling, rocks bow to stern, drifting sideways. The scarred tweaker lifts a flare gun, and the others watch without expression as the flare fires and streaks across the cloudless cyan sky in a long lazy arc at the yacht.

For a moment, Pauly watches the boy dance on the deck, as if delighted by the fiery tangerine tail.

Then he stops, as he understands what it portends.

Zoala yells something obscene and scrambles over the cabin for cover. The flare strikes spilled fuel and combusts. The yacht explodes, spitting flames so hot that the teenage pirates flinch and recoil from them even as Pauly shoves the throttle to send his fast boat leaping around again to catch up with his brother.

CHAPTER NINE

Driving home, under a sky afire with purpled Chesapeake sunset, she can't stop thinking about Port Isabel.

The freshly whitewashed lighthouse that sprouted from a half-dome berm of green grass. The sound of a cheap cell phone ringing as her rental sedan skidded to a stop at a no-parking curb. Sprinting into the building, the bulky duffel bag slung over her shoulder.

The phone nagging. Four times. Five. Circular stairs she took two at a time, willing herself up to the gallery deck, where a throwaway cell phone taunted from the ledge, ringing.

Sentro picked it up, wheezing, "I'm here. I'm here."

The voice and accent she recognized from previous calls said, "Check out the view, why don't you?"

"Nobody's following me. We don't have to do this."

"*Mira*. Look at the view."

Heart pounding, she did: the shimmering channel, the traffic bridge, South Padre Island in the distance, and a quaint little harbor tourist village stretched a couple of blocks north and below her. Boardwalk and the usual little shops and amusements.

"You see it?"

"What?"

"Pirates' Landing. The pier? I give you four and a half minutes."

Sentro was still struggling to catch her breath when the call cut short. "Wait—"

Dial tone.

Down the stairs again, as fast as she could manage, the strap of the duffel rubbing her shoulder raw, Sentro burst from the lighthouse front door and stumbled down the steps, across a parkway, toward the boardwalk.

Unger, lo fi in her ear by wireless receiver, quipped: "Sending you on a little scavenger hunt to make sure you aren't being followed."

No shit.

She heard Falcone wondering aloud, Had they not heard about GPS?

"It's a formality. I think. He knows but wants us to think he doesn't and get careless."

They told her only later about the local deputy texting on his cell phone—receiving and texting, rapid fire from inside the motel room with Falcone—as Sentro sprinted across the landing parking lot, past a clutter of souvenir kiosks, past a theme restaurant, and onto the long wooden pier. Tourists in bright-colored shirts and cargo shorts gaped at her; she was laboring, sweating, not dressed for the marathon she'd been running in the brutal heat of the day.

Another phone ringing, distant; she searched for the source.

A group of little kids were crowding the open mouth of a fiberglass shark mounted on a post halfway down the pier. One of them was reaching inside, where the throwaway phone was making noise.

"WHOA! No—put that down—!"

She shoved her way toward them through a Chinese tour group. The kids looked back at her vacantly, but the boy who'd found it couldn't resist flipping the phone open to answer the call.

"NO!"

Startled by the madwoman running at him, the boy took a startled step back from the shark's mouth, the open phone held out—

"Put it down!"

He did. In fact, he dropped the phone. Dropped it, and Sentro watched it bounce once on the wooden pier planks and cartwheel over the side into the water as she arrived.

The kids screamed and scattered.

She stared down beneath the pier, where the phone had disappeared. Now what?

A vibrating hum. Sentro drew her personal phone from her pocket, flipped it open, answered, "What?"

"Noreen."

Exhausted and disoriented, Sentro asked again: "What?"

"His first girlfriend. Noreen. Correct?"

Sentro said nothing, numb. The kidnapper's high-pitched laughter broke the tension: "Tell me you weren't about to have kittens there, if that phone go in the water."

Her eyes rose. She scanned the area, thinking: *The guy must be close; he's watching me.*

"Yeah. A whole cow, possibly."

"It's all good now, my friend. Almost done."

Falcone described to her later his feeling of utter helplessness, back in the motel, listening along with the cops and feds as the kidnapper told Sentro about the black Corolla in the parking lot—"Key on the rear tire, like we was valets, amiright?"—and knowing she'd be going out of range without backup.

The blue blip computer-screen cursor that was Sentro moved north along a Google map of a thin barrier island, out of communication range: "North, all the way, all the way to the end of Park Road, far as it goes."

And the local deputy kept texting.

Falcone never formally reported what happened next in the motel room, but Unger confirmed later how he'd seen Falcone's eyes narrow as he seemed to put something together and leaned back to ask the

Brownsville deputy what the devil he was doing, and how the deputy just looked at Falcone, smug, which, Unger long afterward pointed out, Vic did not and still does not appreciate, ever. Cops and feds were in the room only as a courtesy, to observe the drop, but clearly this officer was communicating with someone on the outside, somewhere else.

"It's a free country," Unger heard the deputy say.

"Yeah," was what Falcone purportedly replied. "Where you're free to fuck this up? I don't think so. No."

Though he'd deny it when asked to give his deposition, that was when Unger witnessed Falcone spring up out of his chair and drive the texting man, backpedaling, out of the video frame. Some almost-comical punching and heavy breathing ensued off screen, after which Unger saw the deputy reappear, wheeling rapidly headfirst into the wall behind Falcone's laptop, leaving a half-moon crater in the plaster before he fell to the floor, out of sight again.

"Pretty quick and slick" was how Unger described it. After Falcone picked up the deputy's phone, saw then who he'd been SMSing, and said something along the lines of, *Oh shit, no,* both men realized they would never get to Sentro in time to warn her that her race to pay the ransom was doomed.

———

Rocky emerald atolls dot translucent seas overhung by quicksilver romance-novel mist. Black checkmark terns wheel over photoshopped sampans with dragon sails; shredded cotton clouds ride the far horizon.

Everything so hyperreal, Instagram colors and lively promotional prose; Sentro clicks mesmerized through postcards of paradise on a travel agency website. And when she finally looks up, bleary eyed, at the big framed vanity mirror opposite, she can see, on Jenny's bed, the faint ghost of her face looking back at itself over her laptop screen.

White text from the website header reflects off her reading lenses: *FREIGHTER CRUISES. THE ULTIMATE EXPERIENCE. GET OUTSIDE THE BOX!*

She can read it backward.

Don't drift, Aubrey.

Get outside? Sentro hasn't even been *in* the box for such a very long time.

Marta has suggested a voyage on a cargo ship; Marta with the three perfect children and ex-husband, Jumbo, a coal-industry lobbyist who lives with his twenty-two-year-old girlfriend and their love child; kind, earnest neighbor Marta, who has blithely believed for years the lie that Sentro works middle management for an insurance company and who stayed beside her like a saint through the endless, bleak first days after Dennis died. Might they have been best friends, in another life?

The photographs on the travel website do look beautiful; the cruise sounds restful and restorative, or so Sentro says to the voice of Marta from her cell phone speaker, which is flat on Jenny's old counterpane.

"It's not like a *cruise* cruise, the ol' floating petri dish, with a gajillion people milling around, screaming kids and poolside Zumba and so much sensory overload you feel like you're going crazy—those are stressful," Marta notes, because she's been on more than a few of them. "After a couple of weeks you need a vacation from the vacation."

The placid freighter sounds perfect. Isn't rest and restoration what the doctor said she needs?

Sentro's Guilford Avenue row house is unchanged from when she and her husband and children all lived there together, its painted lady facade chipping and sun faded, perhaps, but everything perfectly maintained inside by a service that comes twice a week. Big, bright, spotless, cold, and empty now. As if someone left and took all the life with him. But then, she always thought of it as his place. She grew up in a world where the woman makes the home; Dennis made this one.

Which begs the question: Where is hers?

She sleeps in Jenny's old room, uses the hall bathroom the kids shared, the small study for her home office, and the kitchen only occasionally. It's hard to cook for one; she never really got the hang of cooking, anyway. Dennis perfected the fast-food takeaway buffet (Clark burgers and Abbey Burger Bistro fries, Charmery chocolate shakes, Verde pizza, Kiku sushi, and Shun Lee's Chinese), and the kids loved it, growing up. Their master bedroom has become a dusty memorial to a life interrupted; the living room looks staged, like a furniture-store display. She has no attachment to the house except for the memories it holds, many of which she only heard about later from Dennis and her children, when she came back from a caper.

Will the house help her hold on to them?

"It's just, like, seven or eight other passengers. There's private cabins and a library of movies and pulp novels and a chef that cooks for you and the crew. And there's mostly the sea and the sky and the roll of the ocean for however many days," Marta is saying. "I could go with you." Her voice is thin and strained on the tiny cell speaker.

"I think I just want some time alone."

"Why? What's going on?" For a moment Sentro thinks she might tell her. But Marta doesn't wait long enough. "Oh, Aubrey. You're always alone."

"At work, no. We have teams."

"Work." Marta's judgmental inflection recalls Jeremy's.

"Maybe you could fly down and meet me somewhere along the line during a layover," Sentro suggests, but she's already chosen from the website offerings a trip that offers little in the way of glamorous ports of call and includes a special place in hell, where Marta is concerned.

"What are you thinking? French Riviera? Mediterranean?"

"No. South America."

"Ugh. Rio." Sentro knows that Marta went there with her beloved Jumbo to try to save their marriage and wound up flying back in tears, five pounds heavier, sunburned, and alone.

"I've never been." This is another outright lie, but Sentro is so used to lying about her life she's almost come to believe the fictions.

"It's beautiful, of course," Marta adds sadly.

———

Lush green, lumpy islets punch through glassine azure seas.

Haloed by a silvery romance-novel mist.

The burned boy, Zoala, lies curled in the cool shadows of the coconut palms. They grow thick along the black sand beach of this unnamed scrap of land to which he somehow swam and floated after he was blown free of the pleasure yacht the Zemes had set ablaze. The acrylic cricket jersey having been incinerated, he shivers with fever, and his throat is raw. Uncovered, the flash-broiled skin of his back, arms, legs, shoulders, and one long starboard swath of neck and face course with the exquisite pain of a hundred thousand slender needles being slowly shoved into him.

He drifts in and out of fractured dreams: international test matches against teams of fantastical, delirium-spun creatures he won't be able to remember.

When the sun sets, the beetles find him and feast on the burn blisters, a shimmering sweater of undulating iridescence that shelters him from hypothermia and keeps the wounds from festering. Their shells clatter and click as the bugs settle and stir, settle and stir. Shore birds circle and descend on the bugs, and a strange triage ensues, bugs eating bacteria, birds eating bugs, and Zoala is able to survive for three days by sucking morning moisture from the salt grasses and remaining very still.

———

Shrimpers in long boats find him at twilight after sailing past the charred wreckage of a luxury yacht hung up half-submerged on the reef. They observe an apparition wandering, armored in beetles, along the dusk-misty shoreline like a creature in a monster movie.

At first, no one is willing to go closer.

One of the men, the son of an Obeah woman, is convinced the creature is some kind of *douen*. His fellow fishermen are not so sure. For many generations, long before the priests and the missionaries came with promises of salvation and their son of God and saints' bone relics and mystifying incantations, it's been common knowledge among the coastal people that water remembers whatever has been lost in it. And since water touches everything, this provides a limitless source of malevolent trouble loosed back onto the land in the mist or the rain or the steam from a boiling pot. Like this small evil spirit on the beach.

Dip a hand into the ocean, the old ones say, and you have at your fingertips everything you've ever done, dreamed, everyone you've ever known, and everything every man or woman who has ever lived has thought or cared to remember. Water is ancient, here since the beginning of time. The difficulty is in knowing how to gather the memories you want; they're swift and elusive, cruel and capricious, happy to be free of you.

Sometimes it's wise to just let the current carry them away.

After a short deliberation, this brave man strips his shirt off, murmurs as much of his mother's protective spell as he can remember, then angles his boat through the surf, runs it aground on the beach, and climbs out. His small pistol gripped in his pocket, he's ready; he intends to kill with it if he needs to. But after a cautious creep up onto the sloping black sand, the shrimper sees that the creature's feet face forward, and this suggests, as his mother has taught him, that this is no simple child's lost soul. This is a *jumbee* who has been cleverly distracted by a demand that it count all the sand on the beach. It's how you get rid of them: Make them tally every grain and start over each time they make a mistake. When sunrise comes and they haven't completed their task, they die.

But who could have made such a demand here, on this empty atoll?

The creature makes a mournful sound. Doubting his bullets will kill an evil demon, the shrimper is about to plunge back into the foaming surf when the bug-shrouded monster sees him and calls out to him in a language he understands.

Wise to the spirit's tricky, shape-shifting reputation, the Obeah man sloshes out backward into the shallow water anyway, knowing a jumbee can't follow him there.

The other shrimpers, safe in their boats beyond the break, exhort their colleague to use his gun.

The shrimper fumbles for it in his pocket.

The jumbee stumbles and falls to its knees, shedding some of its luminescent skin. A storm cloud of sooty terns explodes from the date palms and swoops down in a commotion of gray white to attack the pus-drunk beetles, gobbling them up, circling on beach thermals around and around a fallen human boy who has been revealed to all, like a magic spell lifted.

The shrimpers watch, transfixed.

Now they see the raw wounds on the boy's back and limbs. His soft features, half-scorched, a riot of red, turn skyward, eyes rolled back white, tears streaming; he's reciting the Lord's Prayer.

And now the Obeah man recognizes Zoala, a troubled orphan they all know well, and whose sister many of them know too well back on the mainland.

CHAPTER TEN

Sentro has never much liked boats. She grew up in a place with little water; what she knows about them derives from the better part of two winter months spent belowdecks in a scuttled trawler that was taking on freezing water in Kastela basin C, Port of Split, back when she was cashing a federal check. The situation was this: war criminal and self-proclaimed warrior prince Željko "Arkan" Ražnatović had decided to take time out from his cake-shop clubhouse and the Serbo-Croatian conflict to woo his anorexic girlfriend, a pan-Baltic pop singer, on a Red Star Belgrade professional footballer's yacht. Their ensuing hijinks, conversations, and assignations, vigorous, loud, but stultifyingly dull, were nonetheless of interest to the various intelligence services of several NATO countries worried about resurgent ethnic troubles in the region, so Sentro and two colleagues from other eurozone agencies were dispatched to the leaking, listing listening station, where they were mostly bored to distraction.

And drank rakija.

Raw sewage; fuel oil; salt mold; cold, damp blankets; the walls closing in.

Or was that Odessa?

No. Christmas in Split. She's sure of it. Sentro lost $200 playing Yahtzee marathons with the foreign spooks.

Then again, Split is beautiful.

Odessa. And it wasn't Ražnatović; it was the Ukrainian chemist who was fooling with early CRISPR and tubercular genetics.

But a trawler for sure, rotting and dock bound.

A watery coffin—isn't that what they say?

Watery grave?

As was often the case, nothing geopolitically useful was accomplished, and she missed the kindergarten holiday pageant; Jeremy was a wise man. Jenny took her first steps the next day. On a DARPA secure network, Dennis emailed her some pictures of her happy family from his first digital camera, which they pretended she gave him for Christmas. Sentro only heard, years later, after Dennis had passed away, about the bitter tears both children had cried when Sentro hadn't appeared on Christmas morning.

Rectilinear acres and acres of shipping containers on the banks of the Patapsco River wait to be loaded on huge ships or driven away. Gulls slip and weave between loading cranes that lift their heads like giant horses and rotate cargo, deck to shore. A curtain of heavy clouds sheds a wispy rain. The contract carrier cargo ship CMA CGM *Jeddah*, Singapore Shipping Company, Bahamian flag, dwarfs the black Uber sedan that snakes through the containers and stops abreast of the gangway. Sentro climbs out—blue jeans, white blouse, a wool old-style Orioles warm-up jacket she found in Jenny's closet, and her black leather backpack bag.

At the last moment, she ran back into the house for a book to read on the trip, scoured the dusty shelves in Jeremy's room, and pulled out a hardbound copy of *Lord Jim*. She faintly remembered Dennis telling her once that their son had to read it for high school. Conrad. Involving oceans.

Right?

Nothing like a good high sea adventure to help pass the time.

Containers tower above her in rainbow colors, scrambled together like unsolved Rubik's Cubes; the ship is bigger than she imagined. Whatever second thoughts she might have had are overshadowed by a spark of anticipation of the adventure ahead—even if it's as quiet and uneventful as Marta has insisted it will be. Sentro isn't unfamiliar with having downtime between assignments, but it has been a long time since she took a real vacation alone; in the past she would greedily fill the days with family. Even packing for this was something of a challenge. She worries she might have brought too much.

Seabirds whirl white like blown scraps of paper around and through the skeletal quayside cranes. A square-jawed Irish first mate wearing work gloves jogs down to greet her with an umbrella: "Ms. Aubrey Sentro?"

"That's me. I got a little lost getting here; I think I typed in the wrong address on my phone."

"The port doesn't fare well on Google Maps, no. Waze is better but so aggravating."

"Yeah. I'm sorry."

"Nothing to be concerned with, truly." That light melody Irish makes of words. "I'm First Mate Mulligan. We need to hit our window of shoving off. Bit like an airport runway, timing is all. Miss your turn, and you're back of the line." Mulligan takes Sentro's battered duffel and small rolling suitcase from the trunk of the car. "This the sum of it, then?"

"You mean my luggage? Yes. Please, I can carry that."

"You can, and you will, once we get you on board."

A couple of other crewmen have come down to help collect Sentro's luggage, but they just stand staring, awkward, because the first mate can easily handle both of her bags himself.

"Captain says we're set to go, Mr. Mulligan." Sentro catches herself scanning their faces to rank them on a threat scale. *Stop.*

"Groovy." Mulligan waves the crewmen back to the ship and gestures for Sentro to walk ahead of him. "Freight don't wait. Welcome aboard, Ms. Sentro." When she grasps the greasy gangway handrail, she understands why they all wear gloves.

———

"Well, there's a thing."

Tugging her rolling bag off the elevator, she can't at first find the source of the comment, as her eyes are slow adjusting to the gloomy corridor ahead.

"Determined to show us all up, are you?" A woman's voice, disembodied.

"No." Sentro flattens herself against a bulkhead wall as a wheezing, obese male passenger with a trio of huge metal trunks comes the other way and directs a crew member to squeeze them through the narrow door of his berth. Given the size of the ship, the cramped quarters are a slight disappointment and a reminder: boats and their OCD nautical restraint. The female voice asks something else that gets lost in the ruckus of the fat man's luggage. "What?" Then Sentro sees her: a rumpled young woman who clearly knows she looks good in anything has stepped out of an open doorway. Sentro guesses, from the accent, she's a product of the British Commonwealth.

"Fontaine Fox. Hullo."

Pale skin and that tangled jet-black just-had-sex hair Sentro has seen in *Vogue* at the salon where she gets hers cut and always wonders how it's done; the Fox woman seems to take hard note of Sentro's minimal baggage as it comes past her.

"Or is there a matched set of leather luggage and a mahogany wardrobe meeting us at another port, like in the novel."

"What novel?"

"Any one of them. You know what I mean. Where they steam across the Atlantic and dress in tuxedos and have issues."

"Aubrey Sentro."

"What?"

"My name."

Fontaine laughs. "I thought you were speaking in some romance language I'm not acquainted with." And then: "Really?"

"Really."

"Americans and their unusual names."

"I guess." Sentro sparks to an odd, primal thrill of connection, like meeting a possible soul mate on the first day of school.

Her cabin is on G-deck, with all the other paying passengers. Just below the bridge, it's bright, plain, but comfortable. One of the singles, not a suite. Desk. Chair. Love seat. Built-ins. A minibar-size refrigerator and rounded window looking back over the stubby stern-deck stacks of cargo.

Tugs are urging the huge ship out of the crowded port. Sentro dumps her bags on the bed, shrugs off her pack, senses eyes on her, and turns. The Englishwoman is angled in Sentro's cabin doorway now, her body loose, slender but not lean, in the way of a lucky someone who never has to work out.

The wordless pause between them then is odd. A regauging? Fontaine Fox has one of those efficient smiles that doesn't need to ask for any encouragement.

"That's it, then. Your 'things.'"

"What? Oh. Yeah."

"Having a go at us, it would seem."

"I'm sorry; I don't understand."

"Trying to show us all up as dilettantes," Fontaine translates, gesturing vaguely with a long hand of manicured nails lacquered black, "with your oh-so-economical kit."

"Oh." Sentro looks at her two small bags. "Is it? I never know what to bring."

Fontaine says, "Me neither. So I bring everything. You, it appears, bring nothing."

"I don't have much."

"And you're one of those who launder."

"I guess."

Fontaine's bright eyes bear down, amber, intent. Sentro has the dizzy feeling that this pretty younger woman is flirting with her. More awkwardness ensues. No one has flirted with her in years. Sentro feels the dull weight of her age.

"Well."

Sentro makes an effort: "Nice meeting you."

"I hope so." And seeing Sentro acceptably rattled, Fontaine gestures again, vaguely, at nothing and tenders another efficient smile before she disappears from the doorway.

———

As the *Jeddah* slowly leaves the harbor, heads downriver toward the open sea, Sentro walks out to the stairs, where a small open deck allows her to watch the skyline of Baltimore drift away. There's a lingering guilt that she told her children last minute she'd be taking a quiet sea cruise but not exactly where and how. They should be used to it by now. Jeremy seemed jaded but nonplussed ("Of course you'd do this now—have a safe trip; try to make some new friends, for Chrissakes"). Jenny wasn't answering her phone.

She won't miss them because she long ago learned to carry them with her; she has no feelings one way or the other about the city any more than she does for her house; after all these years, entries and exits are second nature; anywhere is interesting; attachments create vulner-abilities that can be tactical distractions. For a long time after she began to work projects in the dark corners, she worried over the way she could disappear Dennis and her children, push them into some safe, soundproof room deep inside her, where they couldn't be touched but also wouldn't disrupt her focus.

Where, for the duration of the assignment, they could cease to exist. An occupational hazard, was what her colleagues called it. Collateral damage. *The price we pay.*

But that's not really what it was.

Dennis had it right all along. The job didn't change her. It suited her.

CHAPTER ELEVEN

Flat-screen TV, comfortable chairs, a game table—there's a welcoming reception in the common room for the eight paying passengers to meet and mingle with some of the officers and senior crew. Crudités, brie, and prosecco; the roll of the ship is barely evident as it makes its way down the Chesapeake Bay. The captain, evidently a Spaniard from his precise Castilian enunciation, presents fit and elegant, with a continental skunk streak of white through his wavy, swooped-back hair, as he delivers a well-rehearsed toast.

"And so I'd like to welcome you all aboard our humble *Jeddah*. It's not a Princess Cruise, but I think you will find it has its own roguish charm."

Everybody has a name tag. The overweight man has written only *Bruce*. There's a shaggy-haired duo, the Gentrys, Jack and Meg, who appear to be newlyweds; two sinewy, ageless Scandinavians have both unhelpfully identified themselves as Nelson; the bashful Tagalog has scrawled something unreadable in an abomination of grade school cursive.

The captain's salutation drones on and on. "You have chosen the waterway less traveled, following the venerable tradition of the tramp steamer, seeking ports of call at the pleasure of its clients . . ."

Again, out of habit, Sentro finds herself idly assessing the tactical exposure of her position in the common room, finding the points of egress, possible cover, the way she always does when she enters an enclosed space. *Stop.* She reminds herself that she's on vacation, where the credible threat level is, well, probably nil. And this leads her to wonder if her concussions have opened some new level of introspection she'd rather not explore. Circular thinking ensues, killing time, really, until she feels a light touch on her shoulder, and someone leans against her from behind to whisper, "So, hmmm, let's see what we have." The Englishwoman. Her breath moist and warm on the nape of Sentro's neck.

". . . Or, as the great novelist wrote," the captain intones, "'in order to attain the impossible, one must attempt the absurd' . . ."

To her frustration, Sentro draws a predictable blank on the woman's name.

"Blushing Bride and Groom." She's nodding toward the newly-weds, and then the Swedes: "Some looks-to-be Scandinavian Gristle. A Man So Fat No One Will Travel with Him. The Tawny East Asian of Mysterious Origins."

Sentro angles her eyes to look over her shoulder at the name tag stuck above a slight swell of breast: Fontaine Fox. *Use it in conversation.* This close, Ms. Fox leaks a splash of expensive perfume, and perhaps a brush of purplish lip gloss, but no other makeup. Sentro, in an aside, asks, "Which great novelist is he talking about, Fontaine?"

"Cervantes." And then, correctly deducing that Sentro has drawn another blank: "*Don Quixote?*"

"I saw the musical at a dinner playhouse with my dad."

"Of course you did." Her eyes are amazing. When was the last time Sentro noticed that in anyone?

"*Man of La Mancha.*"

"Not quite the same, sorry."

Polite applause as the captain concludes his remarks. The Swedes and Bruce No Last Name step up like field trip students to ask him questions about his ship. First Mate Mulligan is on his fourth full glass of wine; two of the junior officers are making side-eyes at Fontaine's plunging T-shirt neckline and murmuring in what sounds like French. The Tagalog pretends to be interested in one of the framed maps on the wall above the refreshments. The newlyweds stand side by side, fumble fingers down low, and smile, mute.

"You've got it all figured out, then," Sentro says.

"Well. Except there's you and me."

Sentro turns to face her. "What about you and me?"

"Star crossed, I should think."

"What?"

"Once we get around to the fucking. You're not married, are you?"

Sentro feels the hot blush race up her neck to her ears and offers a suitably dumbfounded silence to counter the melee that erupts in her head.

As if realizing she's overshared something, Fontaine Fox looks mortified. "Oh hell. Sorry. I'm sorry, I didn't mean—and yes, afraid I am always this candid."

"I mean, I'm flattered," Sentro begins to explain, "but I'm not—"

"You don't need to commit yourself."

"And you're very attractive, but—"

"Very. But."

"But I don't, I mean I'm not—"

"Did I misread where your eyes just went?"

"Probably. Name tag. My memory is a little—"

"Not into same sex, is what you're saying?"

"No. Yes."

"Which?"

"Not really, no."

"Hm."

"And yes, I am . . . was. Married. To a man."

"Me too, how fun." Fontaine is nonplussed and upbeat. "The truth of it is—Aubrey Sentro—I'm a bit hopeless. And, well, randy and impetuous, those who know me and judge me would also tend to say. But. Mostly hopeless, which explains, you know, why I'm here, on a slow boat, avoiding Mr. Fox, as it were. Whilst I drift away and contemplate the best way to disentangle myself from him . . . and, well . . . sizing up my limited onboard options? I'm not keen on swinging, so the Scandinavians and the just-wed White Stripes cosplay band are out.

"I don't do crew; the executive officer seems a bit weedy, his second too Irish by half; the adorable little South Asian has a crucifix around his neck, which tells me he's either Catholic or born again, and I don't wish to be cause of his eternal damnation. Which leaves you and the plus-size bloke. Call me a fat shamer, but I'm confident Bruce won't fill the bill."

This is way more than Sentro wanted to know, but she's been able to gather her composure while it was said; it's not the first time she's been propositioned by a woman, and it just took her by surprise. She's intrigued by Fontaine, thrilled to have the awkwardness of traveling alone so thoroughly mediated. Lurid overtures won't be a problem unless Fontaine Fox chooses to make them one. "I'm sorry."

"Apology unnecessary."

"Good."

"Attracted will do"—Fontaine shrugs—"for now." Then she smiles her see-you-later smile while offering a toast: "Fuck the French."

She chugs her prosecco. Hands the empty glass to Sentro. "Ciao." And glides away to mingle.

———

Passengers dine with the crew in the officers' mess, directly adjacent to the common room. Sentro is seated at the captain's table with the Gentrys, Big Bruce, and the enigmatic Tagalog. Soft light flares in over the mainland from the dying sun; out of the shelter of the bay, the long lazy sway of the ship on Atlantic waves takes some getting used to.

"It was a *Snow White* theme," Meg, the new bride, is telling them. "With a touch of Tim Burton. We wrote our own vows."

Bruce guffaws. "Were the groomsmen dwarves?"

Worried, both the newlyweds chuckle and chime, "Oh no."

"Instead of the exchange of rings," Jack elaborates, "we did the, you know, glass slipper."

There's an uneasy pause, as if nobody's quite sure what they're talking about. Fontaine Fox holds court at the other dining table. Gales of laughter. Mulligan's bloodshot gaze never strays far from the Englishwoman's tremulous décolletage.

"Slipper, that was *Cinderella*," Bruce says to the couple.

A baffled look passes between Jack Gentry and his bride, and Sentro offers, helpful, "Fairy tales share so many common themes." She's looking at Bruce. "True love, for example."

Jack and Meg say, "That's us."

Bruce scowls. "And death." He saws at his rib eye, lips moving, keeping his own counsel.

The captain, who has introduced himself as Gonzalo Montez from Getafe, points his fork at the Tagalog.

"And you, señor. What folly brings you to my ship?"

The Tagalog stares at him, deer caught in headlights. Sentro guesses he doesn't speak English very well. Bruce snorts and, mouth still full, starts to launch into a half-intelligible diatribe about how somebody should do something about "all the unchecked immigration from Islamofascist lands in the South Seas." Irritated, before she can stop herself, Sentro translates the captain's question into passable Tagalog, and the young traveler brightens and responds eagerly. She has to tell him more than once to slow down; her understanding of the language has never been more than serviceable, and she's surprised she remembers anything after all these years. Everybody at the table waits and watches her with a mix of curiosity and disbelief. She's tipped her hand; she'll need to proceed with caution.

"His name is Charlemagne," she translates for Captain Montez. "From a village on the island of Marinduque." Recognizing the word makes Charlemagne grin. "Software engineer, if I understood him correctly"—of course she did—"working on some, I'm guessing, artificial intelligence thing at Johns Hopkins?"

"Multimodal sentiment analysis," the Tagalog interjects, evidently triggered by keywords in Sentro's loose translation.

"He had some time off," she continues, "wanted to take a vacation cruise, but his English is so poor he was afraid to book on a regular tourist ship."

"Those Princess boats have people who speak all kinds of languages," Meg says.

"He heard that freighters often have Filipino crew and thought it would make the trip more enjoyable."

"Likely story," Bruce mumbles and mops his plate with bread.

"It's true!" The captain raises his voice as if it will make him more understandable to his passenger: "Normally I have two, three sailors who hail from the Pearl of the Orient Sea. But I am sorry to say, *lo siento*, not on this trip."

Again, Sentro translates the captain. The Tagalog nods, grins back, grateful, gold incisors gleaming, and then blushes and stares intently down into his food, self-conscious.

"Lucky you speak his language." Montez, studying Sentro, states the obvious.

"Just enough." She leans into the truth to shore up her cover. "I had to learn a bit of Tagalog for my job."

"And what did you say your occupation was, Ms. Sentro?"

"I sell insurance. Why?" This instinctive pushback (*lie, dissemble, deny*) comes out a little more aggressive than she intends, and the temperature at the table briefly drops. She takes a big breath. The hole she's digging feels like it's just getting deeper.

Charlemagne saves her. Gathers his courage, pushes back his chair, stands like a schoolboy and blurts something out, bold, a speech. An aria. Extended, gesturing, passionate, ending in tears. From what Sentro can understand, it's the story of his emigration, his brother's brutal death at the hands of vigilante policemen, part of the savage drug war waged by President Duterte. Was the brother dealing? Yes, of course he was. But only in desperation after he'd been laid off from his job when the mine where he'd worked lost its foreign investors and closed. Poverty came crushing down on the family. Charlemagne was fired from his job because of his brother's reputation. His sisters were reduced to working in dance clubs and hostess bars. Finally, Charlemagne found a way to flee with his mother and family: refugees sponsored by the Mormon Church, relocated to California—an apartment, a new job, safety. America saved him, he says. God and America, which, he posits, may be one and the same. But his mother suffered deeply the disloca-tion from her ancestors and died not too long ago of a broken heart. His sisters blame Charlemagne for her death. For leaving the village, bringing them all to Manila and then across the sea. For his brother Arvin's addictions. On Marinduque, they tell him, his brother would still be alive. He has reeled across the country taking contract work in Denver, Chicago, Atlanta, and Baltimore, where he's found permanent employment, a possible fiancée, and a quiet boat holiday, during which he hopes to gather his thoughts before he undertakes this scary new responsibility. Husband. Father. Yes, she's pregnant. Sentro can't tell if Charlemagne is having second thoughts about his future wife or simply feels the weight of life bearing down again. She wonders if, on this cargo ship, he's running away.

The Tagalog stops abruptly, done; he and the others at the captain's table look expectantly at Sentro. She hesitates, then shrugs apologeti-cally. "Now that—honestly, I have no idea what he said."

Everyone chuckles and resumes eating and chatting. But from the captain's lingering, practiced look of annoyed bemusement, it's clear to Sentro that he doesn't quite believe her.

Dessert is an assortment of aromatic sorbets.

———

Later, unpacking her bag, Sentro hears a knock on the cabin door and half expects Fontaine Fox, but no—

"What was it, really?" Big Bruce fills the narrow threshold. He reeks of cod, wine, and Old Spice.

Sentro takes a step back, frowning. "Excuse me?"

"Your Micronesian friend, his whole confession or whatever dealio he spewed to us at dinner? I could tell you understood it. Some kind of crypto-Islamic thing?"

"Hardly."

"You know what I'm talking about." Coffee and licorice sour his heavy breath.

Sentro angles her head, annoyed. "Bruce. Where are you getting all this?"

"Okay. Or not. Okay, yeah." He backs off. "Whatever floats your boat. But me, I like to know who I'm traveling with. Nobody told me I'd be sharing quiet time with ISIS, and they don't exactly have TSA checkpoints for these junkets."

"Philippines is nowhere near Oceania. And almost ninety percent Christian."

Bruce looks like he's been slapped. Softly: "No shit?"

"No shit." Sentro starts to close the door, but Bruce raises his hands in surrender.

"I'm sorry. Sorry. I had a sambuca and some coffee after dinner and, whoa. Never mind. I'm . . ." Bruce gestures behind him, at a huge strapped leather traveler's trunk. "I was knocking, actually, because I was wondering. Could you help me guide this sucker up the stairs?"

The case weighs a ton, more than the fat man can manage; Sentro provides more than guidance. Awkward clunking tracks their struggle with Bruce's trunk out onto the side deck and up the exterior stairway two levels, Bruce uphill hefting one end, Sentro downhill gripping a hand strap, shoulder to the other end.

They stagger out onto the open deck of the bridge castle—where passengers can marvel at the vastness of the ocean under a spectacular night sky—and they put it down and slide it to the far rail. The dark containers stacked in tidy rows on the main deck stretch impossibly far both directions into the darkness, where a light on the foremast reveals the faint haze of a sea mist she can feel on her face.

Big Bruce, last name Bologna ("And I got a lot of grief for it in grade school, believe you me"), has been confessing to her the whole journey up ("I was always large, but it wasn't from lunch meat"), a whole different side of him exposed as if a switch got flipped. Primarily, he explains, he's a stargazer: "At the equator, we're perfectly positioned to look edge on into the fat of our galaxy: constellations like Ara, Norma, and Lupus. Scorpius, with all its incandescent draperies . . ."

Stepping back as the big man crouches to loosen an array of hasps and latches, Sentro flexes her back and shoulders and considers the thin line of lights on the horizon that must be the Atlantic Seaboard of the United States. Bruce's helter-skelter Milky Way crazes its canopy above the pale halo of civilization's glow and wheels the stars and galaxies up into the vast vault of night.

". . . a central bulge of old, yellow stars, and those spiral arms of blue, younger stars . . . it's crazy to think about. We gape at a past, like, events that happened a million, a billion years ago . . ." A crescent moon vents the darkness. Soughing waves whisper along the sides of the ship. There is magic still on earth, she thinks.

The dull moan of the engines thrums at the edge of her perception, and Bruce's strange soliloquy unwinds.

". . . a firework pinwheel. Distances so vast. And the walls of stars, and the carousel of galaxies. And gas and dust clouds." His mouth open, he cants his head back and stares skyward. "And black holes the size of the orbit of Mercury and bigger. Everything lurking around them gets swallowed and forever trapped. Not even light can escape."

You can't save anyone, not really.

She watches Bruce sit back, prop open the case, and remove a tripod, then the parts of a huge telescope, which he begins to assemble.

"Most of what's out there is dark matter, though," he says gravely. Sentro understands; her life has been largely about dealing with the dark matter, dark flow, dark energy. Nothing magical about it. The unknown that holds the known. "Stuff we can't even see," Bruce marvels. "Or prove or measure, or I don't even know, but . . ."

It separates, it binds, it forgives, it forgets. Sentro's spent a good part of her life traveling through it.

"I don't like to think about that," the big man admits to her, but she watches him aim his tools of curiosity up into the unknown anyway.

———

In the dark cocoon of her *Jeddah* cabin, sheets unfamiliar and crisp across her, she awakens from a vivid jumble of a mission that never happened and that she won't even remember in a moment except the feeling that everything went wrong; she awakens in a cold sweat to a banging and moaning, and she rolls and reaches down under the bed for the gun that, at home, she always keeps there.

Her fingers find the empty floor. The knot of her half-conscious thoughts untangles, and she remembers where she is. Her pulse is racing, her head throbbing backbeat with the percussion that's coming from the Nelsons' room next door.

She tries to shake her lucid dream. *I saved the boy,* she reminds herself.

It never helps.

Vocalizing bleeds through the cabin wall, growing louder. A soft, steady, easily identifiable rhythmic thumping in the adjacent berth, slowly building. Procreation seems to be going pretty well next door.

A couple of deep breaths. Her tension unwinds. She fumbles for her smartphone, left charging on top of her unopened Conrad sea tale, taps the screen for the time: well after midnight. White banners with text messages from Jennifer. In sum: *Where are you?* Sentro calls, on the off chance she still has service, gets sent directly to her daughter's voice mail, but stubbornly decides not to leave a message. She puts the phone back down on the side table. She wants to hear her daughter's voice, not the cold counterfeit of messaging.

In the bathroom, she squints in the sudden light. Sits and pees and tries not to stare at herself in the wall mirror opposite. There should be a rule against putting mirrors facing the toilet. Thoughts tumble, fragments of things she's clearly not forgetting: Jenny, Jeremy, the near catastrophe on Cyprus. She hears the shrill whistle of blood in her ears, feels the tickle of a migraine.

Sentro takes the new prescription bottle out of her overnight kit. *Take as needed for headaches.* She washes three pills down with water.

BANG BANG BANG BANG. Something heavy and hard hitting the wall. Sentro freezes. A man cries out. Pleasure. Then there's silence.

Oh.

"I hope that was his head, not hers," Sentro exhales softly to herself before switching off the bathroom light and climbing back into bed.

It won't take long for the drug to seize her. In the meantime, she decides to try to remember the faces and count, like sheep, all the enemy combatants, malefactors, and blackguards she has personally taken off the board. No safe place to put them. They scream from the darkness until she gives them their due. Since her consultation with the brain doctor, Sentro has grown convinced that these will be the last memories to leave her, if all the rest do go.

Even when she can't remember her children's names, the faces of the dead will linger.

She's asleep before she gets through eight of them. A dreamless peace this time that feels like heaven.

CHAPTER TWELVE

"Now, best guess: Are you of the opinion that was young love last night, conjuring the two-backed beast?" Fontaine Fox sits down with her, a plate heaped with eggs and ham. "Or some unspeakable occult blood ritual we will stumble on later in our journey to the earth's edge? Sailors sacrificing an albatross to Poseidon so we won't be eaten by the dragons. Or is it Scylla and Charybdis? Safe passage and so forth." Airily apologetic: "My A levels got a bit pear shaped."

Sentro was up at dawn, running the perimeter promenade of U-deck as the sun broke over the dark water of the Atlantic. She doesn't like boats, but she loves the size of this one. The crazy distortions, containers stacked five and six high and dwarfing her, interspersed with the bulk cargo, crated machinery, giant bags, grain bins, and then more containers, with narrow, long dark gaps at measured intervals bleeding sunrise as she ran, crevices between the towering mesas of cargo; then the ship itself, impossibly massive and football fields long and yet dwarfed by the vast sea, puny, insignificant, at the whim of the gods.

Having alerted the bridge and obtained approval, she donned the obligatory hard hat and safety vest and began four circuits that included the elevated bow they call the forecastle, where, on each lap, she passed three crewmen fussing with something—the anchor mechanism?—chunky thick steel compartment gutted, parts strewed everywhere. The swirl of languages fell away, like her troubles, for the moment, as her feet trod the deck, steady.

Only one of the men looked up at her, his lean body taut and restless, a deep scar through a ruined eye and the feeble makings of a mustache. On her last lap's pass, the crewman's good eye tracked Sentro with a jaded mien. Had Sentro been in the field working, it might have signified more, but here, on holiday, she is determined to shed her old habits and predilections, hence the running, which has always helped her to find the fine balance and disengage; on this elephantine cargo cruise to the Southern Hemisphere, the disfigured man just strikes her as a bad hire the management of the *Jeddah* could come to regret.

"Sounded Nordic," Sentro answers her new breakfast companion, sipping coffee and folding her laptop screen down on a half-finished email to Jenny.

"Nordic?"

"Finland, Denmark. But probably Sweden."

"Sex has regional distinctions?"

Sentro shrugs. "You're the expert. Come to think of it, couldn't it have been you and our first mate?"

"I told you, I don't do crew."

"Mm." Sentro enjoys the light banter. Has missed it. Dennis always kept her on her game.

"Anyhoo, I'm English. We suffer in silence."

"Of course, my mistake."

"Swedes?" Fontaine considers this. "Swedes, you say, having a rumpy pumpy. That's mildly arousing. I do carry a genetic predilection for getting plundered by Vikings."

"Why is this even a topic for breakfast?"

"I dunno. Would you have preferred to begin with some empty waffle about weather? Or perhaps I could ask how you slept? But I'm sure you didn't, because I didn't, because of the howling of the mystery mating. So."

Sentro smiles. "Not a mystery to me."

"Ha. Nelsons. Brilliant. Ew. Unlikely."

"I'd put money on it."

"I'd feel awful having to take it from you so easily, love." As the Englishwoman digs into her veggie scramble, Jack and Meg enter the dining room. They look cranky and tense. Sentro trades looks with Fontaine, who starts to say something, but as if on cue, the Swedish woman is hard on the heels of the newlyweds, and she's come in smiling and humming.

"Glowing, in fact," Fontaine observes with irritation. "Quite nervy."

After a moment, the Swede is followed by her husband, who has a purple bruise under his eye and a red knot on his forehead and a swollen lip, as if his face has been hitting a wall.

Sentro meets Fontaine's stare again, deadpan.

"Don't gloat," the Englishwoman says.

"I never gloat," Sentro insists, oddly happy, and tries to remember the last time she made a new friend.

———

After breakfast is a nonoptional tour of the bridge castle—also called the accommodations tower, apparently, depending on who on the crew was talking—sold as a hospitality gesture to the passengers but clearly a necessary safety protocol required by insurers in case of emergency evacuation or lockdown. Sentro lags back, disengaged; she did her own thorough recon not long after boarding. First Mate Mulligan looks to be struggling with a nasty prosecco hangover. "Cabins you're familiar with . . . this is the officers' lounge, which the officers never use. Community television, board games, limited library. Donations

from your pulpy beach reads strongly encouraged after you finish 'em
. . . next door, we call this a reading room; you might want to stay
clear in rough seas, as there's no window . . . galley . . . weight room,
please ask if you don't know how to use a piece of equipment . . ."
Blah blah blah.

It goes on like that. Eight lettered decks after the main—U-deck, A
through G—and then the bridge topping it off. Laundry. Sauna. Officer
cabins. Crew quarters. A basketball half court carved from a cargo space
on the second deck. Engine room. Electrical. Infirmary. Boxes linked
by boxes, then stacked. Just like the cargo they carry. Down one set of
stairs, through the bowels of the ship, and back up the elevator. Sentro's
tactics professor at Quantico—or was it the Point?—had a name for the
difficulty of defending this kind of structure. The narrow passageways,
the exposed egress in the event the elevator failed or was caused to fail.
Sentro can't remember it. An acronym, she thinks, surely. BFO: blinding flash of the obvious.

Stop.

Nor can she remember the name of that professor. Rheumy gray
eyes, ruddy gray flattop. She woke up today with a clear head and
thoughts, the dull ache gone. But the unexpected gaps and disremembering persist.

Shit. Pickering? Almost thirty years ago. She was never good with
names, but now every lapse of remembering rattles her. She hates the
flush of helplessness, not being able to trust her own mind. How you
think, what you remember—or forget—defines you. Doesn't it?

Looping finally back to where they began, they linger on the bridge
for another pithy quote from the captain, this time Coleridge:

> The ship was cheered, the harbour cleared,
> Merrily did we drop
> Below the kirk, below the hill,
> Below the lighthouse top.

And he helpfully plots their course with a marker on a glass-topped horizontal map of the Atlantic: "Down to Savannah to pick up bulk paper, cotton, and tobacco, then hop over to Nassau, and then it's about four days to Rio, rounding the shoulder of South America; we'll be crossing the equator right about here . . ."

———

"And this is our secure cabin." A door opening and a harsh light flickering on in a windowless room on C-deck. Sentro looks with some skepticism past First Mate Mulligan as he continues, "Where we'll tell you to go in the event of a nasty storm or other unexpected event. Watertight. Door locks from the inside. Six days' provisions, life vests, scuba gear, and a homing device . . ." Mulligan clearly likes to hear himself talk.

A group coffin, Sentro finds herself thinking. Watery. Grave. She glances at Fontaine, who's not even listening; she's trading short missives with someone on her smartphone, turned away from the group for privacy. The other passengers attend to the first mates with a sober quiet. The Gentrys are wearing matching sneakers and can't keep their hands off each other, as newlyweds do. Jack shows early signs of a cold sore, and there's a faint rug rash on his forehead, which has already caused Fontaine to elbow-nudge Sentro and lift her eyebrows, suggestive.

"Any questions?"

Even if there are, nobody wants to think about having to be trapped in this windowless cell.

Mulligan smiles, reassuring. "Mostly, as you can see from all the crates against the back wall, we use it as a wine cellar, since the temperature stays fairly constant."

The wine list was a big sales pitch on the cruise-trip website. Sentro wonders if, toward the end of the journey, you get so bored you're swilling a spunky Spanish red with the breakfast waffles.

The ship makes odd noises as it powers through wind-chopped sea and flexes. Twenty-four hours in, she's already feeling twitchy.

———

"Well, it was kind of spur of the moment; I'm sorry I didn't get to say goodbye."

The *Jeddah* makes port in Savannah to take on another several dozen containers for which it doesn't seem possible the ship's deck has any more room. A five-hour shore leave encourages most of the passengers to avail themselves of a chartered shuttle to the historic downtown, but Sentro's been to Savannah—one of the road trips she did manage to take with her family—and remains aboard to answer, from the wide stairwell landing off G-deck, where the warm afternoon sun has begun to settle into the coastal cloud cover, Jenny's phone call after leaving several irritable, deliberately unanswered texts.

"I tried to call you before I left."

"You could have left a message."

"I like to hear your voice."

"It's not an either-or." Jenny launches into a familiar lecture on twenty-first-century phone etiquette, and Sentro finds herself hearing words but not paying attention to them. Conversation with her daughter has, for years now, been fraught. The anger, the recriminations, the frustration with what Jenny insists is her mother's fundamental failure to understand what her daughter has endured. "You look at me, but you don't see me." Is she right? Sentro, a victim of her own mother's foundering, has no real point of reference. Sad that Jenny feels a hurt she can't seem to fix, Sentro distracts herself watching a huge rusty-red container with a black-and-white cat logo get swung aboard while, down below, on the concrete quay, five men are clustered, hands in pockets, posed like a boy band, watching. Four of them are comic-book muscular—big shoulders, shaved heads, tracksuits—day players from some low-budget Balkan crime movie.

Bulk paper?

Stop. Sentro's growing weary of having to remind herself.

"What's it like?" Jenny asks, out of nowhere.

"What? Oh. Strangely serene," Sentro says. "Odd. Singular. Not beautiful yet. I'm hoping we'll see something beautiful, but that's not why I came."

"Running away from us again."

"The only running I remember is back to you."

"That's so wrong." Jenny wants to talk about her wounds again. The purported crimes her mother has committed against her, the hole in her heart. How her father raised her to believe the world was fair, and how she's come to discover that it isn't. And somehow that, too, is Sentro's fault. She can't change the past or the grievances her children have gathered on their own; she settles in to let Jenny vent and lets her own thoughts drift.

For one glorious summer season, when they thought Dennis was in remission, Jenny turned thirteen and played softball on a travel team, at first in rebellion against her mother, who was indifferent to sports, while her father had been a high school shortstop phenom and she was a daddy's girl, all the way. But once Jenny discovered the game came easily and that she was quite good at it, mother and daughter found common ground in simple rituals, the pregame braiding of Jenny's hair and tying a ribbon in, the strangely intimate long dawn drives to weekend tournaments, radio karaoke, the shared rooms. Sentro had a rare, long break between assignments, and as Jeremy was touring colleges with his dad, Dennis made a point of "giving his girls some space."

It was, for Sentro, ten weeks of wondrous détente with her daughter that she has never quite found again. In the championship game, Jenny's playing was otherworldly. Sentro had the dizzying sensation of living life's adventure through someone else, someone she loved, marveling at her daughter's ferocity, which Dennis insisted was pure Sentro. And her icy calm when—three and two, two outs, game on the line, just like in the movies—Jenny smacked a single down the line and drove in the winning run and was mobbed and buried by her screaming teammates when she crossed home plate.

Afterward, a number of sharklike parent scouts from better teams approached Sentro about Jenny's future. An elite national travel team even offered scholarship funding in the event Sentro and her husband couldn't afford the steep fees.

Jenny disappeared from the celebration. Sentro found her in the car, hiding, sobbing, insisting that they needed to go home. Now. No goodbyes.

It was more than a hundred miles before Sentro dug the reason from her inconsolable child.

"You were amazing," Sentro told her.

"I wanted Daddy to see it," Jenny said.

"I took pictures. I took videos. I was on the phone Skyping with him when you got your last hit."

"But he didn't see it," Jenny wailed.

Sentro said that there would be lots of other times for that. That this was only the beginning.

"No," Jenny snapped. "I don't want to play anymore. I'm quitting."

Sentro was stunned. "But why? You were great."

"Yeah. And now I'll have to do it again. And again. And again. No." She wrapped herself in a blanket and turned her head away to cry into the pillow she'd brought, wedged against the door. The weird part was Sentro understood her. And thought, naively, *Give her time; she'll change her mind.*

They didn't talk the rest of the way home.

And after Jenny ran inside and hid in her room, Sentro and Dennis discovered that Jenny's equipment bag in the back seat was empty. She'd thrown her glove, bat, and cleats away at the field.

There's dead air on the phone. How long has it been since her daughter stopped talking? Sentro vamps, "Twenty days, Jen. I'll be back before you know it."

A fifth man joins the four on the Savannah quay. Light haired, a hipster, miscast here. Sunglasses, skinny cuffed pants, and a Vince Vaughn porkpie hat. Sun dusts a downy chin nimbus of beard. Sentro almost laughs. Jenny seems to sense the inattention and asks if her mother has heard anything she's said.

"Yes. And I'll email; I'll send pictures. I'll call you whenever I hit a port where I get cell service."

The ensuing silence on the other end of the line is Jenny's favorite current expression of deep skepticism where her mother is concerned.

Then Sentro says, "Promise," before she can stop herself.

Jenny makes a cutting observation that Sentro's promises have always been mostly empty, and it's not an unreasonable criticism, but the next awkward pause between them is Sentro's fault because she's followed the upward tilt of the hipster's gaze to the gunwale of the *Jeddah* forecastle, where Fontaine Fox stands, leaning forward against the rail, hips cocked, with shiny black jeans and an untucked shirt, sexy hair blown everywhere, staring back down at him.

This strikes Sentro as odd. Could they know each other?

She forces herself to back off from speculation: it's none of her business. Shut the sensors off. Her business is what she's set sail to leave behind.

Her business and all it engenders.

Focus, Aubrey.

The men are walking away. Getting into their mobster motorcar. And Fontaine Fox is gone from the deck rail.

A skip in the record, dust on the needle. Wait. Did she finish her call with her daughter?

Sentro looks down at the phone clutched in her hand, its screen dark. Then she gazes out and down again at the empty quay, where a minivan has arrived and drawn close to the gangway and her fellow sea travelers are spilling out with shopping bags ready to reboard the ship. Sentro shoves the phone in her hoodie pouch and worries a hand through her hair, fighting back the disquiet that's overtaken her.

CHAPTER THIRTEEN

It was stupid, taking the scooter. Just like he'd told his brother. Even when the road is dry, the village of San Ignacio is a jarring, tooth-loosening half-hour ride from Porto Pequeno, and in the current downpour, the spattered mud cakes the legs of his pants, and water rivers off the cheap poncho over the hump of his backpack and right down the crack of his ass, and his eyes ache from blinking away rain and struggling to find safe passage between the potholes and furrows and exposed roots and fallen palm fronds. Castor should have fucking come himself if he was so anxious to off-load their haul.

Or they could have borrowed the Colombian's Land Cruiser and come here together.

"Closing the bloody books on that yacht noise," Castor insisted; they already have their next play schemed—contract work, easy peasy— half in advance already wired to Western Union, cashed, and banked. A big flashy job Pauly is proud to have found and finessed. His brother still can't believe it.

He squeezes both hand brakes to cross the narrow stone bridge a swollen stream has already breached, brown water sheeting across it in surges. The bike skids, but he manages to stay upright by using his boot like a mud ski. Brown sludge rooster tails behind when he throttles up. He can see dull light from the few structures that remain around the overgrown Ignacio plaza up ahead. The tiny village is nested in steam rising off the ground.

A signless corner bodega offers a single man framed in the front window: middle aged, unremarkable, European. Merino suit, expensive watch, no tie; it's his sleek crimson Jaguar parked right out front, the back of which Pauly leans his scooter against, because the kickstand is busted.

The man looks up from a smartphone and his chicken and rice as the thickset figure in a hooded rain poncho splashes across the street and enters. The door has a jingle on it. Pauly's boots, dripping wet, squeak across the unfinished floor to the table.

"Robbens?" Pauly has never met him.

"Don't bother to sit. I told your brother—we have no business to discuss."

It's always a pissing contest with the Dutchman, Castor says. An imperious white man determined to prove his birthright of Anglo exceptionalism, whatever that is. Pale forearms are thatched with coarse hair, and slack muscle wobbles when he lifts them from the table to gesture his disdain. The trick, Castor told Pauly, is to just push past it. So, stubborn, he lifts the poncho and shrugs off his backpack, unzips, and empties its contents on the table. Watches, jewelry, credit cards, wallets, and cash and coin from the United States, China, and the European Union scatter, violently. Booty from the weekender yacht the Zemes lately plundered.

"I also have account names and passwords." He shows the soggy piece of paper, with handwriting already smearing.

Robbens stares at it all, unmoved. "Question. Do you know, *mijn zoon*, how young men survive to be old men in this world?"

"My brother said to tell you we got an even bigger play coming up, yeah?" He allows Castor the credit for it, since he's five and a half minutes older and claims to be the alpha. *Sons of Zeus,* their mother would coo, to feed their old man's ego.

Robbens talks over him. "I'm well aware of the bloody source of this shit. Okay? Did you think I wouldn't find out?"

"We burned the boat."

"In water."

"What?"

"You set the yacht afire in water, which, what a surprise, tends to extinguish flames. Debris washed up on Lorenzo Key. Along with the remains of many passengers and crew.

"They were important people, boy. With important friends. And said friends, you can tell your doppelganger, said friends would pay me considerably more than I could get for this plunder, were I even able to find a buyer, in exchange for the names of the lowlife reprobates who thought it was a good idea to rob and kill their good friends."

Pauly stares at him, not sure he's understood everything, but he's understood enough to know that this isn't going to go the way his brother told him it would. Pauly resents always being sent on these fool's errands. Never knowing the full story, always feeling like he's playing catch-up.

"Where is Castor?"

"Busy." Still stubborn: "So are you interested or not?"

"Are you deaf? Have you been listening to what I am saying?"

"What?"

"I suggest you call Colonel Silva and swear to him the cock-up on the yacht was an unfortunate accident and beg him not to kill you, because that is, in fact, the only rational option you have."

The name Silva means nothing to Pauly, but the rank worries him. It's been his experience that the rich tend to look after each other, that the military and the criminal are often separated only by their chosen uniforms. He guesses that the colonel is in the drug trade, connected to the 1 percent of the 1 percent by the very fact of their all being absolutely filthy fucking rich.

Pauly stews. "You told him who we were?"

"Not yet."

"Not ever." Pauly reaches under his poncho for a gun but hesitates when Robbens scolds him, clearly irritated now.

"Stop! Pointless! Think! Kill me, and you will not only have *federales* and the colonel crawling up your ass; you'll have everyone who relies upon my services coming after you."

Using his arm like a blade, Pauly sweeps his bloody bounty back into the open pack and zips it shut. "We can sell 'em on eBay. And you'll be kicking yourself for pissing on us when you see what else we got going."

"This is a business. Yes? You are not remotely pirates; you're high sea sociopaths, and you are out of your depth."

Now Pauly pulls the gun.

Robbens flinches; his slender hands come up to shield his face. The clip empties. Pauly can see the heat of its discharge singe the hairs on the back of the Dutchman's arm as the bodega window behind him shatters and falls in a curtain of glass. Across the street, the bullets thunder off the bulletproof Jaguar like raindrops.

Then it's quiet again. Rain sheets in. Robbens pushes back from the table, slips some folded money under his coffee cup, and stands up. He's already soaking wet. His legs tremble, but he's trying to pretend he's unimpressed.

Pauly is breathing hard, glaring at him.

Robbens says, "How much better you must feel."

He doesn't. Castor should have done this himself. Chastened by their need for this imperious knob, angry at everything, and feeling like a sorry stand-in for his brother, Pauly runs back out into the storm.

Chapter Fourteen

Dinner is served on tilting tables, chairs creaking with shifted weight, half cups of coffee sloshing, and there's a lot of picking at the flattened chicken on flash-scalded kale, but nobody's much interested in eating it. Outside their squared steel refuge, fierce rainfall races in Cristo-like curtains draped over a surging gray sea and splatters against the windows.

They're all given journals, compliments of the captain. "Proteus blesses the seafarer with marvelous insight," he intones over boulevardiers at cocktail hour. "Unfetter your inner poet."

("Hell's bells," Fontaine groans.)

The black Moleskine fits easily in Sentro's hand and includes a very nice ballpoint pen that, lingering alone after dinner when the table has cleared, she holds poised over the blank page for longer than she wants, waiting, but no words flow. Back in middle school, she remembers, as a writing assignment, she was required to keep a diary, but she managed only two weeks before stopping and later more or less made up, in a panic, the subsequent three months of entries the night before the project was due.

She ditches the journal and runs the U-deck twice a day instead. Sleeps. Eats. Banters here and there irreverently with her new friend Fontaine when they cross paths. Tries not to worry too much about the momentary blanks, hesitations, unwanted recall, daydreams, every minor tremor of distraction that may disrupt her thoughts. *Is that an early sign? Should I be making plans?*

The crewman with the scar watches when she runs.

What's that about?

More than once she's discovered him watching—from the observation deck, where he appears to be wrestling with one of the microwave antennae; from inside the containers while he tightens the straps. She considers confronting him, but the next run he's gone. Working below, somewhere, she tells herself. *False positive; move on.*

The wide Atlantic pitches and heaves; waves split by the bow explode upward and away in white, foamy madness. They're fighting the north equatorial current, Mulligan tells her. "We're gonna lose at least a day." An albatross follows the *Jeddah* for almost four hours, magnificent, riding thermals without ever straining its wings.

Her headaches ease; her Cyprus scrapes and bruises heal. She doesn't dream.

She thumbs through dog-eared paperbacks and pulp fiction from the shelves in the community room in order to avoid the book she brought from home; the plots of these abandoned tomes all run together. Most involve hard, handsome, haunted men with secret government jobs that require them to rack up the body count to save the world from conspiracies of evil; some involve hard men whose worthy distrust of government requires them to rack up the body count to save the world from evil secret government conspiracies.

Lord Jim, according to its introduction, is about a flawed, humble man tortured by his own fallibility. This does sound promising to Sentro, but she somehow can't bring herself to start reading it. She's never thought that what she does is special or heroic. Just necessary, sometimes. Or so she hopes.

Hours spent on the observation deck leave her sunburned and mesmerized by the juddering of the mountainous waves, the miracle of dolphins, the ruler-straight horizon, same in every direction, but with an infinite presentation of white clouds piling, shifting, blooming, folding in on themselves like her thoughts and her memories and the nagging suspicion that her work was all that tethered her to the world.

She's a snow globe somebody has picked up and shaken, and she just has to see how everything will settle.

The remaining pages of the Moleskine stay blank.

At a Thai-themed supper, seated between Charlemagne and the carnal Swedes, who are deep in discussion with the Swedish helmsman in, well, Swedish mostly—causing Charlemagne to act interested and nod at intervals as if riveted—Sentro glances to the other table and finds Fontaine staring at her as the captain winds out another of his inexhaustible archive of tramp-trade yarns for the newlyweds and Bruce Bologna.

Sentro holds the Englishwoman's gaze this time until it's Fontaine who looks away.

———

A gloomy, sunless day sends the passengers and some of the senior crew to watch *Titanic* in the common room, which Sentro finds unsettling. Meg Gentry is sniffling back tears before the main titles end; she's seen the movie more times than she can remember. "They both could have survived if Rose had just let him get up on that goldarn door," she insists, with a quaking certainty.

The Swedish woman's knitting needles clack. Her man does Sudoku, ignores the movie, lips moving as if in silent commentary on his math. The Swedes, Sentro has learned during the captain's cocktail hour, are product-branding specialists from Malmö and trying to "make a child." Multiple positions are required, proper temperature, deep penetration, and Kegels plus unbridled enthusiasm, followed by the female pelvis held elevated by the male partner at a forty-five-degree declining angle, ass above head, for no more than twenty minutes. And ginger-ginseng tea. Sometimes Jesper brays like a donkey when he ruts. Asta admits she finds this stirring. This is way more information than Sentro wants.

"The baby will have vigor," Jesper insists.

Fontaine seems mesmerized by DiCaprio. She keeps murmuring asides like, "Jack's got a bit of a stonker, yeah?" and "Sweet Fanny Adams, I should think she'd devour him in a matter of minutes, left to it." She also keeps bursting out in laughter whenever Billy Zane shows up on screen.

Sentro leaves when, during the sex scene in the Model A, Meg pauses the DVD to demonstrate how Kate Winslet's hand could have done what it does on the fogged-up window.

───

The forecastle is shrouded in a humid darkness. Distant flares of lightning; the summer squall they weathered has passed but still stalks the easing sea. Star dustings glitter through jagged gaps in the clouds. Sentro leans against the forward railing, feels the grease on her hands, the wind against her face, listens to the torque and moan of the cargo ship, the bump and spray as the sharp prow below knifes the *Jeddah* southward to the rumble thrum of the engines.

And voices. Deep in the stacks of containers on the deck.

A flickering light beam stabs a gap between cargo and blinds her, then vanishes.

She can hear what she assumes is the sound of someone clambering up the container rigging, the squeak of a door or hatch; a shadow bobs in the darkness above the stacks' square flat silhouette. *Don't get discovered here,* is her first thought, because she hasn't cleared her midnight walk on the main deck. But her instinctive suspicions have the day—or night, in this case—and she quietly makes her way down the perimeter of the *Jeddah,* stepping carefully because the runners are slippery with salt mist. Another brief stab of the flashlight through the cargo, like a strobe, helps her orient. Another scrape, metal on metal, and the faintest hint of bodies moving, the sibilant whisper of low voices through thin chasms of steel.

Halfway back to the accommodations tower, she becomes aware that all she's hearing are her own movements. She stops, listens. Nothing but the sea and stacks shifting and the *Jeddah*'s normal complaints about the opposing current.

She cuts through the next gap between the stacks, going in where the darkness is disorienting and the wash of stars above her seems, by contrast, overlit. Near the center she arrives at a small, odd, open area between towering stacks, like one of those tiny hidden public squares in Venice with the roving vendors and used books—her tenth wedding anniversary, she and Dennis would come upon them, like sudden secrets, and could never find them again if they tried. There's a hatch that leads down into a dry-bulk container below her at the top of the hold. It's fastened tight, but she can just make out a spillage of something that smells of land and plants. It feels pebbly, smells organic. She has no light to parse its riddle.

Crouching, Sentro looks up the sides of the stacks rising on all sides of her, trying to puzzle out a mystery she may be inventing whole cloth from her hypervigilant default. A few feet away, an object wedged into the deck seam catches starlight. It feels like a long bolt, half-encased in plastic, the exposed end tapered, almost sharp.

Footsteps behind her. She slips the bolt in the pocket of her jeans, intending to stand up, but a pair of big hands pulls her off balance and twists her and bangs her back into the side of a container, pinning her there.

"What are you doing here?" Portuguese. The crewman with the scar through his eye leers at her with a cruel malice that must be baked into him; he smells of sweat, vodka, and hashish. Sentro is not a close-quarter fighter if she can help it; the fantasy that a small, fit woman can overpower a bigger, heavier, stronger, younger man has led to a lot of tragic miscalculations in the field, and she knows it would be better not to reveal herself to the other passengers or the captain and crew if she can avoid a violent confrontation with this one.

What were you looking for? She thinks that's what he's asked.

"Just trying to cut through, to get to the other side," she says, adding, "Shortcut," and when his good eye darts away to make a quick scan of the clearing and the towering containers, just as she did, Sentro sideslips out of his grasp, wondering if, whatever was going on here in the darkness, he may not have been part of it.

"You're not like the others," he tells her, switching to heavily accented English, and reaches to grab her hair and pull her back to him.

She catches his hand. "No, I'm not." Unable to tug himself free, a flicker of confusion crosses his face, as if there's something in Sentro that he suspects is out of pattern, and she finds herself wondering what this man is really doing on this ship—but the thought is broken by the sound of someone else entering the cargo clearing, and:

"Am I interrupting something?" Charlemagne eases out of a gap, eyeing the curious couple he's discovered, and the scarred crewman leans in and mashes his lips against Sentro's in a vile, clumsy gesture of dominance that causes Sentro to reflexively slap him so hard his whole body pivots away from her.

Cocktease, is what she thinks she hears him hiss.

"Hey!" the Tagalog barks, stepping forward, but the scarred crewman is already moving away from them, spitting dismissively on the deck. Disappearing into the shadows with a defiant, shambling gait.

Charlemagne chases him with Tagalog obscenities, then turns, gallant, to Sentro. "You okay?"

She nods, wipes her mouth with the back of her hand. "What are you doing out here?"

He flashes a slender pack and a lighter to offer her a smoke. Sentro demurs. He blushes and puts the pack in his shirt pocket. "No, me neither, I am trying to quit," he assures her.

As they slip back out to the U-deck perimeter, Charlemagne chirps happily in Tagalog and proceeds to have a one-sided conversation that Sentro doesn't bother to try understanding. His language flows like strange music, percussive, and Sentro's attention strays, distrait, wondering what the fuck just happened and how much of it she's precipitated with her relentless, untethered suspicion about everything.

At the bottom of the accommodation tower stairs, before they ascend, Charlemagne stops to get her attention, repeating something he's just said, and when Sentro looks at him, he gestures vaguely and makes a big show of taking the pack of cigarettes out again, tapping out and lighting two. Sentro's about to decline again when he holds up his hand. Wait.

The embered ends glow in the darkness. He puts one in each ear. Closes his eyes.

"Abracadabra." It sounds alien when he says it.

The two cigarettes wink bright on either side of his head, like disembodied eyes, in unison. Charlemagne puffs smoke rings from his o-shaped lips.

Giddy smile. Gold teeth. "Circus trick," he says.

Sentro laughs, the tension that's wound her body tight finally easing, and she high-fives the Tagalog's offered bony hand.

———

> He was an inch, perhaps two, under six feet, powerfully built, and he advanced straight at you with a slight stoop of the shoulders, head forward, and . . .

The bottle of pills on the night table nearly tips when she puts Jeremy's book down after an abortive attempt to crack the first page.

. . . To the white men in the waterside business and to the captains of ships he was just
Jim—nothing more. He had, of course, another
name, but he was anxious that it should not be
pronounced. His incognito, which had as many
holes as a sieve, was not meant to hide a person-
ality but a fact.

She closes her eyes.

Chapter Fifteen

A dawn chill claws the coastal two-lane, all the way to the stony eastern point. Ghoulish slender black palms rise curving up through it like frozen fireworks.

They need three go-fast boats for this gig, which means they're one boat short, and Castor knows just where to find it, short notice.

The shrimper David Carew has been bragging about is a sweet new thirty-five-footer with a hard chine and twin outboards he keeps tied up at the wharf beyond the Coaster Wheel, and because it's probably true that he isn't likely to let them borrow his boat—which Pauly helpfully pointed out as they stepped up onto the covered porch in the northern hills—when a sleep-starved Carew opens the shack's front door, Castor lifts a .45 and puts two bullets through the little man's head, like a second set of eyes, boom boom. Blood and brain spritz back and sideways, and Carew flops fishlike to the bamboo floor, taking more than a moment to stop juddering.

"Oy," Pauly says, more than a little startled.

His brother shrugs with one shoulder, saying, "We're on the clock, brah," and puts his gun away too soon, because Carew has guests.

Pauly shoves past him, shouldering the AK automatic from their recently acquired arsenal, but the local men inside the dingy room are drunk and unarmed and no threat to the twins; still, Pauly can tell from the terror in their eyes that they're not going to be able to let this insult to their friend slide, so there's more work to be done here.

"I'm sorry," he says, though he's not, and he squeezes a burst in their direction; one man down in a heap, the other crashing out panicked through the shuttered back window. Castor goes after him with a Ka-Bar knife and catches him halfway up Carew's rotting fence.

Pauly loves only his brother in this hard world, likens their wordless twin-syncopated havoc to a short litter of feral dogs, which, when you get right down to it, is pretty much who they are. Who they had to be to get this far, he thinks.

Everything from here on out is going to be different. Fucking epic, in fact.

"The fuck are you gawking at?" Castor asks, irritable, dragging his gutted, bloodied fugitive back to the window and hefting and stuffing the limp body through. Pauly suspects the man might still be alive. He won't be for long.

"I'm gawking at the knob that didn't find out where the key's at before he did Wavy Davey Carew."

"We can jump the twin boards."

"Maybe. Mebbe not."

Castor scowls, sometimes annoyed when Pauly is right. They spend way too much time fruitlessly sorting through Carew's shack, find some coiled rope, a useless pistol that hasn't been cleaned in decades, and a cracker tin filled with Brazilian real. There's paperwork for the go boat in the big tackle box on the porch, receipts and licenses, but no key.

"Carlito can get pretty much anything to start up," Castor insists.

Pauly thinks he hears a car slowly winding up the road. "Okay." Time to go.

The five-gallon can of gasoline they brought won't spread far, but after piling the bodies in the middle of the floor, Castor splashes it up across the walls and gets the sofa pretty good.

Wavy Davey's home is all dry wood and creosote and catches fire fast. Pauly can feel the heat from the flames on his back for a good distance as they scramble down through the trees to where they left the scooter. He was wrong about the car coming; the dirt road is empty all the way to the highway. Pauly considers it an excellent omen.

They can see green-black smoke from Carew's still billowing up like a thunderhead from the pier, where, sure enough, their one-eyed lieutenant works his magic with the ignition wires and in no time at all has the go boat's twin 150s throttled and humming out across the bay to where their new crew awaits.

———

Something about toeing the red line in long lazy circles, casting a silhouette in a bright, clear equatorial sunrise; something about the sense of insignificance, a tiny runner on this huge ship running tiny in a boundless, heaving Atlantic, horizon the same in every direction. Sentro takes care not to trip on the tangle of rigging or touch the railings glazed with an oil that doesn't wash off. On her first lap she passed the newlyweds taking an intimate stroll, unconcerned with her, murmuring to each other, heads inclined, touching the way you do at first and sometimes for a long time after, like Dennis did with her until the troubles started; she often worried it was because he was afraid if he didn't, he'd lose all connection to her—that she'd spin away like one of Big Bruce's satellites no longer held in orbit.

It occurs to her, as she runs, that she's been running like this all her life in one way or another, not in circles so much as in cycles—days, months, years, missions, staying in her lane, avoiding entanglements, and returning again and again to her starting point unchanged, just wearier. The memories, stacked like containers, locked, unmarked, throw their shadows over her, daylight flickering sometimes between them.

Half a year after he died, Sentro decided to deal with everything her husband had left behind: clothes, shoes, unpaid bills, penny stock investments, free weights, road bike, his collection of pins from minor-league baseball parks. In the desk Dennis called his office, she found folders of half-baked projects he'd schemed and abandoned but never told her about: a wedding videography business, a pop-up panini shop in Bethesda, vacation real estate opportunities, a solar farm in the Sonoran Desert, the half-finished outline of a how-to book for stay-at-home dads. Expecting to find in the big bottom drawer the family's important document files, she discovered instead several photo albums and a note from Dennis clearly scrawled late stage in his cancer. He explained how he'd curated from thousands of photographs he'd taken of the kids all the things Sentro had missed while on assignment. Not the obvious milestones like birthdays, holidays, and graduations; these were more like the incremental everyday treasures that a parent collects as children grow. Candid moments he'd shared with no one and saved for her in his final act of love. A box turtle Jeremy had found in the garden. The sofa-cushion forts Jenny had made and kite-string spiderwebs she'd spun in her room on rainy days. The ice cream truck of summer. The lopsided snowmen. Jenny's hair clips. Jeremy's haircuts. The ginormous (Jenny's word) potato bug in the bathroom that had terrorized all of them. An afternoon park picnic in silted August sunlight: Jeremy shirtless, Jenny painting dinosaurs on his back.

Sentro felt light headed as she first flipped through the albums. Transported, dizzy, into another realm she had long ago come to terms with never visiting. Except for what Jenny and Jeremy wanted, she gave all of Dennis's other things to Goodwill. For the next six months, she spent her downtime with her grief and her picture books, memorizing the moments, going through the photographs, in sequence, the way her husband had intended, until she began to feel she had been there when they were taken.

After which she threw them away.

Her reasoning, solid at the time, was that she wanted Dennis's recorded history to become real memory, *her* memory, and have it, with time, grow as imprecise and forgiving as memory, not saved and fact-checkable in photo albums she could go back to when memory failed.

And now? What if these are the memories she loses? Last in, first out?

"Running so sucks." Fontaine rattles down the forecastle stairs, brushing past, breathing hard.

Startled, then pleasantly surprised, Sentro keeps going. "Morning." Up the stairs, past the newly repaired anchor rigging, back down the other side, and into the glare of the rising sun.

Out of the corner of her eye, she checks for Fontaine through the gaps of container alleyways—assuming, since Fontaine was slightly ahead of her, she'll overtake the Englishwoman on her parallel starboard course. But there's no sign of her. The sun has baked the steel on this side of the ship, and it throws off heat in gentle eddies of distortion.

The cat logo on the rusty-red container grins down at her, bright-yellow cargo bolt seals dangling from both door handles. Same as the one she found wedged in the decking before her weird midnight dustup with the creepy one-eyed crewman. She's been back to the little clearing between the stacks once since and found no evidence of the earthy deck detritus from that night. She worries she only imagined it.

Looking angled up at the cat and paying no attention to where she's going, she nearly slams into Fontaine, who's stepped out of the next narrow passageway between containers. Sentro breaks stride and skip-hops around the Englishwoman, hip glancing off the railing and leaving grease skid marks on her leggings. Fontaine reverses, runs after, and finds pace with her, their strides synced; they can't quite run side by side on the narrow perimeter deck, but Sentro feels the steady footfalls right behind her, smells the sour coffee in Fontaine's labored breaths.

"I thought everything spins clockwise south of the equator."

"That's toilets flushing," Sentro says. "And hurricanes. Which are typhoons or cyclones, below the line."

"Why did I know you'd know?"

"I didn't think about direction when I started out," Sentro adds.

They run in silence for a while.

"Do you mind me running with you?"

"No."

"Good." Fontaine is starting to labor. "Because I would anyway, seeing as I went to all the trouble of cutting through that valley . . . of shadows . . . to catch you."

Sentro eases up. Fontaine's stride settles.

"So. Mr. Sentro, where's he?"

Sentro isn't prepared for the question. Feels her face flush red. "How can you be sure there is one?"

"There has to be. And some little Sentros, I suspect."

Sentro slows and stops. Fontaine circles back, her legs heavy, her breathing ragged. Not a runner, Sentro thinks. Pretending to be. For me. "You're trying way too hard."

"Am I?"

"Yes."

"By the way, have you read any of your book? Or is it just for show?"

"Fontaine, I don't know what you expect of me, but—"

"I've never known anyone who willingly read Conrad, is my question, I guess."

"Not to change the subject. Much."

The Englishwoman looks intent on saying something glib, then doesn't. Sentro watches her regroup.

"We're in limbo, love. That's what this is." Fontaine glances away, at the sea, then back, some of the thick armor coming off. "I'm not looking for love or commitment. Just a modicum of companionship . . . someone to hold on to in the darkness . . ." Her voice trails off.

She looks out at the sea. There's a palpable melancholy in Fontaine she seems determined to deny. Secrets. Sentro has always found secrets irresistible.

"Do I scare you, Aubrey?"

"One of my little Sentros is almost old enough to be your boyfriend."

"A, he's not here, is he? And B, who says I want a boyfriend?"

"Fontaine—"

"Say no again, then. My feelings won't be hurt."

Sentro blinks. She can hear the water coursing past the hull below them, the ceaseless shifting of cargo, the visceral grind of the engine room. They stare at each other. Fontaine's eyes. Are they yellow or brown or both?

"Say no."

———

The door to Sentro's cabin unlocked, Fontaine pushes her gently ahead and inside, shucking her safety vest, pink hoodie, and Lycra top in a series of fluid motions—a simple gold cameo on a thin chain jangles between the Englishwoman's small pale breasts. She's fetching, Sentro thinks in Fontaine's continental accent, amused, and then catches the stunned look of Bruce just squeezing out of his cabin when Fontaine kicks the door shut and, body on body, arms around and up and under Sentro's running shirt, kisses her. She's stronger than Sentro expected. Laughing at Sentro's serial blushing, Fontaine dances her back to the bed, eases her down, straddles her, her thighs damp and warm, her hair falling forward and hiding her eyes as she rolls Sentro's loose running shirt over her head and arms and off.

"What is this?"

"This" is the collection of patternless ragged scars on Sentro's shoulder and chest. Violent puncture wounds neatly healed, pink.

"Accident," is how Sentro explains them.

"With what, a drill?" Fontaine sits back, puzzling, her hands warm on Sentro's hips. A faint, curious smile. "Who are you?"

Fighting unexpected tears, Sentro pulls her down and returns the kiss, lightly, brushing dry lips against better ones. Fontaine's body, sour with exercise and spent perfume, has a languid softness, and not as much resistance as she expects. Sexuality has always been fluid for Sentro. Situational, largely monogamous; she found Dennis, or they found each other; it felt right, and random unimportant indiscretions aside, she was faithful only to him, girl on boy. But what she's seen, what she's done, the tenuous thread that she's come to learn tethers a soul to this life, renders so much judgment pointless. And now, with her past probably slipping away, she finds herself riding the indefatigable roll of time, plunging forward to some distant landing she doesn't much care about anymore.

She's lonely. No one has touched her like this in a long, long time.

Fontaine breaks it off first. Taking a husky breath, she says, "It's a love story."

"What?"

"Your book." She nods at the Conrad novel on the bedside table. "That's how I see it, anyway." And just as suddenly as she embraced her, Fontaine is lifting away from Sentro, up from the bed, peeling her leggings off, and heading into the tiny bathroom, pale naked white with accents of pink.

"We need a shower."

Chapter Sixteen

He doesn't need to ask what they're doing out here.

The motley trio of go-fast boats creases parallel white wakes through the waves seven o'clock off the stern, having risen up so suddenly out of the distant rolling water they might have been conjured by the sea itself; two curl off, like fighter jets leaving formation, because the cargo ship *Jeddah* looms in front of them, and they're coming up on it now.

On the bridge, Captain Montez, lowering his binoculars, anxiety biting him, his voice thin, says, "Get the passengers into the secure cabin." He's been watching the meandering approach for the past ten minutes, hoping they were fishermen but sensing, no, this was going to wreak havoc with his schedule. He makes the requisite distress call to the company, knowing that no help will be coming within a reasonable time frame, and sends his wife a satellite text telling her not to worry. Their own private code.

Moments later, outside the passengers' quarters in the G-deck corridor, crew members are herding Charlemagne, Meg, Jack, and the Swedes ahead of them, pounding each cabin door as they pass, the second mate, Salah, shouting, "Everyone below! Everyone below, into the safe room, captain's orders."

Bruce struggles to maneuver one of his big leather telescope cases out of the door, a journeyman arguing with him, "Leave it. Sir. LEAVE IT!"

"Long and deep, sweet pea. Slow. Slow." Asta Nelson is hyperventilating. "Breathe," her husband, Jesper, whispers.

———

"Ms. Sentro?"

She hears a distant, muffled voice—Mulligan's?—and perhaps someone knocking on the cabin door, but in the bathroom, Sentro and Fontaine are well entangled, hot water spitting down on them, steam so thick it tickles. They've tuned out the world, Fontaine holding on to the top of the enclosure with one hand. "Oh my."

"Sorry."

"No—I—wait—oh—"

Sentro can't hear anything except the water drumming against the fiberglass stall walls and the rattle of the glass door and the squeak of their feet on the floor and the soft whisper of her breathing, syncopated with Fontaine's.

———

Deck guns shoot boarding lines up from the fast boats onto the *Jeddah*. Montez, alone now on the bridge, stuffs important papers into a time lock safe and takes one last look at the instruments. Company policy asks for a documentable display of resistance, but the priority is keeping the cargo intact, along with but not to the exclusion of the passengers and crew.

The former, per his orders, should be crowding into the safe cabin, asking the crew their panicked questions. He wonders if the women will be sobbing wrecks; he imagines the Tagalog murmuring silent prayers. The Swede strikes him as solid. The fat man could be a problem. The mysterious American, Aubrey Sentro, he hesitates to predict. Tasked with reassuring them is the ship's steward, a practiced script: *Stay calm. They won't hurt us. This is just about insurance, and our company will pay.*

Nervous nevertheless, Montez glances down at the assault again, gets a glimpse of Mulligan scrambling to the stern. What is wrong with him?

The captain hurries out.

———

First Mate Mulligan rips the cover off a stern-deck water cannon and swivels it down to bear on the attackers. His bonus is tied to profits, and this unfortunate development, he knows, is going to fuck all that to hell. Dark bodies have leaped from the boats to scale the hull of the ship, hand over hand, Russian automatics slung across several bare backs. He pulls the trigger. Water from the *Jeddah* gun wipes two pirates into the sea, but the others keep coming.

Mulligan watches a big pale man at the helm of the closest fast boat duck below the wheel as cannon water pounds across his bow. Two more pirates are sent overboard, but it's a fruitless campaign; the Irishman's goal is to buy a little more time for his crew to get all the passengers safely stowed. He's planning to offer one more salvo and go when the fast boat man pops back up with a compact RPG-29 in his hands and fires up at the stern of the ship.

Mulligan dives for cover. The shell hits and blows the water gun to pieces, along with a good portion of deck and rigging and a bit of Mulligan as well.

———

In her cabin's shower, finished for now and holding each other, Sentro turns her head automatically toward a disturbance she senses more than hears. "What was that?"

She shuts off the tap. The pipes knock. She thinks she felt the whole ship shudder.

"That was us." Fontaine's eyes stay closed, her breath quick.

Sentro listens. Silence, except for the dripping of the drain, the squeak of their feet on the floor.

Fontaine kisses her neck lightly. "What?"

Sentro isn't sure at first. Defenses down, she's in unfamiliar territory and hasn't felt the need to establish a baseline. But instinct kicks in. She feels a change. "Someone's cut the engines."

———

As the full contingent of sea raiders breaches the gunwales of the ship and captures the main deck, Captain Montez hurries the bloodied Mulligan along the C-deck corridor, through the doorway, and into the antechamber, where the door to the secure room is already shut and locked. Passengers and crew, he assumes, are inside. Descending the stairwell from the bridge, he heard the RPG hit and, knowing that his brave and foolish first mate had gone to the gun, assumed the worst. He found him alive, was able to get him up and moving before the attackers breached the main deck. Montez has no delusions of bravery or resistance. He tries to stay pragmatic: A fungible inconvenience. Like turbine trouble or heavy seas.

He steadies his first mate and pounds on the door. "It's the captain. Open up."

———

The new hires have had precious little time for training; they're not their normal crew. Everything the Zemes have heard about taking ships suggest this one won't be heavily defended, but Castor insisted on hard men, not boys. Pauly doesn't give a shit; it's all the same to him.

It takes them a while to make their way up into the accommodations tower. There's no sign of crew, but both Zemes exercise caution on the approach. Castor leads two pairs of the hirelings up the external stairs. Pauly brings another duo, with their AKs and rust-streaked machetes, to clear the lower corridor, where they ride the elevator to the top and work their way down.

When he gets to the bridge, Pauly kicks the door open the way he's seen it done in movies and surveys the empty helm with only a little disappointment.

"Hullo."

———

Sentro pulls on her jeans and a shirt, still uneasy and too aware of the ship's eerie calm. Fontaine has to squiggle back into her sweaty running clothes and hoodie.

"Ugh. At least my walk of shame will be only about twenty feet. Let's just hope Baloney Bruce won't be . . ."

Sentro puts her finger to her lips: *Shhhhh.* Fontaine studies her, bemused, incurious; Sentro shakes her head, still listening. She needs to put on her shoes, but Fontaine, impatient, slicks back her wet hair and decides, "All right, let's see what the kerfuffle is, shall we?"

"Wait."

Fontaine is already at the door. Sentro lunges to stop her from opening it and, failing to do so, discovers a weathered young white man in the doorway staring back at them—broad shoulders, flip-flops, piercings, front teeth laminated an unholy ivory, and feral eyes that slur over both women, vulgar, vacant. Sentro feels a switch inside her flip; she's back in that other, ugly world again.

Holstered pistol strapped to his leg like he's a gunfighter, the young man swings a sawed-off shotgun up into Fontaine's astonished face. "Perfect timing, that."

Hard soldiers float behind him, slick with sweat, eyes empty, their assorted weapons aimed in nervously at Sentro. Fontaine starts to back-pedal into the room, but he grabs her by the hair and drags her out into the hallway.

"This way."

CHAPTER SEVENTEEN

The sun-pinked pirate has an odd accent, surely Australian but, Sentro thinks, also vaguely South American—Chile or Brazil. Shotgun pressed up against the back of Fontaine's neck and that fistful of hair in his hand like a short leash, he leads his captives out of Sentro's cabin. On the ropy forearm that grasps the gun, *Pollux* is tattooed in looping blue cursive. His name? In case he forgets who he is? Sentro walks behind them, feeling a healthy mix of fear and familiarity; she had a therapist who once told her that when 9/11 happened, all the crazy clients got calm. Same for her, now, here: weighing options but keen to stay present and aware of the hard men flanking her, most burned black by the equatorial sun, but nothing like the underfed Somali teenagers she once encountered in the Guardafui Channel. Not as likely to shoot her from jittery nerves, she decides, as from malicious intent.

Mercenaries, then. Not pirates at all.

Through open cabin doorways as they pass, Sentro sees more of them plundering the cabins of the other passengers, looking for cash and jewelry.

That makes seven.

Herded out onto the stairway platform and down to D-deck, where other raiders stare at her from the doorway, faces hungry, bodies tense. Sentro counts another four posted near the stern, sharing cigarettes and tending the lines for their fast boats waiting below.

Nine, ten, eleven, twelve. Sentro marks their positions. Nothing about this will be easy.

On C-deck, impossibly, the pink pirate's clone is waiting for them at the end of the corridor like a mirror reflection, slouching insolently outside the open doorway that leads to the safe room.

"Yo, Pauly, the fuck you been doing?" Incisors filed jack-o'-lantern sharp.

"Castor, brah, lookit these here classy slits."

Identical twins.

"Muff divers." Pauly grins. "Dueling batwings."

Castor is the alpha, for sure.

Just inside, wearing a madras sports coat too big for him, the scarred one-eyed deckhand from the forecastle lets his gaze linger on Sentro and says something in Portuguese that makes the others laugh. The inside man.

Thirteen. And the matched pair.

"That's everybody," Pauly says.

"Hokay then."

The madras man makes way so the sunburned twin can frog-walk Fontaine across the anteroom and shove her stumbling in front of the secure cabin doorway, where she falls to her hands and knees. Helpless, crying, but making no sound. Sentro wants to tell her it's going to be okay but knows that it probably won't be. A gun barrel prods Sentro into the anteroom, followed closely by Castor. The scarred faux crewman decides, just for shitgiggles, to piston-crack her at the base of her skull with the butt of his rifle as she goes past him.

She reels but doesn't fall. Legs uncooperative, a burst of cartoon stars momentarily blinding her, her hands fly up to feel the open wound she knows she'll find there. Blood mats her hair and trickles down her neck. She can't hear anything except the ringing in her ears. She's angry now, feels an adrenaline surge. Tingling in her fingers, hollow in the pit of her stomach; if she's going to do something, it has to be here. Real soon. She watches Castor's mouth move, but for the moment it's all a muddle. He's looking at Sentro but pointing his shotgun at Fontaine. Words gather from the confusion: ". . . get these wankers to open the door?"

Sentro figures out what he's asking her but stares back at him blankly, as if still trying to sort it out. Buying time where there is none. Desperate to find an angle to play.

She watches Pauly lift Fontaine to her feet again. Castor takes one step and presses his .45 against her chest. Right where her heart is. "Do it," he says to Sentro. "Now. Or your little lezbefriend will die."

She blinks and finds herself dissociating, deciding: Fontaine is already dead.

"Oy!"

Her heart is pounding. Her Achilles' heel is believing she can somehow bend destiny.

"Okay. Wait," she whispers and moves to the safe cabin door, slaps it, flat handed, and calls out: "They have a passenger; they're going to kill her unless you come out of there."

But she knows they intend to kill Fontaine either way.

"Louder."

"No. They can hear me," Sentro says. "There's a room monitor." Eyes and ears on the whole ship, which she made note of during Mulligan's tour. "They can hear everything you've been saying."

She glances at Fontaine, on her knees, on the floor, gun to her chest, shaking, arms wrapped tight as if they're all that hold her together.

The door remains closed.

Sentro turns, looks at Castor, and frowns. Something's not tracking. An anomaly she can't pinpoint, a glitch in the playback.

Hostages are currency, Sentro thinks. Why kill anyone?

"Time's up." He licks his teeth. "And see, me? I don't bluff." Pulls the trigger, flash of his .45. Fontaine folds and sags to the floor. Blood spreading underneath her.

She wills herself to feel nothing. Takes a half step backward and collides with Pauly, who, having traded his shotgun for a well-traveled AK, blindsides her down to the floor with its duct-taped butt, then swings it around and down at her.

"Now we do this one. But a little fun first, yeah?"

The precious second and a half Pauly takes to consider having a go at her lets Sentro parry the second blow to the side of her head from Castor and drive the meat of her palm into Castor's kneecap, fracturing it, then stripping him of his .45 as he screams and tilts. Rising, Sentro catches the onrushing one-eyed tweaker with an elbow that crushes the cartilage of his nose, in the same rising movement shouldering away Pauly's Kalashnikov as he finally thinks to tap its trigger, causing it to fire in a wild arc that sends his brother cowering to the floor while the other pirates bail out into the hallway, yelling for him to stop.

The scar-faced tweaker has bounced off the door, leaving a wet skid of bright red from his damaged face across and down it; he's making ugly sucking sounds, struggling not to drown in his own blood.

As Sentro bulls her way out of the anteroom, into the corridor, Pauly's weapon shreds a ragged line across the bulkhead trying to find her, so she stops, pivots low, and fires back through the breach he's created, less to find him than to keep him guessing.

Head creased by one of Sentro's bullets, his shoulder joint blown out by another, Pauly loses grip on his AK, and it hits the floor and continues firing; the other pirates—mercenaries—who thought they'd scrambled to safety do a mad dance down the hallway again to avoid getting hit.

Sentro empties the rest of the .45's clip at them as she runs out and toward the exterior door. Handgun spent, hardly slowing, she uses the side of it to crush the windpipe of a pirate ascending the stairwell from B-deck before the man can even raise his weapon.

She whirls him around her like a dance partner as someone opens fire deep down the C-deck corridor. The bullets miraculously manage to miss her after ripping through his torso, but she's misted by his blood and tipped off balance by the sudden weight of his dying, and letting go of the body, she tumbles backward down the flight of stairs.

Primary colors explode before her. Her senses again splintered and bent. Thoughts begin to plod half a second behind; she's thinking of her next move after already having made it.

Sentro rolls upright and slips through the greasy railing and swings down to the next deck. She can hear Castor come out of the C-deck corridor, deliberate, and start down one step at a time, wary of any movement below, favoring his bad knee.

She takes a few deep, steadying breaths. Her playing field has, at least, leveled considerably. She's running but not fleeing, and the twins are no longer calling all the shots. Through the narrow slots and gaps in the stairway superstructure, Sentro sees a gun poised and searching.

"C'mon, ya fuck. C'mon, then."

Men love to talk when they're poised for sex or violence. But rarely during or afterward.

———

At the B-deck landing, Castor stops, waits, listens, and softly shuffles across to the sea side, where he stabs his weapon out over the rail. No one below.

Again, gimping down the next flight of steps, he stays cautious, stopping every other painful step, cursing under his breath, waiting, listening. She's down there. She's unarmed. He hears the creaking of the ship's rigging, the splash of the sea against the idled hull. His own people mill on the platform above him, waiting for the word.

But no sound of a fucking woman in flight. Below his feet, through the steel mesh step: an open doorway to the empty A-deck corridor, lights turned off. Crouching low to look down it, Castor sees only the daylight cast through the open stairway doorway on the other side of the tower.

Where is she?

———

Halfway down the corridor, she's in the ship's office, pressed up against the wall near the closed door, breathing shallowly. Her pulse is in her ears, her hands and arms are sticky with someone else's blood, her pants are ripped, and she's already lost a shoe. Unarmed, running out of real estate, Sentro strains to hear the alpha twin's light tread on the metal stairs.

Start with fifteen armed antagonists, subtract the one on C-deck and the beta brother, if he's dead from his wounds; a thirteen count of pirates, if that's what they are—and she realizes there could be more—is still too many to separate and neutralize, even in a steady, sustained assault with a weapon she doesn't have.

Footsteps settle softly on the outside landing. She considers her other options.

———

Castor slips to one side of the A-deck doorway and edges his eyes around to peer down its length. Who is she? His thinking clots with rage. He locks his injured knee and sidesteps across the opening to scan the doorways on the corridor's other side.

Gesturing that he will provide them cover, Castor waves his hired men ahead of him, knowing they'll be the ones killed first if this stupid bitch comes out of a compartment shooting. He's willing to take that risk, because, well, it's not him taking it, is it? He can't wrap his mind around how a woman is causing all this trouble. Maybe she's a he? A man would make more sense.

Castor's men gyre down the corridor, kicking doors open and clearing the compartments, one by one. All the way to the other end, where, silhouettes against the daylight, they turn and signal back the all clear.

He follows them, the painful hitch in his gait getting worse, glancing into each open doorway as he passes. A small gym. The ship's laundry. Ship's office. The ship's office, where there are community computers and the paperwork necessary for international travel and tall cupboards containing stationary, supplies, important papers for crew and passengers, and, he realizes too late, the woman he's pursuing, somehow braced over the doorway right above him as he leans in to look.

———

Sentro waits until he's all the way in before she drops, scissors Castor's head while reaching down to try to wrest the machine pistol from his hands. The gun goes off. He bucks and rotates under her, gagging. The mercenaries at the end of the corridor dive back to the safety of the outside landing as bullets shred the corridor bulkheads and punch through the outer walls. Castor reels and slams against the wall, trying to dislodge her. Claws at the groin of her jeans as if hoping to find more there. She claps cupped hands hard over his ears; his knee buckles; she spills onto the floor and loses her hold on him. The machine pistol scuttles away. Sentro lunges for the weapon, but the hired men cowering on the stairwell open fire. Castor screams for his men to stop shooting as bullets plow the carpet, allowing Sentro to kick free and crab walk back out onto the opposite landing, where she manages a clumsy hook slide through that deck railing while more bullets chase her.

She catches the shallow steel gutter at the edge of the platform with her fingertips, arresting her drop into the whitecapped ocean thirty feet below. Momentum carries her out; physics jerks her back, banging her body hard into the side of the tower stairwell's structural support.

Above her, she hears the alpha twin find his feet, recover his gun, and start to hobble out to the landing.

Sentro lets go, free-falls, catches the U-deck rigging a few feet below with her angled upper arm, not for the first time wrenching her balky left shoulder but enabling a clumsy sprawl onto the treaded narrows of the main deck, where she was jogging just half an hour ago.

The barrel of the machine pistol clatters, steely, when he aims it over the rail, but Castor must be unable to see where she's gone, because he sends a wild, sustained, frustrated volley of bullets from his AK that chases her down the side of the ship; they spit off the hull and the spars, spark and make a lot of noise, but accomplish little else.

Racked by a grinding shoulder pain, Sentro pins her elbow to her ribs and keeps going. Cargo stutters past in disconnected fragments, like a badly cut film. She weaves and jogs along the high wall of containers, ducking into the first gap between them she can find to catch her breath.

Pressed against the cold metal, she looks back through a narrow gap. High above her, Castor glares down at the stacks of cargo stretching to the stern, slow on the uptake but figuring out, as she watches him, that there's only one direction Sentro could have gone. As he turns to face where she's hiding, his spooked-looking three-pirate cohort is just emerging to join him on the A-deck landing.

Carried by the sea wind through containers, his muffled, apoplectic "WHO FOR FUCK'S SAKE IS SHE?!" echoes and dies.

There appears to be no response. Maybe they don't speak English.

In French, Castor exhorts them: "*Va la chercher, va!*"

Nobody moves. Sentro files away a thought for later use: this is a crew the twins put together on the fly.

"THE WOMAN HAD NO GUN! GO GET HER! *Allez allez allez!*" Castor lurches through them and limps back up the stairway. She stays still, watching, thinking, until he disappears inside and the men he's left on the deck start to cautiously descend; then she turns away.

———

Deep in the *Jeddah*'s cargo maze, Sentro slows to a shuffle, bent double as the shock from her damaged shoulder overtakes her. She knows how to do this next part; she's had it done in the field, even seen a colleague do it himself, but she can't remember who that was. Her memories are like bingo balls in the rotating cage. It was Kinshasa. Congo. Wasn't it? She recalls the relentless heat but has no recollection of when this happened. Was it her? She squeezes into an even narrower passageway, perpendicular to the alleys that run from port to starboard.

She needs to find the right place.

Containers shift and moan around her as the ship rolls on sawtooth waves. Without needing to think about it, she's been picking up the odd deck detritus as she zigzagged through the labyrinth of cargo: a short snarl of wire, a rag, a crushed aluminum Pepsi can that somehow got left here when the containers were loaded and stacked. Things she may need, later, or not at all. Stuffing them with her one good hand into her pocket, where she feels the shape of the container bolt seal she found in a deck seam days before.

She stops. Sags sideways between the container walls and vomits. Tears of pain streak her face, and her lungs burn. She struggles to concentrate, settle. Wind rips, funneled through the container canyons; she can't hear anything but this and the raw keening of stressed metal. A slash of deep-blue sky flares high above her. Sunlight breaks off partway down, leaving her concealed in the cool shadows. The smell of sea and oil is dizzying. She shuffles farther on, to an intersection, where she can see a thin slice of bright ocean in either direction and the U-deck perimeter track, where, sooner or later, the mercenary search party will pass by looking for her. It's a risk she has to take. She tries to straighten her arm as best she can, then swings around into the perpendicular passageway, wedges her arm in the steel locking mechanism of a container's access end, and braces herself with her other hand pressing against the facing container.

Deep breaths, pulse racing. Her body knows what's coming.

Sentro lifts a shoeless foot, her running sock filthy with deck grit, and she kicks out against the facing container as hard as she's able, jacking her shoulder joint, popping it back into place.

She can't help but scream.

Chapter Eighteen

Aubrey is on autopilot.

Reality itself comes to her in fragments, flip-book animation. The world has splintered. The base of her skull throbs where it impacted the stairs.

Fragments, torn, spread, fixed.

A decoupage of time, unglued.

She's afraid if she stops moving, she won't be able to start again.

———

"What a cock-up, yeah?"

Carlito has stanched his split nose with a scrap of towel, the scar creasing his eye and face bled pale, but his breathing is steady, if labored.

"Fucking mess," Pauly wheezes.

Carlito keeps looking at Pauly strangely, and Pauly's thinking, *You're the one who's a bloody mess, mate.*

The bodies of two hired men are splayed out dead on the corridor's linoleum floor because of one fucking lesbian cunt, and Pauly has only managed to push himself into a sit against the secure room door before losing strength. Someone has wrapped his shredded, blown-away shoulder in the other cunt's blood-soaked shirt. He doesn't remember when that happened. Time lurches in fits and starts.

Pauly spits red, tasting metal. *I just need a minute to sack up,* he thinks.

Some of their remaining crew has gathered just inside the doorway, as if held back by invisible tape, as if what Pauly has is contagious. They're staring at him like Carlito, somber, surly grown men surely wondering what they've gotten themselves into now, ivory eyeballs hooded in blank sun-blacked faces, stalled.

You gobs got nothing better to do? is what Pauly wants to ask, but he's not sure it comes out as more than a mumble. "Find a fucking first aid kit. I'm gonna be fine."

Pauly doesn't feel fine, though, and nobody moves. He struggles to fill his lungs; he's punched out and woozy. But not so gone he can't cast a rictus grin at his brother when Castor limps in from the hallways and assesses him with a horror he can't hide. "Brah, shit."

"Fucked, brah. I am. Yeah. But it'll fix."

Castor goes quiet. Maybe he didn't understand. Pauly wraps his lips around the consonants and vowels this time: "Where's the running girl?"

"We'll find her."

"Wait. You lost her?"

"She ran."

"Aw, you lost her, ya gaseous knob."

"Misplaced her, brah. Don't talk."

Pauly frowns. Castor is scaring him.

"Lord almighty." Pain webs across his chest, and all his muscles there cramp up. "Oy."

"Middle of the fucking ocean. Where can she go? Save your strength, yeah? We'll getchu back and sorted out."

"What of the other slit?"

Castor cocks his head down the hallway. Pauly nods.

"Fine fit she did us."

The others in the room are blinking in and out.

"Carlito?"

A labored wheeze, eyes closed, the scar gone white. "Right here."

"She mashed your nose good, man."

"Local problem, boss."

Pauly closes his eyes too. His body trembles. "You go get her, Caz. And bring her back here. So I can watch. Yeah?"

His brother doesn't seem to know what to say, which is surprising, because Castor always wants the last word, but eventually he says to Pauly, in French: "I'm telling the boys to throw the dead overboard. Make a whole scene. Just in case."

In French: "Me included?"

Castor looks stricken. "Shut up."

"I feel weird."

"Don't talk. Save your strength."

"Sure."

———

The lips and crannies, flanges and straps of the shipping containers provide a slow, sore ascent for Sentro, who has clambered to the top of a short stack, where, in cover, she tries to catch her breath and discovers the mercenaries are heaving bodies off C-deck to plummet into the sea.

Awkward, angular dropping shadows are set off starkly against the slate-blue sky. One, two, three. A pink hoodie flutters away from the last of them; it floats down for a long time, like a dying bird.

Do I scare you, Aubrey?

Sentro looks away from it, eyes watering, resisting the hollow chill rising from her heart.

Say no, then. My feelings won't be hurt.

People wink out all the time. It's staying alive that's hard.

When he was on death watch, she would slip away from the office and go to the hospice, curl up next to her husband on his bed, careful because just touching sometimes hurt, but watching him, counting his breaths, the pulse of his heart in his neck, wondering what her life would be without him, knowing that it would be the same. But without him.

Once he woke up, his eyes clear despite the morphine drip, looked into hers, and said, "If this is God's plan, the evangelists can have Him."

Does she believe in God?

Sure. Why not?

But surely She's not a supreme being who punishes or rewards or has anything to do with the affairs of men on this earth. Maybe She lit the fuse of the big bang and called it a day. Or made the rules by which the universe behaves, the Ten Commandments (or however many, Sentro thinks) of quantum physics (or whatever comes next).

And evil? Oh yeah. Baloney Bruce's dark matter and black holes exist; these phony pirates and all the other malevolent zealots and clans and cartels and despots and free-market monsters she's bumped up against over and over are what get born out the other end.

Fontaine and Dennis? Collateral damage.

Palming away cold tears, Sentro catches the movement she's been expecting down on the starboard U-deck perimeter track. Three hired men hunting her. They move gap to gap, guns out, looking impatient and lost, small heads, big ropy bodies. Pay-to-play soldiers with death-dealing weapons. That men come to this as much out of necessity as choice always discourages her.

Sentro slides from her container perch into the cargo canyons and becomes one with the shadows.

———

Castor Zeme has discovered, on the *Jeddah*'s bridge, in an unsecured safe, the passengers' passports, billfolds, paper money, credit cards, and IDs. He spills them across the glass of the navigation table, intending to flip through the passports for the pictures, figuring it's time he familiarized himself with his leverage. But mostly he craves a moment's distraction from the woman running loose on his ship. *His* ship. The simple fact of her, of what she's done to his brother, blinds him with a bitter rage.

"Castor."

"Yah?"

Carlito steps up behind him. "Man, what about the other hostages?" The scarred man has taped a splint and bandage from the plundered sick bay across his mangled nose; there's blood streaked on his pilfered madras coat, and his voice is a shredded croak.

Castor manages a shrug and, in French, says, dismissive, "What about them?" He's found the running woman's passport, and his chest tightens, looking at her unsmiling picture. "Sentro, Aubrey." When they catch her, he'll let Pauly make her scream. "Gotcha."

"We should still tryta get 'em outa that room, no?"

"Why?" Castor looks across the helm at his number three, a round-faced Colombian with a wishful mustache and soul patch. "They've done us a favor, Berto. Locked themselves in a very lovely jail."

He goes through Aubrey Sentro's wallet. Cash, bank cards, driver's license. Snapshots of grown children, a few stray business cards, including: *JEREMY TROON, Summer Associate, Sterling Financial Fund.*

"Jail that we can't get into."

"That they can't get out of. Boom."

Carlito cackles into a coughing fit.

Gunfire pops like a snare drum out in the ship's vast cargo; Castor reacts and snaps his head toward the doorway, where the burly, moon-faced hire from San Pedro Sula peers in, a little spooked and tentative. "Master Zeme? Man, you better come."

Stones. Gravel?

    Grain.

    No. Beans.

    Legumes. Thank goodness for Berlitz French.

Hunting the hunters, she again found the odd clearing between the stacks where she'd encountered the Zemes' disfigured lieutenant, and she opened the top hatch of a dry-bulk container to hide in a dank, musky sanctuary of bulk cargo thick with the smell of soil and plants and herbicide.

But when she lowered herself, her feet at first found nothing solid; she hung by her hands from the hatch lip, gauging the drop, thinking: *Why isn't this bin full?*

Hearing movement on the deck above her, her damaged shoulder cramping, she lost her grip and dropped.

The fall was less than a meter, and the landing was soft. Her legs sank deep into the fat seeds this bin holds, and after she kicked her feet free, she sprawled sideways, ungainly, stretching her good arm out to stall and stabilize herself in the pebbly mass. Hoping they hadn't heard her.

Dry, hard beans.

She twists onto her stomach to make her body bigger, spreading herself across the surface of the grain to keep from sinking farther.

Soybeans, she decides.

Feet shuffle on steel. And men speaking muffled Portuguese above her.

———

A young, ashen-skinned, acne-ravaged Sentro hunter midship fires blindly from a crouch at the edge of the clearing toward where he thinks he saw movement. No way he'll let the woman get a jump on him. Another young mercenary in a faded knockoff Arsenal kit crowds him. Bullets ricochet off the containers, and the sound kicks back sharp at them.

A third man, older but somehow outranked by the younger men, darker, long and lanky to the extreme, hangs back in a slot, trying not to be scared. His Portuguese is halting, not his native tongue. "Lucas. What is it? Is it her?" He eases carefully forward to join them.

The two younger hunters cease shooting and listen. Language is noise. Wind rushes through the narrow spaces. Clouds skitter and gather overhead, shrouding the sun.

"Don't know."

"Go see," the older man suggests.

The deck just past them in the passageway shows deep crevasses of steel bracing, where the full depth of the *Jeddah*'s lower cargo hold falls away dark beneath them. The Arsenal man looks down. One misstep could break a leg or, worse, send them plummeting down the slot.

"You go see."

"Go. Both of you. Falcao, you take point." The youngest man, Lucas, shoves Arsenal forward onto the struts and into the gap. The senior man follows.

Falcao tugs on the neck of his jersey and throws Lucas a wounded look but goes. It's just a matter of being careful, he assures himself and eases toward the clearing, the lower hold dark beneath them. Falcao and the old man, fingers on triggers, nervous. They've seen what this woman is capable of.

———

Pauly Zeme is still angled up against the secure cabin wall like a sack of something, but now he's listing, limp, when his twin brother comes into the safe cabin antechamber to check on him. "Pauly? Brah?" Bloody compression bandages from a medical kit are wrapped tight around

Pauly's chest. The English twist's ruined training shirt is wadded in the corner, where someone threw it after using it to stanch the wound.

Bloodshot blue eyes open, dilated, fixed stare.

Pauly's dead.

Unable to crouch down to him because of his knee, Castor reels from his brother, making a guttural keening noise. Turns his head away so no one can see his face get utterly wrenched by abject grief. *That cunt. That fucking cunt.*

His eyes burn; he tries to cry, can't. Emptiness swallows him. Castor pivots, limps, threading between Carlito and Berto and, in the doorway, nearly knocking over the San Pedro Sula hire who brought him in here to see this outrage.

He staggers into the hallway and vomits.

———

Falcao and his wingman climb and stalk the staggered grid of cargo canyons for the woman who's eluded them, who's killed their employer and mates, who's made them for fools. Lucas watches them angle across an interior gap where the blue shadows lighten. He sees their weapons pivot, low, high, constantly seeking a target, and ready, Lucas thinks, in case the woman has somehow climbed up above them. The flexing metal of the ship, the container stacks, and the rigging's crack and moan spook him. The sorry slant of cold, overcast daylight high above them casts its feeble help down as the sky opens up to rain.

Their shoes slip; their sweat-stiffened clothing is flogged by the squall gusting through. Neither would admit to being scared, but Lucas can tell they're jumpy for sure. His senses are acute, still a little buzzed from the bolus of Mexican brown he chipped for courage before they set out from the beach hours ago.

Eventually they circle back to a gap, an empty space, where a rustling flutter causes Falcao's gun to worry upward as a seabird explodes from its nook. The older lanky hire opens fire without taking time to ascertain what it is.

"Don't waste bullets!"

They step out of Lucas's line of sight.

"Falcao?"

There's a thump of a corpse landing, and then moist bird parts rain down, and the two men who disappeared start laughing, and the sound of them rattles out to where Lucas waits, nervously touching the ulcers on his face, confused by what he's hearing and further agitated by an angry yell from the stern. He slips back out to the perimeter deck and sees striding toward him the boss man, Castor Zeme, and his broken-nosed, scarred meth-monster majordomo, whose name Lucas has never been told.

They look so unhappy. Lucas wonders if this cargo ship has been cursed.

Inside the cargo corridors, Falcao and his wingman can't seem to stop laughing.

———

Standing firm on a container clearing poised above the hold, rain spattering down on them, the older man watches young Falcao flap both sleeves of his threadbare jersey and mime the exploding bird, setting off a whole new round of laughter. He's embarrassed that he's wasted bullets, glad that the kid finds it entertaining. It feels good to laugh. Falcao says something the older man doesn't understand, then shuffles, giddy, backward to an open hatch that neither of them noticed before, where something takes hold of his leg and pulls. Falcao looks down, perplexed; the older man watches, helpless, as the woman they've been searching for yanks the kid violently off balance and drags him inside the bin below.

The older man shouts, "Look out!" and raises his gun way too late.

His younger colleague shouts what must be *shit* in his language as the crimson jersey disappears.

———

Bullets chip the lip of the hatch behind Sentro, spitting slivers of steel. No way can she go back and pull it closed. A shadow crosses the opening; hands jab an automatic rifle blindly down to fire three more short bursts into the darkness of the bulk cargo hold.

Sentro flattens herself on the flailing young mercenary she's acquired, then rolls to the safe side of him as bullets burrow through the soybeans they're swimming in. The boy jerks twice and coughs as stray shots rip through him. Sentro feels him deflate. Stripping him of his weapon, she presses his head under the surface of the soybeans and holds it there as he shudders and stills.

Someone calls down into the container: "Falcao?"

There are heavier footsteps, more voices: French, English, Portuguese, Spanish, in an incoherent, angry jumble. She's succeeded in disrupting them; there's no coherent strategy to their search. Now she will see if she can play that to her advantage.

The dry-bulk air thickens with stirred soil, preservatives, pesticides, and the acid smell of gunfire. She's still scared but no longer angry. Not planning her next move like this is a chess game, just determined to survive and regroup. Desperate but resolute, she forces her aching shoulder to move, snaking away from the open hatch, shoving the dead kid's rifle ahead of her, over the grain, and into the turgid darkness until her hands strike something sleek and solid beneath the surface, and in the faint light she can just make out the shine of a couple of heavy aluminum carrying cases buried in the soybeans. Something familiar about them. A car company logo. SAAB BOFORS DYNAMICS. She's confident she's seen these cases before, many times, in stockrooms and weapons caches, arms depots and stacks on tarmac, waiting for their due mayhem. But her mind draws a blank on precisely where or when or why.

She hears the scuffing of the heavier shoes and boots directly above her now, moving apace toward the open hatch. Three men. At the other end of the long bin, maybe twenty meters still to go, a thin shaft of daylight, thick with dust, beckons. She keeps crawling.

———

Following the steely echo of voices and gunfire, Castor has located his newly hired senior man huddled wet in the rain and squatting between stacks, staring worriedly into an open space and the open top hatch of a dry-bulk bin. A former FARC rebel, Colombia by way of Fortaleza; Castor and Pauly've never used this man before. They heard he had a drinking problem. Castor has never bothered to learn his name.

In a thick, rural Spanish dialect, the rebel explains to the pimply one, Lucas, how Falcao got pulled belowdecks by the woman.

Castor gets the gist of it, but Carlito translates anyway, and when he's finished, Castor nods for the FARC man to go in and get her. The old rebel hesitates. Carlito snaps, smacks him on the back of the head. The lanky man sprawls on the wet deck, cursing in Spanish, but nevertheless belly crawls out of the safety of his narrow slot to the top hatch opening and, after murmuring what looks like a prayer, sticks his head and gun down into the container, expecting to be killed.

For a moment it's a still life. He stays there, upside down, rain soaking his legs, before finally shouting something back at them. He can't lift himself up without dropping his deadweight rifle. He yells, "There's another hatch! She's getting away!" in his inept Portuguese, so distorted by the bin that even Lucas is slow to understand: their Arsenal man is dead, and a woman's legs have just disappeared up through another hatch at the far end of the hold.

CHAPTER NINETEEN

The squall whistles, compressed, a strange incantation through the containers; it catches on rigging and straps and trembles them like a warning. But the sudden rain has stopped.

Having effectively doubled back toward the accommodation tower, Sentro scrambles up out of the dry-bulk bin's second access hatch and onto the main deck behind another row of containers, with the unfortunate Arsenal fan's automatic rifle slung across her back. She could get out to the perimeter from here, but then what?

Still outnumbered and outgunned, she wants to take the higher ground.

Because her shoulder makes her whole arm balky, back braced against one side of a cargo stack, feet pressed flat against the other, she begins to chimney climb upward, using whatever tie lines and rigging she can for better hand- and footholds.

Halfway up, she rolls onto the flat of a container and looks down over the edge, not surprised to discover the alpha twin and his three hired men hurrying back toward the hatch from which she just emerged. She repositions for a better sight line. The AK rattles as she swings it into use; her pulse of gunfire drives Castor and his crew scrambling back for cover in the steel canyons. She shoulders the gun again and crosses to another stack to continue climbing.

Toward the top of this ascent, her shoe catches on and dislodges the lever on a container's loading door. She's startled when it swings outward but manages to grasp the handle and go with it as she feels the bullets from below punch into the door's back side and tear up the boxed cargo exposed inside.

Hundreds of Korean hair dryers waterfall out of the open container and cascade down onto a startled scattering of her pursuers just as they appear to have regrouped for another assault. It allows Sentro time to haul herself the rest of the way up to the top of the stack before the door swings closed again, revealing, as Sentro rolls to cover, Castor down below, trying to find footing on the landslide of appliances and aiming up at where Sentro just was.

He must get a glimpse of her leaping over the next gap, because he fires wildly and misses, and from her new position Sentro can track the other three men on their awkward scramble out of the hair dryers to the main deck to regroup.

Sentro has climbed to a wide plateau of evenly stacked containers, and she's exhausted. Open sea stretches vast to muted horizons on every side of her. The bow of the ship seems impossibly far away, and just the top of the accommodation tower shows its squat square face above a higher stack of containers behind it.

She listens for her pursuers but hears only the slap of waves against the side of the idled ship. They can't be far.

Whatever adrenaline has driven her this far is waning. Her legs shake; her hands and arms are cramping from the climb; she can't catch her breath. She starts running, or what passes for running given her fatigue, using the strength she has left to jump the breach between stacks, shoe and sock skidding on steel slick with rain, heading back toward the cabins and the imprisoned crew.

It's not all that selfless. She needs their numbers to survive.

Before the next jump she stops, listens again for sounds of Castor and his crew, who she guesses are somewhere behind her, stalking the perimeter. She imagines their eyes scanning the ridgeline of the stacks and seeing nothing but the cloudless blue sky.

Faintly on the wind, she hears French, Castor's voice, warning, "Get back to the hostages before she does!"

So much for another element of surprise.

She waits for the pounding of their shoes and boots on the U-deck perimeter. All four men, but in opposite directions. One of them is moving away from her, toward the bow.

Why?

She can make out another man's stilted, "*Où allez-vous?*" It's the scarred one Pauly has called Carlito, and he doesn't get an answer.

Sentro jumps the gap and quickly climbs to the top of the next, higher stack of containers. She's still intent on reaching the exterior stairs and platform outside C-deck; it's almost level with this checkerboard mesa and runs clear all the way to the accommodation tower.

Her shoulder throbs.

Murmurs of Portuguese, a brief back-and-forth, rise on her left from the main deck. She crawls to the edge, peers over, and locates two of the mercenaries who have been chasing her struggling to carry the body of the Arsenal man back to the stern, where the fast boats are tied.

No sign of Carlito or Castor, but bullets begin to skip off the top of her current container, and when she looks that way, she sees other men firing at her from the tower's C-deck landing.

Fuck.

Swinging the AK off her shoulder, she rolls and slides to the edge and eases over it, but her toes can't find purchase on this container's steel side. For a harrowing moment she's exposed to the disfigured tweaker, Carlito, who is positioned underneath her, good eye keen, his face where she broke it a swollen bruise.

He raises his gun.

Fuck fuck fuck.

A sharp knife of pain stabs her rotator and causes her to lose her grip.

She falls. Gunfire from the hired men on C-deck chases her.

Carlito must have darted into the narrow gap too late to track her short descent. His speculative bullets rattle around corners, and Sentro feels steel splinters scrape her face.

She kicks out and propels herself backward, arresting her plunge downward but landing hard on her back on the top of a lower stack. The impact knocks the wind out of her; she gasps for air and loses grip on the Kalashnikov and, helpless, watches it clatter across and over the side and down to the main deck.

There's an odd, soothing quiet, as if someone turned down the sound.

Then Sentro hears, distant, in accented English, "SUCK THIS!"

Arching her head back to look to the bow, she discovers that Castor Zeme has climbed to the crow's nest beneath the forward masthead light.

He has a cannon tucked on his shoulder.

She knows what it is.

Castor triggers his RPG: the flash, the trail of smoke, so familiar and predictable, like an old friend. She can only watch, helpless, feel the hot projectile pass over her and slam into the face of the higher level of containers she just fell from.

They're a bitch to aim, she remembers, even if you know what you're doing.

The struck container explodes. Or rather, the ordnance explodes and blows the container apart. Pressed prone by the concussion, throwing an arm over her face, Sentro only imagines she can see Castor lower his weapon and crack a grim payback smile.

The blast momentarily blinds her.

But she feels the stack of containers she's on come unbalanced. It and all the other stacks around it shift and tilt precariously to the port side, steel rigging snapping as part of the top row slides free and tumbles into the sea.

Sentro claws for a handhold as the whole cargo ship *Jeddah* rolls from side to side, the weight of its disrupted containers leaning out over the water.

Black smoke billows from the afterburn of the RPG. She's on a half-collapsed house of cards. And blazing, insubstantial bits of lacy silk cargo are fluttering down from the sky like incendiary ticker tape: burning lingerie.

Dazed and exhausted, stunned passive, Sentro is a rag doll slung in slow motion by the violent pitch and roll of the ship. Gravity has its way with her. She tumbles over and off into the skewed black grime of darkness below.

PART TWO:
~~GIRL~~ WOMAN ON THE SHORE

CHAPTER TWENTY

Say no, then. My feelings won't be hurt.

———

Like a distant memory:

Smoke clearing, the naked Grey Wolves femme from her Cyprus acquisition gone sideways rushes out, grim determination, gun in her outstretched hand, aimed point-blank down at the client and her and

an unsteady thumping sound that might be a heartbeat

and faces, all the faces of all the dead, and

oh

her son Jeremy's long face, ten years old, he's talking, the smile ironic, his eyes already judging her, but that could just be the Dennis of it, no? No. And all she hears is the ragged thump of her own heart and she hopes it's hers.

But where is Jenny?

and her heartbeat and that crazy MRI of her skull and brain, vibrating, as if alive, as if the resonant image of Aubrey Sentro in real time scans deeper and deeper, through the gossamer tissue, to the sparking telodendria and synaptic bouton of—

———

Rattled, restless thoughts dance and skip across decades like a badly scratched record but find the groove again on a slender spit of sand barrier off Port Isabel, where the blacktop park road on Padre Island deadended at a **NO TRAFFIC BEYOND THIS POINT** sign nailed to the wooden hardware that forbade further access, behind which stretched endless grass-studded dunes and a deserted beach washed by a long, low, rolling tide.

The boy—Andy Yoder—was alive when she found him. Wasn't he?

She remembers how the winds tugged at her hair as she emerged from the black Corolla; she pulled the duffel off the seat and felt the strap cut into her shoulder and started walking north, where the small man in the filthy singlet stood at the top of a high dune, waving his arms and gesturing to guide Sentro where he wanted her.

The boy was alive.

A narrow old getaway skiff had been dragged up out of the surf, its paint-flaked sides nearly salt blasted down to the bare wood. The man on the hill gestured for Sentro to stop, then skated down the sandy slope to her. Small, Mexican national, stout. Sunglasses and a Texas Rangers cap. She was circumspect, on edge, fearful as always; she had promised herself long ago that she would quit the game if it ever happened that she no longer felt the dull scrape of fear.

"Hola."

In English, the kidnapper said, "Hi." His wasn't the voice from the phone, which meant there were two kidnappers. The hostage was still at risk. This man seemed skittish, unsure, even scared. Not the mastermind. A messenger. Sentro glanced up and down the empty beach while the little man motioned to the bag: *Put it down; open it.* Inside were the shrink-wrapped bricks of cash the clients' bank had delivered to the motel.

The kidnapper's eyes widened. He crouched to remove one of the bricks and split it open with a boning knife to examine the money. Different denominations, well traveled, hastily gathered from Brownsville sources.

In Spanish, she asked him when he would set the hostage free.

In Spanish, the small man said it would be soon.

"That's not good enough."

The small man shrugged, put the cash back in the duffel, zipped it closed, stood up.

"I've kept my word. Now you. Make the call; let him go. Let me see you do it. For his mother's sake."

The small man cocked his head to one side, as if considering not just what she said but who she even was. What she was. The hot wind howled around them, pulling at his loose shirt like a flag.

She remembers him saying: "Why do they send a woman?"

And that was when the helicopters, wise to the ransom exchange location by way of the surreptitious texts from their inside man, came thundering low over the hill from the channel side, feds and cops, breaking their promise and making it all go to hell.

No no no no no—

The little man screamed into the wind something ugly meant for Sentro, dropped the knife, yanked the duffel full of money off the beach, and started sprinting to his boat.

Waving her arms angrily, pointlessly, at the advancing air cavalry, Sentro tried to convince the cops to divert and let this play out—

Oh, don't do this. You morons. WHAT ARE YOU DOING?!

—but the choppers dipped noses and floated past her, and the leader banked sharply, twenty feet above the beach and water, tail pivoting, exposing a sharpshooter tethered and leaning out of the open door with his high-powered rifle aimed down at the Mexican, who was throwing the duffel of cash into the fishing skiff and trying to push it back into the surf.

Sand and water eddied. The kidnapper stumbled, his feet slow in the sand, body torquing as he heaved the bag in the boat and fell against

151

the gunwale. He pulled a gun of his own from a dingy waxed-cotton pouch in the boat as sniper bullets danced in the sand around his feet and punched through the hull, rendering the boat useless and ripping into the bag of cash.

Doomed where he stood, the man waved his weapon like a crucifix warding off demons and didn't return fire. Sentro remembers him just watching while the second chopper flew out over the surf and floated there, another sharpshooter centering the green bead of a laser sight on the Mexican's chest as a voice drawled from a loudspeaker, telling him to throw his weapon onto the sand and get prone.

Sentro had made it partway down to the boat and the man, shouting at him in English or Spanish; this she can't remember: "Listen to me—listen to me—I can talk to them and—"

Cornered, terrified, the small man then turned his gun on Sentro. "You were followed. You lied."

Here in the eye of the storm she felt only the small man's unbearable sadness. The helicopter loudspeaker screamed distortion—*PUT THE GUN DOWN! NOW!*—and Sentro sidestepped and shuffled in an abbreviated arc, trying to position herself between the sharpshooters and the kidnapper, despite the gun still aimed at her head.

She spoke, low, calm, quick: something about how they could still work this out, how the local cops had made a promise and they'd broken it, yes, but he still held all the cards because the important thing, what everyone still wanted, was that the boy got back with his family.

"The important thing."

Yes. Save the child.

Gesturing skyward: "They should have thought about that."

"Let me deal with them."

"You think everything is negotiable?"

Sentro didn't, and she watched in horror as the man then turned his weapon to his chest, heart high, and pulled the trigger. *Negotiate this.* The gun kicked, made the softest popping sound that got swallowed by the wind and the rotor wash, and she watched the kidnapper fall backward into the shallow water, dead.

All hope of recovering the hostage had surely died with him.

Bills loosed from the punctured duffel were sucked up in sandy paper twisters as the helicopters circled and looked to land. The loudspeaker kept asking a question Sentro didn't answer and can't recall.

She sank to her knees in the sand, exhausted, furious, lost.

The lead chopper touched down close, disgorging the Cameron County sheriff—what was his name? Full uniform, head shaved and sunburned, pony-keg belly and more politician than cop. He yelled at her as she dragged the Mexican kidnapper's body from the surf and peeled away the bloody, waterlogged singlet, intending to rifle through the dead man's pockets, but not before turning and barking back at the blowhard lawman that "you get the hostage back first; then you go after the fucking kidnappers."

"You learn that in girls' gym?"

"No, it's common sense. Unless you're up for reelection in some backwater sewer of ignorant redneck fools, I guess."

Emergency vehicles came screaming in over the dunes from the Park Road barrier, including a dusty Jeep Cherokee from which Falcone emerged, as the sheriff continued to bitch at Sentro, something about something something something and how Cameron County could not abide every miscreant Mexican with cash flow issues snatching sacrificial lambs from its sovereign citizenry and something something something get away with it.

In the dead man's pants, Sentro found a cheap cell phone, waterlogged, bricked, and flipped it to Falcone, who popped the SIM card and confirmed that it was useless but that they might be able to pull the phone number and trace any movements of the cell over the previous few days, maybe find a pattern. She filled him in: two kidnappers; one must still be with the hostage and waiting for his partner's call.

Two shiftless Houston feds spilled from the second helicopter in their creased chinos and cross-trainers and joined them. What rock had they crawled out from under? Law enforcement was unanimous in the opinion that Sentro's two-man theory was bullshit, but then her phone began to ring, and when she answered it, the voice she knew was soft and sardonic on the other end.

"You give him the money?"

"Yes."

"No. No, you didn't."

The voice sounded hollowed out. The shore wind blew a flutter in her phone's tiny speaker. She looked out and scanned the dune ridges. *He's watched us. Where is he?*

"Now is when you ask me where your client is."

Sentro acquiesced, heart sinking: "Where?"

"The boy is in God's hands. Like my brother."

"Your brother shot himself. His own hand," Sentro told the caller. "I couldn't stop him."

There was a long pause.

"It's an unforgiving world."

Sentro felt chilled. "You're not a murderer." Did she believe it?

"Shit happens. God decides now."

———

Her eyes flutter open, glistening in a twilight darkness. She blinks away the haze of filmy mucus and tastes smoke and rust and her own stale blood and oil.

Lying in an abstract of twisted steel and shredded fabric.

A full moon above.

The long, gentle roll of the sea, like a baby's cradle.

She doesn't feel like moving yet; as if in time lapse, the moon travels a narrow slice of ink-black sky, neither day nor night, the moon huge and bright, slipping left to right, eclipsed by the sharp edge of a shipping container.

She revels in the steady sound of her heartbeat.

A gentle mist salts her face.

———

It was their Jeep Cherokee that led the caravan of county patrol SUVs down a dusty dirt levee road along the Pilot Channel, pretty much the middle of nowhere. Headlights bled yellow in the dying day. Pulling over to the shoulder, Sentro leaped out before Falcone had fully stopped, and she scrambled down a shallow dry ditch and up the other side, to the edge of a rolling field, scanning it for any sign of life. Windmills on the ridge spun helpless arms, the low light silvering off them in fluttering sci-fi pulses.

"This is the place," she shouted back at the deputies and their chief and the search team spilling from the other arriving vehicles.

They'd lost precious time on the Padre Island dunes trying to convince various bureaucratic telecom functionaries to provide Unger with the necessary tower feedback to generate a GPS map of greater Brownsville and Cameron County, with data points overlaid, so they could pinpoint where the dead kidnapper's phone had traveled over the previous ten days.

Chief Lewis had dismissed Sentro's scheme out of hand. "This pooch was screwed out from start gate, with all your fancy spy-girl tomfoolery, dragging us all out to this here goddamn catastrofriggin' circus."

Falcone and Sentro ignored him. Eventually, with the help of a black hat hacker who had recently dimed on some compatriots for federal sentencing leniency, Unger ginned them up a scatter of repeated locations that, at first blush, seemed to be without pattern—as if the kidnapper had simply driven around in random directions twenty-four seven, but the points kept evolving, converging, as Unger's algorithm worked its magic, suggesting a single location, here, in the barren hills northeast of town, where the boy must be.

Lewis trundled up out of the ditch behind Sentro while she took measure of a landscape they couldn't possibly cover, even with all the town and county resources plus whatever additional volunteers could be quickly deputized for a grid search. Wheezing like a broken Hoover, the chief had brought along with him the Yoders, Beth and Dean, the middle-aged parents of the victim, six weeks of worry etched on their sunbaked faces. They stood on the other side of the ditch and overheard Falcone speculate aloud, as he hurried past them to join Sentro: "He's buried the boy. We'll never find him in time."

Beth cried out. Dean had to catch his wife to keep her from falling forward into the arroyo when, it seemed, her legs gave out from shock.

Sentro had already thought about and discarded the idea of a buried boy. *Not in the ground.* What was it the kidnapper had told her on the beach? *In God's hands.*

Sentro started running.

"Whoa, wait. Aubrey?"

Not in the ground. Held high, *above it.*

The chief barked, "Hey. HEY!"

Falcone raced after her, over corduroy ridges of parched Texas bristle grass blown to stubble, and a blue darkness dropped on them. They crossed the wide barren field to a raised, rotting wooden water reservoir with abandoned, rusting train tracks still stretched half-grown over beneath it.

Sentro started to climb the wooden ladder strung on one side. A rung snapped under her weight, and she went crashing down onto the hardpan. Falcone jumped over her and clambered up the broken ladder, hand over hand, so nimbly it seemed to Sentro like a magic trick.

At the top of the tank, he pulled himself up and looked down inside and shouted back: "Here. He's here."

A fourteen-year-old boy, deathly pale, bound hands and feet, was coiled, fetal, in his ashen underwear and a sweat-stained T-shirt, trembling from a fever. Coughing. By the time Sentro could renegotiate the broken ladder, Falcone had clambered in and picked the boy up in his arms. She flashed on her own children, safe at home with Dennis; how fragile a life was.

"Hang in there, buddy," she heard Falcone whisper to the boy. "Don't go anywhere on me."

Sentro looked back from the water tower to the open field and saw cops outpacing the police chief and emergency personnel and, farther back, the Yoders, lagging, but clearly moving as fast as they could. A bright bleed of red and orange was all that remained of the day. Sentro sidled aside on the narrow ledge that circled the tank, testing her turned ankle and keeping a grip on the lip in case her feet found another feeble section. Cops took command of the ladder then, formed a chain over and into the tank, helped Falcone lift the boy, and brought him down to the tower's base. Chief Lewis was waiting with the Yoders, who touched the boy and tearfully embraced him and praised Jesus while paramedics wrapped him in a silvery thermal blanket like a gift. Flashlight beams crisscrossed through gathering darkness, over the growing crowd of first responders at the water tank, and found Falcone helping Sentro gingerly limp back to their Jeep. Fire trucks and a four-wheel-drive ambulance and one brave, foolhardy local news rig that would be stuck for a week rumbled past them, bringing searchlights and cameras to bear on the happy ending to a breaking story.

The Yoder boy died two weeks after his rescue.

People did that—died. You could save them from one fate only to deliver them to another.

The Yoder boy died after two weeks from an acute secondary infection resulting from his deeply devout parents' dogged distrust of modern science, which meant all vaccines, including one for the tetanus that he'd been exposed to during his long ordeal. Nevertheless, a grieving Beth and Dean sued, settled, and bought a barrier island vacation triplex in Galveston, which would be later destroyed by Hurricane Harvey.

For this they received FEMA funds, returned to Brownsville, and are active on social media condemning the deep state that conspired to take their son.

Chapter Twenty-One

As if reborn in the broken debris from the blown-up container, Sentro is heaved from the dusty twilight fields of Cameron County with a cold spasm of shock that makes her entire body jump. Her fingers claw at nothing; it takes what seems like forever just to sit up; dazed, she cannot track time. Her clothes are torn, her exposed flesh smeared greasy, black, and bloody.

Did she dream she'd taken a cargo-ship cruise?

No. Blinding colors bloom before her eyes. She blinks them away, and Dennis whispers to her: *Now, baby. Now.*

It all comes back to her. The siege, the run, the brush with death. Her heart pounds, flops with fits and starts when she begins moving. She shivers hard, cooled by a breeze. Her breathing, though, is long, deep, relaxed. Listening for the sound of them coming for her. She wonders at the very faint bleat of a foghorn and assumes she's imagining at least this.

Either it's night or her eyes are damaged.

She feels around herself with palms and fingertips scraped raw. No longer feeling the big roll of open sea and puzzling why.

Folding her stiff legs under and struggling to stand, she feels a searing pain cut behind her eyes and fights the urge to throw up. For a long time, she just stays upright, balances on the rubble underneath her, hearing mostly the shrill ringing in her ears but feeling the low-frequency rumble of a city.

When she's ready, she picks her way down a rutted slope of debris, sinks into the shadows until she feels the level pushback of decking, and gropes forward, arms out, reaching to find the two sides of a container gap and guide herself through. Cool breeze off open water pulls her to the perimeter of the ship.

A dreamlike scrim of lights confronts her, confounds her, and then arranges itself into what Sentro takes for a harbor town curled in a natural cove of glassy black water in which the *Jeddah* has been moored.

The bay's surface shimmers with civilization's reflection, making it difficult for Sentro to discern where the town begins and the water ends. There's a worrisome tilt to this world that she first ascribes to her compromised perception, then realizes is the deck itself. The odd looming shadow of containers knocked out of alignment angles out, bent over the starboard side, midship, causing the boat to list.

In the harbor's elbow, the few modest modern buildings are jammed in the chaos of squat colonial structures lining narrow streets draped with tea lights. Palms tremble like lunatics. A dimmer shantytown scatter of apartment buildings, bungalows, and tin-roofed shelters rambles halfway up steep hillsides thick with trees and brush.

Here and there are flashing billboards in Spanish and French, with random letters unlit; neon signs flicker from the waterfront, where a broken-down Ferris wheel turns and trash fires flare.

In the harbor is what looks to be a small graveyard of hostage ships, their hulking forms anchored together like dead leviathans. Floating, dark. Silent. Seemingly abandoned. Guarded on either side by the distant rise of two dark rocky points.

Another searing blade of pain takes its cut from her, temple to temple, and she doubles up and dry heaves over the railing. She listens for the movement of mercenaries on the decks.

The accommodation tower that looms in front of her now is dark. Silent. Lifeless.

The worrisome lean of the *Jeddah*'s containers, held fast for now by distorted cables and stays, moans with each bay wave's pass under. Legs less quaky now, Sentro flows in and out of the shadows cast by the main deck supports, stopping every few yards to listen again. Distrustful of the oppressive quiet.

Her tinnitus easing some, she begins to hear music, even stray voices, drifting across the water from the town. Laughter. The foghorn again. The flatulent rattle of an engine's busted muffler.

The fevered wind chills her again. Faint whiff of soil and sewage and the smoke of wood ovens.

A clock tower tolls twice.

Night birds. More smells: fish and diesel and the incendiary chemical hangover from the RPG meant to kill her, and for a moment she considers whether they have, in fact, succeeded and sent her to some other world, her own private purgatory.

———

The door to the secure cabin yawns open. A single light bulb burns inside. No hostages. Sentro recognizes flip-flops in the corner but can't remember who they belong to; she notes the crumbs of some dry biscuits the passengers and crew must have shared, thinking they were in for the duration. There's no clue how the ship's attackers got them to leave the security of the room.

Killed? Kidnapped?

Not pirates, she reminds herself. Something else.

A pink hoodie plummets across her thoughts, uninvited.

Do I scare you?

Someone died; someone had no chance.

161

Sentro steps back into the antechamber, where, shiny in the spilled light, thickening blood is splashed and smeared on the floor and walls. The funk of death lingers. Clarity usually sharpens for her in crisis mode, but the veil she's felt cast over her since Cyprus remains. She can't trust the instincts that are telling her she's alone.

Hugging one dark corridor wall and creeping cautiously to the opposite exterior stairway, she clears sight lines out in both directions and then, with an overabundance of caution, for a long time just waits and listens to the kiss of water on the hull, the pop of loose rigging, the steely complaints from deep in the restive ship.

A new headache crawls up and away, behind her eyes. Her shoulder throbs, sending electric tendrils down her arm.

On G-deck the corridor is lit, and the doors of all the passenger cabins are thrown open, clothing and personal detritus strewed out from each across the carpet like the plunder it became. A disembow-eled telescope has left a glitter of lens glass that sparkles like fallen stars.

Her suitcase, in her dark cabin, has been looted, the clothing and contents dumped on her bed. She kicks off the ruined running shoe and laces up high-top sneakers, then turns the soft bag inside out, rips the bottom lining, and finds what she concealed out of habit for contingencies: a dozen twenty-dollar bills, a debit card, a pocketknife, and a matchbook.

She can't find her cell phone. *Lord Jim* lies open upside down against the wall, some of the pages creased, the cover ripped. For some reason she picks it up, and a sudden movement on the periphery of her vision spooks her; she whirls and finds herself facing a cut, battered, broken version of herself reflected in the mirror, lit cruelly from the hallway. The faucets still work, so Sentro takes a quick pass at cleanup, washing away the blood and grease and running wet hands through her frazzled hair in a futile try at taming it. Marginal improvement, and it makes her feel better, somehow. But a deep laceration on her forehead starts to bleed again. She searches the other cabins, finds in the pocket of a half-emptied suitcase a tiny travel sewing kit with needle and thread.

A candle she fashions from a bottle of perfume, using yarn for a wick; its soft light flickers off the bruised face staring back from her own fractured bathroom mirror as she sterilizes the needle and sews closed the gash along her hairline that won't seem to stop bleeding. Nobody mentions, when they teach you to do this, how painful it will be; each stitch makes her eyes water, and she has to stifle a series of tiny screams.

She hears no human movement penetrate her tinnitus. Just the tug of the thread through her skin, the squeak of her high-tops on the bathroom floor, and slow water dripping in the shower.

She ties off the last suture and snaps the thread.

Dips her head to the washbasin and gently flushes the wound with warm water that makes it throb. When she looks at herself in the mirror again, there's only a pink skim of liquid running down one side of her face, which she blots with a towel before she discovers with alarm the acne-scarred face of a young mercenary behind her.

He presses a handgun against her head.

The cold barrel chills her. It's a Glock or a Bren. She's never cared to learn the difference, since they'll both do what's required of them. Pidgin Portuguese, a threat mumbled. Shaking off a stab of panic, Sentro angles her head to stare into his eyes and sees uncertainty there that she can work with.

She lets her hands float up as if in helpless surrender and in a blur of practiced motion simply rope-a-dopes away from the barrel of the gun. The startled mercenary tugs the trigger. Closing her eyes to the flash from the muzzle, she smells it burn her hair; the vanity mirror explodes like a firework, but she's already turning, ducking, and the flying glass finds the face of her startled assailant instead. He screams, Sentro's rising forearm wedges under the man's chin, and her legs plant and thrust and drive them both out of the bathroom into her cabin, where they crash to the floor. With the side of his gun, he manages a glancing blow above her ear. Fire spits from the muzzle again, harmlessly upward this time, and Sentro's world splits, shimmers, tilts; a wave of vertigo overtakes her; she falls, rubber legged, away from him, digging into the pocket of her jeans as the mercenary pirate, screaming, face peppered with bloody cuts, looms over her, intending to shoot again, point-blank. But she deflects the barrel with the heel of one hand and with her other plunges deep into the side of his neck the sharp yellow bolt seal she found on the deck.

He goes rigid, arches his back, gasping, clawing at the bolt, eyes wide.

Don't do it, Sentro wants to tell him.

But he does—pulls the bolt out—and from the gaping carotid puncture his blood sprays like one of the Rain Bird sprinklers in Sentro's hopeless Baltimore backyard garden, which, every time she went away, Dennis would replant with fresh healthy things and then insist were the originals when she returned to find the garden blooming.

The man's eyes roll back; he dies and collapses.

Sentro pushes away from him, struggles to get to her feet, spattered with blood again, but this time it's not hers. Stumbling out of the cabin, she falls, still dizzy, but wills herself to crawl to the next cabin and roll inside before pushing the door closed. She senses and then hears a second mercenary come worrying into the G-deck hallway from the stairwell deck, alerted by the gunfire, calling for his friend.

She forgot to take the dead man's gun.

More telescopes, cases, and broken equipment are strewed here. She recalls a large pale man and that this is his berth and belongings. Brad. Brian? She knows she should get to her feet, but the room keeps rotating like a teacup ride when she tries. A low, angry keening tells her the second mercenary has found his fallen friend bled out. She listens to his rage trundle into the corridor, where he kicks open the door to another cabin, hollow wood booming and the man yelling what she assumes are obscenities as he hunts for her.

She can hear his angry breathing rasp outside the door behind which she's hiding. Her hand grasps the huge optical tube of a dismembered telescope, and when the door crashes inward, she raises it out and up and puts all her weight behind it. She jams the wide-aperture convex lens between the onrushing hired man's eyes, pivots, redirects his momentum into the corridor wall, and crushes what's left of his face.

The pirate drops to the floor and doesn't move.

Are there more of them? She listens but doesn't believe what she's hearing, which is nothing again except for the aggravated ringing in her ears.

Steadying herself, Sentro finds a grimy .22 pistol the second mercenary has dropped and hurries out onto the stairwell landing to make her way down deck by deck, rattled because she's fearful that everything in front of her—ship, water, sky—roils on a troubled sea of concussed misperception. And she can't afford any more mistakes.

On the main deck she discovers the accommodation ladder has been lowered and the shore boat is gone. In its place, ghosted by the big freighter's dark shadow but betrayed by a steady slap of water, is a battered, rusted, and overloaded Boston Whaler with a tiny outboard motor and a pair of oars.

The skiff sits low and stays stable when Sentro steps into it. She pulls back the tarp and discovers all kinds of pilfered items from the *Jeddah*: rope, tools, pots, pans, kitchen supplies, new boxed hair dryers, wine . . . compact LCD TVs. A pair of her own shoes. Jesper's fancy binoculars. The crew's PlayStation. A plastic sack filled with video games.

Somebody's been pirating from the pirates.

Looking out across the water at the harbor town's shoreline, Sentro estimates it's not more than a quarter of a mile to the nearest quay. She senses motion above her and looks back up at the stern railing of the *Jeddah*, where the ladder is secured, reaching for the .22.

A small dark shape drops down on her, causing her to fumble the gun, lose her footing, and fall. The creature proceeds to hit her repeatedly with a cricket bat while shouting in a broken form of French.

Sentro curls fetal, catches the cricket bat under her good arm, and uses it to flip her tiny attacker down hard onto the deck of the whaler. She's on top of him; her hands go by habit to the neck, thumbs against the larynx, squeezing, a filthy, raw-scab-pocked face revealed to her in the dim starlight: a boy.

A small, shirtless boy. Writhing, wheezing, thin. Blistered arms pounding uselessly against Sentro, who is astonished by how young her attacker is and decides to let him go.

The boy gasps for air. His body looks boiled, covered with fresh, weeping scabs.

A voice not the boy's cries out, "Zoala!"

Something crashes hard against the base of Sentro's skull. She reels, feels consciousness slip away yet again, goes limp—the last thing she sees as she rolls to her back is a pretty, ebony-skinned teenage girl with rainbow orthodontia and a Hollister sweatshirt, gazing down with lovely, angry, liquid brown eyes.

Chapter Twenty-Two

"*Il est vivant.*"

Standing clear of the blackened blood soaked into the cabin carpet, Castor Z. considers with revulsion the sorry corpse of the hired man the American woman has mashed to death with a telescope. He was always a problem, this one: sloppy, overconfident. Castor is not all that surprised that the American, Aubrey Sentro, prevailed here, considering all the other carnage she's left in her wake. She's like some kind of wild animal they've set loose. A crouching smaller local hire in silky Laker shorts has a seemingly hopeful ear to the man's chest.

As good as dead, though.

Castor has no visible reaction—or any remorse for hired men incapable of surviving a lucky, lucky woman—he just itches to find her nearby, dead. He steps over the body and winces when his damaged knee locks up; he limps out into the G-deck corridor and from there into the Swedes' cabin, where, striped by sunlight, the unfortunate Portuguese has bled out, dispatched by Sentro's fatal long bolt, still clutched in his bony fingers like a tube of ChapStick about to be applied.

Blood everywhere.

Mort.

Unsteady footprints that stagger out into the hallway. The bullet-shattered mirror in the bathroom. The upended sewing kit. Castor's expression darkens.

To himself: "Still alive." Meaning the American bitch. His mouth twitches. Thinks: *Bloody useless.*

A grind of gears draws him to the cabin window, where he looks out over the displaced containers at the small salvage crew working from an old yellow sheer leg crane cozied up against the side of the *Jeddah*. The rusty-red container with the cat logo swings free of its stack and rotates out over where it will settle on the deck of a ship-to-shore barge.

His brother's death rubs raw. Castor's never known a time without Pauly, and it's difficult for him to process the finality of what has happened. He catches himself carrying on conversations with the twin in his head; he aches over how they could have celebrated their success and strategized their next move.

Rage turns to anguish; tears leak down his cheeks. He turns away from the window. Carlito has come in the cabin, and Castor catches him trying to pretend he didn't see his boss crying.

——

The Caribbean harbor city of Porto Pequeno is, depending upon whom you ask, either an unmapped rumor nestled on stateless, disputed coastline between Venezuela and Guyana—or perhaps some other equatorial realm entirely. Isolated by a ring of sharp, arid mountains, tropical, fertile, rotting, and alive, once a provincial capital, now a crowded clutter of traditional Caribbean clapboard buildings interspersed with decaying midcentury moderns from a brief infusion of foreign investment. Crowded streets show the neglect of no government; Renaults, BMWs, Ferraris, Vespas, Brazilian Trollers, and Soviet-era Lada rust buckets rendered useless, in a state of constant gridlock, on narrow cobblestone streets.

Huaraches, pastel guayabera with a palm-frond pattern, a briefcase he found in the *Jeddah* crew quarters and brought with him, although it's empty, to present himself as a serious man—Castor Zeme is all cleaned up and swankified, as Pauly would say, with his usual bling plus pilfered luxury-yacht Ray-Bans. He limps across an intersection, avoiding the swerving scooters, panhandling homeless, and a shopping cart costermonger selling plums and sooty lingerie that looks familiar, somehow. Past two strip club street hawkers, he eases up onto the steep stone steps of what, in Porto Pequeno, passes for chic patio dining overlooking the harbor.

It's like he's entered a parallel universe. In the Malabar House, all the skin is lighter, the sweat swaddled in aftershave and imported perfume. Paris fashion, continental Spanish and French, or cultivated public school English accents as mimosas circulate and iced oysters disappear.

A private club his brother had hoped they'd join when they made it big. Castor couldn't give a shit. Dress it in silk, wrap it in gold—the world is a cold, unforgiving cesspool, and everyone gets fouled.

Pushing his sunglasses back up on his nose, Castor swings his sore leg around straight and slides into a chair opposite the plus-size Robbens, who's wearing small, retro, square tinted wire-rims and a salmon-colored suit.

"How's that breakfast, Masta Robbens?" Castor eyes the scramble Robbens is devouring. "People say the waffles here are to die for."

"I could take that for any of several meanings. Coming from you."

"How 'bout this one." Castor lifts his briefcase up on the table, pops it open, and pulls out ship documents and the pile of passenger and crew passports from the *Jeddah*. "Singapore ownership, flag of the Bahamas. Tramp ship. Assorted cargo, bulk and container. Squint—you can see it out there. North of the tanker I'm guessing is one of yours."

"We all wondered whose ship came in." Robbens wipes his mouth with his napkin. "This is so unlike you."

"How's that?"

"Seems like just the other day, your brother was shooting his gun while drooling into my *café con leche* and trying to convince me to buy some pawnshop bling he'd robbed from corpses you fashioned and had no business looting afterward."

Castor says nothing. The mention of Pauly makes his throat tighten. He takes the Ray-Bans off and puts them in his pocket. "I don't appreciate how you disrespected him."

"I mean"—the Dutchman is on a roll—"you boys've always been more of a slash-and-burn, scorched-earth kind of outfit; am I wrong? You're limping."

This insufferable asshole. Castor feels hot impatience. "I should bring my freight to somebody else, then?"

"Who? You're radioactive. I told your brother. Those sundowners you slew were greatly loved."

"By other rich gobshites. Got the message, yeah. Okay, fine. I'll fuck off, then." Castor turns to go, but Robbens tugs at his shirttail and fashions a grin.

"Not so fast. Sheesh. We'll add big-ship high sea skullduggery to your long list of talents, then. Some kind of injury. Your knee?"

"We won't talk about that."

"And how is the mirror image?" Robbens has his smartphone out, and he's working the tiny keyboard with agile thumbs while he chats. "Two *d*'s in *Jeddah*."

"Yeah." Castor adds, "Pauly's fine. Thanks for asking."

"Cargo?"

"It's all in the papers. This and that. Boxes and bulk. I could give a rat's ass."

Reading an entry: "Soybeans?"

"Yeah."

"You have passengers and crew?"

"Yes, and yes." Anticipating the next question: "Safe and sound, don't worry . . . but for the ladybit who had this unfortunate accident and, well, died."

Robbens looks up at him. "Died."

"Yeah."

The Dutchman stares at Castor.

"Accident, I swear. Fucking tragic, it was. My condolences to the family." Castor opens Fontaine Fox's passport and turns it around. Robbens stares at her picture. His good humor gone.

"Pretty."

"Hot. But bottom-feeder fare, I suspect, by now. Sea chum." Castor smiles mirthlessly, saw toothed.

"That's not remotely witty. Fatalities complicate things, Mr. Zeme. You know as well as anyone," Robbens lectures, brittle.

"Like I said. Couldn't be helped, yeah? You tell 'em I'll give 'em a price break. My bad."

"I'll tell them bubkes until the transaction clears. But no one else gets hurt, understand? You want to work your mayhem on the leisure class, take your chances with their so-called friends, God be with you. But don't screw this freighter insurance market up for the rest of us."

"Or what?" Castor glares back darkly, fighting the urge to stab this fat white fuck in the eye with an oyster fork.

Robbens seems to get that he's pushed too hard, and Castor watches him back down. Sits back in his chair with a look of, *Let someone else deal with this when the time comes.* And Castor thinks, *Yeah, bring it.* "Bad business, is all I'm pointing out," Robbens says. "After such a bright turn of fortune."

Fuck does that mean?

"Why risk it?" Robbens adds.

"Like we could have stopped it."

"I wasn't there."

"What part of 'accident' do you not understand?"

"Oh, right. Accident."

"Mm. Panicked, fell overboard. Women." Castor wonders if Robbens has already snitched them out for the yacht job.

A website gathers on the screen of the Dutchman's phone. "United Maritime Group is the underwriter. London. So. I just happen to know one of the partners."

"Just?"

"They won't be happy about the dead one but—"

"You said that. And you said they don't have to know."

"Let's hope."

"I'm not interested in dicking around, Mr. Robbens. All these mouths to feed and so forth. So."

"You did this with your lost boys?"

Castor wants him to think so.

Robbens sorts through the other passports with an irritating self-importance. "The market right now is running about point eight to one point and a bit million US. Depending."

"On what?"

"Well. When no one dies, for example."

"'Kay. Fuck you. Give it a rest. And let's not bid against ourselves, wot?" Castor wonders if Robbens negotiates for each individual or in bulk, but he doesn't feel at liberty just yet to ask. "Let them make an offer. Who knows? I might just take it."

"Just."

Studying the broker warily, Castor waits.

Robbens approximates a studious frown. "What are you really up to, Mr. Zeme?"

"Up to?"

"Forgive me; I'm slightly suspect at your sudden scale-up. Somebody put you up to this. Is that it?"

Castor takes a moment to admire the Dutchman's trimmed eyebrows and the spidered capillaries on his nose. Affecting his best white-man pomp: "Boat jacking, such a fussy fucking business. Izzat it?"

Robbens roars with what sounds like uneasy laughter. "Touché."

Castor spots Audrey Sentro's American passport among the others; he forgot to separate it and now reaches out and takes it. "I'll keep this one. You can have the tote." He tucks the passport away.

Too smug and incurious to ask why that passport is so important to the twin, Robbens gathers the ledgers and documents and puts them back in the briefcase. "I should have an answer for you tomorrow." He puts the briefcase on the floor by his chair, as if to seal the deal.

Castor rises. His knee has grown stiff, and putting weight on it sends a slow shiver of ache down into his heel. "You should, yeah. Just 'cause I ain't in the club, do not toy with me, Dutch boy."

"Technically, I'm Flemish," Robbens says, and his deliberate, vacant stare confirms for Castor that the Dutchman has already decided that, after taking his cut, Robbens will talk with his Important Friends (like the colonel?) about a reckoning for the Zemes.

But there's only one Zeme now, isn't there? And this one is way ahead of them.

Castor pops his shades down to hide the grief that suddenly twists in him. He pushes away from the table and lumbers off, trying not to favor the leg.

"Give your brother my best," Robbens calls after him.

I can't, Castor thinks. *But if things go right, maybe you'll be getting mine.*

CHAPTER TWENTY-THREE

She's never forgotten bursting out from under the warm water, gasping for air, eyes opening wide to an amber-and-green-tiled West Texas motel bathroom tub almost overflowing with silky bubbles. Or the armada of Polly Pocket shells that rode rough seas while the shower rained down on her gently, like a summer storm. She could hear her mom, through the closed doorway, arguing with her Texas Ranger father on the phone.

She tried not to listen. She hummed her happy cowboy song and watched the clamshell boats take on water, then pretended they were scuttled and that all Polly's friends were tossed into the angry bubble ocean, threatening to sink, one by one.

With the cup of her hand, she'd saved them all.

Her own pale, serious face stared back in the mirror when she scrubbed it clean of steam. Her mother had resorted to mostly single syllables on the landline in the other room: "Yeah, no. No. Sorry." Hair slicked back, cut bluntly short. Her lips magenta from the water, the freckles she hated pronounced, like a spattering of brown ink. Not a princess, despite what her father claimed.

Towel draped around her like a shroud, she came tentatively out of the bathroom after her mother hung up the phone. Sitting on the floor, legs splayed, she slumped back against the bed, something flaring on the terrible television, blown-out color making it impossible to comprehend; tears streamed down her mother's face as she looked up at her little girl, inconsolable.

And took her in trembling arms.

Said she was sorry for the thousandth time, it seemed. Said she was "so, so sorry, honey," with that kind, liquid Lubbock drawl that reeked of cigarettes and Altoids. Said that this wasn't . . . she was just . . . hadn't meant for their magnificent adventure—which was what she'd called it when they'd left Dallas—hadn't meant for their magnificent adventure to end up . . . well, here.

A crazy quilt of colored lights flashed and fluttered across the curtains like a carnival. Sentro kissed her mother's hands and wriggled loose to cross the room, transfixed by the promise of the kaleidoscope outside. She climbed onto the cushioned chair and pulled the curtains to part them and look out at the motel parking lot, where there was gathered a harsh, hard-angled phalanx of gleaming police cars and emergency vehicles, all with their headlights bright and their bubble bars flashing, and men with rifles hunkered down behind them, grim and locked and loaded and staring back at the window and the little girl in it.

Hundreds of identical bushy-haired, sun-faded bobblehead dolls of an American ball player hang by fishing line from the rafters of a ceiling that towers overhead. The name printed on their bases is Pedro Martinez. In the foggy recesses of her memory, she recalls that this person was a pitcher for Boston, because shortly after he got cancer, her husband took her to an Orioles game in which Martinez played. Dennis kept shouting at the field, "Just tip my hat and call the Yankees my daddy." He kept laughing, so delighted Sentro never bothered to ask what it meant.

Big bell heads judder in a faint, swirling breeze.

Sentro has been staring up at them and puzzling if this is a new part of the West Texas dream she was having: sitting in the darkened motel room with her back to the silent *Scooby-Doo* bleed of a color-shot pay television on top of a minibar, listening as her mother sings, small, desolate.

And I come to town just to hear the band . . .

The bullhorn booms again, "MRS. SENTRO?"

Her mom rocks on the edge of the bed in her periwinkle pjs, ankles crossed, the pistol in her lap and both her hands on it, trembling, eyes dry, lipstick faded, singing:

. . . I know all the songs that the cowboys know—

Sentro asks, "Mom?"

"*Está acordada,*" is the answer she receives.

No, not dreaming anymore.

Flat on her back on a sagging *SpongeBob* pool-float mattress, Sentro feels her head nestled in ice packs and discovers the girl with the rainbow braces leaning in to mop her face with a cloth. Colt-like and slender, the girl has a baby bump that brushes against Sentro's arm.

"I'm cold." Sentro tries to sit up. The sudden movement causes the girl to jerk back, scared, but Sentro's wrists are handcuffed to upended shopping carts on either side of her; she's not going anywhere. The cuff chains clatter loudly in the quiet and bring scuttering from the shadows the scarred kid she wrestled on the skiff, his cricket bat poised high for a downswing.

He barks: "*Fique lá.*"

"What? Whoa." A rush of vertigo blindsides Sentro again; nausea wrings her empty stomach.

"Sit back. Take it slow." A weedy, tropical-browned middle-aged Anglo man-child pulls the little cricketer back behind him and looms over Sentro and the girl; he's wearing a lurid Hawaiian-print shirt and filthy, threadbare bermuda shorts. "Your brain, on ice."

His eyes are almost colorless. His riot of bowl-cut hair wants to be blond.

Worrying again that she's still dreaming, Sentro scans her surroundings: some kind of Spanish baroque ballroom with institutional carpets and stacked hotel banquet chairs and bleak faux-ironwork fixtures replete with empty sockets and cobwebs and rust. Heavy velvet drapery bleeds bright daylight from massive lead glass windows that rattle when what must be truck traffic passes close outside. This makeshift residence, once perhaps the faded centerpiece of an abandoned grand hotel, has been sectioned with a maze of packing crates and muslin screens and upended water-stained plywood pallets, and it overflows with multiplying booty apparently plundered from hijacked cargo ships.

The man-child kneels. He's got doctor props—stethoscope and a penlight—which he uses as if randomly for Sentro's pulse and pupils, doing a decent rendition of a physician while picking up where he left off: "It was either that or borrow a skill saw to pop your top until the swelling stopped. Entailing concomitant hazards of blood loss and tropical sepsis." He pulls a can of beer out from under the ice packs, opens it, and drinks half. The girl hangs back, one arm absently cupping her baby bump. The scarred boy is shouting something in Portuguese and threatening her with the cricket bat as Sentro adjusts to her new altitude. The kid wears a bleach-stained knockoff Arsenal jersey too big for him, which now has a couple of bullet-size holes in it and some stubborn stains.

"You're a medical doctor."

"Last I checked." The man belches. "There was some talk of yanking my license before I left Portland, but yo, I think my disappearance made the point moot." He yaps something in a dialect Sentro can't identify, and the boy shuts up.

"What happened to him?"

The doctor looks at the kid as if seeing the scars for the first time. "We don't know. And he's not saying. Doesn't care to talk about it at all."

"You can uncuff my hands."

"Dude."

"What."

"I don't want to be a dick about this, but not so long ago you didn't know if you were animal or vegetable. And you were like some kinda she-wolf when we were getting the clothes off you." He points to a bruise alongside his eyes. "Who do you think did this? When the girl come to get me—"

"The girl?"

Indicating, with a tilt of head: "Eccola. And this mouse is her brother."

"Where am I?"

A shrug and a half turn away to dig through a scuffed old-fashioned black leather medical bag.

"Little fucker hit me with that cricket bat and sent me to the moon," Sentro tells him.

"Zoala takes a good cut, for sure. But his sister—take my word for it. Swings like A-Rod. So. Lucky that."

"No clue what an a-rod is. Do you have a name?"

The doctor locates a syringe and a clear vial. The blistered boy circles Sentro, cautious. His legs and arms are raw and peeling, and he moves gingerly, with a mechanical caution. She meets his eyes and holds them until he looks away.

She can't remember: "Say the boy's name again?"

"Zoala."

"Those look like burns."

The doctor doesn't hear her or doesn't want to answer; instead he turns back to her with, "You've been in and out. Pupillary reflex, I'm guessing concussion. More than one. Which, you know—or maybe you don't—is not good."

"Serial."

"Yes." His eyes narrow, waiting for more information that she's not going to give him. "As your doctor I'd also advise you never to suture yourself."

Sentro absently touches a fresh bandage covering the cut on her hairline and asks again what his name is.

"Oh—whoa, shit. Thanks for reminding me. That's what I should be asking you. Again." He can read her reluctance. "D'oh. It's okay, Lady Secrecy. I have your debit card, man. To cover my expenses. So I already know who you are, but see, the Double Jeopardy question is, Do you? 'Cause you didn't a couple of hours ago."

"Aubrey."

"That's a name?"

"Yes. Mine."

"And?"

"Sentro. Aubrey Sentro."

"Good. Fantastic. Where you hail from, Aubrey?"

"Baltimore. I was born in Texas. I have two children." She hopes sheer momentum will carry her. "My husband died of cancer. I'm not having trouble remembering things. I'm fine. Can you just . . ." She stops short, watching the doctor plunge the syringe needle into the vial and draw out the clear liquid.

As he flicks the air out, he asks her: "What's the name of the vessel you were—"

"We were boarded by an armed crew. They hijacked the ship and killed a female hostage, and I need to call—"

"What was her name?"

"Who?"

"This dead femme."

"What difference does it make?"

179

The doctor just waits, holding the syringe upright and poised like a mad scientist. Sentro opens her mouth to tell him. Stops. Can't remember. A flood of anxiety washes over her; she feels like she's tumbling backward into a bottomless pit.

"You called her name out, I think, in your dreaming," he says, pulling her out of the free fall. "So I'll know when it comes back to you."

"Who undressed me?"

"Name of the ship you were on?"

Sentro tries to get her legs underneath her, but they aren't cooperating. The doctor puts one hand lightly on her shoulder, and a dull electric pain courses down through her, and she discovers that she's too weak to rise any farther.

"No. C'mon, dude. You're still concussed. Give it some more time. Heal. Your whole body is one big ow."

"I need to find the people I was traveling with."

"On what ship?"

Nothing.

"Your dead friend? Either-or?"

Nothing.

"What day is it?"

"How long have I been sleeping?"

"In and out, like I said."

"Okay."

"What if I told you thirty-six hours?"

Sentro hesitates, stunned. She also lost time after the explosion in the cargo. She's suddenly frightened at having lost so much control of things.

"Month? Year? C'mon, you can do it."

Sentro closes her eyes. She has no idea. The helplessness she feels is overwhelming. Her head has begun throbbing. "The people I work with can help me."

"If only you could remember who the fuck they were." The doctor looks like he's enjoying this.

But he's right. Sentro is falling again, legs flailing, searching for some solid ground. "If you have a cell phone—"

"Who would you call?" Point made, the doctor is digging in his bag again with one hand, keeping the needle up with the other. "What's the number?"

Sentro opens her mouth again. Can't remember. White noise.

"Here's a hint: the international code is zero one."

Can't remember who she works for or what she does there, but she knows that it has importance, that she matters, that people count on her to do things that others can't or won't. What happened on the boat is something she needs to correct.

Ring on her finger; she's married.

No. He died. Dennis.

But for a moment she can't remember her children's names. A wave of hollow desperation overtakes her. Tears blur her vision. "I need to go," she says but doesn't move.

"Dude, you are not fine. So just chill. Literally. Head back in the ice. Hijacking is the cash crop here. If that's what happened, your friends are okay; let the market work its magic and give your body time to heal, and everything will work itself out. 'Kay?"

"Market."

"Free market. Capitalism. Heard of it?"

"You think that's what this is?" Something tells her it isn't. She wipes away the tears gathering. Fierce. Not done yet.

"Yeah."

"You haven't told me your name."

"I have several. Morehouse will do." He pulls out a strap of surgical tubing and wraps it around his arm. Sentro sees track marks. Ugly sores.

"Where are we?"

"We're a boil on the forehead of South America. Some say Guyana; some say Venezuela. It's unclear whether this is because each country claims Porto Pequeno or wishes it on the other. Meanwhile . . ." Morehouse injects himself. "WHOA nelly nelly nelly . . ." His gray eyes pin; he sits back on his heels, riding the rush. The needle trembles as if electric, stuck in his arm. "I am. I am. Fine, me. I am."

Losing balance, he topples heavily back against a box—"Oh boy"— legs splayed, arms spread, and nods off, mouth slack. A tendril of blood pools in the crook of his elbow from the puncture just below it, and a single drop falls to the ballroom's worn carpet.

Exhausted, wrung out, Sentro looks at the girl and her brother. Eccola and Zoala. Will she know their names when she wakes up again? They crouch, keeping their distance, eyes dark, expressions grim.

"I'm hungry," she says.

The girl and her brother just watch her.

A breeze makes the bobbleheads shake and chatter again like the dentures of a thousand baseball fans. Dennis loved Fenway, hated the Red Sox.

Why does she remember that?

Sentro lets her head slip back into the icy compress and closes her eyes again, helpless.

Yippee-ai-oh-kai-yay.

Chapter Twenty-Four

"Andrew? It's Leo Robbens. Yes. Hello."

In his office kingdom, midcentury modern and climate controlled, Robbens rules with a wireless headset from his leather Eames swivel chair throne.

"To you too. I see where your Cottagers have been relegated again—yet somehow made it to the EFL Cup." Laughs. "I know, I know they changed the name, but *Carabao* sounds so silly. Carabao is a water buffalo, if you care to know. Appropriate." He laughs again. "You're welcome. Now. Reason I'm calling, Andrew—the *Jeddah*, yes. Has your client—no, no, I've had contact, and I'm happy to report that there shouldn't be any difficulty negotiating this. The vendor appears quite professional."

Are they? The Zemes? Or even rational?

Not fucking likely, but where money is concerned, Robbens feels confident he can keep them in line.

"Although I should mention that—full transparency—tragically, one of the passengers has suffered an accident. Yes. Mortal, I'm afraid."

The underwriter he's calling is someone Robbens has done maritime insurance business with many times before. A humorless actuary, a grammar school product, Fulham man through and through, whose subsequent moody silence Robbens is expecting.

"They know, they know, Andrew. And they're willing to suffer a reasonable penalty discount, although they insist it was utterly out of their control. As I said, an accident, unrelated to their acquisition of the ship. They were beside themselves. Yes."

Through the tall latticed window, he can see the *Jeddah*, cargo ship in question, listing slightly starboard in the argent bay waters, its cartoon stacks of containers bowing out over its beam. While the actuary rambles away, Robbens puzzles over where the Zemes might be stowing their human collateral.

As sometimes happens, though, and more and more often now, he is flooded with bitterness over how it has come to this for him, middleman between criminals and capitalists—a glorified pawnbroker—in a backwater third world anchorage, when, by education and breeding, he should be plying his trade higher up in the food chain.

He could have been an Oxford man, but for the immigrants and the quotas.

"I know. I told him."

Robbens half listens to a boilerplate lecture that the rep should know better than to give. Ah, but then Drew's just doing his job, isn't he?

"I'll be emailing you the ship registry documentation and hostage list so the families of passengers and crew can be contacted. I can scan the passports if that at all matters. Whatever else will you be needing on your end? The holding party is anxious to close."

———

Overlooking another bay, the Chesapeake, a few hours later, from the Carey Business School library (which classmate Farhid has dubbed the Toxic Asset Incubator, because three recent graduates just escaped doing federal time for bundling bad loans), Jeremy Troon has commandeered a coveted cubicle with a view and downed two Red Bulls to get his thinking razor sharp. The seminar presentation feedback was excellent, and he was looking forward to Marketing and Statistics because numbers come easily to him, concrete and predictable. But a phone call from some thick-accented travel agency representative has him up and pacing, agitated, trying to keep his voice modulated because a few of his annoyed classmates are already looking up from their notes and textbooks with incurious expressions.

"Slow down; say again?" But he doesn't wait for the rep to repeat anything. "Well, she didn't specify a container ship, but yeah, my mother is taking a cruise. Aubrey Sentro. Correct. What's up?" The answer he gets is droll, dry, and matter of fact, but it stops Jeremy short; he shakes his head, struggling to process what he's hearing. "What? Pirates. No. No. That can't be right."

For a moment he just listens, the rep's words jangling, random vowels and consonants, as if Jeremy needs to translate them from a foreign language. Ship seizure? His mother unaccounted for?

"This is nuts. When was this? Where?" He starts to move again, just to be doing something. "Well, if she's on the passenger list, why isn't she on the hostage list?"

Jeremy wanders through the stacks, looking for privacy, unable to find it. "Who did you say you worked for?" The caller repeats a generic name that slips out of Jeremy's head again as soon as he hears it. He can't stop walking. Some corporate ass covering ensues, so Jeremy cuts the man off. "Look, I couldn't give a shit about insurance—what are you, what are you—?" He's never been good at this, crises. Or surprises. What the hell is his mom doing on a freighter? He thinks: *I gotta call her. I'll just call her, and she'll be at home, and this is all some kind of crazy mistake.*

"Wait. Who died? What are you—is my mother dead?" His mind goes blank, his stark panic spiking, fueled by caffeine. "How do you know that? How do you know she's not?"

An undergraduate seeking an empty carrel squeezes past him, smelling of sweet-scented vape and giving Jeremy a worried side-eye. "That one's taken," Jeremy covers the phone to hiss when the student heads for his vacant window-side carrel.

"Oh Jesus, what does that mean, she's not part of the package?" He knows he's on the verge of shutting down. He needs to get outside; he can't concentrate. "What are you telling me? My mother's on her own?" The caller tries to explain again in the irritating accent: no need to panic, fluid situation, so much they don't know yet.

Fuck.

Fresh air. Privacy. Clear his head, and yes, deal with this—Jeremy can deal with this. He steps from the stacks into a cavernous central atrium, its long maple tables filled with students, and he beelines for the exit. His free hand slaps a rhythm against his thigh. He's trying to keep his voice low, measured. "What? Can you just—can you just tell me—what the hell *do* you know?!"

His voice breaks. Everybody in the library is looking up at him.

He shouts, "Fuck."

And keeps walking.

———

The internet café—ByteMe—is dim, cooled, crowded with mostly young men wearing headphones and playing online games or poker or streaming porn, except for Castor Zeme, who's been running a Google search for *Aubrey Sentro* and all variations of it on a filthy Dell computer and getting no results.

Or nothing for *Aubrey*, anyway. There're other Sentros on social and business sites: Facebook, Instagram, Ancestry.com, and one confusing listing for a Jeremy Troon at the Carey School of Business in Maryland, USA. At first Castor thinks it's some kind of search engine glitch. He's on Twitter, Tumblr, LinkedIn—Castor clicks through to Jeremy's online résumé. No mention of Aubrey Sentro, but clearly there must be a connection. There's one smiling photo of a young man with the eyes of the woman who killed Pauly.

Castor double-checks Sentro's passport photo. Not really a resemblance, but for the eyes.

He digs in his pocket for a cell phone, the woman named Sentro's Android, which he's had hacked open by a one-eyed computer repairman in a shop off Central Avenue.

It takes a while for the phone to turn on. He thinks about his brother, already buried and cold in the hard potter's field clay of Saint Ignatius Cemetery on the rocky hills to the south of town. There has to be a reckoning. This woman is more than just part of the cargo.

The home screen glows with a picture of two young children; Castor flips through the menus, finds Aubrey Sentro's address book, a "friends and family" sublisting, and there it is: *Jeremy*.

———

"Hi, yes. Yeah. They connected me to you, said you might be able to—yeah."

Sentro's son has found his secluded space outside the library to make another fraught call, and he's weathered a few layers of federal bureaucracy to get this far.

"Well, I'm not sure how this works. My name is Jeremy Troon; I need to talk to someone about a missing American citizen." The functionary on the other end of the call proceeds to recite some bureaucratic boilerplate, but Jeremy is growing pretty frustrated with all the runaround and keeps going. "She's a passenger on a cargo ship that's been hijacked, and—" He's interrupted again, something about jurisdiction, so Jeremy just keeps talking over her. "Sentro. Aubrey Sentro, S-E-N-T-R-O. I just learned about it from—" The female voice on the other end tries to cut him short, some kind of accent—is it possible an

American law enforcement agency would use a call center in another country? "What, no, no, please, don't put me on hold again. NO, wait, can you just . . . wait." She puts him on hold, lo-fi hip-hop on a loop. Jeremy's cell phone is humming with an incoming call; his juddered brain is redlining; the screen caller ID says *Mom*.

Thank God.

The voice returns, offering to connect him with someone else, probably a low-level drone in the State Department.

"No, can you just. Wait. I said WAIT. Shit. No, no, I'm getting a call coming in from her; can you please just"—the hold music bumps again—"fuck."

He toggles and accepts the incoming. "Mom?"

"No."

———

No.

"Who is this?" The voice of this Troon sounds agitated and strained. Castor Zeme crafts a faint mournful grin: *All for the better, yeah?* What he'd be saying to his brother, if not for the bitch.

"Izzit Jeremy I'm speaking to now?" Finger in his ear, Castor tries to block out the gamer din of the ByteMe main room.

"Who's calling?"

"Jeremy, how are you, mate? I'm calling about—"

"Where's my mother?"

"Ah, that's it, innit?"

"Is she alive?"

"C'mon. We're civilized men here."

"Are we?"

"Yah."

"But you have her."

Castor tries to imagine the American on the other end of the call: callow, rich, in a cold sweat over his missing ma. "We have her." Troon comes across a lot older than Castor expected. That's helpful. Be his own man, make decisions. "We have her, my friend."

"What?"

"Yeah."

"What? Where is she?"

"Ah, I'mma say no to that, just yet."

"What?"

Gotcha. "You want to take a sec to catch your breath?" Castor tips back on his café stool. The kid sounds thoroughly gutted. It's all good.

"Where is she? What do you want?"

"Wind down. I'll be getting to that directly."

CHAPTER TWENTY-FIVE

"He wanted a hundred and fifty thousand dollars; I got him down to eighty."

"You haggled with them? For Mom?"

An agitated Jeremy talks across the barista station to his sister, who he sometimes forgets just turned twenty-five, all grown up, small boned and pretty, with breasts and so forth, hips, long legs, raccoon mascara and ashy lipstick, bright tattoos on pale biceps peeking out under her sleeves, and several examples of what Jeremy believes to be unfortunate piercings.

When was the last time she cared what he thought?

"I wasn't sure he'd respect me if I didn't—"

Jenny bites this thought off before he can finish it. "Pay it! Get Mom back, Jemmy!"

"Wait."

"Use my fucking half of Dad's trust, if that's what you're acting so squirrelly about." Jenny turns her back on him and guns a Frappuccino blender.

"Will you wait and let me explain?"

"Just do what you have to do."

Jeremy resents that he needs to justify to her his reservations. "Look. We gotta be smart about this. It could be, I dunno, a Nigerian scam or something. Old people are susceptible to all kinds of online nonsense. They had a whole series on NPR. What if they don't even have her?"

"What does Nigeria have to do with anything? You said it was South America."

"Figure of speech. Nigerian scam, it's like . . ." He decides not to elaborate. "Trust me on this; it's an internet thing, Jen. Where you make wild demands and get people to send you money. An online grift. Focus for me?" The cute cashier pushes three more empty venti cups down the line for Jennifer to attend to.

"They have her phone. And her passport."

"So they say."

"Do the people she works for know?"

Chagrined at having completely forgotten about calling Solomon Systems in his consternation and embarrassed that his sister thought of it first, Jeremy tries deflecting by wondering aloud if the kidnap insurance they carry, if they carry it, would even cover employees on vacation.

Jenny presses. "Did you talk to them?"

"I put in a call to them, yes," he lies, feeling trapped. "Getting back to me. First they'd heard of it," Jeremy insists with as much sincerity as he can, hoping to get the conversation back on track.

"Capitalist fuckers."

Jeremy frowns. "I thought Mom hates boats."

"That time Dad took us all waterskiing."

"Exactly. She stayed on the dock and fed Beer Nuts to the seagulls."

"Mom." Suddenly emotional, fighting tears that slick her eyes, his sister lets steam blast from the milk foamer and swipes it truculently with a towel. "She did hate boats. Still does. I talked to her."

"When?"

Jenny packs espresso in the portafilter, cranks it into the machine. "She phoned me, from a port in Savannah, I think. That's Georgia, right? Or down there, anyway. Called to tell me she was taking a cruise,

Sorry I didn't connect before I left, last-minute thing—you know, her usual yak-yak—and *Oh, don't worry about me, Jenny.* I don't know what to think.

"And I was like, *You fucking leave without talking to me?* And then we got in an argument and . . . anyway." Visibly rattled, Jenny fumbles the handles and knobs of her espresso machine like the stops on a pipe organ she's never played before.

"She tell you about the cargo ship?"

"I can't remember. Shit. Anyway."

For a moment, Jeremy watches her try to work, spilling ice, fumbling for cups, and he broods about his sister's complicated relationship with their mom. He may look like his mother, but Jenny shares every shred of her singular, fervid, and resolute spirit, despite both their endless denials. Sometimes, when they clash, it's like they're fighting with themselves.

Jennifer almost spills the next order as she sets it too hard on the counter. "Grande half-caf skinny latte, no foam, for Ginger, on the bar!" Her voice sounds strained.

"Typical Mom, huh?" Jeremy thinks out loud.

"Not really. Normally we don't know what the hell she's up to." Jennifer wipes her eyes with her shoulders. "I'm sure she didn't mean for this to happen."

"Are you crying?"

"No."

"Look at you."

"Shut up." She says it without enmity and smiles at him sadly.

"Says the daughter who keeps insisting she's disowning her mother for not being around enough growing up."

"Shut, Jemmy."

"Dropped out of school? Shacked up with a pangender videographer."

"They were just a friend." Another frantic spin around the espresso dials; he can see she's distracted, and over the squawk of a double shot squeezing out without a cup to catch it, Jennifer says, "Shit," then looks up at him. "We have to go get her."

"We? What?"

"She's out there by herself." She looks past him into the shop. "Ginger! Grande half-caf skinny latte, no foam!"

Jeremy says, "I'm meeting at six with this federal agent I talked to."

"FBI?"

"He says he can't officially open an investigation—"

"Why not?"

"No jurisdiction. Plus the US doesn't negotiate with kidnappers or terrorists."

"He fucking said it?"

"In those exact words, yes. But maybe—"

Waving her hands like a traffic cop, Jennifer cuts her brother off. "No no no. Jeremy, the kidnappers are going to kill her. Isn't that what the guy said? If we don't bring them the money?"

"Dude said he wants it wired."

"Fuck that. Into the void? No. Straight swap. Money for Mom. And we gotta have eyeballs on it, make sure they let her go."

"Listen to you."

"I know. This is insane."

"Face-to-face is not what they said."

"Are they going to turn it down if you bring it? Cash? I don't think so."

"Me? What happened to 'we'?"

"Fine. I'll go. I'll just quit here, but you'll have to put the ticket on your—"

"No, it's just, goddamn it"—he rambles over her—"so unbelievable. What a fuckup. You know, yours wasn't the only life she ruined." It just blurts out, and Jeremy is shamed by this childish accusation. He gropes for justification. "What if this is just another one of her lame-brained escapades, you know? Like that penny stock thing I had to bail her out of when Dad was dying? Fifty thousand dollars—she thought she'd make some extra money right during the whole depressing ordeal with his chemo and blood stuff, which you were too young to even—"

"No, I wasn't."

"And the time she totally missed your graduation. And I had to go to the fucking parents' buffet."

"She had that emergency, with work."

Jeremy stares at his sister, all wound up, incredulous. "You're defending her?" He feels his face flush; his hands are trembling. "What the fuck, Jenny? How does a goddamn paper pusher for some reinsurance company get kidnapped?"

"I don't know." Jenny looks broken. "I don't know."

Jeremy tumbles back from his tantrum, chastened. "Okay. Sorry. Okay."

"Excuse me?" a third voice interjects.

But he's still griping: "Who takes a cruise on a goddamn cargo ship, anyway? Fail. Fail. She's always doing this, Jenny; she's always . . ."

Jenny asks, "Always what?"

"You know."

"Excuse me."

"It doesn't matter." Jennifer says it so softly her brother barely hears her. "We have to get her. She's nobody, the person who slips through the cracks. And nobody else cares."

"Miss. Excuse me." A short, burly customer in a coat and tie shoulders up, having evidently overheard enough to know this can't be as important as his order. "Miss?"

Jennifer ignores the man. "One of us goes; one of us stays here. In case," she says, leaving the obvious apprehension hanging, eyes shiny with anxious tears. Jeremy stares at his sister. Small and fierce and hopelessly delicate. They were forced to rely on each other growing up. But oddly, she was often his protector.

It scares him to say it: "I will. Go, I mean." He needs to do this, for her, for his mom, for himself.

"You sure?"

"Absolutely."

"Miss, but do you plan on making me my cold brew sometime this year, or should I talk to the manager?"

Jeremy spins on the man, spits out, "If you don't back the fuck off, Jeeves, I'm gonna rip you a new piehole and feed you a Cleveland steamer. With extra foam."

You could hear a pin drop, suddenly, in the city-center coffee emporium. All eyes on the barista station. The suit-and-tie man's face has stewed to an unholy shade of red.

"Jeeves?" Jenny cracks a brittle smile for her brother. "Save some for the bad guys, Vin Diesel. Damn." And to the customer, as if this were all in the course of normal business, she says sweetly, "I'm so sorry. Coming right up, sir. On the house. My bad."

"Fucking Mom." Jeremy slaps the bar hard and walks out, pissed at the world.

———

Ice tumbles into a big translucent cup, iced coffee from a temperature-controlled carafe, plastic straw that will wind up with all the other trash in the North Atlantic Gyre. Her hands won't stop shaking.

Maybe she should go.

She's the one who gave him the hated nickname, but he let it stick; they were best friends growing up, despite his four-year head start on her. He irritates her; he annoys her; Jenny worries about him, even if he is sometimes an insufferable asshole. Maybe she *should* go, to wherever, and get her mother, instead of him. The day their father died, Jeremy's junior year at Hopkins, he was a chocolate mess—blew off two finals, flunked the classes, got put on academic probation. He said he didn't want to make excuses, never told their mom. After she simmered on it for a couple of weeks, Jenny biked to campus, tracked down both professors, and, aided by copious and only slightly inauthentic tears, got them to agree to let her brother take the tests late.

And then he still flunked them. On purpose, she suspects.

She's never thought of her mother as helpless, never worried about her. And now this. Jenny is terrified. So much of their childhood feels like it was spent waiting for their mother to come home or trying to pack too much in before she left again. In her stays and her absences, though, things calmed; life settled. Somehow normal, either way. That Jenny resented her, felt abandoned sometimes, lonely and aggrieved— that was upsetting and true as well. But she took for granted that her mother would always be there, good or bad.

What if Jeremy fucks up?

"Cold brew on the bar for—" She doesn't know the chubby man's name.

"Doug," the customer mumbles.

"Peace out, Doug," Jenny tells him. And takes her break early to go into the bathroom and cry.

CHAPTER TWENTY-SIX

This hotel, she's discovered from the covers of some dog-eared matchless matchbooks discarded on the floor within her limited reach, was once called the Simón Bolívar. And in its grand ballroom, with dusk shedding its dander light through the slit curtains, Sentro's eyes have opened from another dreamless sleep or loss of consciousness to discover Dr. Morehouse gone.

And pregnant Eccola gone.

And no ice pillowing her head.

But the fire-blistered Zoala remains sentinel, crouched at Sentro's feet in the long shadows, motionless, watching her. Half-boy, half-ancient, wearing a dead man's football jersey, so many questions in his restless gaze.

Sentro says to him, "What."

Zoala lifts a handheld device and types. Then scutters over to Sentro and shows her the green-and-gray LCD screen. It's a tiny first-gen computer translator like people had back in the nineties. Portuguese to English:

i help you kill pirates

Sentro considers Zoala. His round, willful face. The chunky gold Rolex loose on his bony wrist.

His burns.

Sentro gestures to them as she asks: "What happened to you?" She tries various languages: "*Pourquoi? Por quê?*"

The boy types; the device translates:

pirates

Zoala stands abruptly, pulls up his jersey to show Sentro the full extent of the wicked, suppurating, and peeling welts on his body. He spits out what must be the story of his injury and abandonment and near death at the hands of pirates, perhaps the same ones who plundered the *Jeddah*, but Sentro can only nod and guess and listen until he stops talking just as abruptly.

There is then a silence of his waiting. For what?

"Okay," she says, nodding.

The boy types.

help you kill them

"I need a phone. Do you have a phone?"

The boy holds out the translator. Sentro rattles her bound wrists, looking at Zoala. "I can't use that, not with these on me."

Zoala seems to understand this and makes a long, careful calculation to consider the risk. There's a key around his neck; he draws it out from under his shirt, kneels, unlocks just one of the handcuffs.

He puts the translator on the floor in front of her. She types on the tiny keyboard: *Do you know where the pirates are?*

Zoala reads the Portuguese translation, looks up at her warily, but doesn't offer a response. She guesses that he doesn't know, but she's tempted to enlist his help finding them. Then she makes the hard assessment: a brain-fogged stranger and a blistered boy who the twins, for some reason, wanted dead. What are their chances, really? Fool's errands are what Sentro has been trying to put behind her.

So she types, *Can you get me a phone,* and mimes holding one and talking on it. She's confident that if the boy can just get her something with which to call for help, the act of holding that phone will trigger her elusive memory of the number she should dial.

The boy types.

dr say no to you

Not for the first time, Sentro wonders if Morehouse has an agenda of his own. "I need to pee," she says.

She types: *bathroom.*

The boy's eyes narrow with suspicion. Playing her bluff, Sentro shrugs, points to a chipped bedpan nearby someone must have helped her use when she was cuffed, less conscious, and in need. It's not a wholesale lie, and sure enough, from the look of disgust on his face, it wasn't Zoala who was tending to Sentro, nor does the boy seem to have any interest now in playing nurse.

He scoots forward with his key chain, pulls it from under his shirt again to reach and unlock the other cuff from Sentro's wrist. As soon as he's done so, she grabs the kid by the leg and snaps the cuff around one of his skinny ankles, binding him to the shopping cart. He screams and flails at her. The translation device slips from his grip and shatters on the floor, scattering parts.

Catching one of Zoala's arms, she secures it to the other cart with the opposite cuff, snaps the chain from around his neck, and slides out of reach as he kicks at her with his free leg.

"Sorry," Sentro says and gets up, only to regret it. Her head spins. She reaches for a support to steady herself. "I'm sorry," she says again. "But you have helped me." She finds some rudimentary Portuguese has come back to her: "*Eu sou . . . pesaroso.*" Was that even right? Unsteady, she takes a tentative step farther away, stumbles, collides with a packing box that falls and scatters sex toys across the floor, including more handcuffs and other cheerful bondage accessories. She's wearing a loose cotton shift that doesn't belong to her, with nothing under it, feet bare and tingling with unfamiliar movement, a pressure headache building. And now, looking across the ballroom, Sentro takes in the full measure of all the motley goods Zoala and his sister appear to have lifted from pirated cargo ships: mini flat-screen TVs, running shoes, laptops, microwave ovens, several boxes of the handheld translators, automatic coffee makers and espresso machines, basketball shoes, yoga pants, sweatshirts, tennis rackets, Chinese smartphones, Christmas lights, industrial drain cleaner, underwear, socks, rice cookers, hot pots, toaster ovens, high-heeled pumps.

Zoala is bellowing angrily and tugging at the cuffs. The carts jangle. His voice echoes across the ballroom, but no one seems to be in the building to respond. After finding underwear that seems adequate, sunglasses to cut her headache, and a familiar-looking pair of high-top sneakers that are, in fact, hers, Sentro slips all these on and, ignoring the plaintive cries of the boy behind her, strolls across the vast parquet floor on ungainly rubber legs to a pair of huge, heavily bolted, carved double doors, which she unlocks and opens to join the world outside.

Well. A lobby, anyway.

The vaulted, stone-tiled lobby of the once-grand Simón Bolívar now evidently functions as a huge, bustling third world flea market that spills outside into the driveway and overgrown front courtyard of the defunct hotel. The sky is black, awash with stars; what she thought was daylight fighting through the ballroom curtains is the bright beams of old carbon arc lamps fastened to rusted scaffolding that, perhaps, is all that remains of a distant effort to restore the Bolívar to its former function. Fruit stands and fishmongers, fried-meat kiosks billowing black, fragrant smoke, and hung fabric fluttering in a brisk wind off the bay. The clamor is disorienting as Sentro tries hurrying through.

From all sides, vendors bark; their clientele is a strange pastiche of global diversity, as if someone shook the world and a sampling of unfortunates all tumbled to rest here. Sentro recognizes at least five different languages spoken and several more she can't identify. It feels like a dream.

The market thins and becomes ramshackle where the driveway abuts it, overgrown with tropical foliage and crowded with cars and trucks and pulled trailers and motorbikes. A stray street vendor sells from his cart more of the sexy lingerie Sentro last saw raining in bits and tatters to the deck of the *Jeddah*.

An old green-and-white Checker taxi rumbles up the driveway, catching Sentro in its headlights, and for an instant, she can see the surprised faces of Morehouse and Eccola in the back seat. The cab rattles up to the hotel's service entrance, and Sentro hurries off and disappears into the streets of the crowded city center.

―――

There's a gap. A slip in time. Empty, black.

She's in her mother's arms and they're crying, in the motel, with the carnival blue-and-red lights dancing across the curtains, the heat like liquid night, crying and holding each other, and her mother is whispering:

Sing.

―――

Bright.

Hectic.

Neon signs spit and flare in Spanish, Chinese, and Portuguese; girls in tight skirts and Spandex roost on stools tucked into smoky alleyways at entrances promising Vietnamese massage or the girlfriend experience or sex acts in voyeur rooms. Families lumber past, lugging groceries in translucent plastic sacks, and those same sacks are everywhere, guttered, blowing, fluttering from dead trees in median planters, car lights raking them as they snake through the city, stereos booming rap and K-pop.

The smell of grilled peppers, sewage, and hashish.

Half the men strolling the sidewalks and staggering into the street have automatic rifles slung over their shoulders or handguns on their hips. And with every step, Sentro realizes the immensity of her mistake in running off:

—she doesn't know where she is.

—her head is in a fog.

—she has no idea where she's going.

—no money, no papers, no phone.

She stops couples who look approachable, asks, "Excuse me, do you speak English? *Você . . . você fala . . .* English?" If they hesitate, "American? *Parlez-vous anglais?*" They all regard her with suspicion and slip past, muttering apologies.

———

There's a shorter gap, or a gap that seems shorter, anyway—nothing in this one, white noise, then—

———

Circling a small city park with towering mangroves, she feels a pack of boys no older than Zoala that has been shadowing her for several blocks. Mocking her. ("Parlay vooz!") A brave one cuts across the grass along the corner to step in front of Sentro as another, darting up from behind, tries to pick her shapeless dress's pocket (which of course is empty). It rips easily, and Sentro, reacting automatically, sets her feet and rocks her elbow; it whams into the side of his head, and the pickpocket goes reeling into traffic, where horns blare and tires skid and two cars collide. He screams obscenities at her, and the other little punks join the shouting, mounting their attack on Sentro en masse, but Sentro lays another one out with a straight arm and darts through traffic to the other side of the street, where two Porto Pequeno policemen, with whistles screaming, catch her by the arms and wheel her up against a wall, riot sticks ready.

"Is there a problem here?" A sweaty face presses into hers and asks this, in French.

In French, Sentro tells him she's an American.

"Tourist?"

Yes.

"Passport."

Knowing she has no identification, Sentro pats her ripped pocket as if she did, realizes she's exposing more flesh than she wants, and holds it closed, explaining that her documents were stolen from her—and that she needs to speak with the American consulate. The ship she was traveling on was hijacked and—

"Which ship?"

Sentro can't say. In truth, she can't remember. Her hesitation suspicious, the partner cop puts his hands on her shoulders and spins her around against the wall to pat her down with probing hands.

"Don't touch me like that," she warns him, switching to English, hoping it helps.

"Like what, madame?"

"Take your hands off me."

"I'm looking for drugs."

"Not there, you're not."

"You'd be surprised."

Actually, she wouldn't. Sentro jerks away from him but resists lashing out. His tiny yellow teeth gleam in the night light. She's scared. It's a new, raw feeling. Glancing speculatively at the weapon holstered on his hip, Sentro studies the buttoned strap that holds it in and decides she can't hope to get the gun free and useful before his partner reacts.

"Is there an American consulate here?"

The cops ignore her, conferring in French. "No identification."

"Drunken tourist."

"North American."

"Yankee slut."

Daniel Pyne

The sweaty one asks, "At which hotel are you staying?"

Hesitating, Sentro spies, across the street, a familiar filthy madras sports coat striding back the way she just came. She recalls its pirate owner—what was it? Spanish surname. A metal splint taped over his nose glints brassy in the old mercury-vapor streetlights, the scar slashed across his face obscured by it. Sentro wouldn't have recognized him but for the jacket.

"Which hotel?" the handsy cop echoes.

Sentro says, "I'm not exactly sure."

The cops exchange a wolfish look. "Perhaps we can take you somewhere quieter so you can remember."

"*Tia! Tia!*" Zoala shoves through the crowd that's gathered to watch the show and embraces Sentro with a big awkward stage hug. A green-and-white Checker taxi swerves to the curb, and Dr. Morehouse hops out.

"You found her, thank God." He flashes some kind of ID and switches to French. "I'm a doctor; this is my patient"—gesturing—"mental patient. We've been looking all over for this woman. Thank you."

Disappointed, the sweaty cop takes a stance and folds his arms to study Morehouse. "Why does the brown boy call her 'auntie'?"

Ignoring him, Morehouse calls into the cab in Portuguese, and Eccola slides out of the back seat to take Sentro by the arms and starts leading her to the taxi, making weird baby cooing noises. But the cops aren't ready to release anyone.

"What hospital?"

"It's a private guardianship, Officer. Up in the hills."

"Sisters of Mercy?"

"If only. No, no. Secular. Public."

Sentro looks back to see Morehouse shaking both cops' hands and pressing some folded money into them.

"Gentlemen. I am deeply indebted to you. Thank you so much. I tell you, we've been looking all over. She's a firecracker, this one. Walked away during evening meal."

Eccola is desperate to get Sentro back in the taxi, but Sentro stalls, holding on to the lip of the roof and searching the street behind them for her madras sighting.

"*Por favor*," Eccola pleads. "*Entre no carro.*"

Morehouse takes leave of the cops and comes to them. "Get in the fucking cab," he whispers and shoves Sentro in and follows. Eccola slides into the front seat with the driver, and Zoala squeezes in back beside Morehouse as the door shuts. Sentro sees her friend Handsy the Cop step out into the street, helpful, and blow his whistle so the cab can merge into traffic and drive away.

CHAPTER TWENTY-SEVEN

"Dude. Get a grip. You really thought taking a runner was a good idea?"

Sentro is pretty sure he doesn't want an answer. Her head is woolly, and her shoulder has stiffened.

"You suicidal or just stupid?"

"Was that my money you used for the bribe?"

"Yes. Well spent too."

Sentro tells him she needs to find the hostages from the cargo ship the pirates attacked. If they're pirates at all.

Morehouse just stares at her, incredulous. "Find them. And do what?"

Sentro stays quiet, eyes on the street beyond the windshield. Concentrating. She's a specialist. She does this for a living. Saves people. Names float through her head, in and out of reach: Bug, Unger, Drewmore, Scott Chang. Bobbing for memories like apples in a tub.

Chang is a client she saved once. But from what?

"Dude."

Zoala echoes, "Dude."

From the front seat a giggle, and Eccola's withering, mocking, "Duuuude."

Morehouse continues, "The hostages're gonna be fine."

"You don't know that."

"I do. For sure, I do. This is how the game is played: boats are caught up, deals are struck, money changes hands, nobody gets hurt. It's totally chill. You are harshing the flow."

Everyone keeps telling her this. The taxi slows, locked in traffic.

"Somebody already got hurt," Sentro says.

A pink hoodie flutters down from a stairway deck through the pale-blue sky of her memory.

Morehouse shakes his head. "God is indifferent. That's why they invented life insurance."

She's starting to like him, despite everything.

But over the doctor's shoulder, out the window, she has seen a madras coat again, slaloming through the sidewalk crowds. Before anyone can react, she flicks the taxi door handle, steps out clumsily, and falls into the street, and the traffic thins and the cab accelerates before Morehouse can stop the driver, and the door slams shut.

Sentro gets back on her feet. She makes one full rotation, up over the curb to the sidewalk, where she shoves through a pack of men gathered outside a windowless bar, the green field of a *futebol* game glaring down at them. She stops and scans the street to the intersection, spies the madras jacket settling astride an ancient yellow Vespa. He guns the throttle, pops the clutch, and takes off, hurrying down a hill toward the docks in a fog of exhaust.

Driven by habit, by instinct, by inclination, Sentro gives chase. Sprinting on heavy legs, or what she can approximate as sprinting, it's a losing cause. She's bruised and aching and too old for this.

There was a run like this in Cairo, wasn't there?

A chase. Or was it a flight?

A mad sprint through a warren of dark, narrow streets and alleyways, fetid pools of water, huddles of men, the hue and cry from Tahir Square, flat-screens flaring bright colors through open windows, laundry flapping from overhead lines, the thump of electro shaabi blaring from cheap speakers, mercury lamps casting down their dirty ocher light.

It's the struggle and the hunt and the chase she got addicted to—everything leading up to the end.

When the possibility of a happy one is still very much in play.

———

Gap.

Here or there?

The vacuum of space, time out of phase. No idea where she is or why.

An apple-shaped man in a yellow three-piece suit. Leather eye patch tooled with a starburst.

Farhid.

Human trafficking in the sub-Sahara. He'd been chopping up the evidence (children) and scattering it across the city while the Arab Spring bloomed.

Fled to the open arms of the Muslim Brotherhood and was disappeared. A long run for nothing.

———

This fugue spits her out on the waterfront, where the Porto Pequeno Coaster Wheel whirls, gap toothed, on the end of the boardwalk, spitting colors across the bay waters, dozens of its carnival lights broken.

Clarity.

No sign of the scarred man, the madras coat, or the pastel Vespa. Out of breath, her pulse in her head, but no ache from it, Sentro slows to a walk.

Now what?

A crumbling concrete boat ramp leads to the damp, low-tide beach, scrubbed ruler flat for a small, rowdy crowd gathered around a make-shift ring in which two amateur ultimate fighters are kicking the hell out of each other. Sentro stays clear of the event. She walks the water's edge and dips a hand in to brush cool salt water on her flushed cheeks and neck. She turns her back to the boardwalk and skirts the shallows. Local fishermen's jangadas are pulled up in a cluster and tied fast to iron rings in the break wall, dark with the shadow of the working quay and its shabby warehouses and rusted cranes.

———

Gap.

———

Are they more frequent when she's fatigued? Or is she breaking down?

Another skip in time, then surfacing to the cool, hard embrace of sand against her back, the Milky Way canopy mocking her, and water lapping her heels.

Sparks spit in the darkness and scatter on the sawtooth waves of the bay. An arc welder. Working on the doors of a red container lit by the spotlights of a wooden-sided icehouse. As the revolving klieg light at the end of the boardwalk flares across the water and then the dock, Sentro can see some of the logo on the side of the cargo container. Cartoon cat.

She knows it from somewhere.

She sits up and shakes the sand out of her hair, clouds clearing from her fragile sentience. A crude wooden ladder goes straight up the side of the quay from the beach. Some buried memory tells her to test the rungs before putting weight to them, before climbing, one at a time, to the concrete jetty.

The cartoon cat came from Savannah, she remembers.

A group of men stand, watching the welder work, a hundred feet from Sentro, bayside. It's slow going, cutting the doors open, and the men smoke and laugh and shuffle their stiff legs. Their talk rattles, incoherent, indistinct.

There are other steel shipping containers open and discarded like Christmas packages on the dock, some empty, some with pillaged merchandise spilling out of them like entrails. Sentro uses these for cover, weaves among them, trying to get a closer look.

In an alley between two of them she finds the yellow Vespa, parked. Sentro slips into the deep shadows and edges along the container's side until she has a better view of the welder's efforts. Sand shedding inside her dress prickles her ankles as it falls. Sparks flare; watching, impatient, the man in the madras coat can't seem to come to rest, his arms restless, his head jerking as if pulled by an invisible string. Talking with great animation to a man who, when he turns and the overhead spotlight sharpens the features of his sunburned face, Sentro recognizes as the counterfeit pirate king who plundered her ship.

There's a young, white-blonde woman standing next to him.

Blinding blue light flares from the welder like a tiny blazar. The woman smiles, beautiful, and Sentro feels a tremble go through her.

I know you.

Hair bleached and chop cut, but no question about it; she's alive.

I saw you die.

Chapter Twenty-Eight

Jeremy Troon and three special agents sit at a small maple table in a conference room of the Baltimore federal building. Jenny declined the invitation to come. "You're better at this, Jemmy. They're gonna say something assholey; I'll lose my shit. It won't be helpful," she advised her brother. "Record it all on your phone," she added, "so they can't lie to us later," but they took his phone away during the security check out front.

Only one of the feds does the talking: polite and not unsympathetic. He introduced himself as Agent Warren, but he reminds Jeremy of his high school swim coach, Mr. Kalman, who had hair everywhere except the top of his head. He would come into the locker room with his hands in his sweatpants, scratching his balls and telling the boys that it would make them faster if they shaved all the hair off their bodies, but he couldn't require them to do it because the principal, Ms. Belasco—a "friggin' feminist," Kalman would never forget to add—forbade it.

"You called her employer."

Jeremy did. After Jenny reminded him that he should have. "They have a receptionless system. You had to give a name; I got her vacation voice mail."

"You don't know anyone she works with?"

"No."

"Odd," the female fed says.

"No shit," Jeremy tells her, "but that's Mom. I've never dialed the main number before, either, because we could call her cell." He expects a follow-up and is prepared to explain to them that this is what life was always like with his often-absentee mother and her mystifying job, but the feds just trade looks and move on.

"Solomon Systems," Warren says.

"Reinsurance."

Warren tilts an eyebrow. "That's a real thing?"

"Risk management," Jeremy says.

"How long has she been with them?"

"I don't know. Ten, fifteen years. Pretty sure she was with the government before that. And in the army. But it's not like you pay a lot of attention," he adds, self-conscious. "I was just a kid. My dad raised us; Mom worked."

"Sure."

In school, teachers always asked him what his dad did, not his mom. "Mom works in an office" seemed to be sufficient for the incurious. And his mother and father were so opaque about what she did, never talking shop around their kids, only the occasional souvenir from a strange place Jeremy had to look up in the world atlas. He and Jenny had lots of friends whose fathers worked in government or the military, traveled, extended absences. Their dad stayed home: the natural athlete, the crazy-good dancer; the one who could fix anything, cook paella, dog-whisper, explain binomials; the one who knew the best movies and the best books, told the best bedtime stories, got the Frisbee off the roof or the mood ring out of the sink trap. Their mom did little magic tricks and worked hard in a job that never seemed all that special but paid the bills. And that meant she was the one who was gone.

"You're sure you have the firm's name right?"

"Yes. That's why I'm here."

"Okay. We'll look into it," Warren says. The two others are pretending to take notes. Idle doodles on long legal pads. "Could it be that your mother—Aubrey?—got off the boat before it was hijacked? In Savannah, maybe? Or Nassau?"

"She would have called me. She would have called my sister." This is a lie, of course, but Jeremy needs them to take this situation seriously. "Can't you track her phone? Now that you have the number?"

"We can try." Agent Warren runs his hand over a hairless head. The femme fed stares at Jeremy, lost in thought. Her male counterpart—clean shaven, Republican haircut, and Men's Wearhouse two-for-one suit—slouches back from his legal pad like a truculent senior in study hall.

"Maybe she got off the boat with someone else and didn't want you to know," the female agent says.

Jeremy tosses her a sharp look. "No. My mother doesn't fuck around."

That you know of, is what the male agent's shrug seems to say, but instead he speculates, looking at Warren, "Okay. So what if one of the pirates got ahold of her cell and her passport as a consequence of the shakedown, and now he's trying to make a little pocket money for himself on the side. The frontline grunts are notoriously underpaid."

Warren nods, as if considering it.

Jeremy imagines this is about where Jenny would explode on them in frustration. He takes a breath, tells them how he was hoping there was an American consulate "down there" and that the FBI could help him negotiate his mother's release. "We have the funds."

This seems to get them itchy. Uncomfortable. "We?"

"Me and my sister."

"Where's your father in all this?"

"He passed. A while back."

"I'm sorry. Look," Warren says, a little more gravity in his voice, "believe me, we'll do everything we can from our end, but you should know that—"

"Or," Jeremy interrupts, forceful, to finish his own previous thought, "maybe you could at least talk with the local police. Tell them I'm coming. Grease the wheels for me." He offers up what he hopes is a brave smile but admits, "I don't really know what I'm doing here."

After the three agents all share more knowing looks, Warren shakes his head. "The thing is, Jeremy, you've got a Chinese-owned company sailing under a Bahamian flag, and we don't have any jurisdiction over how they choose to conduct their business, and—"

"Business?" Now he's bummed Jenny isn't here, with all her unbridled outrage. They could have good-cop-bad-copped them. "This is an American citizen held for ransom."

"And the United States government does not and will not negotiate with hijackers. Officially."

"Yeah, thanks, somebody already told me that. I call bullshit. Isn't kidnapping a crime?"

"Sure. But again, jurisdiction. Territorial waters, we're not allowed. And not to argue a fine point, but in fact, modern high sea piracy is capitalist enterprise, like it or not. Sometimes best left to play itself out. A variation on, well, the Wall Street hostile takeover. Shippers and their insurers routinely pay millions of dollars in ransom to get their boats and cargo back. Nothing we can do to stop them. There's kickbacks and commissions, middlemen and brokers, support services, codes of conduct."

"The one who called me said they'd kill her."

"She's not worth anything to them dead," the female agent says.

Jeremy blinks, his heart in his throat. "What?"

"Yeah. That sounded wrong. Let me rephrase. What I mean is, it's just an idle threat."

"You're guessing."

"Risk assessment is a big part of our job," Warren assures him.

"Are we still talking about my mother's life?" Agitation is creeping into Jeremy's voice, pushing it to a higher register. His hands skip restlessly on the tabletop.

"We are. And I'm confident telling you she's most likely going to be fine as long as she and the other passengers and the crew cooperate with their captors. Which I'm sure she and they will."

"Most likely," Jeremy echoes, hollow.

"There's no upside in harming her," Warren says, more artfully.

Jeremy feels his panic peak. His eyes must look crazy to these people. His palms are wet; his chest hurts. He wants to scream. "What would you do?" he asks them.

Agent Warren takes a moment, probably deciding whether to tell the truth or the lie he thinks Jeremy wants to hear. "I'd let the shipping company do their thing. They've been through this before. Work with them; trust them. You're right that you don't know what you're doing or what you're getting into, so don't try to be a hero."

"And if you're wrong?"

The windows in the bright room are all black with night. No stars, no cityscape. Jeremy wonders if they're actually windows at all. The agents are quiet, respectful, useless.

Part of an indifferent world that coils around him.

"And in the meantime, what am I supposed to do?" He can't go back to his sister with nothing; it will crush her. It's already crushing him.

Warren, as if this is the right question to be asking him, nods. "Wait. Pray. Let us know if they call again." He raises his chin and seems to read Jeremy, darkly. "But Jeremy. I can't stress this enough. Do not, under any circumstance, try to handle this on your own."

CHAPTER TWENTY-NINE

The Lazarus blonde watches the welder work on the cat-cartoon container door, and Sentro watches the blonde.

The woman's name may be a blank. But the rest has come rushing back.

Perfume, unlike anything she had smelled before, expensive and complicated, and she recalls intending to ask about it afterward.

Afterward.

The quicksilver of hot water guttering down.

The shiver from her touch.

Before the so-called pirates intervened.

Still tucked away between two already empty and rusting cargo containers farther back on the quay, Sentro watches the blonde watch the welder and cut quick, worried sidelong glances at the boss pirate. The blonde's body language is confusing. She leans into him now and then. Her hand on his arm, her smile clearly a ruse.

Are they partners? Are they lovers?

Sentro is surprised to feel herself blush.

She wants to walk out and say something. The part of her that is not fine tuned, the raggedy wreck of a woman that she's always feared emerging, the shitty mother, the jealous wife, the bitter, helpless, motherless, hollowed-out child that she buried but that her fraught condition threatens to exhume, wants to walk out of the shadows and call out to this beautiful, treacherous woman, *What the fuck?*

And see where that takes them.

The machine-milled woman she has become remains in this distant quay's darkness. Watching. Waiting. For what?

Cut free, finally, the container door falls away, edge smoking, glowing red hot, clattering to the wharf deck as flashlights strobe the inside.

It's empty.

The pirate goes inside, disappears for a moment, whatever he's saying lost in a lo-fi booming, then comes out, staring daggers at the blonde, clearly furious.

Empty.

". . . kind of joke?"

Sentro can barely hear them.

The blonde is saying, "No."

". . . is the shit?"

"I don't know." British accent.

"WHERE IS THE SHIT!"

The blonde flinches, expecting, Sentro guesses, a blow. "I don't know," she pleads, and a sudden breeze off the bay carries away the rest of what she tells him.

The pirate does hit her. She staggers. After he hits her again, the blonde cries out. Sentro feels her fists clench, her nails digging into her palms.

"What is your game, eh? Is this a game? 'Cause you'll find that I DON'T PLAY."

He pulls the Englishwoman into him and taps a gun against her temple. Sentro gauges the odds of sprinting out and getting there before the man sees her, puts a bullet in the woman, and empties the rest of his clip at Sentro.

But the blonde has already jerked her head back and is talking, fast, low, defiant, and some of it carries. "Why would I be here if I knew the container was empty? Think . . . my husband . . . double-crossed us both . . ."

Sentro loses the rest of what she says.

There's a fragment of the man's deeper voice: "Gonna go call him and—"

The rest gets buried in the clatter and rattle of equipment the welder is packing up, his part done. The pirate lowers his gun, and Sentro remembers that he's not a pirate. That his twin is dead. Pauly. That she killed him. This twin is Castor.

The scarred man in the madras coat helps carry welding things to a compact pickup truck that looks scavenged together speculatively from several American brands.

"I can't!" The blonde's voice surges up again. "He thinks I'm dead! Please . . ."

Dragging her to a dusty Range Rover, Castor murmurs inaudible instructions back to the madras coat and the welder. Sentro watches as doors slam shut. The headlights blaze. The Rover powers away.

Hidden, Sentro runs swiftly through the containers, tracking the Rover as it goes. She'll never catch it. She looks back to see the madras coat strolling back to where he parked his Vespa. Passing the place where Sentro was hidden only to discover, where he parked it, that his scooter is gone.

She can see the man's frown in the quay lights as he must be puzzling this, wondering: *Where could it be?*

Sentro turns away and, from the shaded cover of other containers, watches the taillights of the Rover disappear into the urban jumble of the waterfront city.

A soft squeak behind her causes her to jump, but it's only Zoala, his cricket bat strapped to his back like a samurai, pushing the madras man's Vespa as fast as he can and calling out softly to Sentro in Portuguese.

He hops on the scooter, wobbles, his bare feet unable to touch the ground at the same time. Kicks the starter, fires it up, and veers crazily toward Sentro, shouting what he was whispering, something she takes to be *Hop on.*

So she does, behind him, tucking her dress under and holding on as they accelerate out of the docks in pursuit of the Rover. The scarred man, madras coat flapping behind him like a cape, comes hurrying out of the containers to see only a pair of shadows stealing his Vespa.

"HEY!"

They've left him behind before he can even start running.

———

Zoala, Sentro swiftly comes to understand, has never been on a Vespa before, much less driven one. His familiarity must be from having watched them go by him; he knows to twist the throttle but does it in uncertain pulses, rocketing them herky jerky through narrow cavern streets between checkerboard tenement apartments, veering up on sidewalks and down alleyways, paying no attention to any laws or common courtesy.

Shouting at people to get out of his way.

She goes with it for a while because it feels like a theme park ride, and her hair blown back cools her head and calms her jangly mind. But when they pop out onto a main thoroughfare and nearly get T-boned by a truck, Sentro reaches around to grab the handlebars and swerves them to safety in the proper lane.

"Let go of the throttle," she says, but Zoala either doesn't understand her or could be willfully ignoring her. He points ahead, and sure enough, the Land Rover carrying the resurrected blonde woman and the fake-pirate twin is only half a block ahead of them, turning right onto another angled street.

The scooter weaves between traffic, and Sentro bumps it up onto a sidewalk. Zoala waves for her to veer down a pedestrian walkway between buildings parallel with the Rover's new direction, a passage so narrow the scooter's handlebar brake levers scrape and spark against the walls on either side as they swerve through.

Zoala's bare foot pushes off walls and vendors' handcarts, and locals are jumping into doorway niches to get out of their way, screaming as they pass.

After bouncing up some stone steps, Sentro curls the Vespa around a couple of oil-drum grills; she can smell the bacon and sausage and peppers and, stabbed by hunger again, tries to remember when she last ate. The aroma is fleeting because they crest the climb and pop out into another narrow street, this time in a quieter residential area pooled with more honey-colored mercury-vapor lamps. The Rover is just up ahead, taillights flaring as it pulls under a brick arch and up the driveway of a massive tropical art deco apartment building.

City police cars are parked out front. A couple of khaki-uniformed cops stand guard, smoking.

The Vespa motors past the driveway, and Sentro watches as the blonde and Castor emerge from the Rover, still arguing, and go inside the building with the cops.

She drives the bike farther, onto a dead-end side street, hops off, pulling the boy with her, and lets it bury itself in an overgrowth of stunted palms. Zoala twists free and looks like he's about to yell at her.

Sentro puts her finger to her lips: *Shhhhh.*

———

The side street is lined with smaller, plainer, blocky clapboard apartment buildings nestled thick in overgrown palms and a heavy hush of trees. Some soft incandescent lights burn here and there in upper-floor windows. The blue cast of televisions ghosts empty walls.

The tallest of these old pastel structures flanks the one into which Castor and his friends disappeared. Rusted iron grillwork and meaningless Moorish details, plus big faded yellow awnings and carved decorative shutters like wings on clumsy glass butterflies. Sentro walks around the block to get to its entrance, with Zoala trailing behind at a moody distance. They haven't spoken since the quay.

The front door is broken, propped open with a cinder block. Rap music blares from somewhere upstairs. She leads him to an unlit staircase, past scattering cats, abandoned appliances stacked against peeling walls, a sleeping man, and the closed doorways of more apartments than were originally designed.

Four flights of stairs, then a narrower climb to the roof-access door, which is stuck. Sentro thinks about forcing it but remembers her shoulder. Zoala tugs on her dress; she steps aside, and somehow, after he jimmies the handle, it's open and yawning to the night.

Crouched low behind the back parapet, they can look down on the courtyard of the art deco building. An algae-clouded pool glows eerily under canopies of palms. Empty steel tables and cushionless loungers. Castor sits with the two policemen, all smoking and arguing in French.

"You'll get paid when I get paid. Isn't that how it works?"

"Sometimes," one of the cops concedes. "But sometimes a retainer is required, to secure the cooperation of those in the public arena."

A giant black moth flutters past on the muggy night's thermals, and Zoala makes a sudden lunge over the edge trying to catch it. Sentro pulls him back.

Below, in the courtyard, Castor snaps, "No retainer. No up-front payment. My rules: we are all in this together."

He flicks his cigarette into the pool and walks into the deco building, leaving the chastened cops to confer. For a long time, there is a scatter of their low murmuring through the whisper-shaking of the poolside vegetation. Night birds dart out and back. The odor of burned tobacco. They don't seem to be able to decide anything. Their cigarettes burn down; they both light another. And fall silent.

Curtains draw open on the third floor. Castor appears backlit, pushes a casement window wide to scowl out. When he turns away,

Sentro sees the blonde step into the light behind him. She's on a cell phone, pacing, pleading her case with someone.

Zoala taps Sentro on the arm. Holds out a small eyepiece Sentro recognizes as once belonging to a fellow passenger. *What was* his *name?*

Lens to her eye, Sentro gets a closer look at the blonde on her phone.

I should remember you.

The woman looks played out. A faint bruise purples one side of her jaw where Castor hit her. Her voice drifts across, distant, frantic, and it rattles incoherently around the courtyard and through the palm fronds, but Sentro can read her lips for some of it. "There was nothing in the container. That's what I'm trying to tell you. Who told you? Who said I was dead? No. I don't know! Believe me, I don't . . ."

When she turns her back to the window, her voice becomes inaudible.

Another room light turns on, same floor. A plus-size man from the *Jeddah*, owner of the eyepiece—Bruce?—looks out and up into the night sky. Bruce. Two other men she recognizes are behind him. The captain. The first mate. More names she can't remember.

A fifth man crosses the room, shirtless. The Tagalog—Charlemagne.

Why that name and not the others?

Sentro sinks behind the parapet, overwhelmed. She's light headed; she needs to eat. But the circumstances of the night have calmed her; this feels like familiar ground. Cairo, Split, Istanbul, Lagos, Kiev. Cities tumble through her thoughts, flicker jumbled postcards of distant assignments she's always ticked off like chores on a to-do list.

This is what she does.

This is what she's good at. Focus narrowed. Task at hand.

Zoala kneels beside her, watchful.

Locate the assets. Check.

Risk assessment.

Strategic plan. Drawing a blank, there, sorry.

Tactics. Not yet.

A low rumble has them both scrambling to the other edge of the roof.

On a street corner beyond the art deco building, a decrepit city bus finishes its crawl up the hill and pulls to the curb, brakes hissing, its doors clattering open to disgorge a small woman with plastic bags in both hands. As the woman slowly makes her way up another street, Sentro grasps Zoala's wrist and pulls it toward her to read his Rolex. She finds a small, torn triangle of roofing and uses it to scratch the time on the back side of the parapet flashing.

Mopping the perspiration from the night's oppressive heat off her face with the hem of her shift, Sentro sits back again to think.

Locate the assets.

Risk assessment. Skip the plan.

Assemble a team.

Recover and return.

It's not such a long list, once you break it down.

CHAPTER THIRTY

WHAM.

WHAM WHAM.

A steel door with a red cross on it is unlocked and opened by a clearly sleep-deprived Morehouse only to discover Sentro glaring back at him. He glances past her, with obvious worry, out into the hallway of his decrepit building as if expecting someone else to cause him trouble.

"I found them."

"Good on you. And?"

"I need your help."

"Christ on a cracker." He makes like he's going to shut the door, but Sentro squares herself to him.

"This is what I do. This is how I'm built. You don't wait for things to work out; you make sure they will."

"Dude." Morehouse shakes his head. "You barely remember your own name." Behind him, in a shabby one-room, green-walled clinic, are the cluttered trappings of his so-called medical practice and paraphernalia from his heroin addiction, organized around a battered examining table on which Eccola, bra and skirt, sits, hunched, hugging her knees.

Sentro estimates the girl is six months pregnant. It's hard to tell. When you're young, Sentro knows, you can carry it so well.

"How'd you find me?"

Zoala steps out of the shadows, where Morehouse must have sensed him. Locks eyes with the bad-boy doctor, then shifts them to his sister, impassive. They exchange sharp words in a pidgin Portuguese Sentro can't begin to decode. Zoala spits dryly on the carpet and turns away, walks to the end of the hallway, where it looks like he intends to wait.

Sentro says to Morehouse, "Listen to me: these are not your normal pirates. This is not business as usual."

"You need help," the doctor says. "But not my kind."

"I make my living untangling knots snarled by clueless people who think evil can't touch them."

"A bottomless well, no doubt. Are you sure? How's your head?"

Light as a balloon. "Feels like someone's trying to push my eyes out from the inside. So not so bad now."

"Pupillary reaction time, that tremor in your right hand. Anybody ever evaluate you for concussion syndrome?"

"You're not going to help me." A statement, not a query. Her attention strays to Eccola, who has taken up a clinic blanket and wrapped herself in it. It looks like she's hiding a basketball in her lap. Sentro thinks: *She's so young.*

"Is that yours?"

Morehouse knows what she's talking about without even turning to look. "Might as well be." He flattens his mouth, petulant, sheepish looking, shifts his weight, and gets defensive. "Dude, look. I know—"

Words appear to fail him. He doesn't, or can't, finish. But if Morehouse expects outrage or criticism, he's not getting it; Sentro believes she has no moral high ground from which to judge him. And she's feeling storm clouds gather behind her eyes.

"What?"

"Give me a sec." She's going weightless.

"You better come in and sit down."

"This is no place to raise a kid," Sentro observes, enigmatic, and then collapses to the floor as her world goes blank.

———

Lights out.

———

She sat there in the hot darkness with her back to Scooby-Doo and Shaggy, listening to her mother sing and watching her sway, cross-legged, on the edge of the bed, feeling her father outside with the other rangers and the lights and the High Plains drama she was too young to understand then.

The AC had shut down. Water pooled underneath the window unit, silvery in the TV's cold light. The handgun they had brought with them from their house in Austin was in her mother's lap, the handgun her father had instructed his little girl never to touch, and both her mother's hands were on it, slender fingers trembling, gimlet eyes dry. The chapped, faded lips that Aubrey thought were peeling lipstick sang in a voice so high and thin it could have been merely air escaping.

I know all the songs that the cowboys know.

The phone in the room rang and rang and rang. Her mother was no longer interested in answering or talking to them.

"Mom?"

'Bout the big corral where the doggies go.

"Please, Mommy."

We learned them all on the radio.

Gentle, fragile, as if her body were breaking, her mother moved the gun to the side and pulled Aubrey onto her lap.

"Sing, sweetheart," she said. "All we can do is—"

Chapter Thirty-One

—Sing.

———

On the street corner beyond the building where the hostages are being kept, another rainbow-painted local bus pulls to its scheduled stop. An old man gets out, sets his walker with the yellow tennis ball feet, and begins to make his way home. The engine revs, but the bus remains, and when the doors open again, Zoala recognizes the scarred face. Even though there's no way Carlito can see him, he sinks lower behind the parapet and watches the madras coat flap in the bellowing bus's wake before the tweaker crosses the street to the art deco apartment building's entrance.

The police cars are still parked out front. The cops who drive them are somewhere inside.

On the parapet's inner edge, Zoala marks the new bus arrival time with one of the doctor's marker pens the way the strange American woman taught him to do it.

Another hour has passed.

He can hear their voices in the rear courtyard before he sees Castor and Carlito emerge below him, deep in a private conversation the gist of which Zoala can easily guess: Carlito is still furious about his missing scooter.

Good.

Zoala would like to find a cinder block and drop it on them both and crush their skulls. The American woman wants him to watch and wait until she returns for his report, so he does so because he finds he doesn't want to disappoint her.

His peeling skin itches, but scratching makes it bleed. The island beetles are a fading fever dream, but being set adrift, the fire, the explosion, the fear of dying are things he will never forget.

When he thinks of the future, he draws a blank. All that matters to him is payback.

Exactly one hour later, the same battered rainbow bus pulls to a stop at the bench, coming back the opposite way. A couple of waiting passengers climb onto the empty vehicle.

The doors clatter and hiss. The bus rumbles away. Zoala checks the wristwatch that hangs loose on his arm like half a shackle and notes the arrival time again on the back side of the parapet.

———

The carnival glare made her eyes hurt as she peered out at him through the motel curtains, but she couldn't look away. His face painted pale red by the whirling emergency lights, his thick angular features were sparked sharp by white searching beams that roamed over the motel while her mother rocked and sang in the room behind her.

Rand Sentro wasn't, factually, Aubrey's father.

Laundry-crisp white-yoked snap-pocket shirt, khaki chinos, and those Lucchese boots he lived in; the star that gleamed on his breast; the ivory-handled .45 always strapped to his hip and never to be touched without asking. That her stepdaddy was a Texas Ranger was a source of great pride when she was growing up, and not only because her playground friends were awed by it. A big, stern, quiet, inaccessible man whose righteous violence was legendary in Lone Star law enforcement but never shown to her, he would come and go like panhandle summer storms, thrilling and unpredictable, just as likely to take her up in his arms as walk right past her to the high cabinet where he kept the Jim Beam.

Her biological father never factored. The way her mother looked at Ranger Rand Sentro when he came home to them was unwavering and absolute, as if there had never been anyone else. Once, as a teenager, Aubrey had searched through what remained of her mother's things in the basement, looking for a clue to this other man who had helped create her. She found nothing, but the following weekend Rand Sentro was down there "cleaning up," and the next time she dared venture into the cellar, all her mother's things were gone.

Absent her mother, theirs was a relationship fraught with polite silence. He was kind to her, a sad gentleness that saw a hole in her heart but was helpless to fix it. And he was nothing if not a fixer. So he was nothing: a taciturn, tentative single parent who, when her rebellion began, withdrew into his work and threatened to leave the rest of her upbringing to the rigid, righteous Baptist catechism of his spinster cousin Jean, who he'd ask to move in with them.

Dennis saved her. Loved her, impregnated her, married her with a promise to shield her with his unwavering devotion, which he did, and which, looking back, she often feels she didn't deserve.

But in that oppressive midnight heat of the West Texas motel room where her mother sang one last time, a girl too young to understand what was happening watched through a gap in the curtain—the man who wasn't, factually, her father pacing the parking lot behind the circled wagons of first responders and repeatedly removing his white Stetson to mop his face and squint into the temporary crisis lights, as if he'd run out of ideas.

The phone kept ringing. Her mother wouldn't allow her to answer it.

Rand Sentro called out to his wife from a bullhorn that made his deep, warm voice hard and splintered. It felt like the night terrors from which she sometimes woke to find her mother looking down at her, smiling, stroking her face, telling her everything was okay.

To lift a gun from lap to temple takes only a moment. It happens so fast it's done before you know it, and you're wiping the warm bits and pieces of a lost cause off your cheeks while salty tears fall.

———

An IV tube snakes from her wrist to a yellowing saline bag dangling from a coat hanger hooked over a ceiling water pipe right above the examining table where Sentro finds herself surfacing, naked again and wrapped now in what Eccola was wearing, which must be the only blanket Morehouse owns.

Sitting up doesn't make her too light headed this time, but the crackle of her bare ass on the paper covering the table padding causes a sleeping Eccola, slumped in a corner chair, to wake up with a start and shout for help.

Morehouse fills an interior doorframe faster than Sentro thinks possible. The pupils of his eyes are huge.

"Welcome back."

"How long was I unconscious this time?"

"Sleeping. You were sleeping."

"How long?"

Crossing, Morehouse cradles her wrist in one hand and with his fingers takes her pulse. "Couple of hours." His stoned gaze makes her uneasy. Maybe clarity is too much for him; she wants it back. Desperately.

"What time is it?"

"Why does it matter? You need to rest."

"Where are my clothes?"

Looking at Eccola, Morehouse starts to say something, but Sentro pulls her arm away and tells him she wants her own clothes, "not the dress you put me in at the hotel. Or was it her? I hope it was her."

"I am a doctor. Nothing you've got I haven't seen."

"You're a man, you're a junkie, you're fucking an underage girl, and you may or may not have a medical degree."

"Your pulse is still racing. Do you feel dizzy?"

"I need to go."

Morehouse shakes his head and assures her he sent Zoala back to the rooftop after the boy filled him in about what Sentro found in the deco building. "They're not going anywhere," he adds, meaning the passengers and crew. "The pirates will contact a broker; the broker will contact the insurer. And then they dance. I've seen this business get wrapped up inside of a day; I've seen them draw it out for several weeks. You never know."

"I'm not waiting for that. The men who did this won't wait either."

"How do you know that?"

How can Sentro explain her unshakable instincts to him when she still can't quite remember why she has them?

Morehouse frowns, steps back, and folds his arms. "What did you mean when you said you make your living doing this?"

Sentro doesn't want to get into it with him.

"Doing what, exactly?"

"Please. Give me my clothes; I'll get out of your hair."

"Your clothes are ruined."

"There's some things in the jeans I want."

"Dude."

"Listen to me carefully. I was in the US Army," she tells him, impatient, itemizing the fragments that have come back to her. "And afterward have worked for government and NGOs that specialize in . . . security issues."

"Ah. Some kind of black-ops girl ninja?"

"Woman. And no."

"Still your gig? Spook for hire?"

It's just a job, she wants to tell him. *I'm pretty good at it.* A set of skills she's developed over a long and productive career. Like anyone, she gets satisfaction from a good result. The dead don't haunt her.

Or didn't. "I need to go."

"You can't remember who you work for."

She can't. She feels a hollowing in her chest and looks away from his opioid eyes. "It'll come back," she says, hoping that's true. "It's like I've dropped a fancy plate in the spot I dropped one with the same pattern years ago. I'm picking up pieces, but they don't always fit together."

"Short term, long term, jumbled up."

"I guess."

"They mention CTE? Last time they did a checkup from the neck up?" It's as if Morehouse has opened her head like the hood of a car and looked in. "Me, I'm unconvinced."

"You're stoned."

"Selective memory loss, no confusion. Attention drift, but you don't have problems organizing your thoughts. Balance and motor skills obviously still there. Depression?"

Sentro doesn't want to talk about it anymore. "Can I please get some clothing?"

"What kind of issues, specifically? Your job, I mean."

"Troubles like this."

"Kidnapping."

"Yes." Phrases come back to her, rote: "Crisis management. Conflict resolution. Extortion and murder."

"You gonna take the bad guys on all by yourself?"

"No. I'm not stupid. I thought I explained this." Sentro slides off the examining table; her legs feel stable, and her head doesn't hurt. She wraps the blanket around herself and stares her challenge at the junkie doctor. "You're going to help me."

It occurs to her after she says it that she can't be sure it was a statement and not a question.

CHAPTER THIRTY-TWO

> He was an inch, perhaps two, under six feet,
> powerfully built, and he advanced straight at
> you with a slight stoop of the shoulders, head
> forward, and a fixed from-under stare which
> made you think of a charging bull.

Salt mist slicks the flat roof tar paper, and a muddled moonlight
has fractured across the shine to where Zoala sits in the shadow of the
balustrade, waiting and struggling to sound out and read aloud English
words in the book he took from the American lady's cabin.

A translucent fog hangs curtained over the bay, throwing back the
city lights with a gray foreboding.

> A water clerk need not pass an examination
> in anything under the sun, but he must have
> ability . . .

Bored, he checks the watch again. Time crawls. Blood seeps through
his faded *Minecraft* T-shirt where he's scratched his skin raw. He's hungry, the liter of Mountain Dew the doctor left with him having been
rationed out and finished off.

Most of the lights in the deco apartment building have been turned off. A single low lamp glows behind a curtain. A big round white man in a patio chair stirs on an unlit balcony and stares up at the shrouded stars.

Black witch moths have discovered the single landscape light in the courtyard and dart back and forth through its beam.

> To the white men in the waterside business and
> to the captains of the ships he was just Jim . . .

Zoala has long ago grown oblivious to the night sounds of the Porto Pequeno hills: the frogs, the bugs, the broken air conditioners, the frightened dogs, the all-night televisions, the distant thrum of downtown traffic, the thump of a strip club, the lonely whoop of a car alarm. What he hears is his own heart beating, a hiss of blood racing through his ears. Since his ordeal on the island, the noise of his body refuses to quiet.

> . . . he was just Jim—nothing more.

Just Jim. He doesn't understand her book. Restless, he digs in his pocket for a crushed pack of Kools, pulls out another cigarette, and is going fishing again for his lighter when a white hand snatches the fag away from him.

"Don't smoke."

He does understand a little English. The American woman has crept up on him like some kind of duppy, which unsettles him, and now she stares at him without emotion, her eyes a liquid wall. Something about her calms him, though. The only woman he has ever been close to is his sister, but this one is nothing like her.

"Someone can see it; someone can smell it," she says. "Plus it's bad for you." Only some of this makes sense to him; he can read a little English but gets lost hearing it spoken. The American turns the cigarette between her fingers, and somehow it disappears. Gone. Shows both hands to him. Gone. Zoala looks down for it, then back up at her, mesmerized.

"That's my book," the woman says, but she holds her hand out like a schoolteacher, not for the novel but for the pack of Kools.

Zoala stuffs it back in his pocket, aping her blank stare. She's unfazed.

"Keep reading."

Zoala puts the book down, folding the page corner to mark his place. She's not the boss of him.

The American smiles faintly. It's the first smile he's seen from her. She rocks back on the heels of her running shoes and proceeds to empty from a plastic shopping bag a familiar pocketknife, plus a soda can and scrap of wire. She's wearing black leggings and a collared shirt his sister wore regularly until her stomach got so big with the baby.

"You really want to help me get these guys? *Vous voulez vraiment m'aider à attraper ces gars?*" she translates for him, in a flat accent.

Zoala nods.

"Say it in English."

He won't. She lets it go.

"*Puis-je te croire?* You'll need to do exactly what I say."

Zoala understands, nods again. He watches as the American flips a pair of tiny scissors out of the pocketknife he knows belongs to Morehouse, and she begins to cut into the aluminum can.

"*O que você está fazendo?*"

She nods to his question but hesitates responding; he can see she's not exactly sure what he asked and that her nod came reflexively, automatic, because she needs him to help her, and it helps him feel strong.

Making tools, she tells him in schoolbook French.

Zoala frowns. Tools? From a can and some wire?

She struggles to explain what she wants from him, and he mostly understands. He fills in the blanks when he doesn't and hopes that it's right.

She's very clever, Zoala decides, as she talks and cuts the can into strips, but she's not a man.

He's decided that he will want to have that knife when Zeme and his hired men kill her, so, of course, he should stay close.

———

"We can put you on the red-eye tonight to Miami."

The cute airline rep Jeremy has estimated to be about his own age works her keyboard behind the counter and scowls at the screen. He feels clearheaded and resolute about his decision. He'll just go and check things out. As he told Jenny, if the feds are right, he can be there when their mom gets released; if they're wrong, he'll do the money swap and bring her home. Boom.

The threat of real danger, of course, hangs over him like the blade of a guillotine, but he'll try not to think about it. Right? He'll try like hell not to think about it.

"From there we can find you a connection to Venezuela," the girl behind the desk is explaining. "In Caracas, there are several commuter flights to Guyana, but they tend to arrive and depart without a firm schedule. And once you've arrived at Cheddi Jagan, you'll need to charter a plane to take you the rest of the way."

"Cheddi what?"

"*O nome do aeroporto.* That's Portuguese; Cheddi Jagan is the name of the airport."

"They speak Portuguese in Venezuela?"

"They speak everything in South America. French, Spanish, English, Dutch, German, so many local dialects. And Brazil is close."

"You've been down there?"

"I wish. I'm, like, a virtual traveler." She looks up at him. Her eyes are blue. "But I am learning Portuguese."

"Never would have guessed."

"Cheddi Jagan is in Timehri. Outside Georgetown." She offers him a wary, polite, professional smile. "Might be a little warm for that leather jacket."

"You think?"

"Nice look, though. Indiana Jones?"

"Not exactly." Is she flirting with him?

"Business trip, Mr. Troon?"

Jeremy adjusts the travel bag strapped over his shoulder. Maybe she's expecting a glib retort, but he stammers, exposed. "Um. No. My mother . . ."

He lets that thought float, unsure how to finish it. She studies him with a curious expression and, flashing a more sympathetic smile, slides back his credit card and passport.

"All set. I'll light a candle for her at Mass."

"Oh. No. It's not like—I mean, she's—"

"Still. Couldn't hurt, could it?"

Jeremy stares, dazed by her unexpected kindness. "My mom isn't Catholic."

"I don't think it matters. Thanks for flying with us, Mr. Troon."

He hesitates, then takes both items from the counter, rotates them between his fingers, and makes the passport disappear. Slots the credit card in his wallet.

The airline rep giggles, charmed. "That was pretty slick."

Something she taught me. "Just something I picked up."

Another deliberate sleight of hand, Jeremy produces a business card and flips it down on the counter in front of her.

"Very cool. I love magic."

Humblebrag: "Parlor trick, really." His mother's simple magic routines awed and delighted him when he was little.

The airline rep cocks her head and looks intrigued. Not the millennial asshole she first assumed, Jeremy guesses.

"Agora estou curioso," she says, "That means 'now I'm curious.'"

He grips his carry-on and feels brave for the first time. "Maybe I can tell you all about it when I get back."

Shivering in the tropical chill, Sentro scratches a fifth bus arrival time on the parapet wall, beneath Zoala's previous notations. One hour between each. Down on the street corner, the idling rainbow bus has no passengers and waits about as long as it can. The driver climbs down, stretches, looks up and down the empty road, then reboards, shuts the doors, grinds into first gear, and resumes his route, taillights dying as the brakes ease.

A sleepy Zoala fusses with a scrap of the cut-up soda can. Trying to make it disappear, it seems, like Sentro did, but having little luck. He's looking very vulnerable, Sentro thinks, and all of his age. He yawns and fidgets and fights fatigue.

Sentro checks Zoala's watch. Three hours until dawn.

No sense in rushing this.

Sentro gathers from the roof's weathered tar paper all the other key-shaped aluminum strips she's cut from the can and puts them into her shirt pocket along with the knife, not unaware that the boy can't take his eyes off it.

"*Dorme*," she whispers, hoping that's the right word.

"*Estou sem sono*," he argues, and of course she doesn't believe him because she knows little boys and how they will fight sleep until the bitter end.

He flicks the last scrap of can at her and turns his head away. In a moment, he's breathing steadily, dead to the world. Both her children, she remembers, were the same way with sleep. Down and peaced out, Dennis would say.

She settles down beside him and closes her eyes.

Jennifer Troon dozes on the cat-shredded sofa bed in her cramped Federal Hill studio. The love seat is a shabby piece of bargain-store furniture her mother has offered to replace, but Jenny rescued it from her father's so-called home office and won't give it up until it falls to pieces.

Soundless late-night TV casts its pale colors across her. A pair of tiny, unblinking, luminous yellow spheroids leer from the dark shadows of hell beneath the breakfront. The upholstery-offending cat. She and Jeremy gave their mom a kitten to keep her company after Jenny moved out, but then Jenny became the de facto cat sitter when her mother went off on assignments, and eventually, the cat became hers.

She has secretly renamed it Aubrey. Mercurial, inscrutable, affectionate and aloof, gentle when it chooses to be, but a fierce hunter of mice and roaches in the night; sometimes Jenny will awaken to find the cat sitting impossibly high (*how did it get there?*) on the bookshelf, staring down at her with those electric eyes.

Protecting her or plotting her demise?

Cats. Mothers. Complicated coffee drinks she inexplicably can't remember how to make. A shallow dream carries Jenny Troon lucid along a horizon of her consciousness: she's flying, soaring, and her mother is just beyond the gathering clouds, if only Jenny can get to her.

Her phone vibrates, rouses her. She sits up, blinking. Text message from Jeremy:

k i'm going

Jennifer stares at the screen for a while, wondering if they made the right decision, and starts to text him back with a confidence she doesn't exactly feel.

———

Although his conversation with Jeremy Troon was discouraging, because there really is nothing constructive he can do to find the man's missing mother, Special Agent Warren is on his office computer terminal, searching for information about Aubrey Sentro.

He's reasonably surprised when nothing comes up.

Nothing.

Which is, well, weird, considering the array of public and private databases to which he has access.

There's a simple explanation, but the special agent's mind hasn't wrapped around it.

The better half of Warren's watchful team of wingmen enters the office bullpen, carrying flat whites in a cardboard tray with one hand and a printout in the other. She offers a fancy coffee to Warren and pops the plastic sipper lid off the other so she can empty two packs of Splenda into the nimbus of steamed milk.

Warren stares at the computer screen. "How is this individual so completely off the grid, Cassie?"

"How do you think?" The female agent flops the printout on Warren's desk. "Solomon is an NGO outside contractor. I thought I recognized the name. That idjit from COINTEL, what's-his-name, used to work there."

Warren tilts his head to study what his agent has brought him while he samples his lukewarm beverage. Then he types a URL into his browser window, accesses a secure NSA database, and goes through the ritual encryption and two-step verification, whereupon Aubrey Sentro's passport photo pops up, followed by a full dossier: military records, honors, citations, assorted civilian contract operations, and a detailed eyes-only précis on Solomon Systems, its federal entanglements, recent contracts, and so on. There are over a thousand official government entities and almost twice that many outside contractors doing intelligence work for the United States government. Paranoia is a booming business. A million people hold top-secret clearances. But not many like this.

"Hey, look—that private-contract clusterfuck in Cyprus. Minneapolis software guy."

"Scott Chang?" Warren remembers hearing about it.

"Yep."

"Holy shit."

"I know, right?"

Pages and pages of more of this he could scroll through, but Warren has found what he needs.

"Old gal's an ex-spook."

"Duh. And a half." Eyes still glued to the screen, the female fed nods, pretending she saw this coming all along, which Warren knows she didn't, but then, lowering her flat white, Cassie asks the smart and unanswerable next question: "Does that help us or hurt us here?"

————

Zoala, awakened by the faint alarm chime of his wristwatch, discovers his peeling skin cooled and slick with condensation and the American woman gone. Moment of mild panic, and then he sees the scrap of endpaper torn from the book about Jim, held down by the telescope eyepiece he liberated from the *Jeddah*.

Sentro has drawn him a three-panel picture note. First, a crude stick figure waves down a cartoon bus, while a group of other stick figures hurries toward it from a big rectangular box with smaller boxes arranged inside it. Next panel has a crude cartoon SUV with comically flattened tires—the Range Rover, Zoala decides. Big darkened arrows point to the tires. Exclamation points. A knife sticks out of one of the tires.

Zoala digs in his pocket and discovers that Morehouse's folding knife has been stowed there. Sweet.

In the drawing's final panel, the American has drawn a clock with its hands frozen at twelve and six.

When he pops up to look over the parapet and across the courtyard, past the inky-black pool water and the crazed canopy of palms, Zoala senses movement along the deco building in the shadows. He picks up his pilfered eyepiece and locates the American woman half-concealed by the thick tropical overgrowth abutting the first floor, already beginning to scale the wall using window trim and a downspout.

Zoala glances at his wristwatch. Big hand at eight, the little one nearly straight down.

He watches the woman climb.

Faint bleed of a sunrise sharpens the ocean horizon beyond the harbor, where the *Jeddah* is anchored, a silhouette, obdurate, black on lavender.

Twenty minutes until six o'clock.

Zoala slips into his laceless Nikes and hurries across the rooftop to the stairs.

Chapter Thirty-Three

Breaching the casement, pushing the third-floor bedroom window open, Sentro wriggles over the sill and through, cushioning her fall with her uninjured forearm, making not a sound. Her shoulder aches again, stressed from the climb. Her eyes are slow to adjust to the room's darkness. She's in the bedroom of a small suite, more a furnished boarding-house than an apartment. A sprawling california king with a cushioned headboard, bureau, framed mirror that catches the interloper as she softens into shadows and sidesteps a small leather club chair. A slender shape is asleep atop the bedcovers in her underwear, sweltering, long pale legs glazed with sweat.

A faint bruising of perfume Sentro knows.

The blonde from the dock.

Sentro listens for a long time for any movement in the outer room, waits until she's satisfied there's no one else in the tiny two-room flat, then rises beside the bed and clamps her hand over the blonde woman's mouth while using her own body weight to hold her down until she awakens with the expected start.

For a moment the blonde claws at Sentro's hands. Her eyes flutter open, but when she recognizes who's on top of her, she goes limp. Her breathing steadies; Sentro can feel the heat of the woman's body through the fabric of her borrowed shirt.

"I'm having trouble with my memory," Sentro whispers, "but I remember you being dead."

They stare at each other, inches apart. Uncomfortably intimate. Tentatively, Sentro lifts her hand from the woman's mouth.

The deep breath that follows Sentro can feel against her own chest. "I was. But it proved too inconvenient."

"Do the others know you're alive?"

"Others?"

"Passengers? Crew?"

The woman quakes and shakes her head and manages to make tears. Sentro wonders if they could even be real.

"I never meant to use you." The undead blonde reaches up and lightly brushes stray hair off Sentro's face to inspect the scabbing wound where she got clipped. Her fingers are warm. "You're hurt."

Sentro rolls off and tells her to get dressed. In doing so, she glimpses herself again in the mirror and even in the gloaming can see hollowed eyes looking back at her. The ugly bruises and cuts cause her to turn away and run a self-conscious hand over the riotous hair that hasn't seen a comb in days.

"I'm sorry."

Sentro has no response for this. Just waits.

Sitting up, the Englishwoman covers her breasts with one arm, as if modest. Part of the performance? "That husband I told you about?" Sentro pretends she remembers. "Well, he's a skanky, wife-beating, two-timing sod bastard hoodlum who's been shipping dodgy black-market arms and munitions to equally skanky sods in the Persian Gulf. Regional mayhem and skullduggery to ensue, I guess."

Sentro dredges up an image of a rusty-red container with the cat logo on its side. The five men watching from the Savannah dock; the Balkan mafia; the hipster with a porkpie hat.

"But he's mostly about the money," the blonde admits. "I'm a bloody fool for marrying him."

The blonde stood at the *Jeddah* main deck rail. Looking down at the hipster. Her expression so deliberately neutral.

Sentro blinks herself back to the present, to the same Englishwoman, who is rambling on, possibly nervous: "Have you ever noticed, in internet pornography—which is, I would argue, kind of our cultural mirror anymore—how the women are all fantastic-looking specimens, while the men are generally hairy little hedgehogs with joyless rodent eyes? Utterly devoid of tenderness or feeling. Yet we select them. And shag them. Resulting in more little evil bastards who—"

In a rush, the name comes back to Sentro: "Fontaine."

"What?"

"Fontaine Fox. That's you."

"That's me. Yes." Her eyes narrow. "What's wrong? Did you take a knock?"

"Repeatedly, as it turns out." Sentro goes to the connecting door and cracks it open, confirming that the suite's outer sitting room is vacant and offers only the hint of a hot plate kitchenette. Meanwhile Fontaine shimmies her lanky pale body into leggings and a black sleeveless T-shirt.

"Well, I had my fill of it, if you want to know the truth. I hired some local freebooters to hijack the *Jeddah* and pretend to kill me in order that I could get a redo on a life misplaced."

"Twins."

"Zemes."

"Castor and . . . Pauly?"

"Exactly. And their merry men. Yes. They come quite cheap, actually. Or seemed to." A crooked smile plays on her lips. "They're very disturbed by you, love. Warrior woman."

Having crossed the darkened sitting room, Sentro opens the hallway door and cautiously peers out into the corridor. Vacant. There's the faint bleed of chatter and canned gunfire coming up the main staircase at the end that at first she thinks is a television movie but then recognizes as a video game. First-person shooter. Fontaine's freebooters, possibly next floor down, killing more than time.

"What are you doing?"

"Listening." Sentro glances back at Fontaine. "You hired them?"

"I did."

"Had them storm the boat, pretend to kill you."

"Is it to shame me that you're repeating everything I say?"

"No, my head is in a fog. It's a good story; you tell it well. I'm not sure I followed all of it, but—" She frowns. "Blanks in the gun that I saw you shot with."

"Obviously."

"And all that blood—"

"Your Halloween stores carry the most brilliant props. It was a good show, yeah?"

"Convincing. Very."

"Thanks, I guess. You were the unexpected guest. Gunplay Kabuki was designed for the cameras in the safe room—odd bit of luck we were able to pull it off without a hitch."

"I don't think 'luck' is the word for it."

"Last Twin Standing's pretty gutted, you having punched his brother's ticket," the Englishwoman added.

"Pauly's dead."

"Yes."

It's how Sentro remembers it, but she wanted confirmation. "This is not playing out the way you planned."

"No." Fontaine goes quiet. "He must've figured out what I was up to," she says finally.

"Who?"

"My guy. My husband. And fucked me. One last time. Literally and figuratively, go back far enough."

"Cat logo."

"What?"

247

"On the container that got loaded back in the last US port we stopped at. That was your husband on the docks back in . . ." Sentro can picture five men, can't recall where.

"Savannah?"

Savannah, Georgia. Sentro says, "Empty, though."

"I suppose, yes, he is. Poor judgment would be my only explanation."

"No. The container. Was empty."

"Ah. Right. Of course, you saw it. Double-crossed."

"By your husband."

"Who else? Sod's law. But truly," Fontaine pleads what she's pled before, putting her heart into it, "I never meant to use you."

"What do you mean?"

Fontaine looks at her with what seems like real remorse. Does she want forgiveness? Does she need it?

"Would you have let them have their way with me?" Sentro asks.

"Have their what?"

"While you were on the floor, pretending to be dead." Sidelong, Sentro watches Fontaine torture her way back through a decision she hadn't had to make. "There were the makings of a negotiation. My suitability for the usual unspeakable violation before they then killed me for real."

"Unspeakable violation? You're quaint."

"Not so much, no."

Fontaine's mouth slants down. "No. I guess not. But then you—"

"Yeah." Sentro finds she wants to believe her. Some of it, anyway. It's important that she does. She glances back into the corridor. Still vacant, no one coming. The faint gaming ruckus steady from the stairwell.

"I'm so sorry."

Sentro shivers then and frowns, still remembering only fragments of what came prior to it, in fits and starts, but guessing: "Did we . . . ?"

"Yes."

Oh.

"Was that part of the plan? Distract me?"

"Decidedly not. A, I had no idea you had these otherworldly talents, did I? And B, I wasn't expecting the boys for another day at least." Oh.

"Freak you out, does it?"

"I don't know. I have no memory of it right now."

Fontaine frowns, looking less sure of herself. For once, she has no glib riposte.

"Only the feeling of not being alone," Sentro adds. Taking a deep breath, she narrows the door, leaving only a slot through which to keep monitoring the hallway, and turns around to face the bedroom and Fontaine Fox, while trying to gauge what she—Sentro—is feeling *now*. And why.

"Sorry," Fontaine says, her refrain, this time making it sound simple, plaintive, as if she's sensed a need to really sell the idea.

"You keep saying that."

"All I got left, really."

Sentro shakes her head to clear it, not from brain fog but from an overload of—what, exactly? What is this? What was it? Not love, surely, but a longing, an aching, for connection. For something she hadn't felt for a long, long time.

Which is, bottom line, just weakness, isn't it?

"Not part of the plan, though, you," Fontaine confesses. It's convincing. "I mean, the plan was for me to disappear and for my piratey hired help's remuneration to be whatever they could get from ransoming the *Jeddah* and its cargo and—"

"Passengers. Crew."

"—including the contents of my husband's container."

"You only wanted your freedom," Sentro says, not believing it.

"Yes."

"But now you've come up short, payroll-wise. On your end."

"Yes. No buried treasure for the boys."

"That's why you called him." Fontaine approximates an unconvincing look of bewilderment, so Sentro specifies, playing along. "Your husband. I saw you, through the window, just a while ago, talking."

"He made me."

"Castor."

"Him. Castor Zeme."

"What did your husband say?"

"He claims he doesn't know why the container is empty and that he was told by a shipping-company representative that I was dead."

"The official story. Do you believe him?"

Fontaine says, "No. He's set me up. I just told you . . ." She doesn't finish.

"Right. Double-crossed. Do the mercenaries you hired believe him?"

"I don't know."

Sentro puzzles over it. Something isn't settling for her: pirates who aren't really pirates, cargo that doesn't seem to exist. Games within games. It doesn't alter the objective, but it may impact how she achieves it. Sentro says, "I'm taking the hostages and crew back to the ship tonight."

"Why?"

All of a sudden it's a question that stumps her, one that everyone keeps asking, and maybe she just didn't hear it the way it comes at her now and—and what? What can she say?

This whole violent charade offends me?

Sentro walks back to watch the corridor through the gapped suite door, unable, suddenly, to come up with a clear answer.

But Fontaine doesn't seem to be expecting one and, rushing ahead, as if to a child, explains, "Everyone, everything—crew, passengers, ship, cargo—will be released when the money comes. That's how it works. You don't need to do this."

"So I'm told."

"By whom?"

"Almost everyone who has had an opinion about it during the past thirty-odd hours." Or in the abstract, she thinks, for most of her adult life. "They're all so certain."

Fontaine says she doesn't understand why Sentro doesn't find this persuasive. "You're stubborn."

"I'm skeptical." Changing subjects: "You know, he might actually kill you now. Given how his field of play has changed. Your pirate partner."

"He might. But there's still a profit to be made from the crew and the cargo. Plus, I think he fancies me for a rousing shag or four, even from the depths of his fraternal grief, so . . ." Fontaine makes a dismissive gesture. "Anyhoo, he's not thinking so much about me, is he? You're the one who topped his twin. And some others. Went off like a berserker on the boat, I'm told. 'The bloody she-wolf,' he calls you. Among other less polite epithets."

"Where were you, while it was happening?"

"Roll over, play dead." Fontaine shrugs, as if helpless.

For a while they study each other like strangers. Sentro knows Fontaine is right about Castor Zeme. But it's never been men who worry her; their unfortunate mash-up of testosterone and entitlement makes them easy to read. Only their evolutionary edge in size and strength needs to be accounted for. Women are where the danger, for Sentro, always lurks, like the naked terrorist in the Cyprus hotel hallway: sudden, unexpected Gordian riddles of emotion, intention, and contradiction.

Fontaine Fox is still playing her. The question is: Why? What game?

Sentro says, "You can come with me or stay here. Up to you. But I'd appreciate it, should you decide to stay, if you'd give me a good head start."

The Englishwoman says nothing.

Sentro slips out the door, into the corridor, leaving it open.

Vacant except for the tattered sofa facing a monstrous flat-screen TV, the second-floor single room, into which Sentro can surreptitiously peer from the third-floor landing, guards all access to where Fontaine has said the crew and passengers are being held. A sprung floral sofa is presently occupied by two mercenaries plus the scar-faced tweaker; all three, facing away from the open doorway, are fully engrossed in a fire-fight video campaign. Sentro knows about first-person shooter games from the homeless boys she tutors. This one, she's fairly certain, is *Call of Duty: Modern Warfare* with the surround sound cranked up all the way. She decides to descend via a fire escape on the other end of the third-floor hallway, trusting that the alarm won't be functional and that the mercenaries will remain insensate in their virtual adventures. It's a wise decision. Not only are the fire doors disarmed, they're propped open for any cooling breeze that might kick up off the bay and provide the apartment building some relief from the heat.

Voices murmur behind a doorway midway down the second floor. The door is indeed locked, an old-world keyhole mechanism that can be done from either side.

Keeping a wary eye on the game room down the hallway, she takes the aluminum can cutouts from her shirt pocket and inserts them in sequence into the keyhole and between the door and the jamb, along with the bent length of wire from the *Jeddah* deck that she's recovered from her jeans. She fiddles with and jimmies her makeshift tool the way she learned at Quantico years ago and is pleased when (she can't recall ever having had the opportunity to try it before) the door clicks open and she finds herself looking into a large, mostly unlit suite where Captain Montez and a few of his crew are at a table playing poker, while Bruce and the Tagalog are just awakening, astonished to see Sentro slip inside.

Montez sees her last, but he's first to say something. "You."

First Mate Mulligan is a mess. Improvised bath towel bandages on his arm and leg, a sheen of flop sweat, and his jaw set hard against pain.

"Where are the others?"

The captain gestures across the hallway to a closed door opposite. For a moment, there's just the male gaze, the unmistakable disbelief, that look of *How did she survive?* But Sentro gets right down to it.

"There's a city bus that stops on the corner in ten minutes. We'll take the fire exit to the street, catch the bus to the harbor and a skiff to the ship." She locks eyes with Montez. "You can be in open sea within the hour. They won't follow."

"You don't know that."

Sentro is growing weary of the serial resistance to what she thinks is common sense. "I'll make sure they don't." She's not sure that's true but says it with conviction. She checks the hallway, then crosses quietly and begins to work on unlocking the facing door there, anxious eyes on the open room, where the game play continues.

Summoning all the withering continental conceit he can seem to manage, Montez gets up, stretches, comes to the open doorway of his room, and lectures Sentro's back in an angry whisper. "They shot the woman who resisted. You saw it. Ms. Fox. We must stay here and do as they say."

Sentro mouths her question: *Which is?*

"Wait for a resolution."

The door Sentro's been working on cracks open. Another bachelor flat, no furniture. The women passengers are in here, on the bare floor, dozing. They blink away the darkness in sleepy confusion. The Swedish woman and the newlywed sit up. Their names will come back to her.

Sentro ducks inside with them, then turns to murmur back to the captain, low, hard, "The resolution of this is everyone dies." She allows this harsh truth to settle on him. "Where are they keeping the rest of your crew?"

The captain offers only worried hesitation, because, as Sentro has correctly guessed, he doesn't know; there's been no communication between the pirates and their hostages because, as Sentro has also surmised, they're not really pirates in the conventional sense, and this is anything but business as usual.

Voices in the captain's room begin to protest, overlapping: "You don't need to do this" and "You're only going to make this worse." Sentro puts a finger to her lips—*Shhhh*—and Montez waves them quiet. The women get to their feet but, visibly apprehensive, make no move yet toward freedom.

Montez gives her the company line across the hall, low: "It's just business, señora. There are even secondary markets. Men who buy and sell shares in upcoming attacks in a bourse in Port-au-Prince. Always US dollars, delivered in sacks dropped from helicopters or parachute boxes or waterproof suitcases sent out in neutral intermediaries' skiffs—"

Sentro tunes him out. The tragic certainty of certain men.

A violent surround sound explosion rolls from the game room, and Sentro hears the mercenaries burst out laughing, delighted about something they've done in the virtual world.

"No more killing," Montez pleads, as if he has any control over it.

Beyond impatient now, Sentro rolls her eyes, checks the hallway, and dashes out toward the fire escape. She hears the captain hiss after her, "*Señora*, please."

She steps through the open door, checks back to see that she hasn't been spotted, and hurries up squawking metal stairs to the third floor to retrieve Fontaine.

———

The only way Sentro can tell the Englishwoman has moved during her absence is that she's put on shoes. Standing by the bed, startled by Sentro's reappearance, she offers no resistance when Sentro takes her hand like a small child and leads her out and back down the fire escape to the second-floor hostages.

But now there are local cops in the corridor. Talking to one of the mercenaries from the game room near the main stairwell. Sentro pushes Fontaine back and stays in the fire escape shadow, straining to hear what they're saying. Something about breakfast; a disagreement about the best rum; the voice of Carlito; and then the scarred man himself, briefly, peeling cash from a roll of bills that they pocket and exchange for a bindle of tin foil, which Carlito dances on his palm as they depart.

Carlito glances toward where Sentro is in shadow. Stares for longer than she would like, as if he senses her there in the darkness, but finally walks back into the room.

Sentro feels a need to quicken the pace. Tugging Fontaine with her, through the door, down the corridor, she ducks into the room where all the hostages have reunited; shocked by Fontaine's resurrection, they stare, disbelieving, cold, their agitated murmuring silenced. Mulligan turns away from the Englishwoman and exhales. "Unbelievable." Captain Montez stares at Sentro, angles his head, at a loss for words.

"You think you know what this is, what's going on here," Sentro tells the group quickly. "You don't. Nothing is what it seems." From the corridor comes a loud argument between the mercenaries strategizing their next video game campaign.

Fontaine says, "I can explain," but then doesn't.

"Horseshit." Big Bruce shakes his head, face flushed dark, stubborn. "This is such horseshit."

"They have the police in their pocket," the captain agrees. "We will never get close to the docks, if that's your plan."

Sentro shrugs. "That just makes the police not police, which is helpful. And we will make it. If you do what I say."

Fontaine stays apart from the rest, her eyes evasive.

"You're going to get us all killed," Bruce whines.

Yeah, that's what I'm doing.

She ignores him and asks again if anyone has a guess where the rest of the *Jeddah* crew is being kept. Montez starts to say something, but

Charlemagne blurts that he overheard the kidnappers talking about people up on the fourth floor.

Bruce warns her, "I'm not going to let this happen."

Sentro doesn't even give him a glance. She tells the captain, "Get everyone ready to move; I'll bring the others down." Checking once more to be sure of a clear path, she slips out into the hallway, leaving Fontaine with the fruits of her deception.

Carlito's demented laughter leaks from the mercenaries at the other end of the corridor as Sentro disappears into the fire escape darkness. Another battle beginning.

CHAPTER THIRTY-FOUR

A deep gloaming predawn enfolds the Baltimore waterfront, where Reno Elsayed is running, running, in watch cap and sweats, but the blue-black Atlantic sky weeps its promise of another day. Wires snake from earbuds to the phone in his hand, and he sings along loudly in a tremulous baritone:

You? You? You? You? You? You? You?

Little God! Love, my loooooove . . .

Headlights pin him, and a beige sedan angles to the curb; Elsayed feels the vehicle slow to a crawl and follow, and he correctly guesses it's going to be some kind of official intervention. The bureau fleet car that eventually comes abreast is a dead giveaway.

The passenger window hums down as the hair-challenged G-man behind the wheel keeps pace with his target. They trade professional looks, and Elsayed keeps jogging. His natural inclination is to make this as awkward as possible for the fed.

For your pure eyes,

muor But-ter-fly . . .

Warren fumbles with his wallet, extends his ID in one hand.

"Mr. Elsayed? Special Agent Warren."

Elsayed isn't impressed, continues running. Retired military, he has a thing about civilian law enforcement. He's always polite but pointedly dismissive.

"Reno Elsayed." Warren keeps rolling along next to him.

"Lucky. Yeah, that's me. And?"

"Lucky?"

"What pretty much everybody calls me."

"Why?"

"We're not having a conversation."

"You work with Aubrey Sentro," Warren says.

It's not a question, so Elsayed keeps running.

ButterFLY! dun, dun dun da-dun—

But-ter-FA-LY! dun, dun dun da-dun—

BUTTER mo-ther-fuc-king FLYYYYYYY!

"Solomon Systems." Warren struggles to keep his sedan from scuffing on the gutter. "Her son's been calling you guys; he thinks she lied to him about her employment there. That's kinda fucked up, if you don't mind my saying."

Elsayed slows to a walk, remembering that Aubrey was a fed for a short time before they met and the exquisite darker arts subsumed her. He's never held her past against her, but she's the exception to so many rules. What in the world could this be about? He tugs the buds from his ears, stops abruptly, his breathing steady. Waits while the fed, slow to react, hurries ahead in his federal car and has to jam the sedan into reverse to glide back to him.

"How's your day going?" Warren asks, smiling like a guy in a drive-through breakfast window.

"Normal until now."

"I wouldn't have pegged you as someone who listens to opera while you run."

Elsayed touches the screen of his phone, and the faint bleed of Puccini from his earbuds dies. "What do you want, Officer?"

Warren seems to ignore the slight, slides across to the window, and drops his voice low, though there isn't anyone on the sidewalk or street in front or behind them. "Appears like your buddy's in a bit of a situation."

"My buddy."

"Ms. Sentro."

"Aubrey?"

"Yes, sir."

Elsayed frowns now. His stomach churns. "Aubrey's on vacation," he says but understands as he utters the words that the fed is about to tell him otherwise.

Agent Warren nods. "Was."

And then he opens the passenger door for Elsayed to climb in.

———

After the harbor cops drive off in their patrol car and vanish down the hill, Zoala crawls out of the shrubbery on hands and knees and into driveway shadows to the side of the Range Rover. The sky is growing brighter, but it will be a while still before the sun breaks over the hills east of town. The boy can hear a raucous cacophony of video game gibberish from inside the building and finds himself wishing he could see what it was.

He only knows the game *Fortnite*, and that only from a few times watching other kids playing it at the internet place.

Zoala sits cross-legged when he reaches the back fender and jams a stick from his pocket into the inflation nipple on the right rear tire and jiggles it around until he hears air wheezing out.

Then he crawls to the front right tire and does it all again, the way the American told him to.

———

Captain Montez and Jesper monitor the corridor from facing doorways, tucked back, looking twitchy and unsure and listening to the mercenaries play their game. When Sentro's face ghosts outside the fire door glass, Montez motions that it's safe for her to join them. Crew members she's brought down from the fourth floor remain out on the fire escape landing, shadowed faces peering in.

Montez opens his hands: *Now what?*

Sentro gestures and whispers, "Down, out, and across, to the street corner. There's a bus coming. No sentry posted outside the building."

Charlemagne begins to lead the passengers and crew out of the room, staying silent, pressed to one wall, women first. Shoulders round, Fontaine stays back, no reaction, just staring at the carpet. As if unable to will herself to move.

Sentro warns her, low, "If you stay here—"

She looks up. "I know." Tears that Sentro can't trust. "I know."

"All right." The room has emptied. Sentro starts to follow the last men out.

Eyes hooded, Fontaine asks, almost inaudibly, "Do we have a future?"

"You and me?"

"Yeah."

Sentro shrugs. "You're dead." She adds, "The future is wide open for the dead," wanting to say more, but in the hallway she sees Bruce go the wrong way, trailed by newlywed Jack and the gimpy Mulligan. Headed down the hallway toward the main stairs and the room where the mercenaries are holed up.

Sentro whispers, "Bruce, what do you think you're doing?"

"Can't let you do this," he hisses back at her, jaw set.

Charlemagne has led the women to the fire door, but the remaining crew have stopped in their tracks at the sound of Bruce's voice, and they look scared, pressed to the wall. Sentro goes after Bruce. Jack and the first mate take a stab at blocking her, but she easily feints and evades them.

Bruce decides maybe he should run.

Shit. "Don't."

Sentro can't make up the ground she's lost and can only watch, dismayed, as the big stubborn man lumbers heavily to the open doorway, where Carlito and his cohorts are engrossed in their virtual bloodbath.

She sees him call in at them, "Hey." Out of breath, Bruce wheezes, "Just wanted to tell you—"

Sentro can imagine the men inside reacting, startled, fumbling for their weapons, because now Bruce is backpedaling, his terrible mistake dawning, hands out in supplication. "Oh. Wait. Whoa, no, whoa whoa whoa."

A mercenary inside barks a warning Bruce can't hope to understand. But a young man emerges, underfed mustache and soul patch, waving his short-stock AK automatic in front of him like a spear, saying, more or less, if Sentro's translation is right: *Go back to your room.*

Her momentum has carried her far enough to smell the cat-piss smoke of crystal meth and see the scarred Carlito on the sofa angled away from the doorway and facing the screen, oblivious, surround sound cranked to deafening in the little room, as he puts a pipe down and laser focuses on his kill tally. "*Vê isto.*" Watch this.

The other mercenary, no doubt equally tweaked and standing behind where Carlito sits, for the moment does.

Trapped in her no-woman's-land, Sentro is tactically naked and exposed, her pulse thumping in her ears, fighting the expected flood of fear, too far from Bruce to stop what she knows too well is coming. The emerging young mercenary's bloodshot black eyes flicker to her, confused. And then past her, down the hallway to the last of the *Jeddah* hostages ducking out the fire escape.

Shit.

Sentro flashes on the only time she was ever wounded—in a corridor like this one, where a trapped, trembling fourteen-year-old freedom fighter accidentally tapped the trigger on his automatic, sending bullets blindly ripping through cheap drywall corridor walls to drop Sentro and three others before they even knew what had happened.

And just as randomly, in the harrowing second it takes for the mercenary to process all he's seeing, Bruce's frightened, awkward, off-balance retreat ends against the opposite wall, and when he pushes himself back upright, toward the advancing gunman, it registers as aggression, so—BAM—Soul Patch puts a bullet through Bruce's chest, and the fat man is dead before he's dropped to the carpet.

The sharp sound of the kill shot has been swallowed and lost in the *Call of Duty* gunfire in Dolby 5.1 surround sound, not to mention Carlito's delighted screams of "*Morre!* Die! Die! Die!" The hallway shooter looks sheepishly down at Bruce, almost apologetic, then back at his colleague, who's torn himself away from the virtual firefight to step out from the room; the colleague clocks the dead hostage first, so he sees Sentro too late, because she's closed the gap and is on them both before either man can react. Elbow to the shooter's Adam's apple the way Vic Falcone once taught her, which exposes the late-arriving hired man to the backup handgun Sentro has pulled from the sagging waistband of the gagging, disabled shooter. She shoves it into the shocked open mouth—"Shhh"—and leaves it there, staring without expression until he slowly lets his AK fall to the hallway carpet and wings his arms up to either side, hands empty, scared. For a moment they both just listen to the rapid percussion of Carlito's apocalyptic video game mayhem.

On his knees, unable to draw a breath, the shooter is shaking and his pockmarks turning white and blue. If done right, she remembers Falcone telling her, you just bruise the hyoid, so once the guy passes out, his neck will relax, and he can breathe again. *Too hard, you could kill him.* Limp in her grasp, his threat sheds; he's just a frightened young man. Not even Jenny's age. Sentro puts her free hand on the shooter's neck and presses the carotid until the man passes out.

Muscles slack, he tucks over to one side, where his wheezing lungs start to suck air again.

Eyes fixed on Carlito's oblivious back while he continues to game, Sentro picks up the short-stock automatic and swiftly backpedals her captive down the corridor to where a shaken Captain Montez waits in the empty hostage-suite doorway. Jesper yanks the mercenary's hands behind his back and spins him; Charlemagne has ripped the cord off a lamp and with the *Jeddah* cook's help swiftly binds Sentro's captive, hands and feet. The cook stuffs a towel in the man's mouth; they drag him into the room and shut the door soundlessly.

Sentro frisks him and finds a roll of cash. Mulligan is the only other hostage left inside. No sign of Fontaine.

"I'm sorry," the first mate tells Sentro.

She feels no need to judge him or respond. Nobody knows how they'll react in a crisis, and a coward in one corridor can find his courage in the next.

It's all a crapshoot.

Mulligan says, "Leave me."

Sentro glances at Charlemagne and the cook. "No," she says. "Nobody gets left."

After an all clear from the Tagalog, Montez and the Swede help the first mate go out the door. Sentro tells Charlemagne, "Go," and watches four men disappear out the fire door to join the others.

AK automatic slung over her shoulder, Sentro lingers to take one last worried look down the hallway.

The shooter is still curled up limp on the carpet outside the bachelor flat, making a rasping noise. Gamer gunplay has ceased, but the theme music blares. Sentro can hear muffled self-congratulatory gloating from Carlito about a mission that he must have gloriously completed, followed by a slow, quiet understanding that he's alone in the room and perhaps something is amiss.

No general alarm, yet.

"*Berto? Onde está?*"

Hurrying away, she hears the tweaker's voice get louder: "*Onde está, fuckwads? Yo.*"

Nobody answers him. The fire door clicks shut behind her.

"*O que você está fazendo no chão?!*"

———

A huddled trail of hostages jogs down the darkened driveway toward the bus stop, silhouetted when round yellow lights crest the hill and the bus rolls to the curb. Doors hissing open, the hostages climb on, find seats. The driver yells at them to pay the fare. Montez and Sentro are the last to board. Sentro drops in the driver's lap all the cash she took from Zeme's hired man and tells him to take them to the docks.

No one speaks as the released air brakes hiss; there's nothing to be said.

Sentro scans the seats and finds Fontaine sitting alone in the back, eyes on Sentro, blank.

A sudden banging on the folding doors scares everyone as the bus begins to lurch away. Sentro pivots, aims toward the steps the handgun she took from Big Bruce's killer.

The bus jerks to another halt. The doors flip open, and there's Zoala. Chattering with annoyance about almost being left behind.

Sentro hurries him up and in, and the bus lurches onward, and she marvels, not for the first time, how her work life is often not so far removed from a strange, buggy beta version of one of the Nintendo games she tried to forbid Jeremy from wasting his time on when he was growing up.

A helter-skelter oddball race through a dreamy nightscape of obstacles and opposition, and the reward at the end is you live to do it again.

———

On a cross street two long blocks down from the art deco apartment building where his next payday is being kept, Robbens's jaunty old Jag waits for the bus to pass.

He taps his fingers on the wheel. Looks idly out at the dazed white faces staring back at him from the bus windows, surprised to see so many European tourists this late at night (or early in the morning?), but otherwise thinks nothing of it.

Maybe they're headed to watch the sun rise over the Arawakan stone ruins on the point.

He pulls into the driveway and is parking next to the Range Rover when Castor Zeme comes strolling out of the lobby to meet him, yawning away and griping, "Lobby sofa is a foul place to get a power nap on."

Stepping out of his car, indicating the Rover, Robbens says, "Looks like you've got a flat tire."

Castor, still rubbing sleep from his eyes, glances at the Rover and frowns deeply.

"Four of them, in fact."

Castor steps back to the front entrance and shouts back into the building, "Carlito!" then looks at Robbens, peevish. "What's the word?"

"They weren't happy about the dead one."

"Accident."

"So I informed them."

Irritated, Castor yells impatiently back into the lobby, "Carlito! *Qual é palavra?*" No response.

"Seven hundred thousand euros," the Dutchman continues, "random bills, airdrop tomorrow."

The twin circles the car, examining all the flattened tires. "You said it'd be over a million."

Following, Robbens lets his temper get the better of him. "YOU ARE AN AMATEUR. Okay? Seven hundred. Minus my fifteen percent and fifteen for my counterpart on the other end—what'd you promise the local police?"

"Sod off."

"Fifty? That means only four forty, net, then, to you. Because you're a fucking amateur. Sorry. But still." Robbens is thinking Castor, eyes sunken in, bedhead hair, looks like he's regretting the whole cursed operation.

"Fine. Done. Do it. I want to be shed of this. I buried my brother today." He crouches down at one of the flats. Finds a twig someone jammed in the fill nipple.

"*Godverdomme.* What happened?"

Castor just stares at the flat tires, as if confounded, until Robbens gives up on an answer and presses on with the business at hand. "They have asked me to confirm the condition of the passengers and crew."

Castor looks up at him blankly, an eyebrow angled. "What?"

"It's insurer boilerplate. Due diligence. I just, you know, eyeball the asset and say that I've done so."

Castor says nothing, still preoccupied with the car. Without looking back, he screams out, "Carlito!" then scans the street. Empty. Stands, crushes the twig from the fill nipple with his boot, teeth set. Jerks his head for Robbens to follow and leads the way into the building, where Robbens hears the disfigured one they call Carlito finally shouting something back at his boss from upstairs.

———

With downtown Porto Pequeno deadened at the first blush of dawn, the city bus rocks and sways its dogged way along empty, trash-strewed streets, zigzagging toward the docks. The driver, stubborn, insists on making all scheduled stops, though there are no riders waiting and there's a woman standing behind him with two guns.

The deserted boardwalk Coaster Wheel spins, throwing crazy light across the hushed passengers and crew.

Fontaine hasn't spoken to her since leaving the art deco building on the hill; Sentro faces the seats, watching everyone as they avoid making eye contact with her, wondering what they're thinking about her now and also watching the road the bus has just traveled. Her thoughts stray to the operation in Cyprus and getting the wrong door and the likelihood that the deteriorating situation with her brain and her thoughts and decision-making (that's what it is, isn't it?) means she will need to stop doing this, stop trying to save her mother—because isn't that what she's been doing all along? That's what the agency therapists said, as well as the private ones who followed. That's what Dennis kept telling her, especially toward the end. Maybe he was right.

And yet. Why does she so vividly remember knowing she couldn't save her mom? Couldn't stop what happened in that West Texas motel room any more than she could stop the black, towering thunderstorms when it was just the two of them, her and the man she called her father, hard rain that would roll in off the panhandle and rattle the light fixtures and drive her to his room, where she'd wrap herself in a blanket on the big chair and watch him sleep.

If her condition causes her to forget all that, will she feel relief or regret?

A siren startles everyone. Flashing lights swerve from a side street behind the bus. Sentro's hand goes to the gun in her lap, but the bus yields, and the police car flashes past, on a different errand.

The harbor quays are dusted by a morning mist, spectral, and the bus driver downshifts to veer off the wide oceanfront avenue and find its last stop.

Castor Zeme hurries up the stairs to discover a bewildering still life: the bachelor-flat door gaping, the TV blaring some annoying shooter game's main-menu theme in an endless loop, a fat dead hostage gutshot and splayed along the hallway wall opposite, and one of his best hired men, Berto, disarmed, left beached on the floor, coughing, hollow eyed, and useless. A hot curtain of fury drops; he struggles to process what he's seeing: a cock-up of epic proportions. How could this get any fucking worse?

Carlito comes clattering down from the third floor, his good eye jacked paranoid from the meth he's been chipping. "*Foi.*" He sheepishly motions down the corridor to where most of the hostages were being kept. "Gone, gone, gone."

"Our assets?"

Fuck.

And the third man Castor assigned to watch them?

Carlito hesitates, waves his arm down the hallway again, and admits, "I'll need a knife to cut him free." He reeks of a chemical flop sweat.

Castor scowls. "How?" Carlito twitches, nervous, avoiding his boss's fiery gaze. Castor takes the switchblade from his pocket, Carlito holds his hand out for it, and for a moment Castor imagines stabbing his number two in the neck, maybe stabbing him twice or three times, severing the artery, like he did the arrogant rich fuck who tried to defy him on the yacht. The head flapped back like a hatch cover.

So much blood.

He hears Robbens's shoes heavy on the stairs. It just gets better and better. Hand trembling with bridled fury, Castor hands Carlito the knife and asks once more, "How?"

Carlito gestures to the man down the hallway. "Miguel says it was the woman from the boat."

"The American."

"Yes."

Castor Z. does his best to process this, paralyzed by rage.

Now Robbens comes huffing up, joining them. "Somebody in this hemisphere needs to invent the elevator." As if from a great distance, Castor watches the Dutchman's eyes take in the dead hostage and Carlito's shame, consider the dry hacking of the hireling on the floor, then turn as if idly to Castor himself. Poker faced. What a smug bastard.

"Problem?" Robbens asks.

CHAPTER THIRTY-FIVE

Passengers and crew file out of the city bus and hurry to where Morehouse and Eccola are waiting below the pier in the *Jeddah*'s twin-hull ship-to-shore skiff.

A wedge of pink sun just starting to rise out of the eastern ocean table.

The empty cat-logo shipping container looms with its broken promise, mocking Sentro, catching the light and casting its long shadow over the quay and across the bay water. Ever vigilant, she keeps glancing back over her shoulder to scan the oceanfront streets of the port city, wary of a pursuit she knows is coming. This is an adversary she would prefer not to confront head-on; she hopes to outrun it and that its attention span is short. If not, she can lock the passengers back in the safe room and let the big ship be her martello tower.

Zoala fidgets beside her as an argument breaks out.

"No! Don't let her on!" Last in line to board, Fontaine Fox's way has been blocked by Asta and the Gentrys, preventing her from stepping on the boat.

"She can't be trusted."

Jesper coos, "Darling."

She snaps at him, "Be a man. The woman double-crossed us."

Nodding at this, grim, Fontaine turns to go, but Sentro catches her arm. "Just get on the boat."

Second Mate Salah is overseeing crew members manning the mooring lines. "We need to fucking go."

"Yes. Go. But not with her," Jack says.

Sentro walks over, bringing the Englishwoman with her. "Cast off."

Morehouse looks up from the wheel of the boat. "What about you?"

Sentro, without answering him, pushes Fontaine ahead. "Let her board."

"We're not taking her!"

Lines dropped, the engine fires up. The crewmen hop to the gunwales and help Montez over the gap.

Sentro looks from the quay to the passengers and crew crowded in the stern of the skiff. "If you leave her here, they'll kill her. That's their default. Is that what you want?"

Nobody answers. Nobody meets her gaze. Waves rock the skiff, and it drifts from the dock. Morehouse reverses the inboard to keep the craft close while Sentro stares Asta down until, relenting, she and the newlyweds move to the port side of the stern.

But Fontaine is walking away. Back toward the city.

Sentro calls after her. The Englishwoman turns around but keeps walking, backward. A vague shrug, a smile of resignation, as if to say: *I'll make this easy for you.*

Their eyes linger. Sentro tries to think of something she can say that would matter. Nothing comes to her. She needs to let this go; there are bigger issues looming. Fontaine turns her back to Sentro and keeps walking.

The ship-to-shore skiff motors off, parallel to the dock, just as Sentro realizes that Zoala is still standing beside her.

"Get on the boat," she tells him.

Zoala, resolute, tells her in Portuguese something about how he's going to stay to help her kill the pirates. How he made a promise.

Sentro puts an arm around the boy and gets him moving, runs with him, and ("Jump!") practically flings him across the widening gap between the quay and the skiff, where Charlemagne and Jesper are there to catch him.

Twisting angrily out of their arms, Zoala barks something sharp back at Sentro while the skiff swerves out into open water. The sound of the inboard drowns out the boy's complaints. Sentro keeps running along the quay, past more containers, to where she has spotted two familiar fast boats tied up at the end of the berth.

Castor's fleet.

A faint voice draws her look back to Fontaine. The Englishwoman has her cell phone flipped open, her expression all business: "*Bonjour. J'ai besoin d'un taxi pour aller prendre le taxi au quai principal . . . près de la grande roue, oui . . .*" She keeps walking, proud.

Lengthening her stride to run faster, Sentro draws the handgun she stripped off the hired man in the corridor and, when she passes the mercenary boats, fires down into the outboard gas tanks until they explode in flames.

Safely beyond them, Sentro looks down the pier and sees Fontaine react to the explosions, shading her eyes and covering her nose from the smoke, squinting through the billowing petroleum haze. She waits for Fontaine's eyes to find her, trying one last time to solve the riddle she knows is buried there. No luck. The skiff swerves back into the pier. Morehouse cuts the wheel hard; the stern comes around, and Sentro jumps aboard, just the way they planned it. Fontaine is still watching her, opaque, as the throttle kicks and the skiff aims across the harbor, leaving the burning fast boats and the Englishwoman quickly behind.

———

Cresting sunrise strikes the bleached art deco facade of apartments and the hills above Porto Pequeno and lends both a hellish quality as Castor

Zeme, Carlito, two shamed mercenaries, and Robbens hurry out into the driveway. The hired men head for the Rover, but Castor calls them back. No time for recriminations—he'll tally all transgressions and collect for them, once this is over.

"Not that one." To Robbens: "Give me your keys." Castor flips the Rover keys to the wheezing Berto, who stupidly shot the fat hostage and nearly got his larynx punched through by a woman. "Get a truck to come fill the tires. Then, *attrapez les autres*, and, uh, *vena*, no, shit— *venez sur la jetée. Venez sur la jetée.*" The kid nods dutifully, pulls out a cell phone, and walks away to make the call.

Robbens warns Castor, "They won't pay the ransom if you don't have the hostages."

"How would they know? If you don't tell them?"

From the guilty expression on the Dutchman's face, this is exactly what Robbens was planning to do as soon as he separated from his partner in crime, and he even lies: "Well, I—well, naturally they're going to—look, I won't offer, but if they ask, I'm just the messenger."

Castor hopes his dark look makes Robbens's blood run cold. Later for him too. "Give me the keys to your car."

"How am I supposed to get back downtown?"

"Walk."

Robbens musters his best manly defiance. "You won't kill me. If you kill me, you'll never see a cent of the money."

With a dead gaze Castor says, "Correction: if I don't see any of the money, I'll kill you, yeah? You understand the difference?"

Robbens does and, moments later, in the rearview, looks relieved to be watching his precious Jaguar fishtail into the street and away, carrying Castor, Carlito, and the other hired man back down into the city. Away from him.

———

The same morning sun sparks off the struts of the Ferris wheel in long slanting streaks, dazzling the quay and the bay as the skiff carrying Sentro and the hostages powers out toward the *Jeddah*. Growing smaller and smaller.

Robbens's Jag arrives, and men spill out behind Castor, who stares irritably at the dark mark of his assets deserting him, more than half a mile away now on the gray bay water. Nearly there. His smoldering, sinking fast boats mock him from their watery grave beside the pier.

He's shackled by his rage. He can't let this go.

"We'll need a boat," he tells Carlito.

The tweaker sucks a miserable drainage back into his sinuses. "*Où pourrais-je trouver un bateau à cette heure?*"

A cell phone is ringing, somewhere.

Castor screams, "Do I fucking look like I care?! Just find one!"

He shoves Carlito away from him. Nothing has gone right since Pauly died. When the blind anger of the botched hostage detainment eases and he stops and lets the truth settle on him, his anguish and discouragement feel to Castor like they might bury him. Back before the fuckup on the hill, Castor dreamed that none of it had happened. Pauly was sitting across from him, in the fried-fish place off Second Street; they were drinking aguardiente and planning the trip they would take on the profits from some other business they'd done. It was so fucking lovely, just Castor and his twin. Like looking in a mirror all his life, but better, because the other side had its own ideas.

The English one came in, then, and sat down—Fontaine—and Pauly, in the dream, began to bleed from his eyes.

Such as it is and was.

And Castor woke back up to this nightmare.

The phone is still ringing. Ringing. Ringing, muffled.

Finally understanding the sound is coming from his own pants pocket, Castor fumbles for the fucking American woman's phone, which he's been carrying around in the event of just this possibility. He looks blankly at the caller ID (*blocked*) and answers: "Hullo?"

"Hello?"

"Who's this?"

"Who's this?"

———

The tiny regional airport outside of Porto Pequeno consists of a couple of monstrous prefab corrugated-steel hangars and a squat wooden control tower that probably dates back to the Cold War. It is nearly deserted at this hour, but a solitary fat white commuter prop plane has parked on the tarmac behind the austere, flat-roofed, one-room terminal. A few laconic workmen in safety vests and cargo shorts are kicking blocks under the wheels.

Already too warm in his father's old leather jacket and chiding himself for bringing it, Jeremy Troon stands outside the terminal building, tired, overwhelmed, at a taxiless taxi stand, on his cell with the man he assumes must be his mother's kidnapper, repeating: "Wait. Hello? Can you hear me?"

"I can."

"Okay."

"Who's this, then?"

"What?"

"Who's calling?"

"Jeremy Troon. You have my mother's phone."

"Yeah, and? You got the money?"

Jeremy hesitates, nervous. He's so far out of his comfort zone it's ridiculous. But he keeps telling himself that in a rational world a reasonable man can prevail, because the alternative is too terrifying to consider. "I'm here." Here to get his mother back. "At the airport," he adds, rattled. His feet feel dull and fat from the long flight. The light of the day in this strange land seems all wrong. "I have the money. Where is she?"

———

Castor Zeme can't believe his good fortune; maybe fate has turned. Wind fills his sails.

Carlito is staring at him, clearly curious.

"I want to talk to my mother," the voice of Jeremy Troon says, sounding strained.

Castor nods. Back on it. "I'll send a car."

PART THREE:
NO ~~WOMAN~~ GIRL NO CRY

Chapter Thirty-Six

The accommodation ladder they used to disembark three long days ago has been raised and disabled. So one by one, with the gathering heat of the day pressing down on them, the freed hostages of the cargo ship *Jeddah* climb an unspooled pilot's ladder from the skiff tied near the *Jeddah*'s stern up to the main deck walkway, where the worried passengers mill uncertainly while the crew quickly begins dispersing to their stations.

Last to disembark, Sentro helps Zoala hop across to the ladder, but Eccola and Morehouse stay in the rolling boat, and Sentro realizes they're intent on going back to shore.

"They'll come after you."

The doctor shrugs. "I'm a good talker. We have nothing they want."

"What he'll want is payback," Sentro says. "Wherever he can find it."

Morehouse looks unmoved. While there's no guarantee that staying with the *Jeddah* will be safer, Sentro feels it's worth arguing with him about not staying in Porto Pequeno.

"You could do better than this," she says then.

Morehouse just shakes his head at her. "Define better." He looks strung out, pale. Eccola casts off the line that holds them to the cargo ship. Zoala sees what's happening and begins yelling at her to stop.

"Can't do it," the doctor admits to Sentro sadly.

"You could."

"Can't. Dude. Look at me."

Sentro has been looking. The tracks on his skinny arms. The swollen red, probably arthritic knee. His surrendering eyes.

"Stay clear of the pier, at least," she tells Morehouse.

"Duh."

"And thanks for your help."

Securing the AK that hangs on her shoulder, she leaps to the ladder and stands on the bottom rung.

The skiff drifts free. Zoala rubs away furious tears and starts to climb back down. Sentro's arms keep him from leaping off into the water.

She calls out: "Take the boy with you."

Morehouse busies himself with starting the engine.

Zoala's in a panic. It's not that he wants to join his sister. He wants her to stay with him. They talk at cross-purposes, the physical distance between them growing.

The doctor feathers the throttle; the boat pivots, throws a white wake.

"He will do better with you," Morehouse shouts.

Tears falling, Zoala keeps yelling at Eccola, and she's crying now too. But the skiff is already hurrying away.

———

Morning traffic is picking up; buses roll in on grimy diesel clouds to deliver local early-bird air travelers and airline support staff to the sleepy regional airport while, still waiting, fidgety, coat draped across his bag, Jeremy Troon distractedly watches a pretty white woman getting out of a kiwi-green taxicab. No luggage, not even a handbag; in designer leggings and a black sleeveless T-shirt, she pays the fare and flashes through the terminal's glass doors. Something about her holds his attention until she vanishes behind the day's bright reflection, and a late-model Jaguar comes racing in from the gravel access road to the blacktop terminal driveway, tugging a wake of dust behind it. It circles ominously around and skids to the curb where Jeremy stands.

His courage is in his throat. *Here we go.*

A copper-skinned man with a broken nose and a scar-slashed, ruined eye stares darkly across from the driver's seat.

"Troon?"

Now shit gets real, Jeremy wants to say bravely, trying to bring back his coffee shop Vin Diesel. It doesn't do the trick. The hot wind has him already sweating. The Jaguar man's one good eye seems to drill right through him. Exposed, no turning back, Jeremy nods. Swallowing the acid of foreboding and repeating his other, brittle mantra: he's here to save his mother.

The automatic locks jump open. The driver gestures for Aubrey Sentro's son to get in.

———

His ship looks like it's been crenellated with cotton balls. Every horizontal edge is dotted with equidistant white roosting seabirds of a species he doesn't readily recognize. Hundreds—no, there must be thousands of them—stem to stern.

"I want engines operative and moving us seaward as soon as possible, okay?"

Cleaning up the shambles wrought by the mercenary crew, barking out instructions on the ship's comm, Captain Montez has resumed his command and feels the familiar rush of adrenaline it engenders. "Check the payload to make sure it hasn't shifted so much it has compromised our beam."

But the birds are freaking him out.

With the ship's communications room ransacked and their cell phones still in a bag possessed by Castor Zeme, there's no way to radio Georgetown or another port for help. Montez is hoping to get north to a shipping lane where they might intercept a passing vessel and go from there. At worst, once they establish their position, he can head northwest and seek safety among the Lesser Antilles.

They're a bad omen, these birds, every now and then bothered by the movement of the crew below them, lifting like a chorus line, wings beating, hovering a few feet above their roost, then settling again. He shouldn't have let the American bring his people back here.

Montez stares out the bridge windows at the blight of birds and murmurs a Catholic school prayer for strength and courage.

———

The crew scrambles to winch the teetering containers back into a manageable shape and correct the nasty list they're causing. The laughing gulls that dive-bomb them are a nuisance. Up on G-deck, the Swedes stare sadly at the late Bruce Bologna's broken equipment, strewed out from his doorway into the corridor and all the way down to their cabin. Jack and Meg Gentry have locked themselves in theirs. Charlemagne makes short work of returning his belongings to his duffel bag, then, restless, goes out and up to the observation deck and finds Sentro watching the harbor for any approaching craft.

Diesel grime belches from the *Jeddah* exhaust stacks; the ship shudders as the engines power up. Charlemagne tells her, in great detail, something that she finds she can't begin to translate.

"I should tell you, I don't really speak much Tagalog," she apologizes, but the truth is, for the moment she's simply forgotten how.

"I knew this," he says in English. "It's okay." Sentro can see that he's become afraid of her—of who she's been revealed to be—but that his instinct for survival must be telling him to keep her close. "We will not outrun them if they chase."

Sentro says, "Oh, they'll chase."

"So what's the plan?" First Mate Mulligan comes gimping out onto the deck, shadowed by Zoala. Mulligan's leg is freshly bandaged, braced. Surprisingly, the ship's medical supplies were relatively unplundered.

Sentro looks at him with her blankest expression. "The plan is to stay alive."

Mulligan shifts, grimaces, shakes his head. "You shouldn't have messed with things. I'm sorry for saying it to you, but the dead are as much on you as the pirates."

She didn't need him to tell her this. "They're not pirates." With only that answer ready, she waits for him to finish his indictment.

"This is just my opinion. You know." Mulligan seems to be trying to measure his words, as if for a stubborn child. "But like we keep telling you, there is an unspoken but accepted protocol for these transactions."

They're not pirates.

"You think there is," Sentro says. "You want to believe there is. Like in the movies," she adds. "Because otherwise it's all a bloody chaos, and you'd never come this way again."

"You have no plan."

Sentro remembers learning long ago, from a SEAL team captain who didn't make it out of the sandbox: *Plans are what you make ahead of time to keep your head busy and so you can pretend you have some say in the hellacious shit show about to happen.* She wonders if Mulligan would understand.

"'I am come in sorrow,'" Zoala recites suddenly, rote, from memory, but struggling a bit with his English vowels. "'I am come, ready and unarmed.'"

"What the bloody hell is that?" Mulligan asks.

"Book, book," Charlemagne guesses.

Sentro says, with a little more certainty, "*Lord Jim.*"

"This little kid's reading Conrad?" Mulligan marvels, betraying what Sentro suspects must be a university education.

She explains, "He stole it from me. I thought I might enjoy a maritime adventure while we steamed across the ocean, but I never really had a chance to enjoy it."

Mulligan looks at her like he's worried she's losing her mind but offers his opinion that nobody really enjoys Conrad.

"I doubt he understands much of it, but he probably likes to say the words aloud."

"*Lord Jim*," Zoala parrots, nodding gravely.

"Are there any weapons on board?"

"Only the water gun. And it's dusted. The captain may keep a pistol in the safe, though it's strictly forbidden. We're trained not to resist. We're not given any means to resist, save the water gun. So they don't have any reason to harm us."

Sentro nods. "These guys don't need a reason."

Mulligan studies her, deciding. "You have a plan."

"I will if they come after us," Sentro agrees, after a pause. She doesn't have the heart to tell him it never factors.

———

At his usual table, nursing coffee and the tabloid *Stabroek Sunday News*, Robbens shifts his cell to his good ear, multitasking with the latest of a long-running series of BlackBerrys he's been using since aught two. As part of his studied je ne sais quoi, he has a cache of them, purchased on eBay; when one dies, he soldiers on with the next.

"It's all gone wrong, okay?" he explains to his caller. "Turns out he doesn't know what he's doing. He's an imbecile."

The city police captain, who Robbens knows is on the pad for Castor Zeme, sits across from him at a sunny table on the Malabar

House veranda, gazing out through wraparound sunglasses at the sparkling bay and stuffing his face with scones and clotted cream.

Robbens has moments earlier promised the captain a considerable bounty, to be paid by the colonel and his friends, in return for a guarantee that Zeme will not, under any circumstance, live to collect his *Jeddah* ransom. It's a fair deal, better than what the twin promised him. They shook on it. Now the Dutchman just needs to make sure the *Jeddah*'s underwriter doesn't fuck this up.

"*Quel imbecile, oui.* Clueless. *Oui.* Just sit tight. I'll be fine, I will, there's . . ." He trails off and waits impatiently without paying any attention to what the caller is saying, then advises forcefully, "No no no no no. Don't give him the money—he doesn't have the hostages, he doesn't have the cargo, he doesn't have shit. Give me some time to sort this; something is not right here."

Then Robbens sees someone step out onto the patio and cast a shadow over him. He shades his eyes. "There you are. Where the hell is my Jag?"

———

Aimed not quite point-blank, in fact still moving forward when the muzzle spits, the Glock blows away half of Robbens's face. He topples over, very dead, and as Castor Z. lowers the gun, the grinding pain he's felt behind his eyes ever since he learned the woman from the boat had taken his hostages eases; he decided to pop the Dutchman the moment he saw him come huffing up the staircase this morning, red faced, grinning, the little eyes like capers stuck in Spam.

Shuddering as he wipes the bits of Robbens off his face and hands, the police captain pushes away from the table, looking disgusted but unsurprised. Stuffing scones into his pockets, he rises and glances dispassionately at Castor Zeme, then informs the panicking club patrons in an officious drone: "Do not be alarmed. *Tout est sous contrôle. S'il vous plait, restez calme, je suis policier . . . prenez vos affaires et dirigez-vous vers les sorties . . ."* And then, in Spanish, he adds, *"Tendré que tomar algunas declaraciones."*

Castor murmurs, "Asshole," and thinks about shooting the duplicitous cop, too, but knows that will not further his cause, plus he needs official cooperation for the next part of his day. An insistent, distant, utterly confused audio squawking, like something trapped in a plastic box, calls his attention to Robbens's odd phone on the deck. He picks it up and speaks into it: "Hullo? Hullo? Who's this, then?" The caller identifies himself, a name Castor wouldn't recognize but can assume is the Dutchman's continental contact. "Yeah, yeah, listen, you: that was the sound of my shit hitting Robbens's fan. Mmm-hmm. So. Now. Having got rid of the middle fucking man, let's talk about where you'll be delivering my money, yeah?"

———

The momentum of things is a sonofabitch. Time tumbles relentlessly, no matter what you do to slow it. And now she has to worry that she might not remember something important just when she needs it.

On the main deck of the *Jeddah*, with the sun high and an oppressive, windless heat settling, Sentro leads Mulligan and Charlemagne along and under the still-precarious tilt of containers the crew has given up trying to secure, to a midship gap between stable stacks, where Sentro unlocks and throws back with a clang a familiar dry-bulk hold hatch and climbs down into the darkness.

Zoala comes sideways through a different gap, looking curious. He's been following the trio, clearly unsure if he'd be welcome.

Zoala grins big at Mulligan, whose stony face offers only indifference.

"Coming out."

A black-clad equipment case stenciled with **Saab Bofors Dynamics** is propelled from the hold by Sentro's hands. The first mate lunges to grab it with his good arm, but it bangs on the deck before he can pull it, scraping, away from the hatch. It's that heavy.

Sentro climbs out shedding soybeans, while the first mate struggles to figure out the latches to unlock the lid and look inside. "The Gustaf recoilless rifle," Sentro tells him, ruining the surprise. "All the rage with insurgents and jihadists, from Grozny to Darfur." Bits of memories jangle back at her. "These look to be aftermarket, probably stolen military surplus."

Giving up on the case, Mulligan asks the obvious: "What are they doing in the soybeans?"

Sentro takes a dry pause before answering: "Are you really asking me that?"

"Aimpoint sighting," Charlemagne says suddenly. He glances at each of them in turn like a schoolboy who knows his lesson. "In Sweden, they say it is the Grg m/48 Granatgevär. Grenade rifle, model 1948. Soldiers of Great Britain say 'Charlie G'; Canadians say 'Carl G.'"

Sentro and Mulligan stare at the Tagalog, amazed.

"United States military call it 'M3 Multirole Antiarmor Antipersonnel Weapon System.' MAAWS. Or RAWS."

Mulligan frowns at the Tagalog. "RAWS?"

Sentro cracks a smile. "We do love our acronyms."

"Ranger Antitank Weapons System," Charlemagne tells the first mate and makes a vague salute. "Gustaf bazooka. The 'Goose'!"

"Like he said." Sentro adds, "There must be four dozen of these bad boys buried down there, along with God knows what else."

"I don't think I want to know how he knows so much about these weapons," Mulligan muses.

"Probably did a stint back home in the New People's Army, resisting Duterte." She kneels and pops the clasp, opening the case to reveal the cartoon components along with some ammunition neatly packed in lush foam protective padding, like high-high-end audio.

"That's a rifle?"

"As generously defined." Basically, a tube of steel. She feels a surge of optimism; even if the pirates catch them, this changes the game. But then, just as suddenly, she's flooded with doubt.

"You know how to use this?"

She angles her head and stares at the components, drawing a blank. "I did." She blinks, lost. "Shit." She feels the queasy emptiness of another memory wipe. And a dull panic. "Fuck."

Charlemagne steps forward and starts talking, excited, in Tagalog, gesturing to the gun.

"English," Mulligan suggests.

Sentro's attention is split, because from the radio clipped to the first mate's belt comes a squawk: "Mr. Mulligan? This is Second Mate Salah, on the bridge? Over."

Sentro gestures for Charlemagne to stop jabbering; he's making a hash of both his native tongue and English. "What? Slow down. You learned how to use one of these where?"

Charlemagne answers; she still doesn't understand most of it but thinks—is it wishful?—he's saying that he knows how to put this Gustaf together. "NPA, for sure," she confirms for Mulligan. Then, "Go, go, go," she tells the Tagalog, closing the case lid and snapping the latches, and indicates for him to take it. "Do it. But do it up on the tower."

In the meantime, Mulligan has reached for the rover on his belt, but not before the radio crackles again: "Bridge calling. Mr. Mulligan? Is passenger Sentro with you? Over."

Things aren't any better up on the control deck when they ascend to it; the captain holds out his radiophone for Sentro the moment she comes in, murmuring gravely: "It's them. It's him."

She takes the handpiece but hears the voice doubled on the staticky bridge comm system. "I have something you want."

"Who is this?"

"You're a fucking pain in the arse, ladybits."

Castor Zeme. The alpha twin. Game on.

Sentro looks out from the bridge window, back toward the Porto Pequeno docks. She can just make out, fronting the flashing lights of official vehicles, a cluster of indistinct figures and two big harbor-patrol boats waiting just below the edge of the quay, where she scuttled Castor's fleet.

He says, "I have something you want. You have something of mine."

"Look," Sentro says, calm, "Ms. Fox has made her own—"

Castor cuts her off. "Oy. Not the English."

Salah, his mournful eyes wide with fear, hands Sentro some binoculars, and she raises and adjusts them until she has centered all the figures standing not far from the cat container, flanked by police cars with their bubble lights active. Her heart flips because she'd know anywhere the angle and posture of the figure positioned off to one side, sandwiched between two mercenaries with guns.

"Your son. A Mr. Troon?"

Her son.

"Jeremy?"

Jeremy.

"You getting this?" Sentro watches the scarred tweaker lift a pair of binoculars and train them back at the *Jeddah*. It's as if she's looking right into him. And vice versa. Sentro lowers hers first, dazed. Hollowed out.

"Let him go."

"He's come to save you," Zeme says, the amusement bright in his voice. "We gave him a ride from the airport, no extra charge."

Sentro is too stunned to respond anything useful, so instead she just stalls with the stiff, expected, "What do you want?"

She knows.

"I want my brother back, but . . ." Zeme takes a dramatic pause that is his feeble attempt to mask the soul-searing pain saying it clearly causes him. His voice goes thick. "Lacking that, I want my boat, my passengers, my crew . . . and you."

She tells herself, *Breathe*. Her worlds colliding. The one thing she never wanted to happen, that she sacrificed so much to proscribe. The singularity she has meticulously contrived, all these years, through the lies, the dissembling, the careful construction of parallel lives that would not, could not, ever intersect—to make sure, at whatever cost, her children would never be exposed to what she was—

Shit.

—to never, ever have it happen again.

"How do I know—"

Castor Z. cuts her off, cruel. She can hear him gauging his advantage and doubling down on it. "Right, right—" In the whistling audio on the other end of her radio call, she can imagine him holding the phone out into the bay wind for her son, as he shouts, "Sing for Mommy!"

Sing.

Jeremy's voice comes distant, flat, scared. "Um—hello? Mom? Mom, I'm sorry."

Her soul splinters. She hears the twin put the phone to his own ear again. "There. Content?"

"If you so much as hurt him—"

"Yeah, yeah, blah blah. Noted," Castor says. "But you've had your bloody run, Grandma. Fuck off. We're on our way."

A dizzying rush of fear and utter helplessness overtakes her for the first time since her mother died. There is no click of Zeme hanging up, only the sudden absence of cellular static, and it claws at Sentro's heart.

CHAPTER THIRTY-SEVEN

Sagging power lines quicksilvered by headlights slipped past her side window like drooping music staffs, tethering her back to the motel, to her mother, the last threads fraying as they drove back to Dallas, her stepfather silent, his big shadow draped over the wheel of the truck, arms folded across it as if he wanted to sleep, his face etched soft blue by the instrument panel, eyes lost in darkness, mouth set sharp and hard. He was ghostly granite and chiseled like the giant faces of Mount Rushmore that she'd seen the other time she and her mother had taken a runner, but that one had ended in a different way.

Truck tires winged against the asphalt, and a blood moon hung on the horizon for a long time and then was whispered away by clouds.

They didn't sing.

Texas went on and on.

"She wouldn't have hurt me," she told him at some point.

"I know," he said softly. "She wouldn't have."

It was the only conversation they ever had about it.

The gunshot was loud, but the corresponding forced entry by faceless cops in helmets and Kevlar was the greater shock; she had heard him calling her name on the bullhorn but couldn't gather enough air in her aching lungs to make a sound. Her mother had checked out; what remained there at the foot of the bed was no one Aubrey recognized, just a lifeless shape dusted by the spectral light of the fluttering TV.

The tactical squad broke in with their battering ram and rattle-tag guns, awkward armor squeaking, and she screamed and her stepfather stormed in right behind them. As if from a high corner of the room, she watched him glide across the floor to her; she didn't want to be touched, but he took her up in his arms anyway and carried her out into the hot night, where whitewashed faces were all turned to her, so she buried her eyes in his hard shoulder, and he put her in the cab of the truck and told her to stay there, and she heard him tell someone to wait with her, and he was gone for quite a while.

She felt the cab tilt when he climbed in. She didn't look at him. He didn't say anything; they just remained in darkness until she felt his hand warm on her shoulder, lighter than she expected. He didn't leave it there long. There was the turn of a key and the scrape of the starter; the engine rumbled to life.

"Are you hungry?"

She was but didn't answer him.

Somebody outside was trying to talk to him, but she heard him keep saying quietly, "Later. Later." And they drove away.

On that other trip, to Mount Rushmore, she was younger enough that she doesn't trust that her memories of it aren't corrupted by what she must have learned later, growing up—about her mother, from her father, from her mother's friends, and years afterward while going through the boxes in the basement of their Dallas house after her father died.

There was a Rapid City hotel ashtray that her mother had slipped into her purse as a souvenir; there were some snapshots that had been taken with a Brownie Bullet, faded and casually focused, like a fever dream of another life. Aubrey was four, then (or just turned five?), a girl's girl, judging from the clothes she wore in the photographs, or maybe that was what her mother wanted for her; she'll never really know.

He showed up on the third day of their Dakota walkabout, as her mother later called it; she has an image of him entering the lobby café and removing his hat and glasses and looking across the room to where they were sitting, eating breakfast, by the window, bathed in full sun. There was the worry in her mother's eyes and the easy smile that broke across his face to reassure them both, a smile Aubrey is sure she'd never seen before and never saw again: relief, sadness, love.

Or did she add that detail at some point, wish that it had happened? She never asked him, and then it was too late.

Rand Sentro is not her father, but she's his daughter. He raised her as best he could.

His sister in Lubbock offered to take in the motherless child; Ruth Muzzie had two girls of her own and lobbied hard to make Aubrey her third, but Ranger Sentro refused, and then, as if to prove his point, he never remarried. Took a promotion and got a big desk downtown supervising other marshals so he wouldn't be gone so much.

But he'd been emptied out by the events at the motel.

Never remarried. If he even had another relationship, she saw no evidence of it. He was home every night, her taciturn sentinel. He made them dinner until she couldn't stand it anymore and took over.

Theirs was a polite understanding, father and daughter; he taught her what he knew, which was, at its core, how to hold the world at arm's length, how to stay human but not feel too much to be useful, how to navigate violence and havoc and death and come home.

A Vietnam veteran (she only learned of it when, in his will, he asked to be interred in the National Cemetery with full honors), he once told her, "All this posttraumatic bullshit they're saying is bullshit; well, it's real, and it's tragic, because you take a boy and send him to war and ask him to forget everything he knows about being civilized; then you bring him back and expect him to forget all that and live by the very rules he had to break every day in order to survive."

A boy.

His was a world where boys became men and girls became wives, but torn between his chauvinism and prejudice and the sanctity of paternal legacy, he taught her to stand straight, to shoot and to hunt, to defend herself and recognize bullshit when she saw it. Try as he might, he was never able to understand her, so it shouldn't have surprised him when, first chance she got, she was pregnant and leaving home for happily hapless Dennis Troon.

———

When her husband first got the cancer, it hit so hard and fast. Before they could even begin to make plans, Dennis was in the hospital and fading, the aggressive oncological campaign his doctors devised already scuttled by the scorched-earth blitzkrieg waged by the disease, and Aubrey was embroiled in some shady NOC fuckery as a hire-back for Paul Bremer's Coalition Provisional Authority that pulled her away from home and turned out to be her last government assignment. Her husband was dying; Aubrey wanted compassionate release. Dennis insisted that she honor her commitment. Insisted this wasn't his time yet, and they would need the hazard pay from the mission to cover his growing list of meds.

The day she shipped out for Baghdad, she discovered her father in Dennis's room, camped out. Rand Sentro had driven nonstop to Bethesda from Dallas, told her, "I have this under control; don't worry about anything." In the farewells and confusion, she never asked him how he'd found out about it, and three weeks later she got an urgent sat-phone call from the hospital that she assumed would be bad news about her husband. Instead a nurse told her that her father had died, peacefully, during the night while sitting vigil.

He was back and buried in the dry Texas hardpan before her Iraqi nonsense was completed.

Dennis was right: he'd have another five years of hell before the ugly end came.

And now the only men in her life are the ones she works with and the scoundrels that keep them busy.

Like this phony pirate bastard who has her son.

CHAPTER THIRTY-EIGHT

From a distance, looking back across the bay at the harbor, the red-pulse conflagration of emergency lights, vehicles, and official personnel on the veranda of the Malabar House seems staged.

A mechanical bird buzzes overhead, destined for the *Jeddah*, presumably some kind of tactical drone, and as Morehouse points this out to Eccola, she shouts an alarm, and he swerves portside to narrowly avoid the pair of police boats sluicing out toward the ship. The harbor patrol zips past them, following the drone, and the doctor instantly recognizes the white man Sentro called Zeme, but not the other young Anglo they have under heavy guard on the stern deck. Bloated by a life preserver, his head squeezed, he looks terrified and struggles to keep his balance despite sitting.

Morehouse counts half a dozen local gendarmes on each of the two boats, fully armed, plus the pirates, and doing the math in his head, the doctor can only assume that Sentro and the crew of the *Jeddah* will be toast. A wiry, scar-faced mercenary in a windblown madras sports coat has taken command of a big nasty deck gun on the patrol boat that follows Zeme's.

The doctor cuts his throttle and jacks the skiff around to watch the patrol boats recede and tries to make his peace with his coward's choice here.

Eccola has sagged to a bench. Her eyes rise to meet his. There's fire in them. He looks away, ashamed. This girl.

"We go back," she says.

"If I want to kill myself, I'll do it with morphine, thank you very much."

"Go back," she repeats.

"No." In her language he reminds her she's with child.

"Back. For my brother."

To himself, grim, the doctor murmurs, "Yo ho ho." Shoves the throttle full and cuts the wheel starboard.

———

She's lied a little to Mulligan. But not so much to herself.

Making this up as she goes along has been her principal strategy, from the moment the so-called pirates burst into her cabin.

It's when it became personal that the doubts crept in.

After Jesper finishes setting up and focusing the late Bruce's smallest telescope, Sentro and Captain Montez take turns watching the police boats approach from the quay with a shared sense of worry.

"We didn't get out quick enough."

"They'd have caught us anyway," Sentro admits and wonders for one bleak moment what she was thinking coming back to the boat if she knew this. Was it the best bad option? She catches her concentration straying, recommits herself to the task at hand, remembering out of nowhere what must be a training trope from Quantico or Bragg: *When facing superior force, shrink the battleground.*

Right?

A speck of a drone hovers two hundred feet above them, whirring eerily. Salah was first to point it out. The gulls on the masts and containers twitch, unnerved but too stubborn to be chased off.

Jesper offers a different eyepiece to her, and Sentro pans a much closer view across the deck of the lead patrol boat and finds her son, wearing the old leather jacket that she brought back for Dennis, years ago, from Spain. A ragged breath escapes her.

"Is it him?"

Sentro nods, numb, staring at her son's stony features through the telescope.

"How did he get himself all the way here?"

Yes, how?

She wonders at how many other moments like this she missed, all the times he stumbled, got lost and needed direction, got scared and wanted comfort, got himself in some kind of trouble that Dennis—not she—had to help him resolve. She has no memory of the first girl her son liked, whether he ever wanted to learn to play guitar. If he was bullied in middle school.

It's not because she's forgotten. She wasn't there. She wasn't there to know it.

"Do you have children, Captain?"

"Five. In Gibraltar."

"You know the answer to that, then."

"They're resourceful," Montez agrees.

Below them, fifty yards out from the ship, the patrol boat carrying Zeme and her son throttles down and lets the rolling wake overtake it, rising, dipping, gliding sideways, as if worried about coming too close just yet.

"AHOY THERE."

"That's a good bullhorn," Sentro thinks aloud, recalling the harsh distortion of the one she heard in West Texas, in the motel. The captain glances at her, annoyed.

"HEY! AHOY THERE!"

Montez raises a microphone to use the ship's comm, but Sentro reaches out and stops him. The hatch above them opens, exposing the forest of antennae on the observation deck. First Mate Mulligan struggles down the ladder while the Tagalog remains up top, frantically trying to put the Gustaf together and load it. Zoala squats beside him, offering a stream of unheeded suggestions.

"Progress?"

"He's getting the swing of it," Mulligan says without conviction.

Castor Z.'s voice booms across the bay water. "IF WE DO THIS RIGHT? EVERYBODY GETS WHAT THEY WANT."

Um, *no*. Sentro watches the crew on the second patrol boat inflate a rubber pontoon boat and drop it over the side. Its coiled line is thrown to the lead boat, and hand over hand, Carlito pulls the inflatable across to where Jeremy is already being positioned to climb down to it.

Wearing her husband's jacket. In this heat. A worrisome detail. Probably not his choice, she thinks. So what is it hiding?

"AS YOU CAN SEE, WE'LL BE PUTTING LITTLE MAN SENTRO INTO THE FLOATY FOR A BIT OF QUIET TIME. UNTIL TODAY'S SWAP IS DONE."

"The money is on its way," Sentro says to Montez, just realizing it.

"How do you know that?"

"He wouldn't expose himself like this if it wasn't. Too many moving parts." Everyone on the bridge is staring at her with looks of confusion. "He'll have arranged for it to come by plane. An airdrop. He just needs to show them that he can deliver the ship, its cargo, its passengers and crew, intact, and that he has it under his control." Sentro closes her eyes, feeling a twitch of headache that wants to come back. She wills it away.

"HELLO?"

Montez raises his microphone again, and again Sentro stops him, shaking her head. "I'm going down to talk with him face-to-face about my son. Get the passengers into the safe room. As soon as I have Jeremy, if Charlemagne has managed to assemble it in time, put a shell from the Gustaf into that lead patrol boat. Maybe you'll get lucky and kill Mr. Zeme."

"You'll be in the line of fire."

"Don't worry about me." She means it.

"And if we don't kill him?"

"It'll get messy," she allows, then removes the handgun wedged in the small of her back and puts it on the map table, asking the first mate, "Do you keep a signal gun up here?"

"Take the Kalashnikov."

"I can't possibly shoot all of them." Mulligan doesn't seem to understand, and she doesn't have time to explain. "Signal gun," she says again.

He limps to a cabinet to find it, exasperated, while the captain asks one last time, "Why not just let him have his money?"

"There's more to this than the ransom," Sentro replies, almost a chorus now. Cartoon cats, empty containers. Twins and her very own femme fatale. She imagines a bird's-eye view of the *Jeddah*: glassy bay water, police patrol abreast the hull, gulls, drone, fake pirates waving signal flags. Castor Zeme on the bow of his baby frigate, arms akimbo, king of the world.

It always comes down to a dinner theater production number, best intentions, bravely sung. And the buffet sucks.

Some kind of colorful seaplane will make the drop, she guesses, with the clown-shoe pontoons and overhead wing. She imagines it circling, a package tumbling out. The parachute pops; the ransom floats over the bay, to the *Jeddah*, in a lazy spiral, down, down, down.

"Which means he's going to want to kill me as soon as he can." Below her, the second patrol boat has begun motoring slowly around the freighter, trailing Jeremy in the rubber dinghy like some kind of door prize. "Then my son." She can't, won't, let this possibility overtake her. "And kill the passengers and the rest of you as soon as he has the money." She takes a beat to gather herself and let the others process this certainty. "Because this whole endeavor has gone horribly south on him," she tells them. "And that's who he is."

Bloody carnage.

Flies swarming in blue-black clouds.

Everyone on the *Jeddah* dead when the ship's owners finally send a boarding party to assess their losses. And no Marlow to tell the tale.

The bridge has gone quiet. While Mulligan crosses to hand Sentro the yellow flare gun he's located, Captain Montez stares at her, dumbfounded.

"I know," Sentro says kindly. "It'd be wonderful to live in the civilized, transactional world you have always believed was real. But we don't. We live in mine. You'd better get everyone locked down. Now."

And because it's been bugging her, she asks, before he leaves, the impertinent question she probably should save for later, if there is one: "How much did she pay you to turn a blind eye to all those Gustafs hidden in the soybeans?"

The captain turns beet red. He stutters guiltily about how he doesn't know what Sentro's talking about, and even if he did, he had no idea the complications that might ensue.

"Oh, stop. Stop." Securing the flare gun in the back waistband of her leggings and letting her shirttail drop over it, she cuts him off, impatient. "Don't lie to me. I suspect it was you I heard in the dead of night moving them."

Montez blinks guiltily, like a kid caught shoplifting.

"I don't care," Sentro says. "Thieving from thieves, good for you. I hope your kickback is a fortune.

"But don't think for a minute that you will live to spend any of it on your children if we don't take care of this monster now."

Chapter Thirty-Nine

She first noticed Dennis when Euclid Junior High merged their boys' and girls' PE classes, eighth grade. Ballroom dancing was the ruse with which the faculty intended to teach young men and women how to deal with each other as the Niagara Falls of hormones came crashing down. She had known him most of her life, but she noticed him then. Ropy and pale and helmet haired and smelling faintly of a nervous flop sweat that nevertheless never bothered her, even years later. He crossed to pick her as a partner. She assumed it was because of their friendship, that he was too shy to pick the girl she was convinced he was crushing on, but when he put his hand on her waist and she put hers on his shoulder and they struggled with the formal footwork of waltz, something caught in her chest and the world tilted, and she found herself thinking about him in an electric new way long after the class had ended.

The way time sideslipped when she was with him. No one image or gesture settling. An exhilarating smear of right now, the world left behind.

The unconditional freedom it allowed her.

Later, this would be what she felt in the field when she was working. She never told anyone. Not even Dennis. She was embarrassed to confess that the thrill was what kept her coming back into the game, that the joyous freedom she had felt dancing with her forever boy in the gym kept sending her into the field operational, again and again, back to the risks that she should by all reason and convention have rejected to remain with her family and settle into her role as a woman and a wife.

She doesn't regret the choices she made, only the inescapable consequences of having made them.

So it doesn't surprise or upset her when, having discarded her running shoes to climb down the pilot's ladder barefoot, she's shed much of the fear of what might happen. She looks down and watches the one-eyed tweaker's boat motor past Castor Zeme's, tugging grim Jeremy in the trailing inflatable, tethered by a long line. No more doubt, single minded, all Sentro's focus has narrowed to this; she's not going to let any harm come to him.

"Sack up, boyo!" Zeme is taunting him. He has some kind of tablet in his hand that evidently shows him the view down at the *Jeddah* from the overhead drone, because the cop at the controls of it sits in the back of the boat, eyes set skyward.

"You're the mackerel, and we're going trawling!" A swirling bay breeze catches up her son's leather coat and flaps it open, revealing C-4 explosive duct-taped over his sweat-drenched shirt like a waistcoat; it looks to be rigged with a homemade throwaway phone detonator that Sentro makes an educated guess will be triggered by the old-school BlackBerry the malevolent alpha twin is holding up and waving at her smugly.

Acutely aware of how scared her son must be and how brave he has been to come all this way to find her, Sentro tugs down the shirttail concealing her signal gun and begins to descend to the endgame.

———

Up on the observation deck, Charlemagne takes his eye away from the telescope eyepiece. "Oh no."

He watches one patrol boat curl past the other to come abreast of the *Jeddah*, where Sentro has climbed down to face both.

"No no no no."

Charlemagne looks to Zoala, who has taken over the attempted assembly of the Gustaf. There are three pieces left in the suitcase, and they can't figure out where they go.

Carlito throttles back, and his boat rolls on its own lazy wake and drifts sideways, while Jeremy's dinghy goes wide. Sentro makes a quick sea-level assessment of her parameters but still sees only one way forward. Her son is almost twenty yards away, clutching the rubber dinghy's fat sides, rolling on the patrol boats' wakes as they cross and slap and rebound back and forth; Jeremy's drifted to a position equidistant between her pilot's ladder and the closer patrol boat carrying Castor Zeme and his vile sawtooth grin of triumph.

There's a distant, dull droning sound she briefly worries might be a third rogue harbor patrol she hasn't accounted for, but no, the noise she hears is high, steady, rising—a whine that suggests an air- as opposed to waterborne approach.

It's not the drone.

The ransom?

"You're a tough fucking chew, Mrs. Sentro." Wide stanced, facing her like the imperious high sea freebooter he aspires to be, Zeme steadies himself on the bow, his gun hanging loose at his side from a strap. He has the tablet in one hand, the BlackBerry detonator in his other. "I'monna be thrilled to get shed of you."

The gun is an automatic but not a Kalashnikov. Some expensive, manly, and exotic assault rifle he must have stolen from one of his previous death-dealing adventures. Sentro has no fetish for firearms; she can see at a glance it's a killing tool, with an enhanced clip, thirty rounds. That's all she needs to know about it. Her bigger problem, she's decided, is the AKs slung over the shoulders of Zeme's three attendant mercenaries, who, along with two of the crooked Porto Pequeno police-men in the stern, have thrown lines up to the *Jeddah* deck rails and are already clambering aboard, leaving Sentro with Zeme; his aide-de-tweaker, Carlito; and the remainder of the *policías*.

She wants to do this before the climbers can settle and shoot back down at her.

"They've got a big gun up there." She fashions an expression that's calm, open, unhurried. "I told them to take you out if I don't get my son." Zeme keeps grinning back, vulgar but unreadable; nevertheless she can see the first threads of uncertainty twist in his empty blue shark eyes when he realizes she's not bluffing.

"Get him?" Castor Z. bares his pointy teeth and bends the corners of his mouth down in what she decides he thinks is a grand, con-descending smirk. "I see a foolish boy wearing a combustible do-it-yourself kit under his daddy's jacket."

Dennis's name is stitched on the inside label with *Love Always, Aubrey.*

Sentro calls across to her son, a touch of stall, but she means it: "Honey, it's gonna be okay." *Honey?* Where in the world did that mom trope come from? Jeremy just stares back at her dully, numb with fear, quaking. Watching a mother she knows he has so thoroughly misjudged.

She finds the tears she wants next more easily than she expects, clearly confusing Zeme. Maybe they're real. Tears are primal, always unsettling. And the momentary distraction allows her to draw her flare gun from under her shirt and aim it at Castor Zeme's head.

"Hey now."

A clattering of weapons that lift and aim at Sentro; nobody mov-ing, and after a wired moment, Zeme bursts into laughter. "And what's the point of that?"

The dull droning has kept rising, an insistent bumblebee hum as, from the west, a banana-yellow seaplane comes bearing down on them, fast. A lone figure with a safety harness leans out on one of the pontoon floats, holding a parcel with a chute attached.

Even from this distance, Sentro thinks she recognizes the stippled dome and distinctive cant of the figure's sturdy frame. She knows him. A friend? She can't remember his name.

"Getting your son seems, in all honesty, insanely optimistic, Aubrey Sentro," Zeme says, glancing up at the approaching aircraft, looking pleased. "Considering I only needed my boys to get up on that boat long enough to show we have possession and collect my money." There it is. Sentro regrets briefly that the captain didn't hear this.

Zeme waves the tablet and whoops as the yellow seaplane swoops low overhead. The mercenaries on the main deck follow suit; the wings tilt, a parcel tumbles out, and its translucent chute mushrooms open.

It's a beautiful sight.

"But that's already ancient history, isn't it? And your son's a fucking memory."

Zeme stows the tablet and raises the old phone to dial. Her breath catching, Sentro can only hope that, with all the tiny arcane buttons, it will take him a moment to figure out how to key the detonation.

A crack and a high-pitched whine draw everyone's eyes up. The drone has come apart, and it's whirling down in pieces. Salah has shot it with the Kalashnikov from an accommodation tower stairwell landing.

And this second distraction proves perfect.

On the dinghy, Jeremy has risen, his shaking legs beginning to buckle as he anticipates a bad ending, but braced on the bottom rung of her ladder, Sentro has already moved the barrel of her signal gun to the right, and Castor, shaking off the drone's distraction, looks like he can't quite process everything at once. His finger is poised over the BlackBerry keyboard but not moving. As if time has been suspended, he puzzles the riddle of a woman taking aim at her child.

She fires at the swollen prow that curves behind Jeremy. The flare hits the vinyl flush and burns the hole she wants in it but doesn't penetrate; instead, to her horror, it skips up and pinwheels madly into the left breast of her husband's old leather jacket, where it blooms with phosphorous flame on her son. Sentro screams, "No!" as if she were the one hit. Jeremy's rocked off balance backward by both the impact and the dinghy's deflation; he plunges into the water, where Sentro is counting on the weight of the IED vest he's wearing to take him rapidly under so the incoming cell phone signal won't connect.

And to her great relief, it doesn't.

Castor Z. reflexively flattened himself on the bow of the patrol boat when Sentro's gun fired, and as if still catching up with what she's done, he only thought to key the phone after he dropped, so the delinquent call to Jeremy's C-4 pack rings and rings and rings without result. The local cops and hired men on the patrol boats are likewise caught short and even slower to react.

Sentro leaps off the ladder into the ocean, dives deep after her son, bullets from above zipping uselessly into and through the water behind her, quickly losing thrust. She kicks down toward the distant, descending shape of the child she knows has never learned to swim.

Above her, a fractured, bright flash blisters the sea's surface, followed by the dull thump of one of the patrol boats exploding.

And then the dazzling rain of debris.

———

Charlemagne has been knocked on his ass by the recoil of the recoilless Gustaf, but Zoala is already popping another shell into the canister and urging the Tagalog back to his feet. The Tagalog shoulders the tube, shoves it over the observation deck rail, and fires again down at the second boat. This round only clips the stern but blows a mortal wound in it, and now it's all madness below: the flaming wreckage of the first boat, the second one sinking, hired guns and police leaping to the ladder and lines coming up the side of the cargo ship.

The ransom parcel plummets in lazy circles into the vast field of cargo and snags there on top of an uneven Jenga of disrupted containers, parachute sagging and then draping over it.

By the time Charlemagne manages to find his feet again, Zoala has fumbled the remaining ordnance, and they watch as it rolls under the rail and off the edge. Bullets rake the accommodation tower wall from below. They stumble back to the open hatch, where Mulligan hustles them down into the bridge.

———

And Sentro swims.

Kicking down into the murky depths of the bay. No sign of Jeremy. Who can't swim.

When he was little, she promised him she'd teach him, but lessons kept getting delayed. Dennis told her, later, that Jeremy refused to go to the pool at the Y without her, and then life overtook them and Jeremy got too old for his mom to teach him to swim, and they both let it go.

Until now.

Fire and light ribbon around her in miasmic striations of luminous yellow green; the bay is churned murky, plankton-mud stew, visibility negligible; her lungs ache. Above her, rippling through the surface water's glimmer distortion, she can see Zeme hanging from the pilot's ladder, sweeping the aim of his assault rifle back and forth over the oily, smoke-shrouded water where the deflated dinghy bobs. Waiting for Sentro to surface.

When she must, using the inflatable as poor but sufficient cover, she comes up just to take one big breath and kicks down again. Zeme pivots and fires and shreds the dinghy, too late to hit his target.

Elsayed, she thinks, pulling the memory out of nowhere as she swims down into the sea.

What in the world was Lucky Elsayed doing in the ransom seaplane?

———

Passengers and nonessential crew have barely managed to secure themselves in the safe cabin, slamming the door shut just as one of Zeme's mercenaries runs into the anteroom. A burst of frustrated automatic gunfire splinters the compartment's wood laminate, revealing thick steel plating underneath.

The hired man spits on the door and walks back out into the C-deck corridor, where—WHAM—a wide-stanced Zoala, who's crept up to watch this all go down, sets and swings his cricket bat as hard as he can, catching the unfortunate target full in the face with the square drive he learned watching Shai Hope on YouTube.

It feels sweet.

Even as the man falls senseless, Zoala keeps striking him, again and again, reverse sweep, then a cut and a slog, before the man flops facedown on the deck.

"Howzat? Howzat?" he shouts.

And like a good batsman worried about his overs, Zoala keeps hitting him until Captain Montez and his second mate emerge and Montez catches the boy in his arms and pulls him away while Salah kicks the rifle clear and pins the dazed, bloody mercenary to the floor until other crewmen can bring the rope from the safe cabin survival kit, according to plan.

———

The explosion came out of nowhere.

The brief flash of the flare drew Lucky's interest while the seaplane pilot cast a lazy, looping circle around the cargo ship to afford them the full measure of it. But then hell broke loose. A confusion of white carets lifted up from the cargo when the patrol boat blew up. He strained to see through the smoke and fire, searched for a sight of his friend. The plane banked away and gained altitude to avoid getting taken down by the birds. When it came around again, swooping low across the *Jeddah*'s length, from the open doors under the wings on either side Reno Elsayed and the fed sent some provisional bullets down on the armed men cresting the main deck gunwales to see if they might encourage a retreat.

They couldn't.

Lucky sits back into the cabin from the wing strut, out of the punishing wind, and watches another couple of what he assumes are pirates scramble up onto the stern deck, hard on the heels of the others. Directly below, one harbor-patrol boat that was visible on the first pass now lists badly, damaged, sinking, amid the smoldering debris of what must have been the other. No sign of Sentro. Tethered to the other strut, Special Agent Warren can be heard letting loose more pattern fire, which causes the new two-man boarding party to scramble for cover as the plane buzzes over them. But one man rolls onto his back, aims what has to be some fancy new Russian assault weapon at the plane, and shoots with alarming accuracy.

Warren shouts and swings inside as Elsayed watches a couple of rounds go through the belly of the seaplane, just missing him, and pins of light stream in. "Hell's bells. Is that an AK-308?"

The pilot banks away.

Lucky has to lean out wide to observe the selfsame shooter rise to his knees and signal his partner, and together they sprint into the cover of a narrow canyon between containers.

"Going for the money," Agent Warren guesses aloud.

No surprise, really, that the fed had a government Citation X fired up and waiting at Martin State Airport, and he drove Elsayed there directly after picking him up from his morning jog. No time to change, but plenty of time on the long flight to Georgetown to debrief Lucky on Aubrey Sentro's unfortunate intersect with high sea piracy. Or at least as much as Warren claimed he could make of it, given the dissembling and stonewalling of the *Jeddah*'s Shanghai-based parent company and its byzantine web of underwriters and private insurers, who kept insisting that this was a private matter, sheltered from US jurisdiction, and anyway, they had everything under control.

Which was why, Warren said, he decided to track down running Reno.

It's just like Aubrey to get caught up in the random violent crime or uprising or revolution. Some of the independent contractors who cycled through the doors of Solomon over the years, all men, have privately complained that she is a trouble magnet.

Elsayed can only observe dryly that she is still alive and operational while most of them are not.

He doesn't understand why the fed decided to dive headfirst into this but suspects that Aubrey's name rang the alarm in some deep-cover old spook's payback machine. All that she's done for God and country, some of which is so classified even Elsayed can't get the details, must warrant and deserve Uncle Sam's eternal gratitude.

Or maybe Agent Warren was just bored with busting dope rings and Ponzi schemes and rich old pedophiles. Break out the bureau's fancy jet and some M16s; live the dream. Elsayed will take it, either way.

Because of the noisy open doors, they wear headsets to communicate. Warren is asking, "You know that canard about shooting fish in a barrel?"

"Yeah."

"It's bullshit. I saw so on *MythBusters*."

"That's still on TV?"

"Far as I know, yeah. Maybe in repeats, I guess."

"I thought *MythBusters* was bullshit."

"No, no. Straight up. Those guys are good."

"Huh." Elsayed's jogging sweats have been ripening for hours, and while the fed hasn't made a comment, Reno's thankful to be in a steady breeze.

It nags at him that he didn't see Sentro on the last pass over. The pilot has looped back for another run. The fed leans out to fire down at the observation deck of the *Jeddah*. Another pirate drops, unmoving.

"No barrels here, luckily," Agent Warren observes.

CHAPTER FORTY

Like a dark ghost, she can see him below her. What she hopes is him. A shape in the water's half light that must be him: legs limp but scissoring with the current, the heavy jacket billowing out like ventral fins to slow him but still dragging him down. Almost gone.

Sentro has lost track of how long she's been underwater this dive, and Jeremy has been down longer; her lungs heave against her ribs as with one last desperate surge she kicks toward the suggestion of her son.

Giving birth again, she thinks.

Reaching out in the cold water, reaching, kicking, the breath beginning to boil out of her, she's got him, Jeremy, in her arms, his eyes wide, his lips white, pink water blooming from fingertips shredded by his attempt to shed the explosive rigging that was dragging him to the bottom. Sentro strips Dennis's heavy leather coat off, hooks one arm under her son, and swims them both to the surface.

Rising, gasping, into a pool of fiery patrol-boat bits and acrid smoke. Jeremy isn't breathing. But Zeme is no longer on the ladder.

Fuck fuck fuck.

Zoala has Sentro's pocketknife—the one she needs to slice the explosives off her son. She's not sure how long she can hold him up, treading water.

"Ahoy!"

The sharp prow of a skiff slips out of the surface smoke, aimed right at her. She kicks and pulls her son out of the way, the boat already churning in reverse, sliding past, slowing, propellers thrashing close. It slides back with Eccola leaning over the bow, reaching for Jeremy. Morehouse kills the throttle and comes to the side to help his pregnant girlfriend lift the lifeless body up and into the boat.

"He's not breathing," Sentro gasps.

"What a surprise," Morehouse says with the eerie calm of a real doctor. He disappears below the gunwale where Jeremy flopped aboard.

"He's my son," Sentro says, so flush with emotion she's unsure that the doctor heard her. Eccola reaches out again. "I can help you," she says, but Sentro doesn't have the strength to lift her arm.

"Wait," she wheezes. "Wait, let me just, let me just . . ."

From the boat, the C-4 rig Jeremy was wearing sails over her head and splashes down, disappearing. Clutched in Sentro's hand is her husband's waterlogged jacket; she couldn't leave it. There's a charred spot on one side, but knotting the sleeves together, she flaps it and captures a big bubble of air inside to help keep her afloat while she catches her breath.

Eccola gazes down at her with those mournful, liquid brown eyes. "Let me help you."

Sentro worries what she'll find if she comes aboard.

Morehouse has begun singing, off key.

The girl's arm still extended. "Please."

Under his breath, falsetto, tone-deaf flat, but in a steady beat, Morehouse huffs: "Ah ah ah ah, ah ah ah ah—"

Reaching, grasping Eccola's arm for leverage, Sentro summons all her remaining strength, flutter kicks up out of the water, and, using the girl's surprising strength as a pivot point, tumbles over into the boat, dragging the sopping leather coat behind her. She's just in time to see Jeremy tilt to his side and cough up a thin gruel of bile and water. The doctor has brought him from the dead. Delivered him back to her.

"Bee Gees?"

Morehouse nods, looking spent, sitting back. "Pretty much the perfect rhythm."

"Thank you," Sentro says. She flashes on Jeremy's birth, a grueling ordeal, his tiny body slick with her blood, pale and blue from the cord that nearly finished him, her terror, watching, drugged, helpless, terrified that he wouldn't ever take that first breath.

Morehouse makes a face, still trying to catch his breath. "I do 'How Deep Is Your Love' as an encore."

"No need." Fighting back tears, just as she did long ago.

Jeremy, fetal, on his side, stares at his mother with what she hopes is wonder. "You shot me."

There are a million things she wants to say, but all that comes out between gasps as she recovers her wind is, "Flare gun."

Her son just stares, as if at a stranger.

"Sulfur burn," Morehouse realizes. "Explains how your chest got grilled." He frowns, intrigued, at Sentro. "You didn't worry it'd go right through him?"

"Flare gun," Sentro says again.

"Oh man." Jeremy closes his eyes.

No need to get into how she never intended to even hit him. Missions go sideways, but usually not with your own children at stake. Sentro demurs. "Insufficient velocity. And he was pretty well protected. With that coat." But she felt her heart leave her body when her son went backward into the sea.

"A coat which I see you also recovered from the deep. Special meaning?"

None of his business. Jeremy coughs like he can't stop, but the sound to her is as beautiful as anything she's ever heard.

"What if you'd missed?" the doctor asks her.

Sentro wants to say *I tried* and *I was out of options*, but she doesn't know if it's true. When she pulled the trigger, was she thinking, *This is my son?* Did she think at all?

She looks at Jeremy. "I knew what I was doing," she tries to reassure him. Then, as he stares, unconvinced, she hedges: "More or less."

"More, I hope," Jeremy says and then shuts his eyes as another fit of racked wet coughing overtakes him.

She puts her hand lightly against his face, murmurs, "Rest," then rises to take the tiller and aim the skiff back at the *Jeddah*.

CHAPTER FORTY-ONE

All he has left is the ransom money.

Brother dead, the bitch and her boy underwater, the whole point of this latest fiasco now drowned, Castor Zeme limp-skips, knee throbbing again, through the cargo toward the container stack where he spotted the silvery special delivery chute flagging in the breeze. He doesn't understand how the hell this all went so wrong again.

In retrospect, killing the Dutchman was a boneheaded move, but at least it bought him time to collect this payoff and disappear, maybe to Belize or Curaçao, go to ground while the colonel rages. And Castor's sure that old fascist fucker will rage. Demand his kilo of flesh or whatever. If his brother were here, Castor would smack him for answering that bloody online ad that launched them spiraling into high sea cargoship piracy for a duplicitous Englishwoman and the serial calamity that has followed.

Oy, dude, chick swears we'll net a hundred grand, Pauly had crowed.

Dumb, dumb, dumb. The ache of missing him twists inside.

At the base of the tilted stack, Carlito steps up from behind Castor, cups his hands, and boosts the good leg clattering up onto a lateral brace of strapping from which Castor will find decent purchase to keep going. The ship is otherwise unnervingly quiet.

It should be only a short cliff climb up to the prize.

Seabirds flock and dart and complain, made skittish by all the low aircraft flybys. Another, he senses, is due soon.

At the top of the stack, Zeme spots the package right away, wedged one level higher than he thought, in a narrow slot between salt-rusted green containers, but before he and Carlito can cross over for the final climb, sure enough, the seaplane is back, swooping low on a slant, port to starboard. Bullets pluck at their feet; they dance away from them until Carlito loses balance and goes over the side with a startled cry. Disappeared.

Zeme drops to the sun-warmed steel, then flips onto his back and empties half his magazine up at the belly of the aircraft when it zooms over him.

———

Elsayed is reloading when Zeme's return fire peppers the fuselage. More pinholes of light; their punching through sounds like popcorn in a cheap pot. He presses back against the cabin bulkhead, trying to make himself very small, praying that there isn't a stray one with his name on it. Agent Warren leans in from the strut, unhurt. Behind him one of the wing engines has caught fire.

"Hell's bells," Warren says, sounding disappointed.

Smoke pours in on them, and the plane tips when the pilot tries to shut the engine down. Bracing himself so he doesn't slide out his open door, which is angled sharply down, Elsayed spies an open fishing skiff glide up against the stern of the cargo ship, and he watches as Aubrey Sentro, hair plastered drowned-cat down on her head like a bad hat, leaps to climb a dangling ladder up the hull. Her small body moves with such grace that he marvels at how easy she can make some things look.

"I have got to splash down," the pilot shouts back at them in Spanish.

Warren says something that gets lost in the wind.

Elsayed looks again and sees, spread eagled on a stern container, a saggy-ass sniper who has drawn a bead on Sentro as she threads through the starboard rails of the main deck. The seaplane wobbles badly, but Reno makes the adjustment, double taps his trigger, and the prone shooter jerks once and goes still, his rifle clattering away.

"Bada boom."

Sentro is looking up at the plane as it passes over her. Elsayed waves down at his friend, grinning like it's Saturday softball, until engine smoke blinds him; he gropes for a flapping cabin restraint to pull himself in and buckle up for the emergency descent.

―――

The ransom package has turned out to be a suspiciously repurposed Amazon shipping box, duct-taped to the hilt but already cracked open along one seam by the impact of its arrival. Impatient and wary of his continued exposure atop the containers, Castor has dislodged and dropped it to a lower level and the relative protection of looming cargo on either side. Having climbed down after it, he pulls the drapery of its parachute away and jams his fingers in the split to finish ripping the cardboard open.

Blank, money-size slips of paper cascade out at his feet.

Another infuriating fail. Another elaborate fucking ruse.

Castor Z. screams his outrage.

A bullet grazes his head, slapping it sideways, and he falls back.

The box overturned, the plain paper gets swirled by the wind, twisting, rolling, skittering white across the container top and down into the cargo canyons, nearly indistinguishable from the dropping, diving, peripatetic flock of unsettled gulls.

―――

If there is ever an official intelligence white paper on the *Jeddah* siege, Sentro knows that it will be briefly covered and summarily redacted: an abortive high sea extortion by unknown apolitical nonstate actors, thwarted by quick and decisive actions of Captain Montez and his crew. Mulligan may get special mention for his bravery. The casualties will be deemed inevitable and unfortunate. Bruce's family will receive a settlement. The United States government will not comment, and no public mention will be made of Aubrey Sentro, Reno "Lucky" Elsayed, or whomever he brought with him in the seaplane (she's already preparing herself, not uncharitably, for the two-manhattan-cocktail session her friend will require in order to spin a labyrinthian, half-true tale of how he got there with his new federal BFF in a private RICO jet that once belonged to some knucklehead like El Chapo). She further doubts any account of what has actually happened will make it even as far as the internal-eyes-only anecdotes that sometimes circulate among the bureaucrats and NGOs and private contractors through back channels and word of mouth.

Unless, of course, she somehow dies during this mop-up.

Her government does not negotiate with kidnappers.

The *Jeddah*'s shipping company will report no loss of assets, human or otherwise; their ransom insurer will settle privately with the surviving passengers for their emotional distress, subject to a strict boilerplate NDA everyone will gladly sign.

Lowering the Kalashnikov she recovered from where she heard it fall between containers, she watches through a narrow gap as blank white paper waterfalls down on weird thermals from over the lip of the container, where the bottoms of Castor Z.'s shoes just skittered backward out of view after she fired at him.

The gun's sight has been torqued, she decides, which is no surprise; she guesses she missed Zeme by a meter or more. Slipping the rifle strap over her good shoulder, she's beginning to climb containers to find a better angle and try again, when an answering bullet explodes against the corrugated steel next to her and the resulting shrapnel peppers and shreds Sentro's lower rib cage and chest. She cries out and falls back to the deck. The rifle strap is dislodged; the Kalashnikov gets away from her.

More bullets ricochet off the decking before Sentro can heave herself around a container to safe cover. She's hit, and it hurts, and the shock of it hasn't even gathered yet.

Crawling away, she hears Carlito's quick movement to the next intersection and knows what comes next. She turns in that direction; sure enough, he pivots around a corner with his gun thrust out in front of him, but the cricket bat that strikes his face crushes his nose and rattles his brain so badly it causes him to pirouette in a helpless rage as the small shape responsible dances past.

Upswinging: rib cage, kidney, balls.

Carlito somehow keeps his feet. The blows keep coming, but the bat splits lengthwise, and the better half clatters away, leaving mostly splinters in Zoala's hand.

Carlito yells and somehow manages to block the next swing with the forearm of his gun hand, while with the other he backhands Zoala to the deck. He raises his revolver and fires a bullet into the boy before Sentro can react and retrieve the sharp good half of the broken cricket bat to plunge it through the scarred tweaker from behind like a spear.

Carlito gasps, vomits blood, and collapses, dead.

She steps over him and takes the boy in her arms. More gunfire rains down on Sentro through the cascading slips of paper from where Castor Zeme has taken the high ground.

Sentro lifts Zoala and carries him to cover through the open end of a breached and plundered deck-level container. Panicking, she rips open his shirt where the bullets struck and discovers to her astonishment that Jeremy's hardback edition of *Lord Jim*, which the boy had wedged in the waistband of his shorts, has two slugs buried in it. They've penetrated over halfway, but Zoala is unhurt, just the wind knocked out of him. She exhales in relief. His eyes blink; he's dazed.

"*Matei ele?*" he asks.

Bullets jackhammer into the container and rattle around. The sound of Zeme's feet pounds across steel as he circles and then descends, searching for a better angle in on them.

Sentro doesn't want to be trapped. Her ribs are on fire, her shirt matted wet with what she knows, without looking, is blood. She darts out into the open, telling Zoala, "You'll be safer in here," and, using the container door as a shield, grabs ahold and swings back with it, momentarily protected from the gunfire that tracks her and punches into the other side. She jams the door shut, drops the latch, and rolls into a slender chasm between the next group of stacks.

As Sentro crawls away, hands and knees, she can hear Zoala screaming and pounding on the door. Cast down, Zeme's long shadow gimps along the container tops, tracking her retreat through the rats' maze of passageways, popping off single rounds, missing, but not by much.

She hears Elsayed's seaplane buzz past again. Through a slotted opening, she sees it drop low, one engine smoking, struggling to stay airborne, and then it banks out of sight.

Not entirely by chance, she's wound her way into that midship widening that she remembers from the last time Castor had her chased. The full depth of the lower hold gapes beneath her in a slot between the dry-bulk containers. A top hatch of the soybean bin is at her feet; she throws it open and dives into the temporary safety of its darkness.

———

Zeme has seen her go in.

Hearing the yellow seaplane approach again, he flinches, distracted, and turns to watch it pass low, one engine smoking, struggling to stay airborne and loop around the leeward side of the ship to land in calmer water.

Rifle slung over his shoulder, blood leaking warm from the nick on his widow's peak to the ridge of his jaw, he half clambers, half falls down to the main deck, midship, where the bin into which Sentro has disappeared waits for him.

He also knows where the exit is.

From where he stands, he can look through a gap in the main deck cargo to the bin's second hatch, still flipped open from the American's escape days before.

Not this time.

With a stony flash of his sharpened teeth, he locks down the hatch door at his feet, watertight, and then heads for the other one.

CHAPTER FORTY-TWO

The match Zoala strikes sparks the gleaming glass eyes of a thousand shrink-wrapped baby dolls, and they stare back at him, torn from their packaging and piled up like corpses. Startled, he cries out and stumbles away from them until his back strikes the container door.

Ti bolom, he thinks, terrified. Little babies who die before they get baptized. His sister says they lure grown-ups with their plaintive crying so the devil can take their souls. Zoala covers his ears and shouts at the bolom, "Count sand!"

There's no beach in this dark container. But maybe they'll be fooled. His match goes out, and the life is gone from the bolom as well.

Faint light bleeds through cracks in the door. There is an emergency-release handle, painted bright red, high on the inside, just out of reach.

If he can pile the devil dolls high and sturdy enough, he might climb them to reach it.

———

Her strength is fading. She just wants this ordeal to be over. It's not her first injury from gunfire, but she's shivering with shock and exhaustion, light headed from hunger and dehydration, and the deep wound in her side throbs and continues to bleed. Even breathing in this fetid bin proves difficult as she snakes across the surface of the soybeans, lit dimly by daylight that seeps through the hatch she's crawling toward. She's heard the hatch behind her get sealed, no surprise. But after a moment, a shadow eclipses the dim moon of daylight up ahead, the bin goes almost black, and a wave of nausea grips her. Castor Zeme. She's boxed in. Her chest muscles spasm, and as she curls fetal for relief, her buried hands brush across something cool, close underneath her. Scraping, digging, she uncovers what feels like the slick steel of another recoilless-rifle case.

The latches pop open.

She gropes for the Gustaf's components, gauging the different shapes with her hands, desperate to broom the fog from her brain and remember how they go together as her eyes try to adjust to the darkness.

———

Muffled voices ring through the cargo canyons from the main deck perimeter: Zeme assumes that *Jeddah* crewmen have emerged from their safe room to search for Aubrey Sentro and—without a doubt—for him.

His options have narrowed to nothing. It no longer matters. He thinks about the rocky beach near the Port Hedland house where he and Pauly grew up. Running with his brother down a narrow briar-thick path along the cliffs after one of the beatings their father would regularly give them. Hiding there. Making the promise of *never again*. They made the old man pay. They made the world pay, for a while. But Pauly is dead, and Castor is down to this.

Wiping a sting of sweat from his eye with the back of his hand, he sidesteps down a slender cargo gap to the second access hatch into the grain bin, and circles it, wary, testing his sore knee before crouching down to wait, assault rifle draped across his lap, finger on the trigger.

"OY! WONDER WOMAN!"

He's got two extended clips left, plenty of firepower to greet the bitch when she pops up, and maybe even to hold off the bravest crew if they dare to come rashly, but once the rest collect real weapons from his downed boys, Zeme knows all bets will be off.

"I'd seal you in there and call it a day, but there's my brother to think about."

He's not expecting her to answer.

It's not about money anymore. He's resigned to the probability he won't make it off the ship. Now it's a simple matter of pride: undone by a fucking femme?

No, no, no.

———

The Gustaf feels finished, but Sentro's got an extra piece, which must mean it's not. The clipped light from the far hatch where Castor waits weeps poor illumination this far back on what she's trying to do.

Soybean chaff dusts the finely oiled parts. Another swell of nausea racks her.

"You are a fucking Amazon, lady," she hears the alpha twin yelling. "The she-wolf. But I mean, what's the point? You shoulda stayed with the program, because things were gonna work out. But now, shit. . . all this death and mayhem? It's on you. Only cuzza you."

They taught her how to fieldstrip guns in the dark, and she remembers thinking, *When does that ever happen?*

Sentro studies the weapon, runs her fingers over the extra part she knows could be essential to its operation (but how?). She thinks about the absurdity of the soybeans, then fumbles for the shells in the Gustaf suitcase and drops one—and allows herself a raw flicker of desperation.

Her right side has gone numb; her leg feels dead. How much longer before Zeme's patience breaks and he finds the courage to start firing down through the open hatch? Deep inhale, and with aching fingers she begins to break the rifle down to try assembling it again.

"TIME'S UP!"

No response, but again, he wasn't really expecting one.

Without even a look back, Zeme snaps his hand out and snags the tiresome runt he's smelled creeping up behind him with a pocketknife poised. He yanks Zoala off his feet and slams him down onto the deck, stunning him. "You're a mean little rat, boyo." Foot on Zoala's ruddy, peeling chest, rifle barrel nudged up under the boy's skinny chin.

"You want to add the kid to the list?" he yells.

A drop of blood from Castor drops onto Zoala's petrified face. Silence from below.

But voices again, on the deck's perimeter, closer. No more time to wait. Castor chides himself for yelling so loud—stupid, *stupid*—and, taking a fistful of hair, drags the boy to the hatch opening, intending some gruesome demonstration he hasn't yet decided upon.

"You fucked everything up for everybody," he calls down to the American, carefully angling his position to peer into the bin's chiaroscuro shadows without exposing himself too much.

The fat matte-black tube barrel of a recoilless rifle catches the sun and glints dully up from the empty darkness, aimed directly up at him.

"Oy."

BOOM.

Still groggy from Zeme's body slam, Zoala feels a brush of ferocious heat and watches as his pirate nemesis is struck by a shell, thrown backward in a pink mist, blown to bits. The incandescent exhaust of the Gustaf lights up the hold; Zoala smells burning beans and then his own singed hair where the projectile went past him.

The boy wriggles over and rolls and tumbles down headfirst into a sea of hot, musky pebbles, where the recoil from the rifle has punched the American woman backward and set the sleeves of her shirt on fire. Zoala leaps on her, smothers the flames with his arms and body, but she's limp to his prodding, her eyes shut, her face gray.

His hands come away sticky with her blood. He's overwhelmed, eyes filling. Men's voices and their footfalls clatter together above him, and pale faces lower in the hatch opening, peering in, upside down. Zoala hears someone screaming and then realizes it's himself.

———

The yellow seaplane, its engines mute, one wing smoldering, splashes down alongside the *Jeddah* and skis through the gentle sawtooth bay waves toward the stern. A sturdy, balding man is braced in the open doorway, looking back at the silver skiff, where Morehouse wraps his trembling patient in an oilcloth Eccola has found in the equipment box. Shock has settled in on Jeremy Troon. The doctor's hands are steady, his eyes intent.

For the moment, he's not a runaway, not a failure; he's a man of medicine. A healer. It feels good; perhaps it won't last.

But it feels good.

Morehouse glances up at his pregnant girlfriend as she gives Jeremy a worried once-over, then shuffles to the back of the skiff. He loves her, as much as he can love anyone, he decides. In her brief time in Porto Pequeno, the American spook has disrupted his world. He understands that it will never be the way it was, but he lacks the imagination to predict how it will be going forward.

Waves slap at the huge hull of the cargo ship. There's activity on the decks; passengers have gathered on a stairway landing high on the accommodation tower, looking down, not at Morehouse, but into the middle of the stacked containers, where a skim of smoke sifts, rising.

Some sixth sense tells him it's where she finished her job.

———

Not at all sure if it's the shock, the jet lag, or exhaustion, Jeremy discovers he's unable to remember much of the last few hours. The boat rocks him. He stinks of sea and sweat and diesel oil, his lungs aching, feet cramping, nose and mouth still leaking mucus brine.

All he knows: he came to save her, and she saved him.

The shabby doctor hovers over him, taking his pulse again. Fingers firm against his neck.

"How do you know my mother?"

The doctor appears to think about it before answering. "I don't, really."

In the distance, out beyond the twin rocky points that guard the bay, huge rollers of water pulse, up and down, whitecapped here and there, and a wide scud of clouds hangs low over the open sea. A gossamer curtain unfurling from the sky portends rain.

Jeremy nods. "Me neither."

———

Not dead yet, sorry.

She wants to tell them she's okay, but the effort it would require doesn't seem worth it. When they lifted her, sharp pain opened her eyes, and she saw Captain Montez, Mulligan, and Salah gingerly lift her out of the cargo hold from the arms of the Tagalog and Jesper, who were still below. The *Jeddah* officers are joined by more crew members, and together they carry her into an open space, where she looks up into an impossibly blue square of cloudless sky.

When they lower her to the deck, she sees Zoala's face upside down, studying her, intent, his expression somber, curious, worried. And then from behind him, and this she's less sure of, the gathered faces of the dead crowd in on her: the naked shooter in a Cyprus hotel hallway, the Corpus Christi kidnapper, the boy from the water tank whom she thought she had saved. Does Zoala see them? They blink here and are gone like fireflies: a mobster in Montevideo, an NVD assassin on the banks of the Don, the apple-shaped man with the starburst eye patch and mustard-colored suit.

The kidnapper on the South Padre beach.

The boy in the water tank.

Pauly Zeme.

Go away.

Montez is asking her questions, but her eardrums are numbed deaf by the brutish concussion of the Gustaf in the confines of the steel dry-bulk bin. She only hears thrumming and an odd wind and the sound of her own heartbeat.

No, she doesn't see Dennis or her father or her mom.

Jeremy is safe. Jenny—there's a nagging sense of something she needs to tell her daughter, but she can't remember what it is.

It's hard but not impossible to breathe. She's been worse. The square of blue heaven tilts as she feels the gentle roll of the sea, and then something opens up, her heart or her head; she hears the creaking of the cargo containers, the churn of the ship's engines, the chatter from a flurry of white gulls that cross the sky and—

CHAPTER FORTY-THREE

For most of the night, Jenny sat alone by the bed in the ICU, more or less relieved but also, in fitful ebbs and flows, pissed off, like always, by everything she didn't understand. Gathering her thoughts, holding her mother's hand, for some disobliging reason that she knows now only her mom would appreciate, "Did you sleep with him?" was the first thing she asked when her mother surfaced from the anesthesia, saw her, and smiled.

"What?"

They stared at each other for what seemed like forever, and Jenny could see that her mother was expecting the torrent of questions that she had to believe would have been coursing through her daughter's head all these long hours. Jenny, resenting that she needed to ask, stubbornly didn't. And her mother, stubbornly, didn't seem surprised.

"The cute pharaoh," Jenny said finally.

"You mean Lucky?"

"Reno. El-something."

"I don't remember," was what her mother answered, and it sounded true. Neither of them made a big deal out of talking face-to-face again. Despite her mom's long absences, they had an intimate, private shorthand, a fundamental connection that Jenny, whenever she thought about it, always insisted shouldn't be possible, but there it was.

"You did," she said. "Ew. You can totally see it, the gooey eyes."

"Lucky?"

"*Reno.* From Minnesota, he claims."

"He might be."

"And?"

No answer, but none required. Something between them had changed; Jenny felt it. Her mother would come clean, in her own time. On everything. And Jenny felt no real rush.

"Remember when you gave me the sex talk?" she teased.

"No."

"Yeah. 'Cause you didn't."

Too sharp. She watched her mother flinch and wished she could take that back. She'd never seen her so vulnerable. The tubes and the monitors, shrapnel wounds, concussion, separated shoulder, and all these crazy bruises like somebody'd rolled her out of a truck—what the fuck?

A lifetime ago, anxiously enduring what seemed like forever for her brother's screen ID to light up her phone, Jenny had held vigil in her apartment, waiting for Jeremy's report on the ransom payment, praying there wouldn't be a problem, attempting to calm herself with bowls of Kosher Kush and a binge-watch of *One Tree Hill*, the cat, Aubrey, purring on her lap. She'd fallen into an anxious doze twice, had pretty much smoked all her weed to black ash, and was debating the pros and cons of getting more from Shayda when the call had finally come through midday from somewhere on the forehead of South America (she'd googled it), and to her confusion, she'd heard, instead of Jeremy, her mother's frail, distant voice on the other end of the call. *Something something Jeremy's been hurt something Johns Hopkins something something.* It unfurled in a blur; her mom sounded tired.

A few nerve-racking hours later at the hospital, further confusion— she was met by this handsome crew cut Egyptian American who said his name was Reno Elsayed but urged her to call him Lucky, though Jenny was pretty sure neither could be right. While she puzzled over who he reminded her of (an old Rami Malek? A young Omar Sharif?), this putative Elsayed tried to explain that her mother was in surgery and that her brother, Jeremy, was asking for her, and Jenny, who had *talked* to her mother on the phone, was flummoxed, not to mention still couldn't quite feel her face or her arms or her feet or pretty much anything, for that matter, on account of all the smoking and fitful insomnia. She was weightless, a foggy consciousness, exhausted by all the anxious speculating she'd done.

Jenny remembers just thinking, over and over, *Who is this guy?*

Another couple of completely lost hours followed, as she kept asking the Elsa-whatever what the hell had happened (and how in the world he had happened to be there), but his explanation was decidedly vague, and Jeremy, when she visited him, looked like someone had put him in the spin cycle of a washing machine, huge purple-red welt on his chest. But her brother didn't seem fazed. The excited Vicodin tale he blurted between bruised breaths sounded impossible, and he didn't even bother to cast himself as the hero, which caught Jenny short. A bomb in a vest? Their mother with a flare gun? Pointy-toothed villain, exploding boats, and nearly drowning—Jenny just nodded and made sure not to let any grateful tears of relief come until he slipped off into Jeremy dreams probably no different from his crazy account of things.

The Egyptian came to get her. Her mother was out of the OR, stable, and she was going to be okay; would Jenny like to stay with her?

Jenny would, very much. The last time she'd been in a hospital, it was to take her father home to die.

Her mom drifted in and out of consciousness those first few days, more from exhaustion, her doctors said, than from injuries she'd sustained. Jeremy would wheel himself in and out, accompanied by some cute girl he'd apparently met during his travels; Jenny kept forgetting her name. She popped Motrin for her migraines and stayed with her mom, and the setting sun broke striped through the blinds in bright articulation, and the nights were fitful with nursing visits every couple of hours, plus machine coffee and sketchy crullers from the cafeteria, where a sunken-eyed intern hit on her one morning, so Jenny made a point after that of bringing her makeshift meals back to the room.

"I'm sorry," her mother keeps saying.

"Do I know you?" is Jenny's stock reply.

Her brother, held over a few extra days for observation, had the cloying airline attendant (as it turned out), what's-her-name, hovering with board games and suspiciously immovable boobs and reeking of fruity perfume. Jeremy's ribs were cracked, and he had some superficial burns, but otherwise he looked mostly on the mend (make?), and Jenny was so secretly glad that she surrendered to suffer the company of the new girl (Bryce-Ann, for God's sake!) and let her brother regale them both with the latest version of his Porto Pequeno saga. Most of it was bullshit; the hunky Egyptian had provided a more fact-based take in which her brother sounded not quite so heroic. But her brother had done a very brave thing, Jenny kept reminding herself, and the bottom line was their mom was safe.

When her mother got moved to a private room, Jenny was able to shower, but she stayed in her Hollister hoodie and skinny jeans and refused to leave, even when her brother was discharged and offered to spell her vigil.

Slowly some truths have emerged. A snapshot of a woman Jenny Troon barely recognizes, but it was funny—growing up, all those long months when her mother was on the road, Jenny once spent a summer inventing a glamorous, elaborate fiction of an Aubrey Sentro that, in retrospect, with all Jenny has learned, wasn't so far off the mark.

Without meaning to, Jenny feels empowered.

I'm feral, like you, she wants to say. *It's Jeremy you gotta worry about.*

After the first fractured, groggy confessions, her mother gained strength and the tubes were removed and machines disappeared, and they played Hearts and watched daytime television and suffered visits from her mother's colleagues—overweight white men named Drewmore and Falcone and another skittish older woman named Laura Bugliosi (matching earth-tone lip gloss and clogs)—not to mention their neighbor Marta, whose creepy son had once offered Jenny fifty dollars to show him her breasts (fifth grade, she didn't have any). And in the intervals, they fell back into their easy patter, deliberately dancing around the trigger subjects, which were pretty much everything, the way they always had. And Jenny waited.

Outside phone calls became more frequent: work-related conversations for which sometimes her mom requested privacy and Jenny would wait in the hallway listening to the low, expressionless murmur of the mother she didn't know.

"There's some things we *can't* know," Jeremy pointed out to her.

At least, Jenny thinks, *now we know why.*

"I need you to do something for me," her mother said a moment ago, after a long call and another visit from Mr. Lucky Egyptian Lonely Hearts, the dreamy but regrettably named Reno Elsayed.

"He's married," her mom keeps insisting.

"So? You're full of all kinds of surprises."

She doesn't respond to the dig. "It's important. Can you take some time off?"

After her mother's second surgery to clean up the bits the first one had missed, a brain doctor showed up and walked Jenny to Jeremy's room to tell them both about their mom's preliminary diagnosis. Serial concussions, memory loss, possible irreversible CTE, but they'd need to do more tests, and even then, they'd just be guessing. He seemed curious about her history, convinced she'd lied to him about never having been abused by her husband or someone else.

Jeremy, a little muzzy from the painkillers at that point, kept saying, "Dad? You think Dad was a wife beater?"

"There's this beam in the basement you can crack your head on if you're not careful," Jenny pointed out as if helpfully, doubling down on what she hoped could be more of her mother's dissembling covert bullshit but already pretty sure that nothing anyone could tell a brain doctor would convince him he was wrong.

It was after she brought the brain doctor up with her mother that the full story finally began to leak. Like a Catholic confession, her mother, contrite and regretful, took her time; she told it to Jenny chronologically, apologetic for the gaps, the parts she couldn't remember anymore or remembered only dimly, like a shadow play—gestures, feelings, but the goals and the justifications blurred. As Jenny listened, all the rising attendant emotions became a flood: anger, confusion, betrayal, wonder, incredible pride, and relief. All the times when she'd thought her mother's absences were because of something they'd done or, worse, something they *were*. Something she was . . . a burden. A disappointment. A blight.

Not true.

And now her mother is saying she needs Jenny's help.

She explains that Elsayed will make all the arrangements, but she wants—she *wants*—Jenny to do the rest alone. "You'll need to stop smoking pot."

"Mom."

"I'm serious."

"Arrangements to go where?"

"I want you to take care of one last piece of unfinished business."

For so many reasons, this thrills her. There is never any question in her mind that she will do it. Whatever it is. But she asks, a little worried and needing to know, "Why can't you go?"

"I'm tired," her mother admits.

"I'll be in Texas," her mother adds after a while. "I'm done."

CHAPTER FORTY-FOUR

Peckish shearwaters and petrels whirl and swoop under a searing midday Moroccan sun, shrieking up and strafing down into Casablanca's commercial port, poaching the floating garbage while fish lie low in the cool quay shadows. Decrepit cranes twist between the docked ships and the vast fields of containers awaiting land transport.

Like a boned fish, the tramp cargo ship CMA CGM *Jeddah*, Singapore Shipping Company, flag of the Bahamas, having completed its rerouted four-week journey here only slightly overdue, is nearly unloaded, disemboweled to expose much of the lower hull's crisscrossing steel superstructure. An old green Volvo Titan truck winds through quayside aisles of cargo to the side of the ship. Doors opening, tailgate dropped, a dozen day laborers jump out and follow the driver, a confident, striding redheaded woman whose Panamanian passport says she's Astrid Loney, a name she's always liked. Long legs tanned from a stint in Mykonos scissor under her billowing sundress. She leads them up the gangway to the *Jeddah*'s main deck, where the few remaining soybean containers have yet to be lifted out.

After two men open the watertight hatches, the Loney woman gestures for the others to go ahead and drop down; they disappear and after a while begin to pass up the aluminum Saab cases, as well as other crates and containers shedding beans and stamped with military markings. The contraband is carefully stacked and counted before she allows it to be hand trucked down to the dock.

"Your bad husband couldn't make it?"

Startled, the redhead pushes her sunglasses up and turns to find herself facing an American whom, at first, she takes for Aubrey Sentro.

"Oh. No, sorry, I forgot that was your scheme from the get-go, right? Mea culpa."

Hazel eyes, piercings, a tattoo sleeve—no, not Aubrey at all, the redhead realizes to her chagrin, but this girl does have Aubrey's pluck, her sly bearing, and a quite confusing recycling of a few of Aubrey's most pleasing features, only so much younger and less guarded.

"You're her daughter," Fontaine Fox says and thinks: *What in the world is she doing here?*

"Almost didn't recognize you from the description I was given." Tugging her own tangled, pulled-back hair: "Beauty tip. Red's not a good color with your complexion. IMHO."

"I'm Astrid," Fontaine Fox says, extending a hand.

"No, you're not."

"What's your name? Where is Aubrey?"

"It's the reversal in the story, the twist you didn't tell her," the girl continues, stubborn, scanning the deck of the ship. "The part where you made it look as if your husband was double-crossing everybody, when, in fact . . . it was you."

Her gaze comes back level. "Lies, lies, lies."

Fontaine feels a shiver of discomfort and wants an answer to her questions.

"Mom couldn't make it either. Sorry."

"He was a dodgy piece of work, my husband," Fontaine admits. "And for the record, I never lied to your mum."

"You can tell yourself that, I guess."

Studying her, Fontaine wonders how much this girl knows. About her mother, about what happened before what happened. "When—I'm curious—did she suss me out?"

"She didn't. Not really. But she knew you'd ask that. She told me to tell you she's not that smart. Just patient. Stubborn. As you probably know."

"I should have, yes."

"Made an educated guess and decided to send someone to catch the big climax and see if she was correct.

"She says stuff plays out," the girl adds, "if you wait."

Fontaine's eyes dart around. To see if she brought police with her or any sort of backup.

"It's only me; don't worry," the girl says, as if reading her concern. "According to Mom, even if someone could, you know, prove a causality between what she calls your sleight of hand with the"—the girl frowns, apparently uncertain—"Gustos?"

"Gustafs."

"Right. And all the rest."

On the quay, Fontaine has spotted a man in a fine panama hat who has found refuge in the cool shadows of a high stack, smoking. Chiseled Middle Eastern features, but an easy deportment that could only ever be American, even at rest. His sunglasses are canted up toward the two women, as if he's watching.

This girl's shadow?

"Your husband. Is he dead?" Sentro's daughter tilts her head, trying to parse Fontaine's nonresponse. "'Cause Mom was fairly emphatic about how that was what would happen. She had a whole scene worked out: big white mansion in the Deep South, your hipster husband kinda Vince Vaughn–ish and hauling his hairy ass out the back door, fleeing through some gothic antediluvian garden." *Girl can talk*, Fontaine marvels. "Chased by those same mooks Mom says she saw you trade supersecret looks with at the dock in Savannah. Over the cat container—whatever that means. Mooks who, when they heard that their shipment was missing, decided to take their pound of flesh from Vince."

"Your mother has an active imagination."

"Maybe, maybe not. There was a story in the papers, I think. Or on the news?" the girl says, making both a question. "Or . . . no, maybe it was one of her work friends saw some kind of eyes-only report about it." She smiles faintly. "Eyes only. Kinda retro cool."

Fontaine has fallen quiet. Her breathing shallow, thoughts churning.

"Anyway, Mom claims they caught him and dragged him back to the house, where—this part, pretty sure she was spitballing—some kind of professional Balkan hit person stepped out onto the porch and blew a hole in your spouse with a short-stock shotgun."

Fontaine stares, then looks away.

"It makes a terrible mess, Mom said. I wouldn't know."

For a moment nothing more is said. Fontaine watches as, down on the quay, the bed of her truck begins to fill with her black-market weapons.

"But anyway, it's all good. For you. There's no extradition here." Sentro's daughter takes a pack of Egyptian cigarettes from her shoulder bag. "You mind if I . . . ?"

Fontaine shakes her head. The man in the panama hat is gone. Maybe she has this all wrong. "Why isn't your mother here?"

The girl just looks at her blankly, taking a lungful and exhaling. The cigarette dangles between her fingers so loosely it might fall.

"She survived. Surely." Fontaine tries not to sound shaken.

Sentro's daughter doesn't answer the question. "These Cleopatra cancer sticks are vile, but I can't stop sucking on them. Super Luxe. You think they've got more than nicotine?"

What happened after I left? Fontaine studies this girl, looking for clues. "Tell me your name."

"Jennifer. Well, Jenny."

"Following in her footsteps, Jen?"

"Oh God, no. I work in franchise coffee. I've been considering studying to be a shiatsu masseuse, but . . . no. Beans are my life."

"Your mother—"

"I know, right?" Jenny Troon doesn't wait for Fontaine to finish her thought. "We always believed she was some cubicle mouse at an insurance company. Can you fucking believe that?" Jenny does a french inhale.

"Surely you suspected."

"She was a shitty mom, most of the time." Exhale.

"Looking at you, I don't think so." Fontaine finds that she likes this girl, despite everything. But why did Sentro send her all this way?

Now Jenny has gone quiet. *An actor who has been distracted and lost her place in the play*, Fontaine thinks. Jenny looks up at the seabirds. As if she's read the Englishwoman's thoughts, she says, "We're still, you know . . ." She lets the thought go, restarts: "The way my mom finally explained it to us, or tried to—she said she's that guy, the one that does the stuff no one else will."

Tried. Past tense? "Guy—not girl."

"Well, technically 'woman,' yeah. But what she meant by saying it that way is when you say a 'girl' does stuff—or even a woman, for that matter—when you say a girl 'does stuff nobody else will do,' Mom said it kinda connotes only one thing."

"Ah. Sex."

"It explains a lot. If you think about it."

"About Aubrey?" Fontaine still can't quite process this girl's presence here, what the point of it is, this new twist in the story. "Your mom?"

"Who else?" Jenny looks blankly at Fontaine. "Sorry if I've gotten it all tangled."

"Not sure you have; could be me."

"Mom said the world is inclined to think a woman can't do anything else. And that it somehow informs what she did do. My mom. And what she didn't or couldn't."

"Ah." After a beat, Fontaine smiles again, fondly. "I think she's selling herself short. I think you're selling her short," she adds. "On the mothering front, I mean. You are exhibit A."

Jenny drops and crushes her half-smoked cigarette. "Whatever."

"What did she tell you about me?" Fontaine asks.

Jenny seems to want to talk about something else. "For a couple of years, Mom was getting these . . . headaches? And after her last work trip, they got worse. She had other symptoms, I guess. We noticed she didn't want to talk about them. My brother claims her hands had been getting a little shaky. I wouldn't know. I hadn't seen her in a while. Anyway, before she took her cruise, she made an appointment and went to this doctor, and he told her she has some kind of long-term memory trouble. A cumulative thing, from work, you know. So this—you—it's one of those loose ends she was anxious to wrap up in case, you know, she forgot."

"We had something," Fontaine says softly.

One eyebrow arching, Jenny cuts curious eyes to her. "I don't think so."

"Why's that?"

"You probably thought you did. But . . ." Again Jenny doesn't finish; she looks as if she isn't sure anymore that she's right about whatever she was going to say.

"But what?"

Shrug of the shoulders; Sentro's daughter seems anxious to wrap this meeting up. "Mom," she says finally, as if that answers everything.

"You never really knew her, though," Fontaine says. "I mean. At all. Did you?"

"That's what my brother says. Mom said it wasn't so simple as that."

"And you?"

The last of Fontaine's cargo is being wheeled past them. The daughter dissembles: "I've never been to this part of the world before. What I'd like to do is stay for a month and score some righteous hash and get all fucked up. But"—she sighs—"my brilliant coffee career won't wait."

Irritated suddenly by all the cryptic ellipses and impatient to get on with her business, Fontaine says, "Fine. You've found me; you've scolded me. Awfully sorry; boo-hoo. Now be honest, love, because I have to shove off: Has she really sent you all this way out of mere curiosity that her supposition was right? Or has she sent you with some other message for me?"

"Both." The girl avoids making eye contact; she looks past Fontaine, down at the dock, evidently seeing something there she's been expecting. Fontaine is suddenly afraid to know what it is.

"Mom's message is this: she's extremely curious what your Casablanca client will say when he discovers that all those fancy gun cases you've sold him are empty."

Fontaine's head whips around. She scans the dock, sees a few dark birds fly upward from among the stacked containers, chased by the two black Mercedes SUVs slowly snaking toward Fontaine's drab green Titan.

Jenny adds: "She sent me here to witness it. I don't think she trusted you to tell her."

Fontaine looks at Jenny again, numb, feeling a flood of pure panic. "What has she done?"

The day laborers have finished loading their cargo into the truck bed; they wait, smoking, draining water bottles, looking up at the main deck of the *Jeddah*, as if impatient.

"Oh, what have you done?"

"*La Sûreté nationale* appreciates your donation," Jenny tells her.

Sprinting down the gangway, Fontaine shouts at her men to pull one of the stainless-steel cases off the truck. By the time she arrives, out of breath, they have it opened. Just foam and broken bricks inside.

They crack another one. Same.

Her fingers tingle; her scalp winds tight. Too late to put the cases away. Too late to run. Fontaine hears the rumble of the black Mercedes duo pulling up and turns toward them, smiling. Whatever sham needs to be cast she will have to make up on the fly. Heavy doors wing open, big well-fed guys in white shirts, silk suits, dark glasses, and kaffiyeh.

"*Wa'alaykum al-salaam.*"

"*Bonjour, mademoiselle.*"

"Hello."

Trapped, undone, Fontaine Fox glances one last time up at the deck of the cargo ship *Jeddah*, but Aubrey Sentro's daughter is gone.

CHAPTER FORTY-FIVE

The mournful two-week brume has finally lifted from the harbor, washed away by torrential, sweet-smelling rains. Sunshine bores a hole through and dazzles the crenellated bay, and all the whitewashed clapboard houses pop like broken teeth from the dark-green maw of the Pequeno hills.

Racing through the downtown streets, brand-new cricket bat slung over his shoulder, a thin computer case swinging from his hand, Zoala darts across a traffic gridlock on Avenida Segunda and ducks into the bruised gloaming of ByteMe. He throws money his sister gave him on the counter and hurries to a corner desk to plug into the World Wide Web and power up a black laptop with a Solomon Systems logo on it.

Rápido. Rápido. He's been working on his English but falls back easily into old habits.

The burns have healed, but his uncovered arms and legs below his board shorts still bear the ruddy, scalloped tessellation of the island beetles that Dr. Morehouse says saved him, and his dreams are often scaly, crawling, clicking journeys through jungled worlds that, upon waking, dissipate like sea mist from a heavy surf.

Eccola has taken to calling her brother Jumbee. He's not amused.

Earbuds in, software launched, and windows opened and clicked through, all the requisite artifacts of WhatsApp connecting over balky third world Mbps cause half a badly framed boy's face to materialize, herky jerky, on the laptop screen. The unsteady link catching and pixelating, an attractive adult woman in a sea-green airline uniform leans in front of the boy and in halting schoolbook Portuguese asks, "*Você pode me ouvir? Você consegue me ver?*"

Zoala has been practicing his English. "Yes. Okay. Both."

Another figure edges into view behind the uniformed woman: the son who came to rescue his mother and wound up getting saved himself. Zoala wishes it were Aubrey Sentro, but the son is not so bad. Jeremy set this all up; he knows a lot about money, and Zoala thinks there could be useful things to learn from him. Not now, though.

"Zoala, this is Damien," Sentro's son says. "Damien, Zoala."

Sentro's son steps back again, drawing the pretty woman with him. Behind them, Zoala can just make out the bookshelves of what he guesses could be a library behind them, more books than he's ever seen in one place before; then the boy his age centers himself on the screen, leans forward, his serious face getting big.

"Whassup, Z.?" Damien says.

Zoala doesn't understand, panics. "*O quê?*" They've been trading texts for a couple of days, but seeing him, hearing American spoken, this is so much different.

Damien frowns, equally confused. "Okay?"

"*Ele disse olá,*" the woman with the uniform tries to explain to Zoala, her pronunciation actually halfway decent.

"Oh. *Olá.* Hi."

"Hi."

"Hi."

There is the awkward silence of boys.

"*Onde está você?*"

Baffled, Damien looks to the adults.

"He's asking where you are," the woman translates.

"Johns Hopkins," Sentro's son, Jeremy, says.

Zoala wonders fleetingly if a Hopkins and a library are the same thing, how this John came to own either, and how much money it took, before Damien translates with the requisite tween eye roll, "Some big-ass liberry."

This Zoala understands, and also that his guess was right. He lets the mystery of the Hopkins go.

"Cool," Zoala says.

"I guess," Damien allows.

Another not-so-awkward pause.

"Welp."

Zoala has memorized the question his sister's junkie doctor taught him: "You wanna play *Fortnite*?"

"Dude," this American boy says, which in the doctor's language, Zoala remembers, has so many different meanings but in this case must mean yes. He watches Damien slip fire-engine-red wireless headphones over his ears. Beats. The ones Zoala covets.

They look at each other from two separate continents, almost two thousand miles and a vast gulf between them, but actually nothing at all, when it comes down to it. A fast connection that needs no mediation.

Sentro's son and his uniformed woman will watch for only a little while before they get bored looking and leave Zoala and his new American friend to build and shoot and floss their way to a better world.

Chapter Forty-Six

And that's the end. He passes away under a cloud, inscrutable at heart, forgotten, unforgiven, and excessively romantic. Not in the wildest days of his boyish visions could he have seen the alluring shape of such an extraordinary success! For it may very well be that in some short moment of hi [bullet hole] nd unflinching glance, he had beheld the face of [bullet hole] tunity which, like an Eastern bride, had come veiled to his side.

She puts the book down and turns off the light.

"He is gone, inscrutable at heart, and the poor girl is leading a sort of soundless, inert life . . ."

Eighteen-wheelers grind gears down the highway, and the minibar kicks on with a shuddering sigh.

". . . 'preparing to leave all this; preparing to leave . . .' while he waves his hand sadly at his butterflies."

Neon dusts the curtains. Sentro closes her eyes. Someone is moving around in the motel room above her. As she sinks into the mattress, her body thrums with the weary rhythms of the road: sixteen hundred miles from Baltimore on I-40, then south, the whine of the tires, talk radio, the slap of the lane markers, the bright green-and-white flare of off-ramps and mileage signs. Her lungs fill with the air of her father's world.

And she sleeps.

———

He said, "I'm having second thoughts. Is all."

And all the motels, hotels, boats, vans, containers, warehouses, abandoned buildings, rented rooms, safe houses, and sanctuaries run together, all the missions strung together like the lanyards Jenny used to make, an endless litany of waiting and watching and tackling and resolving that she's not disappointed has been fractured by this forgetful condition they say she's suffering.

"Second thoughts about the divorce? Or everything you've done to make it inevitable?" It was a cheap shot, but she was emotionally bankrupt. The only man besides her father who she'd ever loved, her forever boy; she didn't want to lose him but feared what might happen to them if he didn't let her go.

Cellophane streamers taped to the AC fluttered like ashigaru battle banners. She lay on the bed, mute, stared through her angry tears at the blur of the ceiling fan, and decided she would not blame him for his infidelity or herself for being so wounded by it.

"You fight for everything but us," Dennis said. Or that's what she remembers. He recanted, then, regretful: "I'm sorry. I didn't mean that. It's just . . ." And she didn't need him to finish the thought.

"We're all hostage to something," she said then, and in her dreams, now, she and her husband lie together, entwined, and she tells him the tale of how their children fought for her.

———

Three far-flung dust devils line dance, spectral, along the horizon, as if in tribute to the vainglorious emptiness of West Texas, last gasp of endless prairie, and the harsh freedom her mother found there.

Only the big sign remains, like a gravestone, outside of Marfa, rusted, peeling: STARDUST MOTEL.

Sentro eased her Audi and U-Haul onto the shoulder of Highway 17 and walked into the weeds to find the rectilinear concrete stubs of foundation that still survive, and she traced them to the place where she remembers her mother unlocking the pale-aqua door, the blast of air-conditioning, the sour smell of stale cigarettes, disinfectant, and air freshener, and the big bed and soft shadows and scratchy sheets and ice buckets and sodas and sweets from the vending machine in the breezeway.

She stands among scattered trash and mounded prairie dog holes and remembers her mother's sad smile.

I'm a cowboy who never saw a cow,
never roped a steer 'cause I don't know how—

"You're good at what you do," Dennis had said, as she sat in that different motel, Corpus Christi, waiting for her call.

"Bargaining for people's lives?"

"Saving them."

She's forgotten to breathe. Fighting tears. What if she forgets him? What if she forgets her children?

Not for the first time her heart aches, never for what she's done but for what she couldn't because of it.

The brain doctor said to her before she left, getting colloquial, "The jury's out, Ms. Sentro." Her tests showed contradictions; the projections were inconclusive. "The more we study the mind, the less we understand. You won't know if you really have it and what it's wrought until it's too late and you're dead and we crack your skull and get a good look at the gray matter in there.

"It's a crapshoot," he admitted.

Typical. But she can live with that.

An impasse is often the best she can manage.

The distant twisters have been raptured into sandy heavens, where they hang like threadbare curtains. It smells like it might rain. Above her, a hawk floats, almost motionless, on hot thermals, like a scrap of black fabric thrown up there as well by an absentminded God. She hears her mother's song whisper in the relentless wind. She has a long drive ahead of her and no plans once she gets there.

Sentro walks back to her car through the honey mesquite and buffalo grass, high-tops crushing the parched, stubborn, unforgiving soil.

Home.

Acknowledgments

Some say a book is only as good as its editors, and if that's true, I've been fortunate to have worked with some of the best. Benee Knauer is my anchor and my secret weapon; somehow she continues to make me a better writer. Tiffany Yates Martin piloted my story into safe harbor, with notes and suggestions that have proved invaluable. I'm extremely grateful, as well, to Liz Pearsons and the crew at Thomas & Mercer for their support, collaboration, and enthusiasm.

Many years ago, the cinematographer Tak Fujimoto, during a long location scout, told me about a cargo freighter he'd just traveled on between films. The strange setting, the vivid imagery, and the undisturbed quiet of the trip he described stuck with me, and years later, a troubled character who had been rattling around my thoughts unmoored made the decision to book passage on a tramp line, hoping to clear her head, and an adventure unspooled.

The insights of my usual gang of early readers—Scott, Julia, Erich, and Aaron—were instrumental in shaping the story and discovering where it was initially left wanting. As always, I owe a debt of gratitude to my agent, Victoria Sanders, for once more believing in a book and in me. My family sustains me; my old dogs reserve judgment as long as they have chewy treats. Conrad, Graham Greene, and Katherine Anne

Porter were my muses as I wrote, but because (for myriad reasons) I was unable to take a container ship cruise of my own, Robert D. Rieffel's warm, unpretentious *Twenty-Eight Days on a Freighter* helped me get at least some of the factual details right. The *Jeddah's* journey is, however, a work of fiction. Dramatic license has been liberally taken.

About the Author

Photo © by Katie Pyne

Daniel Pyne is the author of four novels: *Catalina Eddy*, *Fifty Mice*, *Twentynine Palms*, and *A Hole in the Ground Owned by a Liar*. Among his many screenplays are *Pacific Heights*, *Doc Hollywood*, the remake of *The Manchurian Candidate*, and *Fracture*. He made his directorial debut with the independent film *Where's Marlowe?* His list of television credits (creating, writing, and showrunning) spans *Miami Vice* to *Bosch*. Pyne has worked as a screen printer, a sportswriter, an ad man, and a cartoonist and has taught screenwriting at the UCLA School of Theater, Film and Television for more than two decades. He splits his time between California and New Mexico with his wife, their two rescue dogs, and a surly turtle.